SERENA'S FUTURE
lay in the hands of the most infamous rakehell in England . . .

SERENA'S FUTURE
had been lost by her father in a game of cards . . .

SERENA'S FUTURE
had become a tempestuous nightmare of terror, deceit and strange love . . .

SERENA'S FUTURE
was now part of the grim secret of MANDRAKE, the eerie clifftop mansion where she was now a virtual prisoner . . .

SERENA'S FUTURE
had become bleak days of sheer despair and shuddering nights of abject fear . . .

CAMFIELD NOVELS OF LOVE by Barbara Cartland

Other books by Barbara Cartland

A HAZARD OF HEARTS

BARBARA CARTLAND

"A hazard of cards may bring ruin, a hazard
of hearts may bring one's heart's desire."

SIR HUBERT STAVERLEY

JOVE BOOKS, NEW YORK

This Jove book contains the complete
text of the original edition.

A HAZARD OF HEARTS

A Jove Book / published by arrangement with
the author

PRINTING HISTORY
Pyramid Books edition / June 1969
Jove edition / January 1988

ISBN: 0-515-09512-5

Jove Books are published by The Berkley Publishing Group,
200 Madison Avenue, New York, New York 10016.
The name "JOVE" and the "J" logo
are trademarks belonging to Jove Publications, Inc.

PRINTED IN THE UNITED STATES OF AMERICA

10   9   8   7   6   5   4   3   2   1

One

SERENA, looking from the window, thought that the miracle of spring at Staverley became more breath-takingly beautiful year by year. Never had the dew-drenched lawns been greener or the lilacs more luxuriant with their branches weighted with white, mauve and purple flowers. The laburnums were fountains of golden rain and the fruit blossom lay beneath the trees in a pink-and-white snowdrift. On the lake the darkness of the water was gradually being hidden by the verdant, rounded leaves of the water-lilies and soon the lilies themselves in all their smooth exotic beauty would be in bloom.

Serena felt her heart reach out towards such loveliness. It was part of her—an indivisible part of herself—and it seemed to her at times that her love of Staverley quickened and throbbed within her as if it were a living thing.

' 'Tis the hour for your chocolate, Miss Serena.'

A deep voice startled her and she turned with a little exclamation.

'I was day-dreaming, Eudora. I did not hear you come in.'

If Eudora's voice was startling, her appearance was even more so. At first sight one supposed her to be a dwarf, but on a second glance it was obvious that her deformities were due not to an abnormality of birth, but to some disablement which had twisted her back and left her hunched and distorted.

Her head was a normal size and yet it seemed unusually large on the tiny, withered body. It was difficult to guess how old she was. Lines of pain were deeply etched from her pointed nose to her mouth and beneath her deep-sunk eyes. Her eyes themselves were surprisingly dark and alive and seemed to miss nothing, often expressing strange and violent emotions so that Serena as a child imagined that Eudora's spirit, wild and untamed, was imprisoned within her dwarfed, foreshortened body.

Serena had known Eudora all her life. There had never

been a time when the little woman had not been beside her, looking after her, tending to her wants, loving her with a passionate, almost animal-like devotion, and guarding her fiercely and jealously.

Serena took the chocolate now from the silver tray and sat down on the broad, low window-seat.

'Is it eleven of the clock already?' she sighed. 'And I have a vast amount to occupy me.'

'Mrs. Beaston asked me to inform you, Miss, that if Sir Giles arrives this evening there will be no roast in the house for dinner.'

'Oh yes, there will,' Serena replied. 'I ordered a lamb to be killed four days ago. It should be nicely hung by now. Sir Giles is partial to lamb, as you know, Eudora; and tell Mrs. Beaston we will have baked carp dressed in the Portuguese way, two Davenport fowls, stuffed, parboiled and stewed in butter, some soup to start with and a fruit pie as a remove. It will be a small dinner but just the sort my father enjoys.'

'And if Sir Giles fails to arrive?' Eudora asked.

'I can manage with one of the fowls,' Serena smiled.

'I will carry your instructions to Mrs. Beaston,' Eduroa said.

'Yes, do,' Serena said; 'then come and help me pick some flowers. Those in the big vase in the hall are fading.' She turned her head as she spoke and looked out of the window. ' 'Tis such a perfect day; I want to be in the garden.'

'My heart is heavy,' Eudora said.

Her voice was always strange and rather gruff, but now there was a throbbing note in it and a roughness, as if she spoke from some impulse which she could not control.

'Oh, Eudora, why?' Serena asked.

'I know not,' the hunchback answered. 'But last night when I lay awake I felt as if a cloud—a dark cloud—was approaching nearer and nearer.'

Serena got up quickly.

'Spare me, Eudora! I am afraid of these moods of yours. 'Tis a goodly time since you have had one and yet always when you talk like this it makes me apprehensive and afraid.'

'I am sorry, Miss Serena. Yet I can but speak of what I feel . . . and know.'

Eudora spoke dully, almost sullenly.

'Yes, I know, Eudora dear, but how I wish you did not

feel such morbid things; not on such a day as this. I want to be happy! I am happy! My father should be home soon, and let us pray that his journey to London will not have proved . . .' Serena hesitated for a word, then almost in a whisper to herself added, 'very costly.'

Her eyes roamed round the room. It was a lovely room, but somehow inadequately furnished. There were patches on the wall where it was obvious that once upon a time pictures had hung . . . there was the discoloured outline of their frames . . . there the nails from which they had been suspended. The room held sofas, chairs and occasional tables; but on looking closer one wondered why there were no cabinets; a space between the windows seemed made to hold a console table and the alcove on the opposite wall was obviously designed for a bureau.

Yes, the room was strangely empty. And as Serena turned and went from the drawing-room into the hall, there, too, was a similar emptiness and similar faded patches on the brocaded walls. The hall was dark after the sun-filled drawing-room and Serena shivered a little.

'You frighten me, Eudora. Go and give my message to Mrs. Beaston and bring me my pelisse from my bedroom, we are going out into the sunshine to forget your gloomy forebodings.'

'Very good, Miss Serena.'

Eudora bobbed a curtsy, which necessitated a strange distortion of her twisted body; then she moved across the marble floor, her feet making a strange uneven patter as she walked. Alone, Serena linked her fingers together and stared up at a great blank space over the marble mantelpiece.

'Oh, please let him have won,' she whispered. 'Please, please! Besides . . . there is nothing left to sell.'

There was a passion and intensity in her voice and in the pressure of her twisted fingers. With a deliberate effort she turned towards the door. She pulled it open and the sharp, sun-kissed spring air came flooding in at her. A breath of wind rustled her hair and she turned her face towards it as if it could blow away the apprehensions of her mind.

The door was at the top of a long flight of stone steps leading to the gravel drive. Beyond was a stone terrace and beyond again was a great park which enclosed Staverley Court, stretching as far as the eye could see and enriched with fine oaks planted there a century earlier. A flight of pigeons winged its way across the blue sky. There were

7

several swans moving slowly and majestically on the lake.

How beautiful it was! How beautiful! Yet Serena knew that Eudora's words had thrown a stone, as it were, into the placid calm of her mind. She was afraid, terribly afraid. The servants had always said that Eudora was a witch and Serena laughed at such statements; yet in her heart of hearts she was often afraid that they might be right.

Eudora was different from other people. No one knew, for instance, who her parents were. Serena's grandfather, driving his chaise at breakneck speed from London to Staverley, had rounded a corner sharply in the twilight, his horses had knocked down a woman walking by the road-side and the wheels of the vehicle had passed over her. He brought her home to Staverley, but she died the following morning after she had been delivered of a child. That the child was twisted and abnormal was due, the midwife said, entirely to the injuries sustained by her mother imme-diately prior to her birth.

All enquiries had failed to find out who the woman was or where she had come from; so Eudora had been brought up at Staverley, becoming, first of all, maid-of-all-work at the beck and call of the servants and then, largely by her own insistence and determination, personal maid to Serena. She had adored the child from the moment she was born and no amount of complaints or even scoldings could keep her from the nursery.

Serena's nurse had said again and again that Eudora gave her the creeps and she would not have her up there 'frightening the baby', but that in itself was a slander be-cause Serena never was frightened by Eudora. As soon as she was old enough to recognise anyone she had smiled and held out her arms to the strange, mis-shapen creature from whom most people shrank away in disgust.

But the times were coming when Serena and other peo-ple too at Staverley were to be thankful for Eudora. Num-bers of servants left never to return; a few old retainers stayed on and often went for months without wages, re-maining, so they said, because of their affection for the house, but also because they had nowhere else to go and could not imagine a life which did not hold for them the background of Staverley.

Eudora became invaluable. She was personal maid, housemaid and general factotum in the house and once, when Mrs. Beaston was taken ill and there was no one else, she even became cook for a few days. And yet she was never too busy to look after Serena. However short-staffed they were, her gowns were pressed, her hair dressed skilfully.

'I could not do without her,' Serena had often said to herself. She said it again out loud to the spring wind as she stood on top of the steps which would lead her down to the garden. Yet she wished with all her heart that Eudora would keep her forebodings to herself.

It was uncanny the way Eudora's warnings came true. Once she had said, 'I can smell danger,' and it seemed, too, as if she could smell trouble long before it appeared.

'What can it be? What can it be?' Serena wondered, and knew that she was already worried because her father was three or four days overdue.

She looked forward to his return and yet she dreaded it. She would know from the moment she first saw him driving up to the front door in his yellow-wheeled curricle whether he had won or lost. If he had won, he would spring out like a man half his age, throw his reins to the groom and come bounding up the stone steps to shout for his daughter as though she were not already waiting for him in the hall.

'Serena! Serena!'

At the sound of his voice, for which she would often have been waiting for days, the relief would be almost overwhelming.

'It is beyond anything great,' he would say. 'We have a fortune! We will give a party, a ball, and you must get yourself some new gowns. We will re-stock the cellar and now, for the Lord's sake, let them serve dinner and I will recount to you the whole tale.'

He would be bubbling over with excitement like a child; and because his cheerfulness was so infectious, Serena would forget everything but his happiness and they would sit far into the night planning the things they would do, the improvements they would make to the house, the money they would spend on the estate. How enjoyable they were, those moments of feeling rich, when no extravagance was too fantastic and nothing was out of reach of their pockets! And yet Serena had known after these occasions that all too quickly Sir Giles would say:

'The money is going; my pockets will soon be to let. I will travel to London on Thursday. When I return, we will

9

consider the plans for the new wing to the house. We must empower Adams to do it for us.'

'Oh, Father, do not go yet,' Serena would beg, but she would know it was hopeless even while she pleaded with him.

There was some urge within him, some need within his blood, which could not be denied. He craved the feel of the cards between his fingers as a man dying of thirst craves water. He had to go. But as the years went on the times when he won grew fewer and fewer. It seemed to Serena when she was young that they were fairly frequent; but as she grew older Sir Giles's return from London was generally a very different story.

The curricle would come slowly up the long drive; even the horses seemed lethargic; and when they drew up at the front door Sir Giles would descend very slowly, almost reluctantly, it seemed to Serena, as if he were afraid to face her. If she was waiting for him at the top of the steps he would kiss her in silence, then he would pass into the hall, relinquish his hat and coat to the butler and look searchingly round him.

How well Serena knew that look! Now practically everything that was worth selling had gone—the Vandykes, the inlaid china cabinets, the Charles II silver, the fine tapestries which had hung in the dining-room for hundreds of years. Now for reminders there were only marks on the walls and empty places in the hearts of those who had loved them.

'Please, God, let him have won.'

Once again Serena whispered her prayer out loud, but the fresh wind seemed to blow it from between her lips. Then she stopped and stared along the drive where a horse suddenly showed between the distant trees.

'He is coming! I can see him!'

She spoke more to herself than to Eudora, whose step she had heard behind her.

'Put on your pelisse, Miss Serena. It is exceeding cold out here.'

' 'Tis my father! He has arrived! What a strange time! He must have left London early!'

Even as she said the words she felt her heart drop. When Sir Giles was gambling he seldom left the tables before dawn; and if he had gone from the Club early and come to Staverley before noon it could have only one explanation.

He had lost all his money and therefore had been able to play no longer.

Instinctively Serena put out her hand towards Eudora. The hunchback took it in both of hers, but she said nothing and Serena was well aware that Eudora had no words of consolation for her. She had seen the horse between the trees before the drive curved a little to hide anyone from sight. Now the horse appeared again and Serena gave a cry.

'But 'tis not Sir Giles! Look, Eudora, 'tis someone else on horseback. Who can it be?'

'It is not Sir Giles,' Eudora said quietly.

'No, I told you it wasn't,' Serena said impatiently. 'But I believe it is Cousin Nicholas. Yes, of course, that is who it is. And I was assured that he, too, was in London. He must have returned, maybe to tell us what time my father will be home. He is riding swiftly. Go and order wine for him and some cold meats. He will be hungry after his ride.'

Eudora turned without a word and Serena, waiting impatiently at the top of the stairs, waved to her cousin as he crossed the bridge spanning the lake and cried out a greeting as soon as he came within earshot.

'Nicholas! How enchanting to see you! I thought at first you were my father! Have you come from London?'

Nicholas Staverley looked up at Serena where she stood, the sunshine on her fair hair, the wind blowing the skirts of her muslin dress. She had no idea how lovely she looked against the grey stone of the old house and Nicholas stared at her as she swept his hat from his head. He dismounted as an old groom came hurrying round the corner of the house to take his horse.

'Ye have ridden her hard, Mr. Nicholas,' he said reproachfully with the familiarity of an old servant. When Nicholas had no answer for him he took the horse away, grumbling a little beneath his breath.

'Come in, Nicholas; 'tis nice to see you,' Serena said. 'It must be nigh on two months since you went to London and only one letter have I had from you. I declare I have a mind to chide you for being so unkind, but I expect you have been too gay to remember your country cousin.'

'Oh, I say, Serena, it isn't that,' Nicholas said, colouring a little like a schoolboy. 'It is just that I am no hand at letter-writing, never was at school, and many a flogging I've got for it.'

'But now you are here you can tell me all the news,'

11

Serena said. 'Eudora has gone to prepare a luncheon for you. But tell me, first of all, how is my father? Is he winning?'

Serena dropped her voice on the last words. Nicholas looked down into her upturned face. He was much taller than his cousin—a well-set-up young man, with broad shoulders and a well-turned leg for a boot; and yet at that moment he looked like a badly scared little boy who must confess to those in authority for some misdemeanour. Serena saw the expression on his face.

'What is it, Nicholas?' she asked.

'Let us go into the drawing-room,' Nicholas said. 'We cannot discourse here.'

Serena opened the door which led into the drawing-room. The room was still bathed in sunshine, yet somehow it seemed to her there was an atmosphere of disquiet and of apprehension, as though it waited for the fulfilment of Eudora's prediction. Nicholas closed the door quietly behind him, then he stood still and looked at Serena. The sun was behind her now, gilding her fair hair with a shining radiance.

'What is it, Nicholas?'

'Uncle . . . Giles,' he stammered.

Serena's eyes widened.

'Ill? . . . Oh, Nicholas!'

'Worse, Serena . . . worse than that.'

Serena gave a little cry.

'Worse? Not . . . not . . . he is not dead?'

Nicholas nodded.

For a moment Serena stood very still. She made no movement, only her eyes searched his face. Then at last, in a voice that was scarcely above a whisper, she asked:

'How?'

It seemed to her as she asked the question that the whole world was hushed and still.

'A duel,' Nicholas answered, 'at dawn this morning. I was one of his seconds.'

'A duel!'

Serena's hand went quickly to her breast. Her heart had started beating again after a moment so breathless with fear that she felt as if she had been turned to stone. Almost she said, 'Thank God!' She had feared something far worse, something of which she had always been afraid.

'Yes, a duel,' Nicholas repeated.

12

'He did not suffer?'

'Not at all! But . . . Oh, Serena, he intended it to happen.'

Nicholas' face was white and Serena suddenly realised how tired and drawn he looked. She took a deep breath, taking control of her emotions and forcing her mind to think of Nicholas rather than of her own chaotic feelings.

'You are tired, Nicholas. Sit down! We can talk as easily sitting as standing.'

Nicholas made a gesture.

'Wait, Serena, there is something that I have got to say to you. You must listen.' He came a little nearer to her. 'I want you to marry me, Serena. Now! At once! Today!'

He spoke with an urgency, and now Serena was staring at him, her eyes wide, the astonishment on her face very plain to see.

'Nicholas, what do you mean? Why?'

'There is no time to be lost, Serena. It can be done by special licence, or if that is impossible we can leave tonight for Gretna.'

'But, Nicholas, are you deranged?'

Nicholas passed his hand over his forehead.

'No, I am being very sane, Serena, and you have got to agree. It is the only thing you can do, I tell you.'

'Nicholas, dear, suppose you tell me from the very beginning what this is all about.'

She looked at him with anxiety. She had known him ever since they had been children together. He was her first cousin, and was indeed the heir to Staverley as she had no brothers. But always he had been a quiet, rather reticent young man. They had played with each other and teased each other as children, but in most things Serena had been the leader. Nicholas seldom took the initiative. He was in character both conventional and careful. His father had left him a little money, not much, but enough on which to be comfortable, and he had recently gone to London to pay his respects at Court. He was fond of his cousin, as Serena was well aware, but it was the affection of a brother for a sister rather than of a man for a maid. The last thing Serena had ever expected to hear was a proposal of marriage from Nicholas.

'Sit down, Nicholas,' she begged.

At that moment the door opened and Eudora came in with a bottle of wine and a glass on a tray.

'A repast will be ready in a few minutes,' she said. 'In the meantime I thought Mr. Nicholas would take a glass of wine.'

'Set it down, Eudora,' Serena said quietly.

Eurodra did as she was told and went from the room, closing the door quietly behind her. Without waiting for an invitation Nicholas walked across to the side table, poured himself out a full glass of wine and drank it off quickly; then once again in a wild, distraught manner he passed his hand over his forehead.

'Now, Nicholas, please tell me everything.'

Nicholas took a breath as if it was difficult for him to find appropriate words, and then at last he started to speak in a voice abrupt, raw and very unlike the slow, fashionable drawl he had recently affected.

'Uncle Giles had been losing heavily for the last three days. It seemed not to matter what he did, he never held a winning card. Then yesterday evening his luck began to change. He made a few thousands, not a fortune, but enough to gain back what he had lost. I had been watching, and when his opponent rose from the table saying he must get to Almack's before it closed, I said to him, "Come and have something to eat, Uncle Giles." He smiled at me. "That is a good idea, Nicholas, my boy," he said. "It seems a long time since I ate." He rose from the table and then at that moment the door of the card-room opened and . . . someone came in.'

Nicholas paused.

'Who was it?' Serena asked.

'Vulcan!'

'The Marquis of Vulcan?'

Nicholas nodded.

'That man!' Serena exclaimed. 'It was because of him we had to sell the Vandykes.'

'Yes, I know. He looked across the room and saw Uncle Giles. "Ah, Sir Giles," he said. "I have been hoping we should meet again. Would you care to have your revenge?" "My lord," I interrupted, "my uncle was just coming with me to have something to eat." He stared at me as if I was a lackey, then spoke again direct to your father. "Well, Sir Giles, are you willing?" Your father sat down at the table. "I am at your service, my lord," he said. I could do nothing more, Serena. I did my best.'

'Yes, yes, Nicholas, I understand. Of course you did! Go on!'

'They began to play. Your father's luck had gone. He lost and lost again. He went on losing. At last he staked . . . this house.'

'Oh, no, Nicholas . . . not that?'

'Yes, Serena.'

'And he lost?'

'He lost.'

Serena put her hands for one moment to her eyes.

'I cannot bear it,' she said. 'Staverley is . . . my home.'

'That is not all,' Nicholas said harshly.

'What then?'

'Uncle Giles rose from the table. "My lord," he said to the Marquis, "you have won from me all the money I possess in the world and now I have lost to you my home. I must bid you good night because I have nothing left to wager." '

'I can hear him saying it,' Serena said, 'and he would have said it proudly.'

'He did,' Nicholas answered. 'Lord Vulcan looked up at him, the cards still in his hands, and said: "It is a pity, Sir Giles. I had hoped to give you your revenge. Have you nothing else on which you can try your luck?" He played with the cards as he spoke. Your father seemed almost hypnotised by them, watching them as if he longed to feel them in his hands again. At last he said, very, very quietly, "I have one thing more".'

'What could it have been?' Serena asked.

Nicholas looked away from her.

'I . . . I cannot tell you, Serena.'

'Don't be ridiculous, Nicholas, of course you can tell me,' Serena answered. 'Go on.'

'It was you!'

'What . . . what do you mean?'

'Uncle Giles said: "My lord, I have one thing left, and this time, if you play me, I believe you will lose. I have a daughter, and when she marries she will enherit £80,000, but only when she marries, you understand. Are you prepared, my lord, to wager your freedom?" '

With a swift movement Serena walked across the room and stood beside the open window. After a moment she spoke, and her voice was steady, if faint.

'Go on, Nicholas.'

'The Marquis smiled. If I had had the pluck, Serena, I would have struck that smile from his lips; but I could only stand there watching and wondering where this madness of your father's would lead him. "You agree?" Uncle Giles asked. "I agree," the Marquis said. "All you have lost . . . against my freedom." They began to play. In three minutes it was over and . . . Lord Vulcan had won.'

Serena shut her eyes. For a moment the world span round her.

'What then?'

'Uncle Giles left White's without a word. I followed him. I tried to speak to him but he shook me off. "Leave me be, Nicholas," he said. "I wish to wallow in the hell of my own making." He strode up St. James's Street and I followed him a little distance behind as I didn't know what to do. At Piccadilly he stood hesitating for a moment. There was a man approaching him, a gentleman by his dress, but obviously, it seemed to me, slightly the worse for drink. I saw your father go up to him and deliberately jostle him to one side. "Out of my way, sir," he said. The gentleman stared at him. "Will you kindly pay a closer attention to your manners, sir?" he replied. "My manners are my own affair," Uncle Giles said in an intentionally provoking tone, and taking his gloves he slapped them against the stranger's face.'

'Oh no!' Serena cried.

'He did it deliberately,' Nicholas went on. 'There was, obviously, only one course for the stranger to take. He asked for your father's card, handed him his own, and said his seconds would call upon him in a few hours. I went up to Uncle Giles and offered him my services. He accepted them and took my arm genially enough. "We will go to my rooms in Half Moon Street, Nicholas, my boy," he said, and somehow he seemed quite cheerful. But I was staring at the stranger's card. I had seen the name engraved there—*Mr. Michael Blacknorton*. "Uncle Giles," I cried, "you must be crazy. Do you know who that man is? He is a much-vaunted shot with a pistol.'" "I thought I recognised him," your father answered, and I knew then that I had not been mistaken. As I suspicioned, he had picked the quarrel on purpose.'

'Why? Why?' Serena asked.

'You know why,' Nicholas answered her. 'Can't you understand, Serena? He had lost Staverley and . . . you.'

'Yes, I think I understand.'

'Mr. Blacknorton's seconds were round within an hour,' Nicholas continued. 'I tried to insist on rapiers, but your

16

father agreed immediately to pistols. He sat drinking and talking until the dawn broke, and then we went to a field outside the village of Chelsea. Surprisingly Uncle Giles seemed cheerful and almost at peace with himself. He shook my hand and said: "Look after Serena as best you can, Nicholas, and tell her to forgive me. I do not deserve her prayers".'

Nicholas' voice broke. There was a moment's pause before Serena asked, with the tears running down her cheeks:

'Did he hurt Mr. Blacknorton?'

'He fired into the air,' Nicholas answered, 'and I think Blacknorton meant only to wing him, but your father turned as if to be square to the bullet. It struck him just above the heart and he died almost instantly.'

'Oh, Nicholas, if only I could have been with him!'

Serena sank down in the window-seat and hid her face in her hands.

'There was nothing any of us could do,' Nicholas said. 'Peter Vivien was with me and I left him to make all arrangements to have your father brought back here while I came on ahead to tell you what had happened and . . . to persuade you to marry me.'

'It is kind of you, Nicholas, but . . . we have never loved each other.'

Nicholas Staverley got slightly red in the face.

'I have always been very fond of you, Serena. We have been together more or less all our lives. We would get along famously, I daresay.'

'Without love? Dear Nicholas, I know you mean it very kindly, but it would ruin your life, and you know it.'

'That is nonsense, Serena,' Nicholas said, speaking as though they were in the schoolroom again. 'We are fond of each other and we know one another well. We could live at The Gables for the time being.'

'. . . Within sight of Staverley, when it is no longer ours?' Serena asked softly, and there was a bitterness more than of tears in her voice. 'I have not forgotten, Nicholas, that you have lost it too. One day it would have been yours, and Staverleys have lived here since the reign of Henry VIII. Oh, Nicholas, I am sorry, both for you and for myself.'

In answer Nicholas walked across the room and sat down beside her in the window. He put his hand over hers and held it close.

17

'For the Lord's sake, Serena, listen to me. You don't understand! You can't wed Vulcan!'

'Why not? Presuming that he will offer for me.'

'I don't even trust him to do that. He is a bad fellow, Serena! No, I am not talking in an exaggerated way. It is fashionable at the moment to be dashing and a roué, but he is all these things and more. He is inhuman. Everyone is afraid of him and there are all sorts of rumours always being repeated and whispered about him.'

'What sort of rumours?' Serena asked.

'I don't really know. I have always kept out of his way because people have said such things about him. But you can ask anybody in London and they will tell you that no respectable woman can afford to be seen in his company. There are women always about him, of course; he attracts them just as sugar attracts flies; but he only takes what he wants and leaves them disconsolate and broken.'

There was so much misery in Nicholas' voice that Serena looked at him, sensing instinctively that he had special reason for speaking so vehemently.

'But what can I do?' Serena asked.

'You cannot wed him,' Nicholas said firmly. 'I will ride over to the Bishop, ask him for a special licence and we can be married before Vulcan arrives.'

'Would that be honourable?' Serena asked.

Nicholas hesitated for a moment.

'There is no question of being honourable where the Marquis is concerned. I believe even the Prince said to him the other day, "Justin, I never actually believed in the Devil until I met you".'

'And because he is bad you suggest that we behave badly, Nicholas?'

'Faith, Serena, how you do catch up on a fellow!' Nicholas said impatiently, getting to his feet. 'I say the only way out of this coil, and a sorry coil it is, is for you to marry me, and when Vulcan arrives to claim you, he will find you are already tied.'

Serena got to her feet and walked across the room. For a moment there was only the soft rustle of her dress to break the silence. At the end of the room there was a portrait of her father. It had been painted about fifteen years earlier and he looked young and joyous and carefree as he sat a great roan mare and held his three-cornered hat in his hand.

Serena stood for a long time looking at the portrait. At length she said quietly,

'I never remember his doing a dishonourable thing, Nicholas. He was a hopeless gamester; he would gamble on anything. I recollect when I was a child I told him I thought it was going to rain. It was of vital importance that it should not rain that day because I had been promised a picnic by my nurse. I desired the treat so much that I felt pessimistic about it taking place, I suppose. Anyway, he laughed at me and said, "I will wager you that it does not." "But it will," I said miserably, "I know it will." "Well," he said slowly, "if it does not, I will give you a pony. You have been asking for one long enough." I gave a shout of joy, but he lifted his hand. "Not so fast, not so fast, what do you stake in return?" I thought wildly of my small possessions. He noticed in my arms the doll that I always carried.

'I adored that doll. It was called Louise and I went nowhere without her; she even slept with me at night. "Your doll against a pony," he said. I agreed, but even as I did so there was a lump in my throat, and I knew that even the joys of a picnic and a pony would never compensate me for the loss of Louise. I was right, it never did. I lost the wager, of course, and later that afternoon I took Louise to my father. "Do you . . . really . . . want Louise, Father?" I asked. He saw the pleading in my eyes, but he shook his head. "A debt of honour must always be paid," he said firmly, and took the doll from me. He locked her up in the cupboard in his study. I used to go in there without anyone knowing and speak to her through the closed door.'

'Did you ever get her back?' Nicholas asked.

'I was too proud to ask for her,' Serena replied, 'and I think it was four or five years later that my father, looking for some lost deeds, came across Louise. "What in the name of fortune is that thing doing there?" he asked, and I thought then of the nights I had crept into the deserted study and asked Louise if she was all right, of the times that my arms had felt empty and aching because there was no Louise to hug. I did not tell him what I felt . . . I could not, but I knew then that one should never gamble with the thing one loves.'

Serena's voice was choked, and she threw out her arms

with a gesture of despair. Nicholas went across the room to her.

'You are going to marry me,' he said masterfully.

'But I am not,' Serena replied through her tears.

'Don't be so bird-witted, Serena,' Nicholas said sharply. 'I know what is best, and you will do as I bid you.'

Serena laughed even as the tears were falling down her cheeks.

"Oh, Nicholas, you are so funny. You never could make me obey you even though you were three years older, and you are not going to succeed now. I am going to stay here and face it out. Maybe, when his lordship sees me, he won't want me.'

'To tell the truth, Serena,' Nicholas said, 'I don't believe for one moment that he will marry you. Everyone in London has tried to catch him at one time or another and no one has succeeded. There is . . . someone now who is very much in love with him and he . . . won't have her.'

Nicholas' voice changed and suddenly Serena understood that here was where Nicholas was personally concerned in the story.

'Who is she?' she asked softly.

'Lady Isabel Calver,' Nicholas answered. 'You will never have heard of her; she is a widow. She was married when she was only a child in the schoolroom and her husband was killed fighting against Boney. She is lovely, Serena, the loveliest person I have seen in my life and Vulcan will have none of her.'

'In which case, Nicholas, he is not likely to wed me,' Serena answered; 'but, dear cousin, thank you for asking me and thank you for your thought of me. I do appreciate it; I do really.'

'That is very nicely said, Serena,' Nicholas said awkwardly. 'But I know you are making a mistake. The fellow is not to be trusted. If he does not marry you, he will somehow contrive to get his hands on your fortune.'

'He will have to be clever to do that,' Serena said. 'You know what the trustees are like.'

'Well, there is nothing more I can do,' Nicholas said.

'There is nothing any of us can do,' Serena said, 'except remember . . . that my . . . my father is on his way here.'

'I had not forgotten, Serena.'

'Will you speak with the Vicar?' she asked. 'I will inform the household. But first you must have something to eat, Nicholas,'

'I will, for I am tired to death. I have been up all night, worrying myself into a fever about you. You will live to regret the day that you would not agree to my plan.'

'Maybe,' Serena replied; 'but at the same time, Nicholas, the Staverleys have never run away, and I am not going to be the first to start, not even though it means marriage with . . . with the Devil himself.'

'VULCAN is late,' the Earl of Gillingham remarked, stretching his long legs a little further over the hearthrug and reaching out languidly towards the glass of wine at his elbow.

'Not yet,' Sir Peter Burley answered, 'and I will wager you a monkey, Gilly, that he will be here before the hour strikes.'

'Done,' Lord Gillingham replied, and raised his eyes to the big marble clock ticking away the minutes on the mantelshelf.

At that moment there was the sound of voices outside and Lord Gillingham remarked:

'Demme, Peter, but I believe you have won.'

But when the door opened it was to disclose a woman's figure wrapped in a scarlet fur-trimmed mantua, the hood framing a lovely laughing face. The two gentlemen jumped to their feet.

'Isabel!' Lord Gillingham exclaimed.

'Good evening, Gilly, I did not expect to find you here, nor you, Peter,' Lady Isabel Calver said, dropping a little mocking curtsy before she went up to her brother and kissed his cheek. 'You are looking extremely handsome, Gilly. Have you found yourself a new charmer or have you been winning at cards?'

'Neither,' Lord Gillingham retorted, then added sternly, 'Explain yourself, Isabel. What are you doing here?'

'The same as you, I imagine,' Lady Isabel replied. 'Good evening, Peter.'

She held out her white hand to Sir Peter Burley and smiled at him bewitchingly as he raised it to his lips.

'Drat it, Isabel, you know what I mean,' Lord Gillingham insisted. 'There is no party here to-night; at least, none was planned when Vulcan invited us to dine with him.'

'We will make it a party,' Isabel smiled, letting her scarlet cloak fall from her shoulders into Sir Peter's arms and moving towards the fireplace, her gauzy dress of green net revealing rather than concealing her lovely figure.

'You have come here uninvited,' her brother said accusingly. 'Stop baming, Isabel; you cannot dine with Vulcan unchaperoned.'

'Unchaperoned?' Lady Isabel echoed. 'Is not my most devoted brother chaperon enough? Besides, who is to know? And I want to see Justin.'

'I thought you were in Bath,' Lord Gillingham said.

'So I was until yester eve,' his sister replied. 'But the coach was so monstrous slow, and I was so weary after the journey that I went straight to bed and slept till noon today, otherwise I would have let you know I had returned.'

'That still does not account for your presence here,' Lord Gillingham pointed out.

'Upon my soul, but you are persistent, Gilly,' Isabel sighed. I have told you that I want to see Justin. I only opened my eyes at noon, but I vow before I had taken even a sip of my morning chocolate I was regaled by some wild tale of Justin's latest indiscretion. I drove round here during the afternoon only to be told that he had gone to Mandrake to his mother, but that he would be returning tonight and that you and Peter were dining with him. Now are you satisfied?'

Lord Gillingham met Sir Peter's eyes as he stood at the other side of Lady Isabel. After a moment's pause he asked:

'What was the . . . er . . . wild tale you heard?'

'Don't pretend to me, Gilly,' Isabel said sharply. 'You have heard it too. All London is humming with it and I want to know the truth from Justin's own lips.'

'Which tale are you referring to?' her brother asked. 'There are so many.'

'I know that,' Isabel said sharply, 'and I have heard most of them. The new 'on dit' is that Justin staked his freedom at cards and won a bride.' There was a moment's silence and then she stamped her foot. 'Well,' she asked, 'is it true?'

She had only to glance at the faces of the two men confronting her to know that it was, and she gave a little exclamation that was half a cry just as the clock on the mantelpiece began to strike the hour.

'Do you hear that, Gilly?' Sir Peter Burley asked triumphantly, but even as he spoke the door opened and the Marquis of Vulcan, booted and spurred and wearing an exquisitely cut grey coat trimmed with pearl buttons, stood before them.

'I was delayed, gentlemen,' he said, 'but I know you will forgive me.' He strode into the room, pulling off his driving gloves and throwing them to an attendant lackey. When he saw Lady Isabel, his eyebrows were raised for a moment, then he went forward suavely, taking her hand in his and raising it to his lips. 'Your servant, Isabel,' he said. 'This is an unexpected pleasure.' Then turning to Gilly, he said, 'Well, Gilly, what news from White's?'

He seemed to fill the room with his presence. His personality was overpowering, almost stupefying. The Earl of Gillingham was a tall man, but the Marquis dwarfed him.

'Justin,' Isabel said quickly, her eyes raised to his so that he could not fail to see the pleading in their depths or the slight tremble of her red lips. 'Justin, I had to see you.'

'Exactly! And I am here,' Lord Vulcan replied smoothly.

'I only returned from Bath last night to learn that all London was talking of you,' Isabel began.

Lord Vulcan held up his hand.

'Spare me the tattling of childish minds, at any rate until after we have dined and wined. I have driven straight from Mandrake and I am thirsty.'

'How long did it take you?' Sir Peter asked.

'Not more than five hours,' Lord Vulcan answered him. 'I only changed horses twice. My new greys are magnificent. They are well worth the thousand guineas I paid for them.'

'You must be tired,' Lady Isabel said solicitously.

'I am never tired when I am driving,' Lord Vulcan replied, 'but I am a trifle stiff, and the Dover Road seemed monstrously crowded for the time of year. Methinks there are too many people seeking the south coast for it to be the lure of the golden sun.'

Lord Gillingham roared with laughter.

'The golden guinea is more likely. I hear that the smugglers grow bolder every day and that the French are more interested in building guinea boats than in winning the war.'

'The French know which is the more profitable,' Lord Vulcan said, and turned to take the glass of wine which a footman in claret and silver uniform was proffering him. 'You will join me, Isabel?' he asked.

She shook her head and Lord Vulcan, taking the glass, raised it to her in a silent toast before he drank.

'Dinner is served, m'lord.'

The butler spoke from the doorway and Lord Vulcan,

setting down his glass, held out his hand to Isabel. As they walked to the dining-room ahead of the two men, she whispered for his ear alone:

'You are not angry with me for coming, Justin? I had to see you.'

'Angry,' he replied, not speaking in a whisper, but lowering his voice slightly. 'Have you ever known me angry with you?'

She gave a quick sigh.

'No, Justin. Sometimes I wish you would be. It would show me that I could at least raise some emotion within you.'

He smiled a little cynically.

'You women are all the same,' he said, 'never content with a man as he is.'

Isabel would have made some retort, but she stifled the words on her lips. She heard a bitter note in his voice and remembered that he was invariably in a cynical mood when he returned from seeing his mother.

They entered the gold and cream dining-room where a footman in claret and silver livery stood behind every chair. A hundred wax tapers in the glittering, iridescent chandeliers cast a mellow light over the long polished table heavily laden with gold plate and ornamental vases filled with orchids. In the great wine coolers bottles of champagne rested on ice. Half a dozen crested crystal glasses to hold the different wines to be served during the meal were laid beside every place. Lord Vulcan sat at the head of the table, with Isabel on his right.

The meal was long and varied. Course after course was brought in on huge gold plates. The Marquis's chef was famous and a special sauce of white grapes and oysters was served with the fillets of beef, while tenderones of veal were garnished with truffles and cream.

While the servants were in the room, it seemed to be Lord Vulcan's object to talk of trivial things and to avoid the subject which he must have known was prevalent in the minds of all three of his guests. At last the dessert was put on the table, everyone's glass was filled and the servants withdrew.

Lord Vulcan looked from one face to another and said softly:

'Speak! For the restraint you have put on your tongues is ageing you before my very eyes.'

'This wager, Justin . . .' Isabel began excitedly and the

pent-up emotions within her came rushing through her lips like a full tide.

'One minute, Isabel,' her brother interrupted. 'Justin, you have heard about Sir Giles Staverley?'

'That he was killed in a duel?' Lord Vulcan asked. 'Yes, I heard it yesterday.'

'He got himself killed deliberately,' Lord Gillingham said, and there was a frown between his eyes. 'You have heard whom he challenged?'

'Blacknorton!'

'Yes, and he himself fired into the air.'

'Poor fool,' Lord Vulcan said softly.

'Blacknorton crossed to France the same afternoon.' Sir Peter Burley interposed. 'The betting is that he will be back within six months. It is a relief to be rid of him even for so short a time. He is a crafty fellow, and I never liked him.'

'Nevertheless he is a fine shot,' Lord Vulcan remarked.

Isabel looked from one to the other.

'Is Sir Giles Staverley the father of this girl? I didn't hear the name. What relation is he to Nicholas Staverley?'

'Uncle, I believe,' her brother replied.

'Of course, I remember now hearing him speak of his uncle.'

'Nicholas Staverley is one of your beaux, isn't he, Isabel?'

Isabel shrugged her shoulders.

'A dead bore though doubtless very worthy. But it is not with him that we are concerned. Justin, it is true then . . . about this girl?'

'Whether it is true or not depends on what you have been told,' Lord Vulcan remarked, leaning back in his high-backed chair and sipping his wine reflectively as if he savoured every mouthful.'

'Justin, you will drive me distracted,' Isabel cried. 'Are you going to wed her?'

There was a pregnant silence before Lord Vulcan's answer came quietly, in his usual tone of bored indifference.

'I have not said so, have I?'

'How can you be expected to marry anyone you have never seen?' Lord Gillingham asked. 'The whole wager was ridiculous, you shouldn't have accepted it.'

'I swear I was but trying to do the fellow a good turn,' Lord Vulcan drawled. 'I had won considerable amounts

26

from him on other occasions and I was willing to offer him his revenge.'

'So in a moment of generosity,' Isabel said sarcastically, 'you took from him his fortune, his house and his daughter's hand in marriage! Fudge, Justin, that tale is too smoky, you can't expect us to believe such fairy stories where you are concerned. Let us hear the truth. You have some scheme for getting hold of the eighty thousand pounds without saddling yourself with the girl? Come now, Justin, tell us the truth.'

Lord Vulcan smiled.

'The plots evolved in your pretty head, Isabel, far exceed my imagination.'

'Then you do not deny it?' Isabel exclaimed, clapping her hands excitedly. 'Oh, Justin, I felt they were all wrong when they vowed that you would marry the girl."

'Has anyone seen Miss Staverley?' Sir Peter asked. 'Lady Rohan avers that she is pitted with smallpox and is as fat as a Jersey cow.'

Isabel laughed.

'I've heard that she squints,' her brother said. 'As a matter of fact I think all the talk about her is only a hum. Nobody has actually seen her as far as I can make out, and Nicholas Staverley, who could have told us all we wanted to know, left for the country the morning after the duel.'

'When did all this happen?' Isabel asked.

'About ten days ago,' her brother answered.

'Ten days ago,' Isabel repeated, 'and you have done nothing about it, Justin?'

She spoke in tones of the utmost relief.

'To tell the truth, my dear,' Lord Vulcan replied, 'the whole episode slipped my mind. My mother sent for me—there were things to be seen to at Mandrake—and until a guest at dinner last night mentioned that Sir Giles Staverley was dead, I had forgotten the whole episode.'

' 'Pon my soul, Justin, that is pretty cool!' Lord Gillingham remarked. 'You win an estate, a famous house and a bride with eighty thousand pounds and it slips your memory. If anyone else said so, I would think they were funning, but, by gad, I believe you.'

'Thank you, Gilly,' Lord Vulcan said gravely; 'and now since you have brought it all to my notice, I suggest that we go down and inspect my new property.'

'When? To-morrow?' Sir Peter asked.

'To-morrow!' Lord Vulcan echoed. 'Why the delay? Why not to-night?'

'But, Justin, that is impossible,' Isabel expostulated.

Lord Vulcan smiled at her.

'Nothing is impossible,' he said, 'not where I am concerned at any rate. Gilly, Peter and I will go and see for ourselves the wonders of Staverley Court and the charms of my squinting pock-marked bride. I believe that the place is not more than twelve miles out of town. We can go there and be back before midnight.'

'Gad, but I would not miss it for a fortune,' Sir Peter exclaimed.

'I am coming with you,' Isabel said firmly.

'Now, Isabel, don't be so ridiculous,' her brother expostulated.

'I am not going to miss the excitement. You will take me, won't you, Justin? And a fig for Gilly's endless sermonising. He is constituting himself my *duenna* and I swear that I can't even breathe without his croaking about the damage I am doing to my reputation.'

'If you only knew the things that were being said about you,' Lord Gillingham groaned. 'You will be barred from Almack's before very long. You see if you are not.'

'Fah! Who cares for Almack's?' Lady Isabel asked with a derisive gesture. 'It is monstrously dull most evenings.'

'All right then, if you must be a rattlepate, you can go your own way,' Lord Gillingham said.

'As long as it is Justin's way,' Isabel replied, looking at Lord Vulcan with a longing in her eyes which she made no attempt to conceal. But the Marquis did not look deep into her eyes then as she wished he would, nor was he any more responsive when, half an hour later, she sat beside him in his phaeton and they set off at a sharp pace from the door of the Grosvenor Square mansion.

Lord Gillingham was driving in Sir Peter Burley's curricle, and they had arranged to race Lord Vulcan to Staverley Court once they were clear of the narrow London streets. The stakes were two thousand guineas.

It was not a warm night, for there was a touch of frost in the air but Isabel, wrapped in her fur-lined cloak, its hood framing her pretty face, was impervious to cold. She was, with the unimportant exception of the groom perched behind them, alone with Justin and that was all that mattered. She had been longing to be alone with him not for days but for weeks and months.

She loved Justin and had vowed to herself that she would marry him. Having been spoilt all her life, it was difficult for Isabel to visualise any object that could not be obtained once she had set her heart on it. Her parents, who loved her devotedly, had made no attempt to check her headstrong impetuosity. So much so that when, a day before her seventeenth birthday, she ran away with a penniless officer in the Dragoon Guards, her family forgave her and received her back into her own home immediately the honeymoon was over. That the young officer in question was killed fighting a year later came as a relief not only to his people-in-law, but also to his own wife. When the excitement of her elopement was over, Isabel found lack of money and dissimilarity of tastes were tiresome appendages to romance.

On her mother's insistence the year's mourning had been reluctantly observed, and doubtless she would have broken even this tradition had not her father died and she been forced to be at her mother's side in the country.

At the first possible opportunity, however, Isabel came to London. She had hardly had time to make her début before her marriage. Now she savoured not only the gaieties which should have been hers when a girl, but also the more heady excitement of flirtations and intrigues which were invariably to be found by a beautiful young widow wanting only to enjoy life to the full. She made herself the subject of a good deal of conversation by her madcap escapades before she met the Marquis of Vulcan. After that there was no limit to her daring and to her defiance of the more sober social conventions.

She was well aware that Justin was not in the good books of the more respectable London hostesses. She knew that eyebrows were raised and shoulders shrugged when she sought his society obviously and openly on every possible occasion. But Isabel did not care. She was in love for the first time in her life and she went at it tempestuously and without a thought for anyone's feelings save her own. To her astonishment she seemed to make little headway where Justin was concerned. He neither encouraged nor discouraged her.

It was no secret that his 'light o' love' was *La Flamme*, a beautiful French dancer, who had recently appeared at Vauxhall Gardens, and who was the toast of all the bucks of St. James's. Justin was her acknowledged protector, but Isabel did not care how many *La Flammes* there were in

Justin's life. It was marriage she wanted from him and she believed that she would succeed where every ambitious mamma had failed for the last ten years.

'Now I can talk to you,' she said to Justin, snuggling a little closer to him as they started off into the night.

The moon was rising and it was not dark. Justin's profile, clean-cut against the sky, gave Isabel a thrill. How handsome he was in his many-tiered cape and a high beaver hat. His eyes were fixed ahead, his fingers busy with the reins. They were moving fast, but Justin was an incomparable whip and Isabel knew she would never be afraid with him.

'Have you missed me lately?' she asked in a low voice.

For a fleeting second Justin took his eyes from the road ahead and looked down at her. She saw his lips part in a sudden smile.

'I never have a chance to miss any other woman when I am with my mother.'

Isabel digested this information for a moment in silence. It was true, she was sure of that. She had heard a well-known wit remark only a few days ago: "The Marchioness of Vulcan treats her son as though he were her lover, and who knows better than both of them what that treatment should be?" Feeling that she had somehow made a false move towards the close intimacy which she so greatly desired, Isabel changed her tactics.

'Are you excited at the thought of your journey's end?' she enquired lightly.

'I have long ceased to be excited in anticipation of anything,' Justin answered.

'What a lot of things you miss,' Isabel sighed, 'for I declare, Justin, that half the joys of life are to be found in anticipating what is going to happen.'

'And regretting it when it does,' Justin parried.

'You are getting old and cynical,' Isabel mocked him.

'Maybe!'

Justin flicked the horses with his whip and they went a little faster.

'I wish I understood you,' Isabel went on; 'you are a strange person, Justin, and no one has your confidence. When one tries to get near to you, here is always a barrier.'

'How unprepossessing you make me sound!' Justin answered. 'It is amazing that you bother with me.'

'Bother!' There was almost a sob in Isabel's voice as she

repeated the word, and then lightly, because she was afraid that he might be bored with any expression of her real feelings, she said: 'I don't believe that you enjoy half the things you do, Justin.'

There was a moment's silence and Isabel suddenly was sure she had said something so true that Justin could find no words in which to answer her. 'Why then does he do them?' she wondered and felt, as she had felt so often before, that she was beating frantically against a brick wall which stood between her and the man she loved.

'Justin,' she said pleadingly, and then was well aware that there was relief in his voice as he said:

'Here come the others; they must have got held up. We will let them get even with us and then show them what we can do. Pray heaven we don't lose the way.'

There was no chance of further intimacies. Peter Burley was determined to win his wager. Apart from the money it would be no mean triumph, as he well knew. His horses were as good as the Marquis's pair of chestnuts, but his driving could never compare with Vulcan's.

More than once the horses were neck and neck, but the chestnuts turned in at the gates of Staverley Court two lengths ahead of Peter Burley's greys. Isabel gave a shout of joy which echoed strangely across the deserted park.

'Oh la, that was grand fun, Justin. Peter was certain he could beat you. I heard him tell Gilly so just before he started. After you had been driving all day he thought he had a good chance of winning.' Justin said nothing and after a moment Isabel added: 'There must be an element of luck in it too. You are lucky, aren't you, Justin? Are you never feared that your good fortune will desert you?'

'What do you call my good fortune?' Justin asked.

In the darkness of the trees the moonlight showing through them wove a strange pattern on the drive.

'Your good fortune?' Isabel repeated. 'Look what it has gained you at cards in the past, and now this. . . .'

They had come to a turn in the drive and the house lay before them; the moonlight was full on its grey beauty; the stone terrace and the great wide sweep of lake beneath were a picture in light and shade. The house was exquisite there was no denying that, and yet Isabel felt for a moment that something was lacking. Then she knew what it was. She had never, if ever, approached a house without its windows being filled with light, without a warm glow within showing forth a welcome across the intervening darkness.

'Have you thought, Justin,' she asked, 'that it is late for country folk? Everyone will be asleep.'

'Then we will wake them,' he replied.

'They will have been watching for you day after day, wondering when you would come, waiting perhaps to curse you for your new suzerainty, and then when they are asleep, suddenly you are there.' She laughed. 'Lud, but it is an amusing thought and, if the poor devils but knew, so like you!'

Lord Vulcan said nothing, but drove over the bridge which spanned the lake and turned into the wide gravel sweep in front of the house. As he drew up at the front steps, the groom spoke:

'Shall I pull the bell, m'lord?'

'Yes, and ring it loudly.'

The small groom sped up the steps to do as he was told. He tugged at the heavy iron chain hanging on one side of the door. They heard the bell clang a long way away—a mournful, empty sound. Isabel shivered.

'Perhaps everybody is dead. Let us go away and come another time.'

Peter Burley drove up beside them.

'Stap me if it wasn't a good race, Justin, for all that you beat me. I thought I had you once or twice.'

Lord Gillingham was looking up at the house.

'This is a nice little place you have acquired, Justin,' he said. 'But they hardly seem anxious to make your acquaintance; no one is astir.'

'Why should they be when they did not know we were coming?' Isabel asked pettishly. 'But I wish they would hurry up and open the door. I would welcome the chance to warm myself at a fire.'

Lord Vulcan's groom was still pulling at the bell. There was a sound of footsteps, a creaking of locks and a clanging of chains; then slowly the big front door swung open. An old man stood there, staring out into the night, an ancient coat of livery held across his chest with one hand.

'What is it ye want, gentlemen?'

'It is the Marquis of Vulcan, your new owner,' the groom remarked in shrill tones.

'I did not instruct him to say that,' Justin said in a quiet voice; but it was obvious that he was amused.

The old man looked startled.

'The Marquis of Vulcan,' he repeated. 'I will tell Miss Serena. Come ye in, m'lord. I will light the candles.'

Lord Vulcan sprang down from the box and went round to the other side of the phaeton to help down Lady Isabel. She clung to him for a moment as he held her in his arms. With the utmost dexterity he set her on the ground and she was free.

'I feel as if I were going to church,' Lord Gillingham said as they walked up the steps into the darkened hall. The old man was lighting candles in the crystal brackets set high on the wall on either side of the fireplace. In a moment or two there was a mellow glow of light and then he lit a fire in the big fireplace.

'I will inform Miss Serena,' he was muttering to himself as he walked away.

'La, but it is cold,' Isabel said holding out her hands to the flames creeping up the logs but as yet giving no warmth.

'It is not a bad place!' her brother said looking around him.

'Do you think your bride will offer us a drink, Justin?' Sir Peter Burley asked. 'My tongue is so thick with dust—your dust—that I can hardly speak.'

'We must do our best for you,' Lord Vulcan smiled.

At that moment the old retainer came shuffling back.

'Is there any wine in the house?' Lord Vulcan asked.

'Yes, m'lord. Certainly, m'lord. I will fetch a bottle right away. I was to beg your lordships to make thyselves comfortable and Miss Serena will be down in a short a space of time as possible. Will ye have a chair, m'lord?'

The old man pushed four high-backed chairs forward so that they formed a circle round the fire.

'Wine is what we want, my good man,' Sir Peter Burley said impatiently.

'Yes, m'lord. Certainly, m'lord.'

The old man shuffled away again.

'I shouldn't keep him on the staff,' Sir Peter laughed. 'He should have been retired half a century ago.'

'If you look closely at the place,' Lord Gillingham said critically, 'you will see that it is somewhat dilapidated. Sir Giles must have been pressed for some time. Shall we have a look at the other rooms?'

'It would be more polite to wait,' Lord Vulcan replied, 'and frankly, Gilly, I am in no hurry to view the rest of my property. The sample I see before me is quite discouraging enough.'

Isabel turned from the fire with an impish smile.

33

'Mayhap the lady is as dilapidated as her surroundings. I would not miss your handling of this situation for anything in the world.'

'We have not seen her yet,' Lord Gillingham reminded his sister. 'If she turns out to be a beauty, you will be ready to scratch her eyes out.'

'She won't be,' Lady Isabel retorted confidently.

'Here comes the wine,' Sir Peter said. 'Let us be grateful, Justin, that at least you have inherited one bottle, if no more.'

The old butler filled the glasses with shaking fingers.

'Have you more of these?' Lord Vulcan asked.

'A few bottles, m'lord. A few bottles.'

'Then fetch another one.'

'At once, m'lord. At once.'

The old man was gone again. The fire burned up and gradually the warmth crept out into the room. Isabel sat down in a chair on one side of the fireplace holding out her hands to the blaze.

'I am feeling sleepy,' she yawned. 'Let us hope your pock-marked beauty does not keep us waiting too long.'

'The night is still young,' Sir Peter replied.

'We shan't be back before midnight,' Lord Gillingham remarked.

'What matter if we are not?' Lord Vulcan answered.

He glanced up. At the far end of the hall was a wide staircase with a balustrade of carved oak. The head of the staircase had been hidden in a deep shadow, but now there was a light approaching, the flickering orange glow casting strange shadows as it moved. Then suddenly there was the light of a silver candelabra held high by the strangest creature his lordship had ever seen—a wizened, dwarfed woman, big-headed with a tiny miss-shapen body, her eyes deep pools of darkness.

She stood at the head of the staircase holding the candelabra high in her hands, while into the light, her hand on the head of a great brown mastiff, came a girl. For a moment she stood very still, looking down at the little group of people by the fireplace; then slowly she moved forward, her fair hair haloed around her head, her sweet face pale in the candlelight.

She wore a simple gown of white muslin; her arms were bare and there were no jewels or ornaments around her neck. Utterly lovely in her simplicity and in complete silence she descended the stairs into the hall.

Three

SERENA woke early in the small oak bed that she had slept in since she was a child. The light was coming through the curtains revealing to her the familiar outlines of the room which had once been her nursery and which she still preferred for her bedroom despite the fact that she could, had she wished, have slept in one of the bigger and grander rooms of the house.

She had loved her nursery as a child and it had come, as the years passed by, to afford her a refuge, a place where she could escape from the cares and troubles of trying to run a household without money, from the grumbles of the old servants, and even from her ever-increasing anxiety about her father.

Her mother had died when she was nine years old. Serena had loved her dearly, but Lady Staverley had suffered from ill-health after a riding accident. As long as Serena could remember she never left the house, receiving guests as she lay on a couch in the drawing-room and later, when she grew worse, retiring to her bedroom and being often in such excruciating pain that death was in many ways a welcome release.

Sir Giles, who had loved his wife devotedly, had few friends. He was liked in the county, but his more stolid neighbours could never understand or sympathise with his passion for gambling; and his visits to London were spent entirely in gaming clubs so he made no friendships there.

It was a lonely life that he lived at Staverley after his wife's death and it was even more lonely for his only child. All too soon Serena realised that unless she made an effort to keep the household together the place would sink from bad to worse and eventually become only a shambles of dust and ill-service, of fretful servants and empty, unaired rooms. Before she was twelve years of age she had taken command. In a year or so the servants learned to obey her, and when anything was wanted on the estate the tenants came humbly to ask her to intercede on their behalf with her father.

It was a strange position for a young girl, yet Serena accepted it easily, finding strength within herself to meet the daily demands upon her. She was rewarded by the affection her father developed for her, and the fact that the Staverley estate was, as far as funds allowed, looked after and cared for as it would never have been without her interest and authority.

It was now for the first time, as she lay in her comfortable bed, that she released the full import of what her father's death was to mean to her. Even when they had laid Sir Giles to rest in the little churchyard at the far end of Staverley Park, it had only seemed a strange dream and unreal. It had all happened too suddenly, too unexpectedly; and though there were tears in Serena's eyes so that she held blindly on to Nicholas's arm as they turned back towards the house, some part of her was still crying out pathetically that it was not true and she would awake and find that things were as they had always been.

The interval between her father's burial and the coming of the new owner of Staverley had only increased Serena's sense of unreality. She was used to being alone and as day succeeded day and there was no sign of the Marquis of Vulcan, she began to doubt the wild tale that had burst from Nicholas' lips and of which there had been no further confirmation. Had Nicholas imagined it all? Had the story of that crazy game of cards which had lost both Staverley and herself to a stranger been only a figment of Nicholas' imagination?

Day after day went by and Serena waited, at first starting at every sound, and scanning the drive not once but a dozen times in the hour for the sight of a strange carriage or an unknown horseman.

'If he is coming, why doesn't he come?' she would ask Nicholas impatiently, always to receive the same reply.

'No one knows, no one can guess what Vulcan will do. I have told you, Serena, he is a strange man and a bad one.'

It was cold comfort, but somehow the delay had the effect of taking the edge both from Serena's misery at her father's death and also from her own dread of the future. Although she had to a certain extent hidden her fears from Nicholas on that first momentous morning, she had been by no means as calm and assured as she had appeared. She had learnt very early in life not to show her feelings too easily and, especially where men were concerned, to hide anxiety behind a smile and to control the questions which rose too quickly to untempered lips.

Every night since her father's death Serena had prayed not only for him and that he might rest in peace, but also for herself. She was alone! She told herself the fact over and over again, and yet her future was pledged, her freedom enchained. She would not have been human if she had not wondered continually what Lord Vulcan was like. Nicholas' description of him had not been reassuring, but Serena knew that Nicholas had personal reasons for disliking the Marquis; even so, because Nicholas was a reliable person, it was wise to take notice of what he said.

When, the night before, Serena had been awakened from sleep by Eudora coming to her room to tell her agitatedly that the Marquis and a party had arrived, she had felt at first only annoyance that she should, as it were, have been caught off her guard. She had never imagined that he would come when she was asleep, and she had planned so often in her mind that she would meet him in a cool and composed manner the acknowledged *châletaine* of Staverly, even though she must hand it over to his keeping,

It had all been upsetting and disturbing, a quick scurry into her clothes with Eudora fussing over her hair, the difficulty of trying to remember at the same time whether the engraved glasses were ready for use and if there were enough candles in the chandelier to light the drawing-room.

'I never thought he would come at night,' Serena cried.

'Maybe it is the time that suits him best,' Eudora said darkly.

'How many people did old Beaston say there were with his lordship?' Serena questioned.

'Three, but he was so bemused that there may easily be more than less.'

'You must see that Beaston brings up the best wine, Eudora, and find two more crystal goblets. I stupidly expected that his lordship would come alone or with only a man of business.'

At last she was ready, and as Eudora lifted the big silver candelabra from the dressing-table to light them through the passages she took one last look at her reflection in the mirror and felt somehow relieved that the wild beating of her heart did not show in the calmness of her face.

She was comforted by the presence of Torqo, her great mastiff. He had slept on the mat outside her room since her father died, although his real place was in the kennels. She had been thankful that he was there. When he walked with her down the long flight of stairs to the hall she did not feel so lonely, so insignificant amongst these smart, elegant people from London versed in the ways of the fashionable world, knowledgeable in all the things of which she herself knew so little.

Slowly she went down the stairs, finding it difficult for a moment to focus anyone's face, conscious only that three men were rising from their chairs in front of the fire and that one person remained seated—a woman, whose dark passionate eyes seemed to burn their way into her awareness. Serena swept a curtsy and she looked from one to the other of the men towering above her.

'I regret that I was not here to welcome you, my lord.'

She wondered which was the Marquis. She had somehow expected him to be old, much older than any of the three men present. Then a deep voice answered her.

'We must apologise for our intrusion at such a late hour, Miss Staverley.'

Her first impression was that he was so much younger than she had expected; her second, that she had been mistaken after all and that the lines of boredom on his face and the indifference in his eyes did not belong to the exuberance and enthusiasm of youth. But he was handsome—the most handsome man she had ever seen . . . and he had won her at cards! She stared at him, her eyes wide. Suddenly there was a movement, an exclamation from the woman sitting in the chair, and a low-throated growl from Torqo. With a start Serena remembered her manners as a hostess.

Eudora was lighting the candles in the drawing-room, the big candelabras were blossoming in flower-like splendour beneath the long taper she held high in her withered arms. Soon the fire began to burn up. Quickly Eudora, far more dexterous than old Beaston who was long past his work, brought some small sweet cakes, which Isabel nibbled disdainfully as if they were hardly good enough for her palate.

It was all very formal, and Serena was well aware that a silence had fallen on the visitors since her appearance. She had heard them talking and even laughing gaily as she came along the passage which led from her bedroom to the

38

top of the stairs, but afterwards they had been silent except for the Marquis who had asked her a few questions and listened with an obvious effort at politeness to her answers.

It had not been long before they departed for London. As they made their farewells, the Marquis said to Serena:

'I shall return to-morrow to see you—alone. I regret the discourtesy which brought us here after you had retired for the night.'

'Please do not mention it, my lord,' Serena said, dropping him a curtsy. 'I shall be waiting for you to-morrow.'

She raised her eyes to his face, but already he had turned away, his broad shoulders silhouetted for a moment against the moonlit sky through the open door. Then he was gone and the only sound was of the horses' hoofs moving over the gravel drive and fading gradually into the distance and silence. She had gone up to her bed with her mind in a whirl. She had no idea what she felt or what she thought of the man to whom she was promised in marriage.

This morning it was difficult even to remember what he had been like. It was easier to recall Isabel's beautiful, sulky face, or the light of admiration in Lord Gillingham's eyes and the way Sir Peter Burley had tried to smile at her every time she looked in his direction. It was all very perplexing and disturbing; and because she hated to lie alone with her thoughts Serena sprang from her bed and crossing the room drew back the curtains.

It was still very early and the dew lay like diamonds over the grass, the mist was rising from the lake and the birds were already beginning to sing in the trees. Far away in the distance, where the wild woodlands came down to join the park, she could see the pigeons winging their way from their roosting places towards the open cornfields. Staverley! How she loved it! And now at last the knowledge that it was no longer hers hurt her with an agony that was almost physical.

There was a sudden bumping against the door of the room and Serena knew that her movements, quiet though they had been, had been overheard. She opened the door to Torqo who rubbed himself against her, his tail wagging. Suddenly she knelt down on the floor beside him, put her arms round him and hid her face in the softness of his great neck.

'Oh, Torqo,' she whispered, 'do you realise what is happening to us?'

He licked her face, thrilled by the sound of her voice, too glad that she should speak to him to be conscious that anything was wrong. Serena raised her head, looked at him and gave a little laugh.

'All right, Torqo,' she said aloud, 'there is no use worrying; let us take things as they come and try to be happy while we can.'

He whined with delight and again she laughed, playing with him as if he were still a puppy, rolling him over on his back so that his great legs waved helplessly in the air.

It was thus that Eudora found them as she entered the room with an early morning cup of chocolate.

'You are laughing, Miss Serena?' she asked suspiciously, as if she thought her ears and eyes might be deceiving her.

'Yes, laughing, Eudora. It is better than crying.'

'I am glad you find something at which to laugh,' Eudora said in a tone of gloom.

'If crying would help matters, Eudora,' Serena replied, sitting down on the side of the bed and picking up her cup of chocolate, 'I would cry. Besides, we have yet to know the worst.'

'That is true,' Eudora sighed. 'His lordship returns to-day?'

'He said so,' Serena replied. 'We had better have a good luncheon prepared in case he arrives this morning.'

'There is little enough in the house.'

'There is the ham we were keeping for Michaelmas,' Serena answered; 'there are plenty of fowls on the farm, and the stable boy can ride to the village for some meat. What is the point of keeping anything, Eudora? I do not suppose the Marquis will live here.'

For the first time her voice broke disconsolately and the fear that had been prevalent in her heart could no longer be denied. Staverley Court would be shut up. Closed and barred, it would gradually sink into a state of decay, the rain would come through the roof, cobwebs would blind the windows, the gardens would grow wild and the flowers would run riot untended. The picture was infinitely pathetic. Then, quickly because she was afraid of her own thoughts, Serena said sharply:

'Let us talk of something else, Eudora. What shall I wear?'

'Will you have your other muslin, Miss Serena? I washed and ironed it yesterday. It is crisp and fresh and vastly becomes you.'

Serena smiled.

'Yes, I will wear that, Eudora. I feel it is important to make a good impression.'

Eudora said nothing and Serena longed to ask her what she had thought of Lord Vulcan, but because she feared Eudora's tongue the question remained unasked. When she was dressed, she went downstairs. The windows in the drawing-room were open; the room smelt fresh and fragrant and looked as usual, with only the half-burnt tapers in the chandeliers to remind her that last night guests had been entertained there.

She glanced at the chair on which the Marquis had sat. She could see him now—a big man, he had an air of proud dignity which bespoke breeding and the whole bearing of a man sure of himself. That, Serena thought, was perhaps the one thing she remembered about him in all certainty—his air of self-assurance. Did she hate him? She was not sure, any more than she was sure this morning of his good looks, his courtesy, or of her own impressions of him. Yet she knew if she were honest that she was afraid of him. Why should he concern himself with her? She was nobody and in this world there were few to equal or exceed his position and power. She thought of Lady Isabel Calver, so beautiful, so exquisitely dressed, the jewels sparkling round her white neck and on her wrists.

'How inexperienced I am!' Serena sighed. 'How little I know about the lives such people live! We are country cousins, you and I, Torqo.'

She felt the dog nuzzle her hand and once again she took comfort from his presence beside her. And Torqo stood by her side in the hall an hour later when Eudora reported that a coach was approaching.

'A coach?' Serena echoed in surprise, remembering the phaeton with its magnificent pair of chestnuts in which Lord Vulcan had driven away the night before.

Eudora was right. Coming down the drive was a coach, resplendent in claret and silver. Postilions were astride the leading horses and there were out-riders in attendance. The cavalcade swept up to the front door, a footman sprang down to let down the steps and open the coach door. Out stepped the Marquis, as resplendent as his *entourage*. He wore a coat of azure blue silk with diamond buttons. This time there was no need to pull at the bell chain or to wait on a tardily opened front door.

Beaston, in his ancient livery and white wig, was awaiting his lordship and Serena came forward the moment he stepped into the hall. She curtsied to him and felt unaccountably shy. She had a feeling that this pomp and ceremony was a gesture, and that in some obscure way of his own Lord Vulcan intended it as an apology for the unconventionality of his visit the night before. He raised her fingers to his lips.

'Your servant, Miss Staverley.'

'Will you come into the drawing-room, my lord?'

She led the way and no sooner had they seated themselves than Eudora was at Lord Vulcan's elbow offering wine. He took the glass but made no effort to drink it, merely putting it on a table beside him. For a moment they sat in silence until the tension was broken by Torqo walking slowly and with a dignity all of his own towards the Marquis. He sniffed at him a little suspiciously and then, apparently reassured, laid his great head upon his lordship's knee.

'Is this your dog?' Lord Vulcan asked.

'My own, and a very dear friend, my lord.'

'I thought so last night,' Lord Vulcan said.

Again there was a pause and Serena, conscious that the Marquis was regarding her steadily, felt the colour rising in her cheeks.

'He is young,' she thought. 'It is the expression on his face that belies his years.'

His eyes, dark grey and somehow steely in their depths, were stranger than any she had ever beheld before in the face of a human being, but try as she would she could not keep her eyes on his. Her eyelids fluttered and her long dark eyelashes swept her cheeks which, flushed a moment ago, had now paled again.

'There is a great deal that we have to say to each other, Miss Staverley,' Lord Vulcan said slowly.

'There is,' Serena agreed.

'First of all,' he went on, 'may I express to you my deep regret at your father's death?'

His voice was clear and disinterested and somehow it seemed to Serena not exactly an impertinence but an intrusion that he should speak of her father at all when he had been instrumental, albeit indirectly, for the way in which he had died. Very proudly Serena drew herself up and in a voice as cool and as clear as his lordship's she replied:

'I think it would be well, my lord, if we did not speak of

42

my father's death. The full facts of the event which led to his death and the reason why he died have been told to me by my cousin, Mr. Nicholas Staverley, who was present at White's when he played with you and was with him later when he met his end . . . in a duel with Mr. Blacknorton. The Staverley estate and this house are now yours and I am ready to give you any information regarding them.'

Lord Vulcan inclined his head.

'Thank you.'

'I have for your acceptance, my Lord,' Serena went on, 'the deeds of the estate, a list of the tenants and the names of those who have received pensions from my father these past years. You . . . you would wish to continue these?'

For the first time there was a note of anxiety in her voice.

'Of course.'

'I am glad.'

Her relief showed through her calmness, then, steeling herself, Serena continued:

'There are lists, too, of the livestock on the home farm. I am afraid the accounts are not in very good order. We . . . my father . . . has not been able to affor . . . er . . . to obtain the services of a man of business lately.'

'My own man will be here to-morrow,' Lord Vulcan said. 'I have given instructions to enquire into all such matters.'

'You will shut up the house?'

Serena strove to keep her voice from betraying any emotion, but despite her resolution there was a slight quiver on the words.

'I suppose so,' Lord Vulcan replied lightly. 'Later, of course, it may be possible to find a purchaser.'

With an effort that was almost superhuman Serena checked the cry that rose to her lips. Her fingers tightened for a moment as they lay in her lap and then she was mistress of herself again. Now she knew that she hated him, hated this man who had come here to destroy the little world she had called her own, to destroy it carelessly and indifferently without a thought and without even obtaining any satisfaction from his destruction.

She did not know until this minute how she had tried to find excuses for the Marquis, finding it hard because of its very exaggeration to accept Nicholas' description of him. She had wanted, because in her heart of hearts she was afraid of the worst, to find the best; she had wanted him to

43

be so much better, so unmistakably nicer than his reputation.

Now she knew she had built for herself but a mirage. It was not the evil Lord Vulcan could do that she feared, but his heartlessness, his careless indifference to the feelings of human beings who must suffer through his very omnipotence.

A purchaser for Staverley!—Thus it was to be lost to her for ever!

Somehow she had hoped that even if she married the Marquis she might come here, that it might still remain her home. Well, she would not give him the satisfaction of showing how much he had hurt her. Holding herself stiffly erect, she faced him with darkening eyes. Her very hatred, new-born, virile within her, made her able to speak calmly of another matter.

'The house and estate were, I believe, the first part of my father's wager with you. The second part concerns me personally.'

'That is correct.'

Serena took a deep breath.

'My father told you, I believe, that on my marriage I should inherit eighty thousand pounds.'

'That, too, is correct.'

'It was my maternal grandfather's money,' Serena explained: 'he . . . he disliked my father because, being religious, he disapproved of gaming in all its forms. He left the money in trust for me until I should wed, and he made it a stipulation that I should not anticipate in any form my inheritance. He was afraid, you see, that I should borrow money on my father's behalf. Were I to do this, the trustees were empowered to give the money direct to charity.'

'I understand,' Lord Vulcan said.

Serena rose from her chair and walked across to the window. She stood looking out into the garden. As always the beauty of it roused within her a feeling half pain, half pleasure. It was so lovely, and now it was no longer hers. She felt for a moment the tears blind her eyes, swimming mistily before her sight so that the garden became indistinct, there were rainbows dancing iridescently on every blossoming bush and tree.

'You love this place?' a voice beside her asked gravely, making her start, for somehow she had imagined that Lord Vulcan was still on the other side of the room.

44

Serena nodded, because for a moment she could not speak.

'I must show you a place that is even more beautiful,' Lord Vulcan said. 'My own home. Mandrake.'

Serena told herself fiercely that she would hate it. How could any place be as beautiful as Staverley? He was looking out of the window over her head and suddenly she was conscious of him, his nearness, of the strength that must lie beneath the languid grace of his hands and the studied elegance of his body. With an effort she turned away from the window.

'As you said, my lord, we have many things to discuss.'

'I thought we were discussing them,' Lord Vulcan answered.

Serena threw back her head.

'What are you . . . going to do with me?' she asked.

Even as she spoke the words, she wondered at her own daring. Immediately the tell-tale colour sprang to her cheeks again. But she forced her shyness from her, making herself face him defiantly even while she felt her pulses quicken and her heart beat faster.

'That, of course, is an important question,' Lord Vulcan said unsmilingly.

'My lord, I have a confession to make to you.'

His eyebrows were raised in one second.

'I rather expected it. You are in love with your cousin?'

'No, of course not!'

Serena's reply was quick, spontaneous and almost indignant.

'I am very fond of Nicholas, but there is nothing . . . like that between us.'

'Then it is another local beau who has captured your heart?' Lord Vulcan suggested, and now there was a note of cynical sarcasm in his voice which Serena resented.

'On the contrary, there is no such person,' she retorted, 'and it was not about my heart that I wished to speak.'

'Indeed! Confessions from beautiful young women invariably involve the vacillations of their hearts.'

'I am afraid I am not as experienced in such matters as you, my lord,' Serena replied and thought for one moment that there was a faint twitch at the corner of Lord Vulcan's mouth as if he appreciated her thrust.

'I apologise,' the Marquis answered. 'I will make no more guesses as to what you wish to confess.'

'We were speaking just now,' Serena answered, 'of my

45

fortune, and you believed, my lord, that on my marriage I should inherit eighty thousand pounds. This is not correct.'

'Indeed?'

'No, it will be seventy-nine thousand pounds to be exact. I must be honest with you. I have in fact anticipated a thousand pounds.'

'But I thought you said,' Lord Vulcan remarked, 'that it was impossible for you to do such a thing.'

'If the trustees learn of it, they will give the money to charity as arranged by my grandfather's will,' Serena said. 'May I explain?'

'I hope you will,' Lord Vulcan said. 'Could we not sit down?'

'Of course.'

Serena returned to the seat she had taken when they first entered the room and the Marquis sat opposite her.

'When I was sixteen,' Serena began quietly, 'I went to London for the season. My godmother had arranged to give a ball for me. I had looked forward to it, yet at the same time I was already afraid of London because of what had happened here the previous year. I had a friend, my lord, who was exceeding fair. She was older than I, but she also loved Staverley. She had lived here all her life. Her father was our head groom, her mother had at one time been my mother's maid. She was a lovely girl; Charmaine was her name, and I think everybody in the place was fond of her.

'She was always happy, singing about her work, and though she worked hard she always had time to play with me; and because I was lonely, being an only child, I grew to love her as if she were my sister. My father had various parties that winter for the hunting and amongst the guests, there was a certain Lord Wrotham. I took little notice of him, being but a child and not even allowed down to dinner. But he was a fairly frequent visitor and I was continually finding him in those parts of the house where the other guests never ventured.

'Once I found him in my nursery, another time in the linen room. One day when Charmaine and I were out for a walk together we came upon him unexpectedly when he should have been with my father and the other guests. Being young and stupid, I was quite unsuspicious that he had any particular reasons for his behaviour until one evening we learned that Lord Wrotham had gone back to London and that Charmaine had gone with him.

'It was my first experience of treachery. I was desperately hurt that Charmaine, whom I loved, had gone without telling me, and I was disturbed by everyone else's reaction to her disappearance. I was told that Lord Wrotham would not wed Charmaine, that she was bold and bad, and that I was never to speak or even think of her again. I did not believe what I was told. Charmaine was so lovely that in my innocence I was sure she must find happiness. I only prayed that she might let me know where she was; but no word came from her.

'A year passed. Her father and mother, broken-hearted, never mentioned her name. The other servants spoke of her disgrace with bated breath, but I continued to love her. It was arranged for me to go to London to my godmother, and on the very morning of my departure I received news of Charmaine. It was a dirty, illiterate letter, written not by her—for I doubt if she could write—but by the woman in whose house she was lodging. Charmaine owed her money, she said; she had obtained my address; would I kindly send her what was owing to her or Charmaine would be turned into the street.

'I said nothing to anyone about the letter, but took it with me to London. For the first two or three days after my arrival it was impossible for me to do anything but go with my godmother to buy clothes, drive with her in the park, and make my *début* at two great balls. Then at last an opportunity presented itself and I set off to find Charmaine at St. Giles-in-the-Fields.'

'Good lord,' the Marquis ejaculated, 'you don't mean you went to that place by yourself?'

'No, I was sensible enough not to go alone,' Serena replied, 'I took one of my godmother's linkmen into my confidence. Luckily he had been a bruiser when he was younger. He warned me what sort of place we were going to and I borrowed clothes from an abigail. We set off. I won't worry you with a description of St. Giles-in-the Fields. If you have never been there, you have very likely heard tell of it—sufficient to say the horror and misery of it still haunt me. I can still see the naked children scrambling among the filth in the gutters for scraps of food, the gaunt, starved, drunken women, and men whose appearance and behaviour offends the very name of manhood. I found Charmaine lying on straw in an attic so filthy that even the rats hardly bothered to scurry away at our approach.

47

'She was so wasted that at first I hardly recognised her for the lovely, happy girl who had been tò me as a sister. She had given birth to a stillborn child a month earlier and had never recovered her strength. She had had no skilled attention since her confinement. She was horrified to see me and begged me to go away at once and leave her. But she was too weak to protest overmuch and we carried her away with us. I took her back to my godmother's house and when the latter, incensed by my behaviour, refused to take her in, I ordered a carriage and came home to Staverley. My godmother cancelled the ball she was giving for me and has not spoken to me since but I saved Charmaine's life and that was what mattered to me.'

Serena took a deep breath.

'What happened then?' the Marquis enquired.

'Charmaine grew better and stronger. She never spoke of what she had been through, but I guessed a little of the agony of mind that must have been hers when the man who had seduced her cast her away when she was about to bear his child. There was a young man in the village who had always been fond of her, and when she returned to us he began to court her again. At first she would have none of him, wanting only to hide herself here in the house where she had always worked. But at length I realised that she loved him even as he loved her, and that the other infatuation had merely been that of an inexperienced country girl for an evil, corrupt man of the world.

'There was only one thing to be done—to get them away from Staverley where people knew what had happened and where their happiness would never have a chance among those who condemned Charmaine unmercifully despite all she had suffered. I went to London for the second time in my life and I visited a firm of money-lenders of whom I had often heard my father speak—Messrs. Hinks and Israel.

'I saw Mr. Israel. I told him the whole story. I told him that I wanted money for this young couple and that I could give him no security save my word of honour that on my marriage I would pay him one thousand pounds. I told him that I could give him nothing in writing because if such a paper were produced, it would prevent my inheriting my grandfather's money. He must take my word and that alone.'

Lord Vulcan stared at Serena incredulously.

'You gave Israel nothing in writing?'

'No,' Serena replied. 'He gave me six hundred pounds and I promised him to repay one thousand pounds on the day of my marriage.'

'I know Israel,' Lord Vulcan said slowly, 'he is a hard-headed, shrewd man. He is owed more money than anyone else in the United Kingdom and no one as yet has ever accused him of being anything else but a skinflint.'

'He was exceeding kind to me,' Serena said. 'The six hundred pounds that he lent me enabled Charmaine and her husband to set themselves up in a small inn in the North of Cornwall. They are very happy there. I can never be sufficiently grateful to Mr. Israel.'

Lord Vulcan stared at Serena. For a moment his face expressed both astonishment and incredulity.

'You understand the position, my lord?'

'I do,' the Marquis replied.

'But I have also thought'—Serena went on, and now she faltered and stammered a little—'that . . . that, should you wish to be . . . rid of me, you have but to inform the trustees of what I have just told you. The money will then be given to charity and you will be absolved from keeping your part of the bargain . . . you will be under no obligation to marry someone who . . . who is penniless.'

Lord Vulcan considered her gravely.

'You think I might be relieved by the . . . er . . . loop-hole?'

Serena met his eyes.

'Why not? It cannot be pleasant to be expected to wed someone of whom you know nothing.'

'Surely that also applies where you are concerned?'

'Yes.'

'Have you considered availing yourself of this . . . loop-hole . . . or of others?'

Serena drew herself up proudly.

'I am bound to you, my lord, by a debt of honour. You were the winner of a game of chance . . . I the loser.'

'I see.'

Lord Vulcan appeared to be considering the matter. Before he spoke again he took a pinch of snuff from an exquisitely jewelled box. Serena waited, thinking his calmness, his air of self-possession was singularly irritating. Every nerve in her body was quivering, but she forced herself to sit still, to hold her chin high.

At last the Marquis spoke, and his lips twisted a little on the words.

49

'The thought of marriage with me, Miss Staverley, is, I gather, most distasteful to you?'

Serena blushed despite her resolution not to do so.

'I . . . I can hardly be expected to welcome the idea, my lord, when I know that your only reason for it is your desire for money.'

For a moment she thought she had aroused Lord Vulcan's anger, that there was a glint of steel in his grey eyes, but the expression on his face of cynical indifference did not alter.

'You are certainly frank, Madam,' he remarked suavely. 'May I make a suggestion?'

'If it pleases you.'

Serena tried to make her voice as unconcerned as his.

'Then let us do nothing for the moment. You have most kindly offered me a loophole. In justice there should be one which you too could accept—honour. But until it presents itself, let us remain, Miss Staverley, as we are . . . two strangers brought together by a game of chance.'

'You mean, my lord, that I could continue to live here . . . at Staverley?'

Try as she would Serena could not keep the ringing lilt of eagerness from her voice. But Lord Vulcan shook his head.

'That, I think, would be difficult, for you have, I understand, no chaperone?'

'An elderly cousin who filled that post for two years died eight months ago.'

'Then it is impossible for you to live here unchaperoned now that Staverley has become my property,' Lord Vulcan said.

'You mean—people would think that you—that I . . .'

She broke off.

'Exactly!'

'Oh!'

Again a crimson tide of colour rose in Serena's cheeks.

'May I suggest,' Lord Vulcan remarked, ignoring her embarrassment, 'that, until other and more suitable arrangements can be made, you pay a visit to my mother at Mandrake? I can convey you there before nightfall.'

'You mean that I should leave to-day?'

'To-day!'

'Oh, but it is impossible. I could not—I . . .'

Serena's protestations died away, the full impact of how helpless she was, how dependent on this man who owned both Staverley and herself stifled the words on her lips. What was the use of arguing; indeed what arguments were there in her favour?

'If those are your wishes, my lord,' she said formally.

'It would be best for you,' Lord Vulcan replied.

Serena rose to her feet. She felt her control was very near to breaking point. To leave so quickly, to go without saying good-bye; it was unbearable! She turned aside so that the Marquis should not see the tears in her eyes.

'There is only one request I would make you, my lord,' she said in a strangled voice.

'Which is?'

'May I take with me the only two friends I have in the world?'

'Who are?'

'Eudora—my personal maid—and Torqo.'

Serena put her hand on the mastiff's head as she spoke as if for support.

'It shall be as you wish.'

Serena tried to speak her thanks, but the words were soundless. With a pathetic effort at politeness she dropped the Marquis a curtsy and went from the room. He did not watch her go. Slowly and with an air of *insouciance* Lord Vulcan took a pinch of snuff.

Four

SITTING on the padded seat of claret satin in the coach, Serena had plenty of time for reflection. The hours of travelling had passed slowly and she had welcomed the two breaks when they changed horses and she was able to repair to an inn for a few moments to stretch her cramped limbs.

She had anticipated that the journey would be far more uncomfortable and it seemed to her that the coach was either surprisingly well sprung or else the roads were by no means as rough as might be expected. She could not help but be impressed by the efficient manner in which everything was arranged on their journey. The Marquis's own horses and grooms were waiting for them when they arrived at a posting inn and there was the minimum amount of time in the changing of the teams. Everywhere they were received with the most deferential bowings and scrapings and it was obvious that the Marquis was well known and respected on the route.

Serena's luggage with Eudora and Torqo had gone ahead. Serena had wished to have Eudora with her, especially when she learned that the Marquis was not to travel in the coach beside her but would make the journey on horseback. But in response to the suggestion Lord Vulcan replied coldly that it would be better for Eudora to be at Mandrake when she arrived, and Serena was not brave enough to press the matter further. Travelling alone, however, had its compensations; in that it gave her time to reflect and to sort out her chaotic thoughts and emotions.

Events had moved so quickly in the last twenty-four hours that it was difficult to know what she did feel or think about anything. In the ten days which had elapsed between her father's death and Lord Vulcan's coming to Staverley she had been prepared for changes, but she had not anticipated anything so revolutionary as being transplanted at a moment's notice from Staverley to his lordship's own home. She had not expected to have to say good-bye to all she had loved and known within the space of time which it took Eudora to pack for her and for the Marquis to eat his luncheon.

They had left Staverley at one o'clock in the afternoon and Lord Vulcan announced that they would reach Mandrake before seven o'clock that night. They were certainly travelling very fast and in the glimpses that Serena occasionally had of him through the window of the coach she saw him riding his horse as if he were increasingly impatient to arrive at their destination.

Once when she had a glimpse of his face she shivered a little. He was so handsome, yet there was something strange, almost uncanny about him. Nicholas had been right, yes, right in many of the things he had said, Serena told herself. She had not wasted her opportunities, while she had been awaiting his lordship's arrival, of finding out more about him. After Nicholas' first incoherent denunciation Serena had set herself resolutely to learn from her cousin all that he knew and all that he had heard about the man who might be her future husband.

It was not easy to get a true picture from Nicholas, because it was obvious from the outset that he not only loathed the Marquis but was also afraid of him. Besides, he had had very little personal contact with Lord Vulcan and based most of his assertions on hearsay and rumours which Serena was certain in all justice should be discounted to a very large extent as being exaggerated.

'Some people say he is a Satanist,' Nicholas said, 'but it is unlikely that he would condescend to belong to any society. What is more probable is that he has sold his soul to the Devil by some sinister means of his own.'

'You cannot really believe such nonsense,' Serena laughed.

'Why not?' Nicholas answered. 'Anyway, the fellow is cursed strange.'

'In what way?' Serena persisted.

'I wish I could explain to you what I mean,' Nicholas answered. 'You will understand easily enough when you see him.'

'What does he do?' Serena asked.

'It is not so much what he does—at least from all I have seen of him,' Nicholas added honestly; 'it is the way he does it. When he is at the gaming table, he is uncanny. There is something inhuman about him. He plays high,

53

fantastically high, yet he does not seem to care one way or another whether he wins or loses. He sits there with that bored, cynical look on his face as if it did not signify in the least, and he wins and wins. No one has ever heard him refuse a wager and yet he seldom loses one.'

'Surely there is nothing really wrong nor evil in that?' Serena asked in bewilderment.

'Not when I tell you about it,' Nicholas said irritably, 'but when you are there it is uncomfortably peculiar. Any man who is a man gets in a bit of a pucker when he is losing or winning a fortune, but not Vulcan. I give you my word, Serena, there is something devilish unnatural about the fellow, and that is a fact.'

'I wonder why he is so bored,' Serena said reflectively. 'After all, he has so much.'

'That is true enough,' Nicholas said bitterly. 'He has money, position and women—all the women he wants, including—though I should not mention this to you—that fabulously beautiful bit of muslin—*La Flamme*. But there have always been women at Vulcan's heels. 'Tis rumoured that he treats them badly; but no one knows for sure as most of them are so blindly in love with him that they will not hear a word spoken against the cursed fellow.'

Now, thinking of Lady Isabel as she had seen her on the night before, she was not surprised that Nicholas was in love. But it had also been obvious that he had not been mistaken in her feelings where Lord Vulcan was concerned.

'She loves him and she hates me,' Serena thought wistfully with a little sigh. 'If she only knew how willingly I would change places with her!'

Poor Nicholas! It was a pity he should lose his heart to someone who would take so little interest in him. Part of the gay, raffish set which moved around the Prince, Isabel Calver, fêted and sought after, would have no time for an inexperienced young man from the country, even if her own affections were not otherwise engaged. Nicholas had seen very few women in the quiet life he had lived at The Gables. Serena sighed for her cousin.

'We are country folk,' she thought; 'the fashionable world is not for us.'

She thought how it would have simplified things if only she had cared enough for Nicholas to marry him. They would have lived a quiet, uneventful life looking after the estate, taking an interest in local affairs, bringing up their children in placid, god-fearing happiness without bothering for a moment about the intrigues, the heartbreaks and the excitements of London.

Serena found herself almost regretting that she had not accepted Nicholas' proposal of marriage. It had been generous of him to make her the offer. He had done it for her sake, putting aside his own interests and his love for the Lady Isabel. Dear Nicholas! She had refused him because of her pride, her sense of honour, and because, too, she could never for a moment imagine herself in love with or married to her cousin.

How funny life was, Serena mused. It was almost easier to fancy oneself married to a man one did not know than to someone one had known since childhood and thought of only as a brother.

The coach suddenly drew up and she looked out expecting to see the courtyard of another inn, but to her surprise they were out in the open country. What could have caused them to halt? she wondered; and then the door was opened by a footman and the Marquis stepped in and sat down beside her.

'We are only five miles from Mandrake,' he said, 'and I thought I would ride with you the last part of the journey.'

'That is kind of you, my lord,' Serena answered, tidying the ribbons of her bonnet, and moving a little further into the corner.

The door of the coach was closed and with a jerk the horses started again.

'You are tired?' Lord Vulcan enquired.

'Not in the least,' Serena replied. 'It has been an easy journey. Your coach is a very comfortable one.'

'I had it specially built for speed,' the Marquis answered, and then, turning to look at her, he said, 'Are you afraid?'

Serena did not pretend to misunderstand him.

'My cousin Nicholas has spoken to me of Mandrake,' she said. 'He tells me that it is a very wonderful place although he has never seen it. But your mother, my lord, what will she . . . think of my unexpected arrival?'

'It will not be unexpected,' Lord Vulcan replied, and Serena fancied that his tone was somewhat grim. 'I sent a messenger to Mandrake early this morning to tell my mother that I was bringing you—home.'

'Will she be displeased?' Serena questioned.

'That remains to be seen,' Lord Vulcan answered suavely. 'My mother's reactions are often unexpected, but try not to be afraid of her.'

'I will try,' Serena answered and then added a little daringly: 'Is she very formidable?'

'People tell me so,' Lord Vulcan answered with a faint smile, 'but they say the same thing about me.'

'And there they are right,' Serena spoke quickly without thinking, then added impulsively: 'I am sorry. I should not have said that. Please forgive me.'

'There is nothing to forgive,' Lord Vulcan said. 'I appreciate frankness . . . occasionally.'

'That is a good thing,' Serena answered. 'You see, my lord, I am only a country girl, but ever since I grew older I have been very much my own mistress. I have said what I thought and done what I wanted and there has been nobody to say me nay. I am afraid you will find me very unpolished beside your society ladies.'

Lord Vulcan turned his head towards Serena again and it seemed to her that for the first time there was an expression of interest in his eyes. He looked at her for a second or two without replying, then at length unexpectedly he asked:

'Will you make me a promise, Miss Staverley?'

'If I can,' Serena answered.

'Then promise me you will always tell me the truth,' Lord Vulcan said. 'The world is full these days of people pretending and lying. Pretence has always bored me and lies I cannot abide. You may hate me, but at least do me the courtesy of telling me the truth. Will you promise me that?'

'Why not?' Serena answered. 'It is a promise that is easy to make, my lord, for I swear to you that I always tell the truth.'

Lord Vulcan sighed.

'I hope you will find it easy to continue to do so.'

There was silence after this and Serena looked at him sideways under her eyelashes. What a strange man he was! For a moment he had spoken to her as if he were interested in what he said rather than in his customary languid manner.

'Is he unhappy?' Serena reflected, and then added quickly to herself, 'Why should I worry if he is or he is not?'

The coach was gathering speed as it went down-hill. Serena looked through the window and saw that the sun was sinking and the sky was golden with its setting.

'Are we nearly there?' she asked.

'You will see Mandrake in a few moments,' Lord Vulcan replied.

Serena was never to forget her first sight of Mandrake. Half castle, half mansion, its roof and chimneys were silhouetted against a red-gold sky. Hundreds of its windows gleamed a golden welcome out into the twilight and beyond, below and almost around it was the sea—a moving mass of living gold. It was all so dazzling that she must close her eyes against its glittering beauty. When she opened them again, Mandrake was looming nearer—so vast, gaunt and impressive that she felt insignificant and afraid.

She heard the Marquis's voice beside her:

'It was originally built as a fortification and each succeeding generation has added to it. My family have been here for hundreds of years and all of them have contributed their quota of improvements.'

He spoke very quietly and yet there was a sense of pride of possession beneath his words which could not entirely be subdued.

'He truly loves the place,' Serena thought shrewdly, and was somehow not so afraid as she had been of its overpowering size and magnificence. To Lord Vulcan, strange though he was, this place was home even as Staverley had meant home to her.

She had one last glance at the sea and the great cliffs and then the coach turned inwards, leaving the coast road so that they approached Mandrake from the north, driving in through wrought-iron gates and entering what seemed like a huge inner courtyard. The coach stopped, a footman sprang down to open the door, and now Serena felt sweeping over her the tiredness she had denied. It had been a long journey and apart from that she felt ill-equipped to face what lay in front of her. She pulled her pelisse around her and stretched out her hand to Lord Vulcan as he waited to help her to alight.

'Welcome to Mandrake' he said quietly as she stepped from the coach on to the flagged courtyard.

Through a pillared portico she could see that a door was open and a row of liveried servants were awaiting their entrance. For one moment she felt sheer panic creep over her and instinctively and without conscious thought her fingers tightened on Lord Vulcan's.

'Your maid and your dog will be awaiting you,' he said, and she understood that he offered her the only possible comfort in telling her that she was not entirely friendless.

Gratefully she smiled at him and allowed him to lead her forward in through the doorway. The servants bowed, lackeys came hurrying forward to take his lordship's hat and gloves. A vast hall lit with hundreds of candles, a long corridor soft carpeted, great banks of hothouse flowers and the feeling that it must all be a strange dream were Serena's impressions as she moved forward. Then suddenly a door opened into a room glittering with light. There were hangings of crimson velvet against green and silver walls, shining, iridescent mirrors, huge portraits in gilt frames, more flowers, yellow, white and scarlet, and the leaping flames of a welcoming fire.

'Justin! I did not expect you for at least another hour,' a voice cried, and a woman came across the room towards them, a woman glittering and sparkling with the many jewels she wore. But however flamboyant her gems, however daring her dress, it was her face which was so arresting that Serena could only stare in astonishment at the Marchioness of Vulcan.

She had expected someone so very different, but first and foremost someone who was older. This woman seemed almost the same age as her son, and it was only when the first surprise was over that one noticed the lines beneath mascaraed eyes and the tell-tale sagging of the ivory throat. At first it was hard not to be overwhelmed, not to cry out in astonishment at such beauty, at the dead-white, magnolia skin and the deep, almost violet eyes with their darkened lashes, at the perfect oval contour of her face, the exquisitely chiselled nose, her eyebrows dark-winged beneath a square forehead, and crowning it all, the amazing, glorious deep-red hair curling naturally at the temples and arranged· over her diamond-pierced ears in the very height of fashion.

'What does this mean?' the Marchioness was saying, speaking quickly and impatiently. 'This letter I got from you this morning? I cannot understand a word of it.'

'It means what it says, Mother,' Lord Vulcan answered, 'and may I present . . . Miss Serena Staverley.'

For the first time the Marchioness looked at Serena. She

58

was tall and Serena had to look up at her. When she did so and their eyes met, she felt a sudden tremor, either of apprehension or of fear, pass over her. If Lord Vulcan's face was inexpressive, his mother's was the very opposite. In the Marchioness's eyes Serena saw anger and also what seemed to her a hatred such as she had never encountered in her life before. For a moment the two women stood looking at each other and then the Marchioness made an expressive gesture with her hands.

'Faugh! The whole thing is ridiculous, Justin, and you know it.'

'On the contrary,' the Marquis replied, 'it is a sober fact, my dear Mother, which I must ask you to accept.'

'A fact that you are to marry this girl?'

The Marchioness spoke as if Serena were not there.

'That is still to be decided,' Lord Vulcan answered quietly. 'In the meantime Miss Staverley is our guest.'

The Marchioness turned from him impatiently and looked again at Serena.

'My son has informed me that you and he are affianced,' she said sharply. 'Who are you and where have you met him?'

That the Marchioness was obviously unaware of the reasons why she had been brought to Mandrake gave Serena a momentary sense of confidence.

'Your son will doubtless explain that to you, Ma'am,' she said quietly. 'The situation is not of my making.'

'What does she mean by that?' the Marchioness snapped.

'I will tell you everything in a little while,' Lord Vulcan answered. 'In the meantime Miss Staverley is tired and would wish to retire to her own room.'

He walked across the room and pressed a bell by the mantelpiece. Almost instantly, as if the summons were awaited, the butler appeared.

'Where is Mrs. Matthews?' his lordship asked sharply.

'She is here, m'lord.'

The housekeeper came into the room, her black silk dress rustling as she moved, her hair hidden by a white cap.

'Good evening, Mrs. Matthews.'

The housekeeper curtsied.

'I hope I see your lordship well.'

'Well enough. Kindly show Miss Staverley to her room and see that she has everything that she requires.'

59

'Certainly, your lordship. Will you come this way, Ma'am?'

The housskeeper curtsied again, and Serena went with her, feeling a moment of utter loneliness as she went out into the great hall. They climbed the stairs, not stopping on the first floor but rising again to the second and going along strange twisting passages.

'We are now in the old part of the house,' Mrs. Matthews explained as the corridors grew narrow and they kept descending a few steps and climbing another two or three to find the level of the floor. 'Her ladyship thought you would be more comfortable up here.'

She spoke in a suppressed manner and Serena knew, as if she had been told so more plainly, that the Marchioness had chosen for her one of the worst guest-rooms in the house rather than 'one of the best.

'You have a nice view of the sea, Ma'am,' the housekeeper said as she opened a door, anxious, Serena thought, to placate someone who was obviously his lordship's honoured guest, if not his mother's.

Serena had an answer ready, but the words went from her mind when she saw first Eudora unpacking a case by the dressing-table and then Torqo rushing towards her with his tail wagging in excitement and bounding up and down on his massive paws like an excited puppy.

'Oh, Eudora, I am so pleased to see you,' Serena said, 'and you, too, Torqo. How did he bear with the journey?'

'With laudable patience, Miss Serena,' Eudora answered primly, and Serena knew from her tone of voice that something was wrong.

'If there is anything you want, Ma'am,' Mrs. Matthews was saying in the doorway, 'would you be kind enough to ring the bell? You will, I hope, understand if it takes a moment or two for the housemaid to answer it, for this room is somewhat far away, although, as I explained, it has a nice view of the sea.'

'I am sure I shall be very comfortable, thank you,' Serena answered, and then as the door closed behind the housekeeper she ran across the room, Torqo at her heels, and put her arms round Eudora. 'Thank goodness you are here! What a frightening house, it is so big!'

'It is more than that,' Eudora answered in her deep voice. 'It is unfriendly.'

'I know it,' Serena answered. 'I had no welcome from his lordship's mother, I can assure you.'

'I have only been here a short while,' Eudora said, 'but I sensed at once that something is wrong.'

'They have give me this room as a discourtesy.'

'I was aware of that as soon as they brought me up here and the bed has not been slept in for years. I put my hand inside it, felt the damp and asked for hot bricks. They could not get the fire to draw, the chimney was blocked.'

Serena looked round the room. It was panelled in dark oak, low-ceilinged and somewhat gloomy; but it was as good as any of the rooms at Staverley and the carved oak furniture, if unfashionable, was ancient and doubtless valuable.

'Why worry about the room?' she asked. 'Her ladyship does not want me and takes a pretty way of showing her dislike. Why should we care?'

'I care for you,' Eudora said.

Serena smiled at her quickly.

'You are a dear, Eudora, but you cannot fight all my battles for me, now that I am grown up.'

'I would if I could,' Eudora murmured.

'Yes, I know you would,' Serena answered, 'but you worry overmuch. You look fatigued. Was the journey a bad one for you?'

She knew it was often agony for Eudora to be shaken about in a coach.

'Not too painful,' Eudora replied. 'His lordship's valet was most kind and got a cushion for my back. I have made a friend of him; maybe he will prove useful.'

'I am glad we have a friend at Court,' Serena smiled.

She spoke sincerely, for Eudora made few friends and many enemies. Now the little woman came nearer to her and her voice sank to a whisper.

'He warned me of the Marchioness. You must be careful.'

'What of?' Serena asked.

'He warned me,' Eudora repeated, 'but since I came to this house I have needed no warning. There is evil here . . . evil . . . and danger.'

Serena put her hands up to her ears.

'Stop, stop, Eudora. I cannot bear any more. It has been a vastly disturbing day and I am very tired.'

There was the sound of tears in her voice and instantly Eudora went to her, uttering soothing noises like a hen clucking to her chickens.

'There, there, my little love, you are tired, and why

should you worry your pretty head about such things. Torqo and I will look after you. Now sit down by the fire and I will take off your shoes. Give me your bonnet, and now your gloves.'

Serena allowed herself to be led to the fireplace, thankful for the moment to let Eudora forget her broodings in doing more practical things for her. When at last she had slipped off her travelling dress and sat wrapped in a soft cashmere shawl, sipping the warm milk which Eudora had fetched her, she relaxed and felt more at ease.

'Dinner is at eight o'clock,' Eudora said. 'I exclaimed that I thought it fashionably late and they said that everything was very up-to-date here. About thirty guests will dine tonight.'

'Thirty!' Serena exclaimed.

Eudora nodded.

'His lordship's valet tells me that it is the same every night. Numbers of people to dinner and some arrive later, then they gamble until dawn.'

'Gamble? Here? At Mandrake?' Serena exclaimed.

'Yes, the valet tells me that her ladyship thinks of little else. "She lives for it," he said.'

'How strange!'

'There is every kind of play,' Eudora went on. 'And ofttimes they dance.'

Serena sighed.

'I shall be sadly out of place, for you know, Eudora, how much I dislike games of skill, and anyway, I have no money to stake.'

'And a good thing if you ask me,' Eudora said tartly, 'for great sums change hands every night. His lordship's valet was telling me how the Duchess of Dover lost six thousand pounds the other evening. A gentleman, I forget his name, wagered his coach and horses when all else had gone and would have had to walk home if one of the other guests had not taken pity on him.'

'Good gracious,' Serena exclaimed. 'It is a good thing we have nothing to lose, Eudora.'

'It is not the right sort of place for you,' Eudora answered ominously.

Frightened that once again Eudora would begin to express her forebodings Serena tried to change the subject.

'Where does that door lead to?' she asked, pointing to a small oak door on the other side of the room.

'I was told we could use it as a powder closet,' Eudora answered. 'It is a strange little turret room.'

She opened the door and Serena saw an almost circular room with small pointed windows.

'How quaint!' she exclaimed, and walking across the room looked out through one of the windows.

It was dark and night had fallen, but there was a faint phosphorescent glow over the sea and the stars were shining in the sky. Below, Serena could see the outline of walled-in gardens ending abruptly as the cliff jutted down to the sea.

'It is lovely,' Serena whispered, but more as if she needed to convince herself than to express a conviction.

'Come back to the fire,' Eudora said, 'you will catch cold.'

Serena shut the door of the turret behind her.

'This part of the house must have been part of the old castle,' she said. 'It is very quiet here. I only hope there are not too many ghosts.'

'It is not the ghosts in the house that I am afraid of,' Eudora replied.

At that moment Torqo lifted his head and growled in his throat.

'What is it, Torqo?' Serena asked, then felt the dog's hackles rise beneath her hand. He growled again.

'There is someone coming,' Eudora said.

At that moment they heard steps approaching down the passage and a moment later there was a sharp knock. Eudora went to the door to open it, but before she could reach it the door was flung wide and the Marchioness stood in the doorway. In the small, low-ceilinged room she seemed even taller than in the great drawing-room, her flashing jewellery, her low-cut, skin-tight dress making her appear a strange fantastic figure from another world.

Serena got quickly to her feet and dropped a curtsy. The Marchioness stood for a moment as if taking in every detail of the room and its occupants, then she pointed at Torqo with an ivory walking-stick, its handle studded with jewels.

'That dog cannot sleep in the house,' she said sharply.

'He is used to sleeping in a kennel, Ma'am,' Serena answered, 'but he is always with me during the day.'

'See that he behaves himself then,' the Marchioness replied, 'or he must stay in a kennel. He is too big for a house.' Before Serena could answer she spoke to Eudora. 'I wish to speak with your mistress. Wait outside.'

Eudora went from the room. She curtsied to the Marchioness, her distorted body a strange contrast to the beutiful, commanding figure towering above her.

'Sit down,' the Marchioness said to Serena when they were alone, taking a chair on the opposite side of the fireplace. 'I have been speaking to my son. He has told me of the peculiar circumstances in which you have met. I understand from him that when you marry you inherit a fortune of eighty thousand pounds. Is that correct?'

'That was the sum left in trust for me by my grandfather,' Serena answered.

'It is a fortune . . . but not an unusually large one as fortunes go,' the Marchioness said grudgingly.

Serena waited, wondering what she intended by such a statement.

'My son wishes you to remain here,' the Marchioness went on after a moment's pause, 'at least for the present. You will understand that your arrival was somewhat of a surprise to me. Justin has always been an avowed bachelor. He has sworn that he would never marry.'

'I understand,' Serena said, and she was aware that this was somewhat in the way of an apology and guessed that Lord Vulcan had insisted on it.

'My son desires for the present to make no arrangements about your marriage,' the Marchioness said. 'Is that your wish or his?'

'I can speak only for myself,' Serena said quietly. 'I have no desire to be married to someone I met for the first time yesterday.'

'Eighty thousand pounds,' the Marchioness repeated, as though she were speaking to herself. 'It is not such a vast fortune and yet at the same time . . .' She shrugged her shoulders. 'Anyway, there is no reason for us to make decisions as yet. Also, I shall not present you to my guests as my son's betrothed. I hear that all London is gossiping about the wager, but we need not concern ourselves at Mandrake with their tattle. You will be an ordinary guest in my house. Is that understood?'

'I have no desire for any other status,' Serena answered, resentful of the Marchioness's tone.

'That is all I have to say,' the Marchioness said and rose to her feet. She stood for a moment in front of the fire, leaning on her ivory stick, the flames glittering on the huge emerald and diamond rings she wore on her long fingers.

'You are in mourning,' she said abruptly. 'We must not forget that.'

'I have not forgotten it,' Serena replied quietly.

The Marchioness looked at her and said nothing, but Serena felt there was something in her mind, some thought formulating that she was not yet ready to express. How beautiful she was, and yet how formidable! When she was young she must have been lovely beyond compare, and even now her beauty was almost unparalleled save that she created an atmosphere not of loveliness but of something far more sinister.

'This money of yours, child,' she said suddenly, 'this eighty thousand pounds. . . . You are quite certain that you cannot obtain any of it until you are married? You will need money for . . . your trousseau, for other expenses.'

'I am afraid, Ma'am, there is no possibility of my touching any of it until I am married,' Serena answered.

It was strange, she thought, that the Marchioness, laden with thousands of pounds' worth of jewels, should be so interested in her small dowry.

The Marchioness made a gesture of impatience.

'Then we must wait,' she said. 'I was, of course, thinking only of your comfort. It is difficult to live without money, as perhaps you have already found out.'

'Yes, I have discovered that,' Serena said with a sudden smile, but she wondered if her financial difficulties in the past could ever be understood by the Marchioness living in this great house and having, it appeared, an unlimited income to expend on all the luxuries and comforts which went with such grandeur.

'I will leave you to dress for dinner,' the Marchioness said after another uncomfortable pause. 'We meet in the Silver Drawing-room. When you come down, there will be a footman at the head of the Grand Staircase to direct you.'

'Thank you, Ma'am.'

Serena curtsied and the Marchioness went towards the door. For a moment she was framed there against the darkness of the panelling and her beautiful face crowned with its flaming hair made a picture that was almost breathtaking; and yet there was something else—something which repelled one, something which had kept Torqo growling deep down in his throat ever since she had entered the room. She heard him now.

'Be sure that dog sleeps in the kennels,' she said and was gone.

Serena shivered and turned towards the fire. As Eudora entered she started as if she was half afraid that the Marchioness had returned.

'Oh, it is you, Eudora,' she said in tones of relief.

'Yes, it is only me,' Eudora answered.

Serena knew without questioning what Eudora was feeling, and yet for once the deformed woman had nothing to say. Serena dressed in silence, putting on a plain white muslin dress which was all she had to wear. When she was ready and Eudora had arranged her hair, she looked at herself in the mirror and laughed.

'A country cousin!' she exclaimed. 'But what does it matter? No one will look at me when they can behold the magnificence of the Marchioness.'

'Be careful of her,' Eudora said quietly.

'She cannot harm me,' Serena answered. 'I am afraid of her, and so are you, Eudora, but she cannot actually harm us. She hates my being here, that is obvious; but why should we complain when we would so much rather be at home?'

'She is dangerous,' Eudora whispered.

'How can she be?' Serena asked, talking more to herself than to Eudora. 'It is obvious that she would like to get my money and be rid of me. Perhaps his lordship is thinking the same thing. Well, we know that is impossible, it cannot be done. Either they have got to dispense with me and the money, or else they have got to accept us both together. Oh, Eudora, if only my grandfather had known when he left me an inheritance what a millstone it was to be about my neck!'

'You are not married yet,' Eudora said.

'No, nor am I likely to be if the Marchioness has anything to do or say about it,' Serena retorted. 'Methinks she will feel well rid of me and my eighty thousand pounds.'

'Trust no one in this house,' Eudora admonished.

'Except you,' Serena said with a smile, 'and Torqo. Find somewhere comfortable for him to sleep and see that he is fed and has a bowl of fresh water. Bring him to me the first thing to-morrow morning. I would feel happier if he could sleep with me.'

'So would I, but I am in the next room. They wanted to put me up in the attics, but I said if I could not sleep near you I would sleep on the floor.'

'Oh, Eudora, you are such a comfort to me,' Serena exclaimed.

She put her strong young arms round Eudora and lowered her lovely face to the older woman's lined and withered one.

'Dear, dear Eudora!'

For a moment she clung to her and then to her horror she felt the wizened body quivering and shaking beneath her touch.

'I am afraid, I am afraid,' Eudora said in a hoarse voice.

'No, no, you are not. We are all right. I promise you we are all right,' Serena said reassuringly. 'We are here together, and no real harm can happen to us . . . not in these days.'

Eudora said no more, and Serena, kissing her good night, turned to go downstairs. At the door of the room she turned and looked back. Eudora was standing by the dressing-table. She had her back to Serena, but her face was reflected in the mirror, and Serena saw it was twisted and distorted with a fear beyond expression.

Five

HARRIET, Marchioness of Vulcan, pushed the gilt mirror away roughly.

'Hell, but I look ugly this morning,' she said; 'I don't want to go on regarding myself, woman.'

Her maid moved from the bed, taking the tray on which reposed the mirror and the gold and diamond-studded brush and comb which her ladyship had been using. On the other side of the bed a small black boy, dressed in gorgeous silks and satins and with a turban bearing a peacock's feather, held out a salver on which there was a cup of chocolate.

'Chocolate makes me sick,' the Marchioness said petulantly. 'Fetch me some brandy, boy.'

'Your ladyship said only yesterday that you would forswear brandy in the morning,' the maid remarked, turning from the dressing-table.

'What else can I take, woman, when I feel half asleep and my head aches? La, but it was a tiring evening last night. Twice I won over a thousand guineas in one call and then lost it again.' There was a sudden glint in the Marchioness's eyes and her voice, which was thick and weary, regained for a moment its usual clear lilt; then she slumped back against the pillows of her great bed. 'But what is the use? My luck is against me. I must speak with Madame Roxana, but first inform his lordship I want him.'

'Methinks his lordship is out riding,' the maid answered.

'So early? Well, find out for sure, you fool, and if he is not back, tell them to send him to me the moment he returns.'

'Very good, m'lady.'

The maid curtsied and went towards the door as the black boy re-entered the room. The silver salver now held a bottle of brandy and a crystal goblet. He offered it to the

Marchioness who seized the bottle eagerly and half filled the glass. She sipped it, coughed and took another sip of the fiery liquid.

'That is better!' she exclaimed. 'For all your croakings, Martha, this is worth a hundred medicines and so-called elixirs of youth. Already I begin to feel young again.'

'Yes, but for how long, your ladyship?' the lady's maid said tartly, and passed from the room before the Marchioness could reply.

'Crabby old hag,' her ladyship said, taking another sip of the brandy. 'She has been with me too long, that is the truth.'

She picked up a small hand mirror which lay on the lace counter-pane of the bed and stared at her reflection. The black boy set down the salver beside her and went to the corner of the room where he crouched down awaiting further instructions should they be given.

In the morning light coming pitilessly through the high windows the Marchioness turned her face this way and that. She touched the tiny fretwork of lines at the corners of her eyes and saw the tired droop of her mouth which no amount of crimson salve would hide. Only her hair, fiery and unfaded, was as lovely as it had been twenty years earlier when she was in the heyday of her beauty. Then it had seemed to her that she would never grow old.

Married when she was sixteen, her son had been born soon after her seventeenth birthday and it was as the Marchioness of Vulcan that she had taken Society by storm. The great Court painters had fought to use her as their model, poems had been written of her, books had been dedicated to her, no party was a success without her presence, and no hostess could afford to ignore her demands, however outrageous they might be.

Harriet was beautiful, and what was more she had a quick wit and an impetuous, sometimes outrageous way of speaking her mind which kept those who paid her homage amused and increasingly enslaved. Success followed success. The Court was enlivened by her presence, honours and positions of dignity were piled upon her, and it was said that she could even make the dreariness of Palace functions tolerable by her gaiety and her wit.

It was not surprising that so much success went to her head. Besides, as people remembered later, there was bad blood in her family. The Rapleys had always been dissolute, and her father, before he died in exile, had twice

69

fled to the Continent after being mixed up in very unsavoury intrigues.

By the time she was thirty the Marchioness of Vulcan's love affairs were the talk of London. People no longer exclaimed at her loveliness, they whispered of her latest indiscretion and the way she flaunted each new conquest. Things grew worse as the years went by. Then as her beauty began to fade and the very first touch of age began to show itself there was a strange change. The Marchioness had long been a byword for all that was fantastic, exotic and unconventional, her love affairs, sensational for twenty years, had become legendary, almost traditional. At forty she found a new lover, one that utterly absorbed all her passions and desires as no man had ever done. She took to gaming. A game of chance absorbed her to exclusion of all else. Inevitably she gambled wildly and without restraint, prudence or common sense—just as she had lived all her life.

Her obsession was so marked that it astonished even those who had thought themselves past being astonished at anything that Harriet Vulcan did. Ignoring those who tried to keep her from disgracing her position at Court, the Marchioness had gambled day and night, winning and losing tremendous sums until the newspapers laughed at her, lampoons were written about her and sold in the streets, and Their Majesties were forced to take notice of what was occurring.

Faro had been forbidden. The Marchioness played it on every possible occasion. Her duties at Court began to be neglected. She would hurry impatiently from the Throne Room to the gaming table. She no longer listened when diplomats paid her compliments or poets read to her their latest odes. Her fingers seemed to twist with impatience to get to the cards and she would brush courtiers aside, her impatience causing more scandal and making her more enemies than ever her love affairs had done.

The elder Peeresses who surrounded the Queen at last spoke to Her Majesty, with the result that Queen Charlotte sent for the Marchioness and talked with her in private. The Queen was gutturally unintelligent, but her meaning was very clear. Either Harriet must give up her gambling or the Court would give her up. It was an ultimatum which the Marchioness solved characteristically, for she found a third solution to the problem.

She gave up the Court. She relinquished her positions,

resigned from being Lady of the Bedchamber and retired to Mandrake. For a moment the fashionable world was too stunned to believe it possible—then they understood. The Marchioness created at Mandrake the atmosphere and conditions she had enjoyed in London, but without restrictions or the tiresome interference of responsibilities.

For years she had visited Mandrake and her husband, who preferred the country, only at infrequent intervals; now that she was permanently in residence she began to spend vast sums on improving the place. A year later she became a widow; but when her only son inherited, it seemed that like his father he, too, would deny his mother nothing. The greatest architects, the finest decorators hurried down from London to enrich the already historic mansion; and while people wondered at what was being planned, the Marchioness threw open the doors of Mandrake.

There were banquets every night and afterwards the guests stayed on to gamble. The stakes were higher than those at the most fashionable clubs or gaming rooms in London. A visitor to Mandrake could indulge in every possible type of game from the sober pool of quadrille or of commerce to the more exciting and certainly the more expensive ones of loo, faro, whist and macao.

The State Rooms of the great house were comfortable and exotic enough to appeal to the most fastidious gambler. The food and wine tempted the palates of the most exacting epicure. All that was latest and strangest was to be found at Mandrake. It was the centre of everything that was brilliant, glittering and daring, while the light and spirit of the whole place was its hostess. Sparkling, shining both in her beauty and in her wit, the Marchioness became Queen of a Court such as historians must have sometimes dreamt of as they wrote wearily of the divine dullness of reigning monarchs.

Mandrake became a meeting-place of the fashionable world; but it soon became evident that only the most wealthy could afford to go there. There began, too, to be nasty whispers that the Marchioness was getting importunate. She gambled vehemently when she lost and hungered for more when she won; but either way no one could escape from her while they had the money to go on playing. She was insatiable, a woman devoured by her own desire.

Sometimes visitors to Mandrake leaving for London

vowed they would never return. The Marchioness might still be a lovely woman, but it was unpleasant to see her avid and pulsating at the sight of money, concerned not with people's deeper feelings or emotions, but only with the depths of their pockets.

Also the new Marquis of Vulcan was not popular, and even those who went constantly to Mandrake felt that he did not make them welcome. Strange rumours grew and multiplied, still there was always a number of people ready to pass their leisure hours in staking vast sums of money. There were also those who were no longer *persona grata* at Court. They came to Mandrake. Persons passing through Dover to the Continent found Mandrake, only fifteen miles to the east, a good place to spend a few days either preparing for their journey or recovering from it. There were plenty more visitors with equally valid reasons and the Marchioness of Vulcan never lacked company. Perhaps the only thing she feared was the thought of being alone in the vastness of that great house.

The door of her bedroom opened suddenly and Lord Vulcan entered. He was in riding clothes, with boots of hessian leather fitting perfectly over tight breeches of the latest shade of yellow, his coat of a rich shade of brown had been cut by the great Stulz himself.

'You wanted me, Mother?'

He moved leisurely across her room, eventually coming to rest before the fireplace in which the fire was already lit. He stood looking around him at the huge four-poster bed, flanked by its great fonds of ostrich feathers, at the furniture of carved and gilded wood and at the curtains of nile-blue brocade which framed the windows.

' 'Tis a pleasant scheme,' he approved. 'I congratulate you.'

'It is not paid for yet,' the Marchioness replied petulantly.

His lordship's eyes narrowed.

'That last sum I gave you,' he said, 'I believed it was for the decorations in the house.'

'It covered but a quarter of the bills,' his mother replied, 'and there is the laying out of the new gardens as well. Besides, my mantuamaker was pressing.'

Lord Vulcan took his snuff-box from his pocket. He seemed utterly unperturbed and yet there was a touch of steel in his voice as he said quietly:

'I can give you no more for the present.'

'What about this girl?'

'I am not yet married to her.'

The Marchioness sat up in bed.

'The ceremony must never take place, Justin. I have told you before and I tell you again that you can never marry.'

His lordship shut the snuff-box with a little click.

'I have always told you, Mother, that I have no desire to do so under the circumstances.'

'Then why bring this puny country miss here? You are crazy, Justin. If we cannot touch her money, she is merely another mouth to feed. She will have to be dealt with somehow, sooner or later. Send her away at once—to-day.'

'Where to? You forget that her home has passed into my keeping.'

The Marchioness made a gesture of impatience.

'What does it signify to us where she goes? Why in heaven's name did you accept the wager?'

'To tell the truth,' Lord Vulcan answered with an amused smile, 'I have asked myself the same question. I was almost certain that I would not win that hand. I had been winning continuously; by every law of chance Sir Giles should have had his revenge on me.'

'But having won,' his mother said crossly, 'what is the point of going on with such a farce? You should release the girl from her debt if you are quite certain there is no way of getting hold of the money.'

'There is no way at all, as I think the child told you.'

'How do you know? Did she inform you that I had spoken with her?'

'No, she did not, but knowing your somewhat direct methods, my dear Mother . . .'

'Well, there is no reason why I should not speak with her, after all I am your mother.'

'There is no doubt about that,' Lord Vulcan spoke suavely.

His mother looked across the room at him and suddenly her face softened.

'Justin dear, I know I have been badgering you for money, but all the same you would not wish to wed this chit . . . this nobody?'

The Marquis sighed.

'I have told you so often, I can marry no one in the . . . circumstances.'

'Then send the girl away.'

'Where to?' He raised his hand to check the impatient

response on the Marchioness's lips. 'No, it is no use saying "anywhere". After all, I am in many ways responsible for her father's death.'

'Justin, I am vexed by such foolishness. You cannot be responsible for every idiot who takes his life because he loses at cards. The girl must have relations. If not, marry her quickly to some good-natured yokel. She will then be able to live on her own inheritance.'

Lord Vulcan smiled.

'Strangely enough it was exactly the idea I had in my mind after I had seen her at Staverley, though it will be difficult to find the yokel—here of all places.'

There was a sneer in his voice as he spoke the last words.

'I do not know what you mean by that,' the Marchioness said, 'but I daresay we shall find someone who will offer for her. She is not without a certain attraction, but her clothes are lamentable.'

'Surely, Mother, you of all people could remedy that?'

The Marchioness looked at him.

'I give you my word I had not thought of it. But, of course, it can easily be effected. I have some enchanting materials, gauzes, *batiste*—sprigged dimity that is the very latest thing. Yvette shall make them up for her. We will find her a husband, then you will be rid of all responsibility.'

The Marchioness was smiling now, her eyes sparkling, and she looked years younger than she had done a few minutes earlier.

'Lud, boy, but you frightened me. I thought the girl interested you.'

Lord Vulcan walked across to the window. He leaned against it, the sunshine on his face; for the moment he looked curiously young and unspoilt.

'One day, Mother,' he said very quietly, 'there will have to be an heir to Mandrake.'

'One day, of course,' the Marchioness said impatiently. 'But not yet, Justin. I could not bear to be a grandmother, Why, Eustace was saying only last night that you looked more like my younger brother than my son.'

'Eustace Carringon is just twenty-three,' the Marquis answered. 'He is also an extremely dissolute young man. I cannot commend you on your latest beau.'

'He is rich,' the Marchioness retorted; then she laughed. 'Dear Justin, you have always been so disapproving of my young men. I shall never forget how blue-devilled you were

74

when you first discovered that I had a lover. I can hardly remember who it was now. Was it Charles Sherringham or William Felton? I cannot recollect, but I can well recall your fury. You could not have been very old at the time, but you raged at me. How I laughed!'

'And I cried,' Lord Vulcan said.

'Did you really?' The Marchioness looked at him with interest. 'I never remember you crying even when you were a very little boy.'

'I was careful not to disgrace myself in public.'

'But you did cry over me? I am flattered. I wish I could make you cry nowadays.'

His lordship laughed shortly and it was not a very pleasant sound.

'It is too late. I am hardened. But all the same, Mother, I dislike hearing your name coupled with that of so young a blade. There is too much difference in age.'

'Age! I am all of a fidget when you speak of it. I swear I am afraid of the minutes as they pass. I can see the lines coming. Oh, Justin, if I could only remain eternally young!'

There was a real pathos in her voice, but her son seemed to be unmoved by it. The Marchioness snatched up the hand-mirror and impetuously reached out for the brandy which lay at her side.

'Brandy will not make you any younger,' Lord Vulcan remarked.

'It makes me feel younger,' the Marchioness retorted, 'and it is very good brandy. It arrived only a few . . .'

Lord Vulcan held up his hand.

'Spare me the details,' he said sharply. 'I have told you before that I do not wish to know.'

His mother laughed, her good humour entirely restored.

'Dear Justin! How ridiculous you are! I vow that if I did not know you well I should believe that you were growing respectable.'

Lord Vulcan walked across the room and stood beside the bed, looking down at the Marchioness.

'I am going now,' he said; 'there are a great many things to be seen to. Does the puppet-show take place to-night as usual?'

'Do you mean—are we entertaining?' the Marchioness asked. 'But of course! The Duchess of Dover is bringing a party over after dinner and some of the officers from the Barracks will be dining here.' Her eyes widened. 'Perhaps, my dear Justin, there will be one amongst them who will take a fancy to your little country mouse. She shall be properly gowned to-night, I promise you that.'

'Who else is coming?' Lord Vulcan asked.

'La! But I cannot recollect,' his mother said vaguely. 'We shall be about thirty to dinner, I expect, maybe more, and there will be dancing in the Long Gallery. Not but what I think it distracts from the play. Pray heaven I win to-night. I was in a rare corner the night before last after you had gone to London.'

Lord Vulcan's expression darkened.

'I have told you, Mother, that this cannot go on.'

'It is only a phase,' the Marchioness said. 'My luck will change, perhaps to-night. I must consult Madame Roxana and see if the stars are with me.'

'Madame Roxana! Is that witch still here?'

The Marchioness looked up at him.

'Yes, Justin, she is still here. I could not do without her. She helps me. Without her guidance I might lose even more than I have done already.'

'Nonsense,' his lordship said. 'And I have told you that I will not have that woman in my house.'

The Marchioness smiled.

'In your house, dear Justin?' she asked sweetly.

Her son looked at her for a long moment, then without a word he walked from the room and the door closed behind him.

The Marchioness lay still on her pillows for a moment or two before she laughed. A second later she clapped her hands together. The black boy ran from his corner.

'Madame Roxana! Fetch her quickly,' the Marchioness commanded.

He sped away to do as he was bid and while he was gone the Marchioness sipped her brandy and twirled round her finger a great diamond ring so that it caught the sunlight, sending forth iridescent rays which reflected themselves above her head.

How well she remembered receiving that ring! The man who had given it to her had loved her to desperation. She had given him in exchange a miniature of herself and he had worn it round his neck until he died. Then his widow had returned it to her with a stiff, frigid note. What a lover he had been! How impetuous! How passionate! She had loved him too, but not so much as she had loved his successor.

He also was dead. He had been drowned at sea, sailing

in search of treasure which he would have laid at her feet.
Oh well, there were still men in the world and she was still
lovely enough to attract them. But she would wager her
chance of heaven that there was no thrill such as could be
found at the gaming-tables. Gold! That was what she
wanted nowadays, and she knew well how to get value for
it once it was hers.

The Marchioness smiled secretly to herself. Someone
came into the room. She turned her head and saw Madame
Roxana—black haired, with her great hooked nose and
shifty dark eyes, she looked what she was—a gipsy. The
Marchioness had found her in a back room in Bond Street
where she was rapidly becoming the fashion. Ladies, veiled
to escape recognition, crept up the narrow unlit stairs to
consult her about their love-affairs. Bucks sauntered in
from the gaming clubs to enquire if the stars would be profitable for them that night. She had been amazingly right
where the Marchioness was concerned, and Harriet had not
found it difficult to bribe her away from Bond Street to
Mandrake.

The servants hated her. They were also afraid of her,
and she had managed by some strange method of her own
to change the atmosphere of the beautiful, high-ceilinged
bedroom in which she slept so that it seemed low, dark and
oriental, and those who entered it were uncannily aware of
an alien influence.

The balck boy who had brought her into the room, having shut the door behind her, scurried to his corner with
something which nearly resembled panic. His eyes were
rolling in his head and it was obvious that he was afraid.
The Marchioness was not interested in his feelings. She
welcomed Madame Roxana with a smile and held out her
hand to be kissed.

'How is my Lady, my Queen, this morning?' the gipsy
asked.

'Tired,' the Marchioness answered, 'but the brandy is
reviving me.'

The gipsy's eyes slanted towards the bottle.

'You would like some?' the Marchioness enquired.

'Later, later,' Roxana said, 'first we will talk of you. You
won last night?'

The Marchioness shook her head.

'I warned you not to play,' the gipsy said. 'The stars are
not propitious for you at this moment. You must wait, you
must have patience. You find it hard, my Queen; but do

not worry, your luck will change; then you will be glad and happy and remember that old Roxana told you so.'

'Do you think my luck will change to-night?' the Marchioness asked eagerly. 'Look at your cards. I need the money.'

The gipsy produced a pack of large, greasy cards from somewhere in the folds of her shapeless garment. She sat down on a low stool beside the bed.

'There is something else too,' the Marchioness said. 'There is a girl here. I want to consult you about her future.'

'The little lady that his lordship brought with him?' Roxana asked.

The Marchioness glanced at her and made no comment on the fact that Roxana knew already about Serena. It was not surprising. Nothing went on in the house without her knowing about it. Harriet supposed that she had her spies amongst the servants or else it was true clairvoyance.

'Read her cards for me,' she commanded.

The gipsy shook her head.

'That Roxana cannot do without her presence. The cards must know her, she must touch them.'

'Then we will send for her,' the Marchioness said. 'I have to talk with her, too, about another matter. Put out your cards for me, Roxana, and let us pray that they are good.' As she spoke the Marchioness pulled the great tasselled bell-rope beside her bed. A moment later her maid entered. 'I wish to speak with Miss Staverley,' the Marchioness said; 'ask her to come here.'

'Very good, m'lady.'

Her maid looked at the gipsy spreading the greasy cards out on the floor and gave a sniff, then she went from the room again.

The Marchioness smiled.

'Poor Martha, she disapproves of you and of my gambling and my drinking. In fact, all my interests and actions are reprehensible to her, and she thinks she is privileged to express her disapproval. But I could not do without you, Roxana; you won't leave me, will you?'

The gipsy looked up at her, hearing the fear in her voice.

'Would I want to leave my Lady, my Queen?' she asked silkily, and added: 'If you win to-night, you will remember your poor Roxana who brings you luck?'

'Yes, of course I will,' the Marchioness said. 'Did not I

give you twenty-five guineas the last time I won? To-night it shall be thirty . . . if I win. Tell me, what do you see?'

Roxana bent over the cards.

'It is hard to say; the stars are rising for my Lady, but they are not in their full ascendancy. You may win, but it will be but a handful of gold. There is a man who comes to the house—very dark—I can see him . . . he frowns . . . he has a peculiarity . . . yes, yes . . . I can see now what it is . . . he is left-handed . . . you will win from him. He is rich, very rich.'

'Oh, I know who that is,' the Marchioness said eagerly, 'and he comes the day after to-morrow. Left-handed? Yes, there can be no mistake! You say I shall win from him?'

'Yes, you shall win from him. Wait, there is something else. You will talk with him. You will make—oh, what is the word? . . . an alliance with him over something . . . it will concern gold . . . but it is strange.'

'Money? More money?' the Marchioness asked.

'Yes, there is the glitter of gold, but . . .'

'Do I get it? Do I win it? Oh, look, Roxana, look quickly?'

At that moment she moved impulsively in bed, and the hand-mirror fell to the floor with a crash and shattered into a thousand pieces.

'Hell,' the Marchioness exclaimed impatiently. 'Never mind, Roxana, go on.'

But the gipsy had straightened herself.

'It is gone,' she said, 'I can see no more. The noise has disturbed me.'

'Oh, I am sorry. How tiresome!' the Marchioness said. 'But you saw me win?'

'A little, a little money to-night.'

'Thank goodness for that. But this man, you say he is rich. Maybe I shall win a great deal more from him, a great deal more.'

There was a knock on the door and Martha entered.

'Miss Staverley is without, your ladyship.'

'Show her in,' the Marchioness commanded, 'and do not go, Martha, I want you.'

Serena came into the room. She was wearing a white muslin dress and over it a shawl of green cashmere to keep out the cold in the passages. By rights she should have been in mourning, but she had no money to make any purchases. She looked very young and very fresh as she entered the great room, dropping a curtsy to the Marchioness, her eyes falling curiously on the dark figure of Madame Roxana.

'This is the girl,' the Marchioness said tersely; then to Serena: 'This, Miss Staverley, is Madame Roxana. She is a great astrologer. We are privileged to have her as a guest in this house and we have found her advice often most profitable.'

'The young lady would like me to tell her cards?' Roxana asked.

Serena drew back a little.

'No, thank you. I would rather not know the future.'

'What nonsense!' the Marchioness exclaimed. 'Everyone wants to know their future. Let Roxana tell the cards for you?'

'No, really,' Serena said. 'If you will excuse me, Ma'am, I would rather remain ignorant of what is likely to occur. So much has happened to me in the last few days that I would rather not be conversant with what further adventures are awaiting me.'

The Marchioness was annoyed.

'Is not that just like a country girl? Here is Madame Roxana straight from Bond Street, having been consulted by all the élite and all the greatest people in the land. Why, the Prince himself has honoured her, hasn't he, Roxana? And a young lady from—what is the name of the place?—Staverley, is not interested.'

There was so much indignation in the Marchioness's voice that Serena felt abashed.

'I am sorry, Ma'am! but if it gives you any pleasure I shall be glad for Madame Roxana to read my cards.'

'There, that is better,' the Marchioness approved.

'Take them in both your pretty hands,' Roxana said, holding out the pack to Serena. 'Shuffle them and wish for your heart's desire. Wish, do not forget to wish.'

Serena did as she was bid, feeling unaccountably repulsed by the worn cards with their strange designs and greasy backs. She held them out to Roxana, who took them from her and laid them out on the floor.

'You wished?' she asked.

Serena nodded.

' 'Tis strange, but you do not yet know what is your heart's desire. That is the truth, little maid?'

'I suppose so,' Serena said.

'But you will know,' Roxana went on, staring at the

cards. 'One day you will know your heart's desire . . . and you will gain it!'

'What do you see?' the Marchioness interrupted.

For a moment there was no answer from the gipsy crouching on the low stool, and bending over Serena's cards as she laid them out in a half circle. Her eyes were half closed and her shoulders were moving a little from side to side. Then finally she spoke, but her voice was low and hesitating and quite unlike the glib tones in which she had spoken to the Marchioness.

'I see danger,' she said, 'but you will save yourself . . . always you are saved when you follow your own heart . . . other people's desires, other people will press upon you . . . I can see them crowding in, men and women . . . there is danger there . . . follow your heart, it will lead you truly . . . you will not be harmed . . . but death is not far from you . . . you stand beside it . . . there is blood . . .'

The gipsy's voice trailed away and suddenly she gave a little start. Her head came up with a jerk and she stared at Serena.

'You are lucky,' she said, 'very lucky. No, it is something better than luck, it shines around you . . . it is a white light, pure and . . .'

'Do not sit there burbling,' the Marchioness said. 'Give us facts, Roxana! What is all this talk about lights? I cannot understand you. Will she marry? That is what we want to know.'

The gipsy gathered up her cards.

'She will marry,' she said.

'But whom? Can you say who it is?' the Marchioness enquired.

The gipsy smiled provokingly.

'We must look another time,' she said, 'now I am tired.'

Her eyes wandered towards the brandy-bottle. The Marchioness picked it up and thrust it into her hand.

'Take it,' she said. 'You have not told me half I wanted to hear, but it is enough to know I shall win to-night.'

'A little, remember,' Roxana said, 'only a little.'

The cards disappeared into a pocket of her dress, the bottle was tucked under her arm, hidden by the folds of the beaded jacket she wore; and now she shuffled from the room, the door closing so softly behind her that Serena was not certain if she had really gone or was still lurking in the shadows.

'Now,' the Marchioness said briskly, 'we have to see about your clothes.'

'My clothes?' Serena echoed in a bewildered voice.

'Your clothes,' the Marchioness repeated. 'You are my guest here and I want you to be a success. There are young men coming to-night and every night. You must dance with them and you must enjoy yourself. Lord, child, but smile at the thought. You are only young once.'

'Yes, but I do not understand,' Serena said. 'I am afraid I have only a few garments.'

'Yes, yes, I know all that,' the Marchioness said, 'and that is exactly what we are going to see about. Martha, open the chest.'

In front of one of the windows was a big velvet chest, braided and jewelled. It was fitted with a gold lock and key. Martha opened it and inside Serena saw that it was packed with materials of all sorts and kinds.

'Yvette will make you something for to-night,' the Marchioness said. 'Where is that silver net, Martha?' she asked impatiently. 'But I had best see for myself.'

She got out of bed and Martha hurried forward to wrap around her a white velvet pelisse trimmed with ermine.

'You will get cold, m'lady. Let me close the windows.'

'Nonsense, woman, it is stifling in here.'

Martha paid no attention to the protest but closed the three long windows while the Marchioness, going to the chest, pulled out materials one by one.

'Here is a silver net,' she said. 'It is the very latest from Paris, and should be worn over dove-grey satin . . . but perhaps that is a little old for you. What about this gauze spangled with silver stars or this shell-pink satin sprigged with pearls?' She picked up a great roll of material and flung the end of it over Serena's shoulder. 'That is enchanting,' she exclaimed. 'Look, Martha, at the sheen against her white skin. And this *batiste* will make a delicious robe for the afternoon. Quick, quick, call Yvette. We must decide which she must make first.'

'It is . . . so . . . kind of you,' Serena stammered, realising at last that the Marchioness intended to have dresses made for her, but wondering why her attitude of the night before had suddenly changed.

'Kind? Of course I am kind,' the Marchioness said, 'and why shouldn't I be? Look how lovely this is.' She held up a roll of white velvet. 'You will not find velvet like that in the whole breadth of England.'

'I have never felt anything so soft!' Serena exclaimed.

'It is from France,' the Marchioness said, 'and it would cost a fortune in Bond Street. But we will have it made up for you. You will look exquisite in it.'

'Oh, but, Ma'am, you must not part with anything so rare,' Serena cried.

'Why not?' the Marchioness asked lightly, and lowering her voice, she said surprisingly, 'Do not be in a fidget, my dear, there is plenty more where this came from.'

Six

SERENA came slowly down the Grand Staircase. It was the sixth night since her arrival at Mandrake, but she was still unable to conquer her shyness, and it swept over her in a full flood-tide as she reached the Great Hall and saw through the open door of the Silver Drawing-room a large company of guests.

The Silver Drawing-room and the ballroom opening out of it, which had been designed by Robert Adam, were in themselves awe-inspiring; but Serena felt that she would have got used in time to the magnificence and exotic luxury of Mandrake if it had not been for the people who visited the place in such numbers.

Yet although they were so many, it seemed to her that they were in many respects so similar as to be individually almost unidentifiable. The men were nearly all middle-aged, rich, raffish and heavily flirtatious, while the women with their glittering array of jewellery, their painted faces, dyed hair and fashionable affectations might all have been related; and they certainly had that similar antipathy to each other which relations so often display.

Men and women bearing distinguished names linked with the history of England met at Mandrake for one reason and for one reason only—to gain money. The mere thought of the cards brought a flush to their cheeks and made their hands stretch claw-like over the green-baize tables. Few of them could control their feelings enough to hide their triumph when they won or their chagrin when they lost.

Serena could hardly believe her ears when she first heard the magnitude of their stakes, and as she watched she thought that the players had lost every human emotion save a consuming hungry passion for money and yet more money.

She was beginning to learn, however, that there were other passions which might be aroused in those gilded *salons*. For the first time in her life she found herself fêted and courted as a lovely young woman. She was well aware that her new gowns had much to do with this. The first night she had been almost unnoticed in the splendidly dressed glittering throng. Few people had time for a pale-faced girl in an unpretentious muslin dress; but, garbed in silver net or resplendent in satin, she aroused a new light in dull eyes which had seemed satiated with beautiful women and interested only in the turn of a card.

Earnestly and with an effort which cost her far more than she would have admitted, she attempted to do what was required of her and to make herself charming to the men to whom the Marchioness introduced her with a marked air of insistence. Serèna was not stupid, and she soon realised what was the Marchioness's intention. It only took time and the quickness of sharp ears for her to realise that to all and sundry the Marchioness murmured before the introduction:

'An heiress! She will have eighty thousand pounds the day she weds, and such a sweet girl. I know you will like her.'

Old men, young men, middle-aged men, paundry or crippled, gross or pock-marked, so long as they were unattached the Marchioness hurried them up to Serena and then left her to fend for herself as best she could. She grew used to ponderous compliments from senile gallants who were old enough to be her father, and to rather embarrassed pleasantries from elderly officers and local country squires who seemed somewhat out of countenance among the *haut ton*.

She had the good sense not to accept invitations 'to look at the pictures in the Long Gallery' or seek out a quiet anteroom 'where one could talk'. She kept with the crowd, and as early as she dared and when she thought the Marchioness was paying no further attention to her she would slip away upstairs to bed.

All the time she had a feeling of being alien, almost a foreigner in a strange, unexplored country. She knew that the women talked about her amongst themselves and were jealous of her youth, for she encountered many a spiteful word, and not once but a thousand times intercepted glances which were anything but friendly.

Luckily, Serena was used to being alone, and she was not as lost without family companionship as another girl of her own age might have been, but she was often desperately afraid of the men. More than once during the evening she would glance round the room to see if Lord Vulcan was there, feeling somehow that his quiet, detached attitude was in itself a rock of refuge. She disliked him and had no desire to seek his company, but compared with the other people who thronged the rooms he was sane and controlled.

As the days went by, she grew more and more afraid of the Marchioness. She told herself it was ridiculous to feel so tongue-tied, so embarrassed in anyone's company, whoever it might be; yet she could not conquer either her feelings of fear or her shyness where the older woman was concerned. There was something so overwhelming about her that the moment she appeared Serena felt submerged, lost, even as someone might feel when drowning beneath swirling waters.

'She is doing me no harm; she is in her own way being kind,' she confided to Eudora, 'and yet I cannot like her.'

'Your instinct is right,' Eudora said sharply. 'I knew the moment I saw her that she was bad.'

'Yet why do we say that?' Serena said, arguing as much with herself as with Eudora. 'She is beautiful. She has given me those lovely gowns, and she has made no further pother about my staying here, and yet . . .'

'It is there,' Eudora said darkly, 'hanging over us. There is never a night when I go to sleep but I do not wonder if I will wake up in the morning.'

'Oh, that is ridiculous,' Serena laughed, and yet her laughter somehow held a false note. 'All the same 'tis obvious that the Marchioness does not wish me to marry her son. You should have seen the men she produced for me last night. I swear one of them was not more than seventeen, while another must have been well over sixty and his leg was swathed in bandages for he was suffering from the gout. "Did you like Sir Cuthbert?" she asked me later in the evening. "Is that the old gentleman with the gouty foot?" I questioned. "Old gentleman!" the Marchioness exclaimed in horror. "Why, my dear child, Sir Cuthbert is in the prime of life and has the most entrancing mansion not far from here. He is a fine catch!" "Indeed, Ma'am," I said demurely, "and I hope he finds an elderly spinster to angle for him".'

Eudora laughed, and Serena remembered that someone else too had laughed at her repartee. She had not known that Lord Vulcan was standing beside her when she was speaking with the Marchioness, but when she heard his laughter she turned to see who it was and realised it was the first time she had ever heard him laugh. He was genuinely amused, and it made him seem younger, much younger, until his habitual mask of cynical boredom crept over his face again.

'*Touché, ma mère,*' he said softly.

The Marchioness looked at him with a glint in her eye. For a moment it seemed to Serena that everyone in the room faded away and the three of them were alone—she, the Marchioness and Lord Vulcan—and that something tense and vibrating was passing between them. It was beyond expression, beyond her comprehension, and yet it invaded her consciousness, making her heart throb a little faster. Serena was aware in that moment of being drawn or rather compelled into some dark depths, into a queer entanglement from which she could not escape.

As quickly as it had come the moment passed. With a shrug of her white shoulders the Marchioness turned away. Someone came up to speak to Lord Vulcan and Serena was alone again, her heart returning slowly to its normal beat. She wondered if she had imagined the whole thing, but the impression of what had occurred remained so that she had thought of it, wondered about it not once but a dozen times.

That afternoon the episode returned to her mind vividly and insistently as she walked through the flower-filled gardens and stood alone on top of the cliffs looking out over the restless sea. Lord Vulcan had been right. Mandrake was lovely! Serena wanted to find fault with it, to discover flaws, to compare it unfavourably with Staverley; but she was forced to admit that it was beautiful beyond the conventional meaning of the word.

There were the gardens blooming to the very cliffs' edge and above them, silhouetted against the changing sky, swirled and shrieked and wide-winged gulls; there was the park, stretching away to the east and west until it joined the untamed, uncultivated downland; and to the north the woods, green and verdant despite their exposure to the force of the winter storms, sheltered the house.

With its wide vistas of land and sea, its far horizons and undulating country it was very different indeed from the sheltered gentleness of Staverley. Serena felt now that her world at home had been a very small one. The contrast with Mandrake was the difference between a summer's breeze and the rough, strong winds blowing over the white-crested waves.

She had expected to shrink both from Mandrake and from the sea winds, but surprisingly she responded to them, feeling invigorated and excited by their strength, and knowing a new and strange emotion within herself which reached out towards their compelling loveliness.

Then there was the house itself. It could never have been conceived in the imagination of one man. It had to be the building of centuries, the amalgamation of generation after generation. There was the Norman tower, grey and stolid, joining the warmth of Elizabethan bricks and blending harmoniously into the Charles II additions of dark timber. The new façade and the additional rooms added by Robert Adam had already, it seemed to Serena, blended in with the rest of the building so that they did not seem new or in any way garish. The whole was so perfectly proportioned, so lovely in itself, that where she had come prepared to hate she could only stand lost in admiration.

High brick walls enclosed the gardens to shelter them and one could wander for hours finding new beauties, new perfections maintained not only by a small army of gardeners, but also by the natural surroundings of the house. It was cultured, and yet there was a wildness about it, a lovely untamed wildness which no artifice could keep controlled.

At night Serena usually pulled back the curtains from her window and crouching on the window-seat would look out to sea. She had never imagined that the sea would have such a fascination for her—a great expanse of water stretching away to the hazy horizon, changing its appearance hour by hour, sometimes stormy and sometimes gay—molten silver, emerald green, sapphire blue or pearly grey—fluctuating, mercurial, mobile and invariably entrancing. Once she surprised Eudora by saying: 'I am glad I have seen this.'

'Glad to have left Staverley?' Eudora asked in horror.

Serena shook her head. She could not explain. She ached for Staverley, and yet Mandrake drew her. She was often alone in the daytime and she was glad of it. With Torqo at her heels she was content to wander freely, disturbed only when she returned to the house to find that the Marchioness had asked for her or that more guests had arrived.

To-night when she was dressing for dinner she had received a message to say that it would be a larger party than usual and that she was to wear her new gown. It had been finished only that morning and the Marchioness had sent for her to her bedroom so that she could see the final result and give her approval.

Serena dreaded these mornings when she must go to the Marchioness's bedroom. She thought that the Marchioness herself looked like some strange bewitched creature from a fairy-story, and that Madame Roxana, crouching on a low stool by the bed, was nothing more than a witch. Serena shrank from her even while Madame Roxana greeted her with toothy smiles and oily flattery. Only the gowns fashioned by Yvette's clever fingers were some compensation for those uncomfortable moments, and Serena knew that the latest creation, which she would wear this evening as instructed, transformed her.

There were silver stars on the gauze which covered the pale satin of the underskirt and there was a silver star in her hair. As she entered the drawing-room Serena saw several people glance at her and the Marchioness made a commanding gesture for her to come to her side. There was a man standing beside her and Serena felt her heart sink. Here, she supposed, was yet another person who had been told about her money, yet another prospective suitor in the eyes of the Marchioness. With a coolness she was far from feeling Serena crossed the room which appeared filled as never before with a glittering, chattering throng.

The atmosphere was stifling. The Marchioness believed that people gambled higher when it was warm, so the windows were kept permanently closed. The heat from the candles combined with the fragrance of the flowers banked in the corners of the room was almost overpowering. It was very hot now and Serena knew that it would be a great deal hotter after dinner when still more people would arrive. Yet what was the use of complaining? This, for the moment, was her life and she must accept it with the best grace she could.

'Oh, here you are, child,' the Marchioness exclaimed, and there was the sharpness of a rebuke in her voice.

'I am sorry if I am late, Ma'am,' Serena apologised. 'My new gown delayed me.'

The Marchioness looked at her with an appraising eye.

'It is vastly becoming,' she said, and turned to the man beside her, adding, 'May I present Lord Wrotham?'

Serena gave a little gasp; then she recognised the dark, good-looking but debauched face, the puffy eyes, the thick, sensual lips.

'Miss Staverley and I have met before,' Lord Wrotham said, bowing.

'I have not forgotten it, my lord.'

'Indeed! I am honoured that I have remained in your memory after so many years.'

'I have thought of you often,' Serena said, speaking slowly as if each word were difficult for her to pronounce.

'Indeed! I am indeed flattered.'

The Marchioness moved away to speak to someone else. Serena held herself very straight. She was conscious of a deep, burning anger rising within her and that her fingers were cold. Lord Wrotham had still not guessed at her antagonism.

'How well I remember coming to Staverley,' he reminisced. 'Your father, poor fellow, was a great friend of mine. You were only a child in those days—a pretty child—but, by gad, you have grown into a beauty. I did not recognise you for the moment. You must allow me as an old friend to compliment you, Serena.'

'A friend, my lord?' Serena asked the question icily. 'You are no friend of mine and never will be.'

Lord Wrotham's eyebrows were raised.

'And what can you mean by that, my sweet Serena?'

'I had a friend, who was unfortunate enough to love you, my lord. Later she bitterly regretted her stupidity; it nearly cost her her life. Have you forgotten Charmaine, Lord Wrotham?'

For a moment Lord Wrotham looked uncomfortable, then he began to bluster.

'Now really, Serena, you are too young to know about such things, or rather to talk about what can easily be misconstrued. Charmaine was a pretty girl—I remember her, of course—but she behaved in a very reprehensible manner. She ran away from me, if I remember right. Heaven knows what trouble she got into after that.'

'You are a liar!' Serena said briefly. 'You turned Charmaine away when you learned that she was having a child—your child, my lord. I took her home to Staverley. We thought she must die, but she lived and, thank God,

90

has now found real happiness. But she will never forget you, nor shall I.'

Swiftly Serena turned on her heel and walked away from him. She had no idea for the moment where she was going, moving blindly, seeing nothing in the fury of her anger. She heard someone speak her name, but she did not stop; then with a sense of relief which she was too incensed to realise, she saw Lord Vulcan's huge shoulders looming above her. She stopped at his side. He turned towards her and only under the intentness of his gaze did she realise that she was quivering and that her lips were trembling, while her eyes were large with unshed tears.

For a moment she could not speak, could only look at him helplessly.

'I was just remarking,' Lord Vulcan remarked in his usual quiet, unhurried manner, 'that it is surprising how swiftly one can travel in these days. The roads are better and carriages are finer sprung. Why, you yourself remarked, I think, the other day that you were untired after a journey of over six hours. Fifty years ago it was a very different story. I am sure you will agree with me.'

Slowly Serena felt her agitation subside. She knew that Lord Vulcan was talking to give her time to recover herself. She knew that above all things she must control herself. She must not break down in front of these strange people. Lord Vulcan drew out his snuff-box. It was of finely chased gold set with emeralds and diamonds. He examined it as if he were seeing it for the first time.

Serena's breathing became easier, the tears receded from her eyes, and though she was unaware of it a faint colour came back into her cheeks. At last she could speak in what was nearly her normal voice.

'That man . . . Lord Wrotham,' she said. 'I cannot be near him. If he is next to me at dinner . . .'

'He will not be,' Lord Vulcan said quietly. 'I will see that it is arranged.'

'Thank you,' Serena whispered, and then impulsively added: 'Could I retire? May I?'

Lord Vulcan looked at her for one moment.

'And run away?' he asked.

Serena's chin went up. With an immense effort she managed to smile at him.

'You are right, my lord. He should be the one to run.'

There was a faint smile on the Marquis's lips, and then as Serena met his eyes she heard a voice she recognised.

'Justin! Are you pleased to see me?'

There was no pretence in the lilting gladness of Lady Isabel's voice or in the eagerness of the hand she held out for Lord Vulcan to kiss.

'Oh, Justin, it is good to be here. I have wanted to see you so much. I thought your mother would never answer my letter asking if I could come. I have brought a friend with me. I hope you do not mind.'

A man emerged somewhat embarrassedly from behind her, and now it was Serena's turn to exclaim.

'Nicholas!'

She ran to her cousin's side. She thought she had never been so glad to see anyone. His rather plain, good-natured face was for her at that moment the most handsome visage in the room, and she clung to his arm in an excess of affection which exceeded anything she had ever felt for him during the years they had been together at Staverley.

'This is a surprise, Nicholas. Are you staying in the house?'

'Yes, we are staying here,' Nicholas answered. 'I came down to-night with Lady Isabel and her brother, Lord Gillingham. It was Isabel's idea,' he added, 'that you might be pleased to see me. It was kind of her to think of you.'

'Very kind,' Serenea answered, too happy at the moment to realise that Lady Isabel's thought for her had much more likely been curiosity or a desire to provide her with a companion, leaving Lord Vulcan free and unattached.

'You do not mind Nicholas coming, do you, Justin?' Lady Isabel was saying.

'I am delighted to welcome Mr. Staverley to Mandrake,' Lord Vulcan said.

'Thank you, my lord,' Nicholas answered somewhat formally.

'You have met Miss Staverley before,' Lord Vulcan went on, speaking to Lady Isabel.

'Yes, of course, but in rather unfortunate circumstances,' Lady Isabel said, 'and I doubt that I should have recognised you again.'

Her bright eyes took in every detail of Serena's new dress, the stars in her hair, the scarf draped in the very latest fashion. But Serena felt that whatever she wore she could never equal the elegance of Lady Isabel.

To-night a red dress made a startling frame for her dark beauty. There were diamonds round her neck and rubies and diamonds entwined in her hair. She had a flashing, gay loveliness which Serena envied, and she wondered how Lord Vulcan could have resisted for so long the enticement of her crimson lips.

'Say you are really glad to see me, Justin,' Lady Isabel pleaded, and seemed not to care that both Nicholas and Serena could overhear her. Serena saw the pain in Nicholas' eyes and acting on an impulse drew him aside, taking him a little apart into an alcove made by the windows.

'I was a fool to come,' Nicholas muttered, intent on his own unhappiness.

'Oh, do not say that, Nicholas,' Serena replied. 'I am so glad to see you.'

'And of course I am glad to see you,' Nicholas said courteously, 'but I have been pretending to myself that Isabel might be a little anxious for my company. I might have known it was only Vulcan she cared about.'

'Poor Nicholas,' Serena said softly. 'I wish I could help you.'

'When are you going to marry him?' Nicholas enquired.

'I do not know that I am,' Serena answered. 'He has brought me here, but as far as I can make out he has no plans for my future, while his mother wishes to marry me to the first man who will offer for me.'

'Do you mean he is behaving like a cad to you?' Nicholas asked fiercely. 'If that is the case . . .'

Serena put a restraining hand on his arm.

'No, no, Nicholas, he has behaved in the most gentlemanly manner, I assure you. The fact is, dear cousin, that he does not care a snap of the finger for me and I think I am only an embarrassment to him. Do not insult him on my behalf, I beg of you.'

'I had hoped that he would marry you,' Nicholas said miserably, 'and then perhaps Isabel . . .'

'I do not think Lord Vulcan wants to marry anybody,' Serena said soothingly.

'If only one could get rid of the fellow,' Nicholas growled. 'If I thought he was treating you ill, I . . .'

'What could you do?' Serena asked. 'If you called him out, it would do no good. Besides, he is not treating me ill! No, Nicholas, you must just hope that Lady Isabel will turn to you in time.'

'If I thought there was the slightest chance of that,' Nicholas said, 'I would wait a century.'

He looked so unhappy that Serena could only pat his arm reassuringly. She looked back at Lord Vulcan and

Lady Isabel. They were still standing together. But Lord Vulcan was looking in their direction, apparently paying little attention to the blandishments of his companion.

'Listen, Nicholas,' Serena said, 'if you are going to win Lady Isabel you will not do it by being miserable and jealous. She wants someone to conquer her, someone to sweep her off her feet. Can you not try to capture her attention? Mooning about the place is not going to help.'

Serena spoke forcefully, as she had spoken to Nicholas ever since they had been children together. She had always made the decisions and had driven him into doing what she wanted. She remembered that he had often been difficult even as a little boy, moody at times over a fancied injustice at not being able to get his own way. She looked at Lady Isabel. There was something sensuous and enticing in her scarlet-clad body, and her attitude as she threw back her dark head to look up at the Marquis revealed the tender roundness of her neck and the passionate curve of her tiny breasts.

'You have got to win her, Nicholas,' Serena insisted. 'I am a woman and I know what women want. They want a man to be a hero; someone who crawls about begging for crumbs of comfort, is not going to capture their hearts. A woman wants a lover, not a love-lorn beggar.'

Nicholas looked at her in surprise.

'Where did you learn all this, Serena?' he asked. 'You have not wasted much time if that is the sort of knowledge you have gained at Mandrake.'

Serena smiled.

'I did not have to come to Mandrake to learn about human beings, stupid. Love is much the same wherever you go.' She looked her cousin up and down. 'You are looking exceeding smart, Nicholas, in your new coat, and your cravat is wondrously tied.'

'When I look at Vulcan's, I know it is not up to snuff,' Nicholas said gloomily, but Serena knew he was pleased at her praise. Then he looked across the room and gave a low groan. 'Look at Isabel now,' he exclaimed. 'What chance have I?'

It was difficult not to be sorry for him. Isabel's hand was on Justin's arm and she was staring up at him almost wildly, obviously pleading for something.

'Oh, lud, do not stand there wearing the willow,' Serena said sharply. 'Go and stop her making an idiot of herself if you care for her at all. Be bold, carry her off, make her see that you are to be considered, and that Lord Vulcan is not the only man in the room.'

She spoke sharply and Nicholas squared his shoulders.

'Demme, but I will do it,' he said.

He strode across to Lady Isabel's side.

'There is something I want to show you, Isabel,' he said. 'Come with me.'

He spoke in such a commanding, authoritative voice that Lady Isabel, bemused by some altercation with Justin, allowed herself to be led away before she realised what was happening. Serena smiled a little to herself as she watched them moving through the crowd. She was suddenly aware that Lord Vulcan stood beside her.

'Are you glad to see your cousin?' he asked.

'Very glad,' Serena answered in all sincerity.

'That is what I thought,' Lord Vulcan said.

There was something so strange in his tone that Serena glanced up at him. She was about to say something, when in stentorian tones the butler announced that dinner was served.

The Marquis was taking down the Duchess of Dover, who was waiting impatiently for him on the other side of the room, but he made no effort to hurry to her side.

'The table has been rearranged,' he said to Serena. 'Your cousin will be sitting next to you.'

'Oh, thank you!' Serena said, and was somehow surprised by the expression on his face.

Dinner was the usual long-drawn-out meal, course following course, with exquisite wines and the usual difficulty of conversation divided equally between two neighbours. Nicholas talked unceasingly of himself when he was not striving to get a glimpse of Lady Isabel farther down the table, while the man on Serena's left talked only of hunting, of which she knew very little.

She was glad when the meal drew to an end and the ladies withdrew to the drawing-room. As Serena moved through the chattering, scented crowd, Isabel came to her side.

'Let us retire to your bedchamber, I want to talk to you.'

Serena led the way up the Grand Staircase, and then as they climbed another flight of stairs she thought that Isabel looked around her a little strangely.

'Why are you in this part of the house?' she asked when finally they reached Serena's room, the firelight casting strange shadows on the massive furniture.

Serena smiled.

'I am not important enough for the guest-rooms on the first floor.'

Isabel shut the door behind her and waited while Serena lit the candles.

'Do you mind if I ask you a question?' she asked at length.

Serena turned round.

'I know what it is,' she said, 'and you may ask it, but I cannot answer you.'

'What do you mean?' Isabel said sharply.

Serena came back to the fireside, holding out her hands to the blaze.

'Why shouldn't we talk honestly between ourselves?' she asked. 'You wish to wed Lord Vulcan; I do not wish to wed him. What you are going to enquire of me was if he intends to marry me. That is a question which he alone can answer. I do not think he does, but I would not know. I have never met people such as this before and they both bewilder and surprise me.'

Serena spoke softly, and as she talked she felt Isabel relax. There had been an air of almost aggressive hostility about her as they had gone up the stairs, but now she stared at her in wide-eyed and open-mouthed astonishment, before she gave a shout of laughter.

'Lud, but I like you for that,' Lady Isabel exclaimed. 'I want to hate you, but I cannot. You are nice, and we must be friends, you and I. Why not?'

'Why not indeed?' Serena asked.

'It is a mistake' Lady Isabel said, 'for I have vowed often enough never to have a friend as pretty as myself. And you are lovely, really lovely, and I cannot think why Justin has not taken you to the altar days ago.'

'Do you love him so very much?'

'I am crazy about him,' Isabel admitted. 'I have been for over a year now and he will have none of me. But I swear he shall come to love me. He is so handsome . . . apart from the fact that I would like to be the Marchioness of Vulcan.'

'Does position matter when you love someone?' Serena asked.

'Oh, lud, but you are simple,' Isabel exclaimed. 'Of course it does. Think what Justin could offer any woman. But apart from his riches, his title and this house, I love him. He attracts me. I adore that deliciously insolent man-

96

ner of his, the way he remains indifferent to everything that happens, to anything anyone says. I will win him one of these days, you see if I don't.'

'And when you have won him?' Serena asked.

'I shall be the Marchioness of Vulcan,' Lady Isabel cried. 'What a triumph it would be! For a whole year I have been pining away.'

Serena laughed.

'I am sorry,' she said, "but you do not look as if you have been pining. You are so lovely, so gay, so alive.'

'Faugh, I told you that we ought not to be friends,' Isabel said in mock severity. 'How dare you say I am not pining! I think of Justin day and night. I lie awake because of him. I have even come here to-day . . . a monstrously uncomfortable journey from London . . . just to see him.'

'It was kind of you to bring my cousin with you.'

Isabel looked at her for a moment, then her eyes twinkled.

'Kind?' she questioned. 'Shall I tell you the truth, or have you guessed it?'

'You wanted to learn from him all you could about me?' Serena ventured.

'Correct!' Lady Isabel exclaimed. 'And I promise you I learnt very little. Nicholas persisted in talking about himself. I could not keep the conversation away from him.'

'Which meant, of course, that he was talking about you,' Serena smiled.

Isabel threw back her head and laughed.

'An absorbing topic, you must admit.'

'Poor Nicholas, he loves you so much.'

'Yes, I know, and never was there such a dull fellow. "Pray, Isabel, give me your attention," and "Isabel, I beg of you . . ." Lord, what fools these men be with their begging and their praying, their pleading and their whining. That is what I like about Justin, he asks favours of no one.'

'But Nicholas would always be very kind to you.'

'Kind?' Isabel asked scornfully. 'Who wants kindness? I would rather a man beat me than cosseted me. And I swear I would adore one who was brutal. They are all too polite nowadays.'

She stretched out her arms, her eyes narrowed a little as if she were thinking of strange delights to be found in the arms of those who were not too polite to love passionately and with an unappeased desire. Then she looked at Serena and her face broke again into one of her entrancing smiles.

97

'Are you going to help me?' she asked.

'To do what?' Serena questioned.

'To marry Justin. Say you will.'

Serena shook her head.

'I want you to marry Nicholas. He is the nicest person I know, and if you but knew it you would be very happy with him.'

'Faugh, but you are baming!' Lady Isabel exclaimed.

'No, I am quite serious,' Serena said, 'and Nicholas being my cousin has my first consideration. I shall help him in every way I can to marry you.'

Isabel laughed again, then she jumped to her feet and put her arms round Serena.

'I love you, I swear I do,' she said. 'I never anticipated such fun would come from this visit. I shall try and win Justin from you, and you will try to marry me to Nicholas.'

'You cannot win Justin from me,' Serena answered, 'for he is not mine to give you. The Marchioness is determined that I shall marry someone else—anyone, she is not particular who it is.'

'Gammon! Is the Marchioness involved in this?' Isabel asked. 'Then, Serena—for I may call you that, mayn't I?—we must be careful.'

'Why?' Serena enquired.

'Because the Marchioness invariably gets what she wants. She has some hold over Justin. I do not know what it is; I wish I did. When she sends for him, he hurries to her side; if she wants something, invariably he gets it for her. It is whispered . . .' and Isabel, looking around her, lowered her voice, 'that he goes to the gaming-tables on her insistence and that when he wins she takes the money.'

'But they must have so much,' Serena said.

'Yes, but look what they spend,' Isabel answered, 'and there is more to it than that. There are many people who say that this house is mighty convenient for many of my lady's activities.'

'You mean her gaming?' Serena asked.

Isabel shook her head.

'No, no—'tis only a rumour, of course—but the sea is very convenient for those who are interested in things that come from across the Channel.'

'Do you mean . . . ?' Serena asked.

'Exactly what I say,' Isabel answered, and added in triumph: 'Look at your dress, Serena. In the whole length and breadth of Bond Street one could not purchase even a yard of such material. I will stake my life on that.'

'You mean . . . that the Marchioness smuggles?' Serena whispered.

'I am by no means the only person who says so,' Isabel replied.

Seven

THE sunshine was warm on Serena's head, and after a moment she set down the embroidery which busied her fingers and laid her head against the wooden window frame.

She closed her eyes. She could hear the wash of the waves on the rocks below the cliffs. She could smell the salty fragrance of the sea on the soft air blowing into her bedchamber. Here she could be quiet and at ease. Torqo slept on the floor at her feet. Eudora was at hand in the next room. There was nothing to disturb her save the busy hum of a bee imprisoned against a pane of glass.

Suddenly Isabel burst into the room, and Torqo jumped to his feet with a deep growl which changed into a yelp of joy and a wagging of his tail when he saw who had entered.

'Down Torqo!' Serena said as he bounded towards Isabel.

'Mind he does not spoil your gown', she added hastily.

'I care not what he does, he is a beautiful boy,' Isabel said, patting the dog as he nuzzled against her, delighted by her attention. 'But put on your bonnet quickly, Serena. We are going to Dover.'

'To Dover?' Serena echoed in surprise. 'Why?'

'I declare it is the most thrilling adventure,' Isabel exclaimed. 'We are to see a smuggler.'

'A smuggler!'

'Yes, to see him and perhaps to converse with him,' Isabel replied. 'It is Nicholas who has arranged it all. The Colonel of the Dragoon Guards was talking with him yester evening and he told Nicholas about this man. A desperate character, it appears, whom the soldiers caught red-handed unloading stores from France. There was a hot fight and some of the smugglers got away, but this man, the ringleader of them all, was taken prisoner. The Colonel said the Dragoons have been after him for years; he is known to have murdered no less than three men in cold

100

blood, and a score of excisemen have been wounded by him and his band. Come, Serena, there is no time to be lost. The coach will be round at any moment.'

'I do not think I wish to see a smuggler,' Serena said quietly.

'Not wish to see him?' Isabel echoed in astonishment. 'Really, Serena, I do not understand you. When Nicholas and Gilly said they were going off by themselves I nearly cried with chagrin. It was with the greatest difficulty that I persuaded Nicholas to make it a party and now a number of us are to accompany them . . . you must come too.'

'Who else will be with you?' Serena asked.

'Oh, but I cannot recollect,' Isabel said. 'It has all been decided so swiftly, but I know that Lady Greyshields insists on coming with us for one, and Harry Wrotham for another.'

Serena sat up very straight.

'You know, Isabel, that I would go nowhere if it meant that I should be in close proximity to Lord Wrotham.'

'Pish! I had forgotten,' Isabel exclaimed. 'How tiresome you are, Serena, to continue your feud against him! I vow that he admires you vastly. Why, he was singing your praises all yester afternoon until I was ready to swoon with boredom, preferring to hear people talk about my own face.'

'Which they invariably do,' Serena smiled. 'But I would take it as a compliment if my name did not cross Lord Wrotham's lips. I hate him, Isabel, and I will never forgive him—never—for what he did to my poor Charmaine.'

'Oh, Serena, and that means that you will deny us your company to Dover?'

'Believe me, Isabel, I have no desire to see your smuggler—a brutal murderer who has killed three men in cold blood.'

'Faugh, but you are squeamish! I have told you before that I like men who are rough and brutal, and it will give me a thrill even to look at this creature.'

'Then go and enjoy yourself,' Serena said, 'and Torqo and I will stay here and be happy by ourselves.'

'I declare you have quite spoilt my pleasure in the adventure. I wanted you to come with us. But if you are so obstinate I must make shift with your cousin Nicholas. I would not miss seeing the man for the price of my diamond necklace.'

Isabel dropped a light kiss on Serena's cheek, patted

Torqo, and with a wave of her hand swept from the room, leaving behind her the fragrance of an expensive perfume and a disrupted atmosphere of excitement and gaiety.

Serena smiled to herself as she picked up her embroidery again. She liked Isabel; in fact it would have been true to say that she loved her. Impetuous and reckless, she had yet the singleness of heart and the happy, sunny nature of a child. A spoilt child, it was true, but nevertheless a child. Though she had lived in raffish society, it had not hurt her intrinsically; and Serena had already learned that, while she would rush hot-headed after some new project, she would cry sincere and heart-breaking tears over a sad story of poverty and want and be prepared to give away even the very gown from off her back if it would help someone in distress.

It was impossible not to be fond of Isabel, and Serena knew that already she valued her friendship. But Lord Wrotham remained an enemy whom she could neither forgive nor forget.

With a sense of dismay she had learned that he had come to Mandrake for a long visit. He was, it appeared, a very old friend of the Marchioness, and while it would not have been difficult in so large a house party to avoid him, Serena was well aware that he was deliberately seeking her company on every possible occasion. In the gaming-rooms she would find him by her side. He would talk to her whether she willed it or not, and though she was as curt to him as she dared be she had no wish to cause a scene or attract attention to herself by being openly discourteous to him.

Since Lord Vulcan's intercession on the first night of Lord Wrotham's arrival she had not been placed next to him at dinner, and she had the idea that the Marquis had spoken to his mother and they had argued about this very matter. She was not certain, however, of this; but she did know that Lord Wrotham was determined for some obscure reason of his own to reinstate himself and gain her friendship. She was equally determined that never would she forget the misery he had caused Charmaine; but she was aware that most people would think that she was exaggerating or making too much of what she be dismissed as just an unfortunate episode in the life of a man-about-town.

Isabel for one had laughed at her for her insistence on his depravity and treachery.

'After all, Serena,' she had said, 'the girl did run away with him. She could not have been so bird-witted as to expect someone in Harry Wrotham's position to marry her. You say she was the daughter of your father's groom. She must have known that she was throwing her bonnet over the windmill, but for a girl like that to be a nobleman's "bit of muslin" is sometimes infinitely preferable to the stolid respectability of domestic service.'

'But you don't understand, Isabel,' Serena replied. 'Lord Wrotham made Charmaine love him. She trusted him . . .'

'In which case she was a fool,' Isabel interrupted. 'No one would trust Harry Wrotham unless they were foxed or crazy.'

Serena laughed and gave up trying to explain to Isabel what she felt about Lord Wrotham. Sometimes she thought that her only ally where he was concerned was the Marquis. She felt instinctively that he, too, disliked the man, but she had no concrete grounds for believing this because Lord Vulcan treated all his guests with an equality of indifferent courtesy.

Serena went on sewing until Torqo jumped up on the wide window-seat beside her and whined.

'You want to go out in the sunshine, don't you?' Serena said promptly. 'Very well then, we will.'

She opened the door of her room and called for Eudora. A few minutes later, wearing a shawl of blue cashmere to match the blue ribbon on her straw bonnet, she went into the garden. She and Torqo had discovered a way which led on to the downlands from the formal confines of the garden. Here they could walk along the edge of the cliffs, hear the waves thundering below and feel the sharp wind blowing breathlessly against them.

Serena liked walking. She had grown used to it at Staverley where it was seldom that she had the chance of driving in her father's curricle and for lack of horses and grooms the family coach had gradually ceased to be used.

Isabel, on the contrary, never walked if she could drive, and she had warned Serena that her feet would grow larger if she insisted on taking so much exercise.

'I am a country girl,' Serena replied with a smile, but Isabel answered:

'You do not look it in your new gowns.'

It was true enough. Serena's new wardrobe was amazingly becoming. There were, too, so many garments that Eudora declared crossly that she was quite bemused by them. But poor Eudora was jealous. Yvette's clever French fingers could fashion anything from a ball-gown to a bow of ribbon so that it appeared to have come straight from the very latest Court dressmaker; and Eudora, looking at the discarded muslins which she herself had made with so much labour and care, could only mutter ominous warnings under her breath while at the same time her heart rejoiced because the gowns framed and enhanced Serena's beauty.

Serena had tried to thank the Marchioness, but her thanks had been brushed to one side.

'If you wish to reveal your gratitude, child,' she said brusquely, 'you can pay attention to the compliments that will be offered you by the other sex. Take my advice and do not bother about women in your life. It is men that matter.'

There was certainly plenty of men to be found at Mandrake, and Serena, on her guard because she knew that she was being dangled before them as a bait weighted with gold, was more frigid in her reception of their advances than she would ever have been had she met them under different circumstances.

It was difficult for her at any time, however, to be aloof or even apprehensive or depressed for long. The sunshine and the fresh air routed even the most sober thoughts. Now she ran along the cliffs with Torqo and was conscious as they turned back towards Mandrake that her curls were disarranged beneath her bonnet and that her cheeks were flushed. She made up her mind to regain her room without meeting anyone, and avoiding the front entrance to the house she crept through the walled gardens to a small door in the old part of the castle which she guessed should be somewhere directly below her own apartment.

She had noticed that the servants used it when coming into the garden with a message, and she hoped that it would be unlocked. She was right; the door was open and she found herself in a long oak-panelled passage which after winding for some way came out at the foot of a flight of narrow stairs she had never seen before.

She was just going to climb the stairs when she heard someone coming. Wishing to remain unobserved she drew to one side, and found that by standing in the turn of the passage she could be hidden in the shadows while able to observe who was approaching. To her astonishment the person coming down the stairs was the Marchioness. She was wearing a dress of emerald-green silk which rustled as she walked and in her hand she held her favourite ivory stick with its jewelled handle.

Hastily, feeling like a child who has been caught playing truant, Serena patted her curls and strove to tidy the windswept ribbons of her bonnet, but even as she fidgeted the Marchioness reached the foot of the stairs. She stood for a moment looking at the opposite wall and then, as Serena gaped in amazement, disappeared.

For a moment Serena could hardly believe her eyes; then she stepped from the doorway and looked for a door in the wall through which the Marchioness must have passed. But the wall was covered in panelling and there was no door. Serena stood staring, half inclined to rub her eyes and think that she had seen a ghost. Then she remembered that she was in the old part of the castle. Of course, there must be a secret entrance here hidden in the panelling.

Curiosity overcame her fear and she drew nearer instead of hurrying up the stairs as she should have done. There had been a priest-hole at Staverley reached by a tiny twisting stairway which could be found through a concealed panelled door in her father's bedchamber. Serena recalled how the oak aperture in the panelling had worked. One pressed a tiny scroll in the carving. Her fingers searched now. She found a tiny knot of wood, pressed it and then with a sudden exclamation knew that she had discovered the secret of the Marchioness's disappearance. A panel of wood opened silently and smoothly.

'You are interested in panelling?' a voice said behind her, startling her so much that she released the panel, pushing it to, and turned round with an inescapable feeling of guilt. Half-way down the stairs with a riding-crop in his hand and a dog at his heels, stood the Marquis.

'I—I was—just—looking,' Serena stammered.

'So I perceive,' the Marquis said. 'I repeat—you are interested in panelling?'

He came slowly down the staircase, and Serena could only stand staring at him, trying vainly to find some adequate explanation of what seemed to her now to have been most reprehensible and undignified behaviour.

'I thought . . . I saw . . . someone pass . . . through here, my lord,' she said at last.

'Indeed! But then of course you have already heard that this part of the house is haunted. You must beware of the ghosts at Mandrake.'

He spoke lightly, and yet she felt there was a serious warning in his tone, and her eyes dropped before his.

'Yes . . . I will . . . I promise you I will,' she said quickly, and she pulled her shawl a little tighter round her shoulders as if to protect herself from his scrutiny.

There was a faint smile on his lips as he noted the disordered curls and wind-swept ribbons.

'You have been for a walk with your dog?'

'Yes, my lord. Torqo always wants to be out.'

'And you?'

'You know that I love the country.'

'You have not yet told me,' Lord Vulcan went on, 'what you think of my home. I remember remarking that it was a very beautiful place and you did not believe me.'

Serena looked at him quickly. It was surprising that he should remember their conversation at Staverley and still more surprising that he should have known her reactions when he had compared the beauties of Staverley with those of Mandrake. As if he noticed her surprise, Lord Vulcan said:

'Come with me, I would like to show you something.'

He walked down the passage, opened a door at the end and invited her to precede him into a room. Serena obeyed him wonderingly. The room itself was small, and it had the air of seldom being used. The walls were panelled, and instead of pictures there were maps hanging on the walls. There was a long table down the centre of the room and on this, under glass cases, were several clay models. Lord Vulcan went up to one of them and pointed to it with his finger.

'This,' he said, 'is a reconstruction of Mandrake as it was originally—a Norman castle built as a fortification; and this'—pointing to another—'is the castle as it was four centuries later. I had them done some years ago. You will admit they are interesting?'

Serena gazed at the models with excitement. They were very cleverly executed and like exquisite toys. It was fascinating to see how the great house had grown from its first gaunt and stolid outline. Her bonnet cast a shadow on the case and she pulled it from her head, forgetting the unruliness of her hair. Then she bent over the largest model of them all which showed Mandrake as it was to-day.

'There are the gardens in which I walked only a few minutes ago,' she exclaimed. 'Look how cleverly they are fashioned; and there is the little gate which opens on to the downs. Oh, now I can see the formation of the cliffs. I often wondered what they were like from the sea.'

'You admit it is beautiful?' Lord Vulcan asked, as if he wished to force her actually to say the words.

'But of course it is,' Serena said. 'It is the most beautiful place I have ever seen in my life.'

'I like to hear you say that,' Lord Vulcan approved.

'Naturally, I still love Staverley best,' Serena said almost defiantly, as though she felt she had somehow been disloyal to her own home. 'But one can hardly compare the two. It is like asking someone which they think the more beautiful—a primrose or an orchid. Surely each have their own beauty and one may admire them both, though . . . one may prefer the primrose.'

'As you would prefer to live at Staverley?' Lord Vulcan said.

'But of course.'

'You are unhappy here?' He asked the question sharply.

'Unhappy?' Serena echoed the word. 'Not . . . exactly. It is all very strange, of course, and I am very shy of your many guests.'

'They are not my guests,' Lord Vulcan remarked.

'But your mother invited them,' Serena corrected, without thinking that she was contradicting him, 'and as it is your house, they are your guests, my lord. I try to be polite to them. But often I think how nice it would be if the rooms were empty and one could enjoy quietly the beautiful things they contain; if one could hear the music without the tattling of hundreds of voices; if one could eat and drink without having to make polite conversation.'

Serena spoke with an almost passionate sincerity. Lord Vulcan laughed.

'At least you are frank,' he said. 'Do you collect that many young women would be thrilled to be here, to have the chance of meeting so many people, or should I say . . . men?'

'You may not believe me, my lord,' Serena said, suddenly irritated with him, 'any more than your mother would, but I do not want to meet men. I like few enough of them.'

'The explanation lying, of course, in your affection for your cousin—the worthy Nicholas.'

'Naturally . . . I am very fond of Nicholas,' Serena said, her eyes widening at the tone of Lord Vulcan's voice.

'So I understand, and yet you told me that you did not contemplate marrying him.'

'I spoke truly, my lord,' Serena said quietly. 'I do not desire to marry my cousin any more than he desires to marry me. You know full well that he is in love with the Lady Isabel.'

'And if he were not?' Lord Vulcan probed.

'I would still not wish to marry him,' Serena said. 'I cannot understand why you should imagine that my heart is enamoured with someone I have known all my life. To be truthful, and I promised you once before that I would always tell you the truth, I am in love with no one.'

'Most certainly not with the man to whom you are betrothed,' Lord Vulcan said ironically.

It took Serena a second or two to remember that he was speaking of himself, and then, before she could find an answer, Lord Vulcan said: 'Shall I make you fall in love with me, Serena?'

It was the first time he had addressed her by her christian name, and his words and a sudden depth in his voice brought the crimson tide of colour flooding into her cheeks. She looked up at him in astonishment and was suddenly aware that her knees felt very weak.

'No!' she cried. 'No! No!'

'So vehement?' he asked, and she fancied there was a new expression behind the steely grey of his eyes. Was it cruelty or . . . something else?

Are you afraid of love, or merely of—me?'

'Of both,' Serena replied, and then wildly, because she felt a sudden sense of insecurity and almost of panic sweep over her, she caught up her bonnet. 'I must go, my lord . . . thank you for showing me these models . . . they are very interesting . . . but I must go.'

She almost ran towards the door. As she reached it she turned back to see him standing in the light of the window. He was at ease, and his habitual expression of cynical indifference masked his face.

'Why am I afraid?' she wondered, and then before she could answer her own question, she fled upstairs and kept to her room for the rest of the afternoon.

It was late before Isabel returned from Dover; then she came hurrying to Serena's bedchamber and began chattering vivaciously of their adventures, saying over and over again that it was absurd of Serena not to have accompanied them.

'The smuggler was a most fascinating brute,' Isabel exclaimed. 'An enormous man, with a nose that had been broken in a fight. I vow I would have swooned at the sight of him if I had not held on to Nicholas.'

'Fiddle!' Serena exclaimed. 'You would not have done that because you might have missed what was happening.'

'That is true enough,' Lady Isabel laughed. 'How well you know me!'

'Did he mind you all staring at him and asking questions?'

'No, I think he gloried in it,' Isabel replied. 'He seemed proud of what he had done. The Colonel asked him to show us some scars he had got in a fight twelve months ago, and he bared his arm with three knife wounds in it. La, Serena, it was a thrill such as I have never had before.'

'I fail to understand why you want to see such horrible things," Serena shuddered.

'I have been born centuries too late, that is the answer,' Isabel replied. 'I want to be captured and conquered. Men of the present day with their foppish airs and limp white hands bore me.'

'They cannot all be so very limp,' Serena answered. 'Eudora was telling me last night that Lord Vulcan's valet had related to her how his lordship wagered five hundred guineas that he would beat Tom Jackson in a mill; and won it.'

'Tom Jackson, the bruiser!' Isabel exclaimed, her eyes shining. 'And Justin beat him?'

'The valet said it was a fiercesome fight,' Serena said. 'It took place in the country, of course, about seven miles north of London. There were not many there to see it.'

'Oh, what I would have given to be present!' Isabel cried. 'But I am not surprised that Justin won. He is so strong, Serena. Methinks he could be brutal too, if it pleased him.'

Serena shivered.

'Do not let us talk about Lord Vulcan. Tell me more about your smuggler.'

Isabel chatted on gaily and Serena gathered she had not been too bemused to note the attractions of the Adjutant of the Dragoons.

'One of the most handsome creatures you ever saw. I put Nicholas into a fit of the sullens by talking of him all the way home.'

'Poor Nicholas!'

'Yes, poor Nicholas!' Isabel mocked. 'I promise you one

thing, that never, never will I marry a man of whom people prefix the word "poor" before his name. It invariably means they are sorry for him, and one should never be sorry for any man. One should respect, adore, worship or even hate him, but never, never pity him.'

'I shall never say "poor Nicholas" again,' Serena promised.

'But still I won't love him,' Isabel retorted, 'although I grant you he is preferable to that beast, Harry Wrotham. He was so sneering and condescending this afternoon that I vow I dislike him almost as much as you do.'

'I am sorry you did not push him off the cliffs of Dover,' Serena said.

'What a pity I did not think of it,' Isabel laughed. 'He is a dead bore and I am glad to say that he was exceedingly put about when he learned that you were not coming with us. "I thought the sweet Serena would accompany us," he said to me. "She asked me, my lord," I replied, "who was to be included, and when she heard their names she decided to stay at home." He looked as black as thunder and knew full well you had refused because of him.'

'I wish he would go away,' Serena sighed.

'He has no intention of it, I am afraid,' Isabel answered. The clock over the mantelpiece struck the hour. 'I must go and dress for dinner,' she added. 'I have a new gown to wear to-night. It arrived by post-chaise yesterday and I warn you it will eclipse every dress in the room, even yours, Serena.'

'I am sure it will do that,' Serena replied. 'You always outshine us all anyway.'

'Flatterer,' Isabel said. 'I only wish I had your fair hair and untroubled beauty. I heard an old gentleman ask last night, "Who is the angel?" and to my chagrin he meant you.'

'Who is being flattering now?' Serena enquired. 'And just to pay you out I shall wear a new dress to-night. It is of white velvet, and I swear you will think it is the loveliest material you have ever seen.'

'If Justin looks longer at you than at me, I shall scratch your eyes out, so I warn you.'

Isabel laughed as she spoke, and Serena heard her singing as she went down the passage. It was unlikely that the Marquis would look at either of them with any particular interest, Serena thought; and then remembering his strange words of the afternoon she felt that same sense of insecurity and embarrassment sweep over her. Why did he say, 'Shall I make you love me?' The sunlight had been on his face as he spoke, and perhaps that had accounted for some quickening interest she had seemed to read in his expression, for the look in his grey eyes and the sudden firmness of his lips.

How good-looking he was! She had always planned that one day when she fell in love it would be with somebody handsome, somebody whom she could admire. Lord Vulcan was handsome enough, but she did not love him, and would never love him. She thought of Staverley—empty, far away—but somehow to-night her heart did not throb angrily at the memory as she had so often made it do before.

Why had he said those strange words to her? But what was the point of wondering? The Marquis's behaviour was beyond her comprehension. Impatiently Serena got to her feet and walking to the door called for Eudora, who came hurrying to the room.

'You will be late, Miss Serena, if you do not start to dress soon. I thought her ladyship would never stop her tattling.'

'She wanted to tell me about the smuggler they had seen at Dover.'

'No need to go to Dover to see smugglers from all I hear,' Eudora snapped.

But when Serena asked her what she meant she would say no more.

It was a large dinner-party as usual, but Serena with Lord Gillingham on one side of her and a young naval officer on the other found she was enjoying herself. She liked Gilly, as Isabel called him, and when he complimented her on her gown she was pleased, knowing that the admiration in his eyes was genuine enough.

He, too, could talk of little but the smuggler they had seen that afternoon.

'A ghastly fellow,' he ejaculated. 'I am not surprised that the excisemen were afraid of him.'

'It is a real feather in their cap having got him,' the naval officer remarked from the other side of Serena. 'But he is only one of many. The gangs along this coast are getting so numerous that it is becoming a hopeless task to try to round 'em up.'

'Surely the Dragoons are a help?' Lord Gillingham asked.

111

The sailor shrugged his shoulders.

'They are only a handful in comparison with what is required, and the real trouble is that the excise ships have been taken to reinforce the Navy. Besides, the authorities in London have no idea what they are up against. This rule that no large boats are to be built in England is just making trade for the French. I am told their shipbuilders are at work day and night on boats with thirty-six oars which can travel from anything to seven or nine miles an hour. What chance have our fellows against such speed?'

'None, of course,' Lord Gillingham said. 'But something will have to be done. They report that over twelve thousand guineas are being carried by the smugglers to the Continent every week, and most of it goes into Boney's pocket. We all know his Spanish troops will take nothing but gold in payment.'

'But what is the solution?' Serena asked.

'If only we knew of one!' the naval officer sighed. 'I would like to have a crack at the smugglers myself, but I am off to the Mediterranean next week.'

'Well, here's good hunting, and may you sink a French ship with every salvo,' Lord Gillingham said, raising his glass, and the sailor bowed his acknowledgement.

There was dancing in the Long Gallery that night, and Serena, partnered by Lord Gillingham and the naval officer who had sat next to her at dinner, found that the hours passed surprisingly quickly.

It was late when Isabel came up to her and asked for the loan of her handkerchief.

'I have lost mine,' she said, 'or someone is wearing it next his heart!'

Serena gave her a wisp of lawn and lace and then decided she would fetch another for herself. She went upstairs and was astonished to see that the clock pointed to after three o'clock.

'I should go to bed,' she thought, 'but I have promised the next dance and the one after, and I would not wish to disappoint my partners.'

The fire was still bright and feeling that the room was slightly airless she pulled back the curtains and opened the window. The moon was hidden behind clouds, but the stars were out and the night was not dark. As she pushed wide the casement she heard a sound out to sea. She thought it was a voice. Curious, she leant out. She could not see clearly, but for a moment she had the impression that directly below her on the sea there was the outline of a boat. Then as she looked again it was gone and she felt she must have been mistaken.

'I am beginning to imagine smugglers,' she said to herself with a smile, and picking up her handkerchief she turned towards the door.

She came down again to the Great Hall and as she reached the foot of the stairs she saw to her surprise that a number of men were coming in through the main doorway. Even for Mandrake it was late for guests to be arriving, but then Serena perceived that they were by no means the usual elegantly dressed company who frequented the Marchioness's parties. She recognised the uniform of the Dragoon Guards; while the other men were more roughly garbed and she guessed they were coastguards and excisemen.

A lackey went hurrying across the marble floor to the gaming-rooms as if in search of someone. Serena followed him leisurely. The band in the Long Gallery was still playing the same tune as when she went upstairs and she knew that the next dance had not yet started. She made her way through the crowd who were standing around chattering and watching those who were gambling. She saw the lackey speak to the Marquis at the far end of the room.

Lord Vulcan continued for a moment to talk with those with whom he had been conversing before the lackey reached him. Then he turned and walked slowly across the room. He made his way through the tables and came face to face with Serena moving in the opposite direction.

The Marquis stood on one side to let Serena pass him and then as she smiled up at him a little shyly he suddenly bent down with an incredibly quick movement and pulled at the lace handkerchief she held lightly between her fingers so that it fluttered to the floor. Swiftly he picked it up as if he had retrieved it for her and handed it back to her.

'Your handkerchief, I think,' he said with a courtly politeness, and as she took it he added in a low voice so that only she could hear him: 'Warn my mother that the coastguards are here. Go to her through the door in the panelling.'

Eight

HARRIET VULCAN staked a pile of gold and lost it. A second pile went the same way. She looked across the table and caught the gleam of triumph in Lord Wrotham's eyes.

'The devil take you, Harry,' she exclaimed, 'for undoubtedly his luck is with you.'

Lord Wrotham looked complacently at the big pile of winnings on the table beside him. He tidied them with his left hand, stacking the guineas one on top of the other.

'Poor Harriet,' he commiserated, 'you are certainly out of luck.'

'It will change! It will change!' the Marchioness said angrily.

'Do you challenge me again?'

'Of course,' the Marchioness replied. 'Do you think I am chicken-hearted?'

'Never that, Harriet,' he replied softly. 'Shall we say a little reckless? The first rule for every gambler, my dear, is never to go against your own cards.'

'Fiddle, I tell you my luck will change.'

'Then if you desire it,' Lord Wrotham smiled, 'we will continue. Shall we put up fifty guineas, Harriet, or a mere twenty-five?'

'Fifty! Fifty!' she said feverishly.

It was at that moment that she was aware that somebody stood at her elbow. It was her black boy, and it passed through her mind that he was bringing her a much needed drink. Then his small black hand stole forward and laid something beside her. Harriet's heart gave a sickening thump. For a moment the table with its money and its cards swam before her eyes. Almost automatically her hand went out towards the pack. Then she heard Harry Wrotham say:

'I am sorry, Harriet.'

There was no sorrow in his voice. She pushed what was left of her money towards him.

114

'I am about thirty guineas short. I will let you have it in a few moments.'

'No hurry, Harriet. Pray do not incommode yourself,' he said. 'I can trust you!'

Was he mocking her or being genuinely courteous? She was not certain. She rose from the table, her hand closing sharply over the small object which the black boy had laid beside her. It was only a tiny bottle of smelling-salts and she felt the crystal facets cut into the flesh of her fingers. Only a bottle of smelling-salts, but it carried a message which made her blood quicken and her heart sink in apprehension.

She moved across the room towards the door. She appeared in no hurry and several people spoke to her as she passed. An elderly duke, slightly the worse for drink, laid hold of her arm.

'I want to drink to you, Harriet,' he said thickly. 'The most beautiful woman in England.'

'Thank you, Barty,' she replied, and her smile was automatically flirtatious, but she disengaged herself cleverly so that for the moment he was not aware that she had left him.

The way to the door seemed interminable. People were laughing, talking, chattering; there was the clink of money and the quiet, unhurried voice here and there calling out numbers.

At last she reached the door, and now she was able to quicken her pace, to speed across the marble floor of the Great Hall and run swiftly up the wide steps of the Grand Staircase. She reached her bedchamber. Martha was waiting for her there with an anxious face.

'They are here, m'lady.'

'So I supposed.' The Marchioness opened her hand and threw the glass bottle on to the bed. 'To-night of all nights,' she murmured, 'and yet, fool that I was, I might have expected it. The sea is calm.'

'You are worried, m'lady.'

'Worried?' There was no mistaking the anxiety in the tone with which the Marchioness echoed the word. 'Where is their money, Martha?'

The maid moved across the room and pulled open the bottom drawer in the dressing-table. A canvas bag lay there. She took it up and feeling its weight with both her hands stared at it in surprise.

'It is curiously light,' she exclaimed.

'I know that,' the Marchioness snapped.

'You mean, m'lady,' Martha said in tones of horror, 'that you have taken some of the gold?'

'Yes, yes, of course I have. Isn't that obvious, you fool? I had no idea that they would come to-night. I borrowed a few guineas. I thought there would be time for me to pay it back.'

'What will they say, m'lady?'

'They must wait, that is all. Here, give me the bag, and do not stand there yapping.'

The Marchioness took the bag from Martha and at the same time picked up her ivory stick with the jewelled handle which lay on a footstool in front of the fire.

'Shall I come with you, m'lady?' Martha asked.

'No, of course not! Hold the door here. If anyone comes to ask for me, I shall be returning to the salon almost directly.'

'Very good, m'lady.'

The Marchioness looked around her wildly as if she expected help to spring from one of the shaded corners of the room.

'Lud,' she muttered to herself, 'but I am a fool,' and then she turned and hurried down the passage, the light gauze of her scarf flying out behind her like wings.

She traversed almost the whole of the first floor of the house until she reached a small staircase in the ancient part of the building. She went down it, stopping only at the foot of the stairway to take a taper from a table which stood there and light it from a candle in the wall bracket. Then she felt for the secret spring in the wall opposite and the panelling opened.

The air was damp and cold in the tunnel-like passage in which she found herself. She moved briskly forward, stopping only now and then to light a candle so that the way before her was clear. After she had gone forward about fifty yards she came to a long flight of stone steps leading downwards. The air grew colder, there was a smell of seaweed and far away the faint sound of waves. The steps were narrow and the Marchioness moved carefully, steadying herself with her ivory stick.

When she reached the bottom, there was still another long passage to be traversed, a passage hewn from solid rock, the floor being of earth which was both damp and dirty. There were candles held in the wall by iron brackets and the Marchioness lit them as she passed. The passage

116

curved and there was light ahead. Suddenly she came out into a huge cavern where men were carrying bales and barrels up one dark passage and depositing them in another which opened to the west and was opposite to the one from which the Marchioness had come.

She stood for a moment watching the activity going on around her. Men glanced at her as they passed laden, and several of them returning, having rid themselves of their burdens, touched their forelocks, but none of them spoke. There was a speed, a smoothness and regularity in the appearance of the laden men and their reappearance unhampered which bespoke good management.

The Marchioness glanced down the passage from which they were emerging. The cold wind blowing in from the sea whipped her skirt tightly around her, fanning the warmth from her cheeks and stirring the curls arranged skilfully around her forehead. A man came striding into the cavern carrying nothing on his shoulders, but wearing an air of authority which belied the tattered seaman's jersey he wore, his patched leather boots and the dirty handkerchief tied around his neck.

'Good evening, your ladyship.'

He spoke politely, yet there was a strange lack of servility in his tone.

'Good evening, Padlett. Everything all right?'

'A fine crossing—two hours and fifty minutes. This new boat is worth every penny your ladyship paid for it.'

'I am glad of that. And the cargo?'

'Here is the list, your ladyship, just as the Froggy gave it to me. I have checked it over and it is all correct, only a bottle of brandy can, be crossed off.'

'And why?'

The Marchioness's question was sharp.

'One of the crew, m'lady. That man we took on last month. He's a bit troublesome. He snatched a bottle when I was not watching.'

'You know, Padlett, that I will not stand for pilferers.'

'I am sorry, m'lady, but if we hadn't taken him I would have been an oar short. Your ladyship is aware that good men are hard to come by these days.'

'Nonsense, we have never had any trouble before.'

'Maybe, m'lady, but there's other people offering them higher pay and bigger rewards.'

'I have always paid generously,' the Marchioness remarked.

'I am not saying your ladyship has not been fair,' Padlett retorted. 'But men desire to work for themselves. They get the money, that is true enough, but you don't allow them anything else.'

'They can spend their own money when they get ashore in France, but I have made it a rule from the very beginning, Padlett, not to hand out drink or materials to men who will display them in local villages and bring suspicion not only on their heads but on mine. We have discussed this often enough.'

'Yes, I know, your ladyship,' Padlett replied, but it was obvious that he was not convinced.

'As it happens, I was not expecting you for at least two nights,' the Marchioness said.

'That is true, your ladyship. I did not think that we would be likely to get here before Thursday or Friday, but the cargo was ready for us and the weather was good.'

'It is very clear,' the Marchioness said doubtfully, looking towards the end of the passage from which came the sound of waves. 'And there is a moon for all 'tis clouded.'

'That is so.'

'Then why?'

'To be frank, your ladyship, it was Matthew—you remember him, he has been with us right from the beginning—his wife is expecting and he was mighty anxious to get home if it could be arranged.'

The Marchioness's lips tightened.

'Demme, Padlett, do you think I am concerned with the expectations of every hen-witted clog that works for me? What do I care if his wife is having twins or triplets? The thing you have got to do is to take no risks and a risk it is on a night like this.'

'Now, now, your ladyship,' Padlett said smoothly. 'No harm's been done as far as I can see.'

'How much more is there to bring up?' the Marchioness asked.

'A few more barrels of brandy, I think. I will just go and make sure, your ladyship.'

He turned away and Harriet stood watching him go. She tapped her foot impatiently on the ground and her fingers holding the ivory stick grew restless. She glanced at the list Padlett had given her. It was a good cargo. There was tea, lace, brandy, tobacco and materials. She hoped there was some velvet amongst them, for that had sold well last time. Yes, it was a good consignment.

There was no doubt at all that she could easily get two thousand guineas for the stuff, once it had been moved to London. It must not stay long in the passages below Mandrake. There lay an added danger to that of a boat coming in unexpectedly. She must send word at dawn and tomorrow night carts would come secretly to the passage which ended beyond the walled-in park. Covered with a load of turf, they would rumble their way to a small, secluded inn about four miles inland. There they would be met by the London agents and long before daybreak all the goods would be clear of Mandrake and on their way to town.

It was a well-thought-out and cleverly calculated organisation and hers were the profits. The Marchioness smiled a little at the thought. More than once she had been tempted by pleading or bribery to take partners, but she preferred to work single-handed. She wanted all the money—yes, every shilling of it—for herself.

How worried she had been when she purchased one of the latest guinea boats! It had cost a vast sum of money, but there was not an excise craft in the whole length of the South Coast that could catch up with thirty-six oars. Two hours and fifty minutes! It might be a record, but unfortunately she was not able to compare the time with that done by other crews. It was enough, at any rate, to know that they had arrived safely. There was a risk, of course, but really it had become an almost infinitesimal one. The coastguards were so feeble and if it came to that afraid, too, of the smugglers.

The Marchioness glanced at the great knives each man wore at his waist. The Dragoons might have firearms, but in a hand-to-hand fight she would back her own men every time. Despite the chill air the Marchioness felt a sudden warmth run through her veins. Her men were not afraid, any more than she was afraid. She had taken the risk and how worth while it had been!

She remembered the first time she had sent gold to France. She could think of nothing else for the days and nights which had elapsed until the crew had returned with the cargo. She had known very little about it in those days. It was very shortly after she returned to Mandrake. She had heard people talking of smuggling and she had known that the well-to-do inhabitants of Folkestone and Dover were all making a little money on the quiet. An old friend had told her how easy it was. He had been abroad for a year, escaping from the consequences of a duel after which his opponent had died.

' 'Tis simple, Harriet,' he had said, 'and for those who have the money behind them there are great fortunes to be made.'

He had spoken truly. A thousand guineas in gold sent to France would more than double itself on the return journey. There were, of course, those who alleged it was unpatriotic. Napoleon wanted gold desperately and it had been said even in Parliament that the gold which was smuggled to France was all collected by Bonaparte's agents. Yet how could anyone be sure?

Harriet had shrugged her shoulders, and by the time the great outcry began she would rather have lost an arm or a leg than have forsworn her very profitable smuggling activities. It had been difficult lately to get hold of the gold. Justin had been tiresome. She was afraid he was becoming suspicious that all the money he gave her was not spent on Mandrake. At first she had been able to bribe him into obtaining more and more money for her because she had told him it was for the house. How he loved his home! It had been easy to inveigle him into providing her with gold when he thought it was all to be expended in beautifying the place he adored.

'Mandrake is your mistress,' she had said to him once, and he had been almost pleased at the phrase. Then she had tried being pathetic. She told him that her losses at cards had been overwhelming; that she wished to pay her doctor . . . her dressmaker. But to those excuses Justin had been unresponsive. No! Only for Mandrake would he make sacrifices and now she was well aware that he was getting more and more reluctant to hand over the gold she needed so desperately.

If only she could be more fortunate at the gaming-tables! She had lost vast sums in the last three months. Madame Roxana had promised her that her luck would turn, but still she continued to lose night after night. That was how she had come to take the money from the canvas bag where the wages for the crew were always kept ready for their arrival. Five guineas a man! It was too much, in all truth, and yet Padlett had assured her more than once that the men often asked for more.

They wanted perquisites—a bottle of brandy, tobacco, or maybe a roll of cloth for their wives. Harriet set her face firmly against this. She knew how easy it was for men to talk in local inns, and that a new dress on a fisherman's wife or a child wearing a new coat would be noted and speculated about by the whole village. No, they could take the money and be content with that. If they did not like it, they . . .

Even as she thought of an alternative, Harriet's heart turned cold. If they did not like it, they could leave her; but she was afraid of that. One could never be certain of their loyalty as she knew she could be of the loyalty and affection of those who served her at Mandrake.

These men were coarse and rough. Padlett himself was in a slightly better class—his father had been a man of business to a big estate, but he had lost his job, turned poacher and been hanged at the Assizes. Padlett could read and write, but the rest of the crew were educated in one thing and one thing only—to evade the law, and to take what they wanted by any means, however lawless. Force was what they understood, and Harriet thought sometimes that they were no better than animals.

Once it had been possible to find fishermen who would take a risk of an extra guinea or so. They were decent chaps, most of them, who did it more for the fun of the thing than for greed and gain. Those days were past—the decent fellows had got frightened or been caught, and if they had escaped being hanged had been transported for life. To do the job systematically one had to have men such as this—cruel and bestial; men prepared to take a risk and equally prepared to slit each other's throats if it suited their purpose.

Harriet shivered a little. In a moment or two there was something she had to say to them. The canvas bag in her left hand felt horribly light. She was suddenly very cold. For some minutes now she had been standing with the wind blowing full against her. Surely Padlett should be coming back? She looked down the dark passage towards the sea. How few people knew that the channel between the rocks deepened so that a boat could ride right up to the very cliff's side and that cargoes could be unloaded at the mouth of a subterranean passage which led into the centre of Mandrake!

It had been a secret for years. Even the old plans of the house did not show it; there was no record of it except on small private maps held only by the head of the family.

Harriet had discovered her husband looking at these small maps soon after they were married and had forced him to tell her the secret, finding it momentarily amusing.

'The passages might have been built so that spies could enter the country without being discovered,' had been his explanation, 'or it may merely have been an easy way of ridding the dungeons of unwanted prisoners.'

Harriet had been interested at the time and then had forgotten all about it. It was only when smuggling became a fashionable topic of conversation that she remembered what she had learned. How useful it had proved! How very, very useful!

Padlett was coming, the loose leather uppers of his boots slapping against his legs as he walked towards her.

'It is unloaded, your ladyship,' he said. 'We have finished now.'

The last two men passed her with their backs bent, while those returning from the other passage stood around waiting. There were two torches stuck in holders at the sides of the cave which cast a fierce light, showing the beads of sweat on the foreheads of the men who had been rowing with all their strength for the two hours and fifty minutes. They revealed, too, rough-cut faces, square jaws, cruel, bestial lips and crafty, calculating eyes.

Harriet looked round her. Some of the men met her glance boldly. They had seen her before, but she never ceased to be an astonishment to them. Her naked shoulders glittering with jewels, the curves of her figure revealed by her gauzy, semi-transparent ball-gown, her flaming hair, the proud and exotic beauty of her looks—it was little wonder that they stared at her. Yet there were those who glanced aside craftily through veiled, shifty eyes and through sandy eyelashes. It was those she disliked the most. The others she could understand. They were pirates; they were the type of men who in earlier and more adventurous times would have sailed with Drake or plundered foreign sailors on the high seas.

To them a woman was a woman whether she was a Marchioness or the slut who waited to drink with them in the dark alleyways of Dover. Yes, she could understand men like that, and she did not think it a presumption, as most women in her position would have done, that they dared to look at her with an appraising eye.

She remembered once a lady of quality had sent her linkmen to thrash a fellow who had called after her outside

Carlton House Terrace. 'There goes a buxom bed-warmer for the Prince.'

'I would not countenance such insolence,' she said later to the Marchioness. But Harriet had laughed at her.

'It was a compliment, my dear, and compliments are not always so truthful.'

The story had gone the rounds of the Clubs, and Harriet had made an enemy.

But such men were men, Harriet thought now. Whether they wore powder and satin and smelt of scent, or were merely covered in tattered garments and reeked of sweat, the passions in them were much of a muchness.

Men . . . strong, passionate and demanding, their very virility an excuse for the lust they made no effort to hide—those were the sort the Marchioness understood, whether they were gentlemen—or smugglers.

It was the other type she disliked, and never so much as when she employed them in this difficult and dangerous game. The men who could not look her in the face and who turned their heads away when she spoke directly to them. There was one of the crew whom she had noticed on recent occasions and for whom she had a particular loathing. He was a big man, but his features were thin and pinched; he had a shifty eye and a twitch at the corner of his mouth which made him appear as if he were perpetually smiling.

As the men gathered round now waiting for payment, Harriet saw that it was this man who had stolen the brandy. He was very tipsy, stumbling against the others who shoved him off with a muttered oath or the admonition to 'pull himself together'. He was talking to himself and to the others, thereby infringing yet another rule that there should be as little conversation as possible while they were unloading.

Padlett glanced sharply towards him, but he said nothing, and then he looked impatiently at the Marchioness, suggesting silently that the quicker the men were paid the better it would be for everyone. The night's work was over. They had only to take the boat along the coast to a small creek where it was usually hidden and then the crew could disperse to their homes and rest for a day or two.

The Marchioness hesitated, and Padlett moved forward.

'Shall I pay them, your ladyship?'

The Marchioness held out the bag to him.

'Yes, pay them,' she said. 'But we are short to-night. If

123

you will come to me to-morrow, Padlett, I will give you what is lacking.'

'Short?'

One of the men repeated the word beneath his breath.

'I was not expecting you until Thursday,' the Marchioness said firmly.

'How short?' another man asked.

'There should be two guineas there for each of you,' the Marchioness said. 'As I have already said, the rest will be here to-morrow.'

'Yus, but how's us a-going t' get it?' someone asked.

'I will see to that,' Padlett said sharply. 'You have heard that her ladyship said that she was expecting us on Thursday. You can wait a few hours for your money.'

There was a murmur and some of the men looked surly, but it was obvious that they would accept the inevitable, though with a bad grace. Then the man who had drunk too much staggered forward.

'Oi wants m' due,' he said.

Quiet and sly by nature, the fiery spirit he had drunk emboldened him. Now he was aggressive. His head was thrust forward and his great hands were almost clawing the air around him. He pushed two men on one side and confronted the Marchioness.

'Oi wants m' money now, and by Gawd's teeth Oi means t' have it.'

'You will be paid to-morrow.'

The Marchioness spoke quietly, but there was the sharpness of a lash in her voice.

'Oi've taken t' risk,' he retorted. 'Oi've risked m' blasted neck to bring t' stuff here for a swell-mort and Oi'm not going to be fogged off wi' promises. 'Tis m' money Oi want; gold—that's what Oi've done it for—gold.'

There was a murmur of agreement from the men around him and quickly Padlett intervened.

'You have been told what you are going to get,' he said, 'and those that do not like it will get something they do not want from me. Is that clear?'

He spoke so peremptorily that several of the men instinctively took a step backwards, but the drunken one paid no attention.

'Oi wants m' gold,' he repeated stupidly.

At that moment the Marchioness heard a step in the passage outside. Swiftly she turned her head, and to her astonishment saw Serena. The girl came forward from the shadows, the light shining full on her white dress and her shining golden hair. Her eyes were wide, but she did not seem afraid. She looked at the men, who stared back at her curiously, then she spoke to the Marchioness so that all could hear.

'Lord Vulcan asked me to tell you, Ma'am, that a party of Dragoons and Excisemen are upstairs.'

The Marchioness gave an exclamation.

'Lud, they will search the place. They will watch for any boat passing along the foot of the cliffs. You must be quick, men. My son will doubtless delay them for a few minutes, but there is no time to be lost.'

Padlett was already doling out the gold pieces from the canvas bag. One by one the men took them from him and ran down the passage towards the sea as quickly as they could go. But the drunk, swaying tipsily on his feet, remained where he was.

'Oi shall be hanged by m' neck for this,' he cried. 'T' soldiers will catch Oi. Before Oi be hanged Oi want m' gold, t' gold for which Oi've risked m' neck.'

'Go to the boat at once,' the Marchioness said sharply.

He towered above her, but she faced him defiantly.

'If Oi aren't t' have gold,' he said, 'Oi'll take that gaudy bit.'

He put out his great hand and grabbed at the diamond necklace which encircled her neck. Serena instinctively gave a little cry of horror. Padlett, who was paying another man, dropped the canvas bag and the guineas and, turning, doubled up his fists. But the Marchioness was quicker than he was. There was a faint swishing sound and the sheath of ivory slipped from a flashing, tapering rapier of tempered steel. She made one movement forward, and the sword passed through the base of the drunkard's neck. He staggered and there was an astonishment on his face which was almost ludicrous to behold. Then he crashed sideways to the floor.

He lay there for a moment, his fingers twitching, his legs writhing as if in agony, before he gave a low croaking cough—a sound terrible and strange to those who heard it—and a stream of thick dark blood poured from his mouth on to the damp ground.

As he fell, the Marchioness drew the sword from his neck. It was stained with blood, but she slipped it swiftly into its sheath. The torches flamed towards the ceiling and there was of a sudden an awful quiet in the great cavern.

Then the Marchioness laughed. It was a light, lilting laugh of sheer untrammeled amusement. It echoed and re-echoed itself until there was silence again and only the distant breaking of the waves could be heard. The Marchioness touched the fallen man with the toe of her shoe.

'See that this is removed,' she said contemptuously to Padlett.

Then with her head held high and a smile on her lips she turned to face Serena.

Nine

SERENA felt as if she were gripped by a paralysis which made her incapable of movement even while her heart thudded and she felt the horror of what had occurred creep over her in the sickening waves of dizziness. She almost craved oblivion so that the sight of that dark stream of blood issuing from the smuggler's open mouth might be shut out, so that she could wrench her gaze from his eyes clouding over with the film of death. Some voice within her told her that she ought to do something to help him, should try to staunch the flow of blood; but she could not move, her body had ceased to obey her will.

Then the Marchioness turned, and there was in the expression of her face such cruelty, such stark bestiality, that Serena wanted not only to cry out but run away, to fly from the horror of a human being so depraved that she could glory in the murder. The Marchioness's eyes were shining brightly, there was a delicate flush of colour in her cheeks, and she flung her head back defiantly as if she faced the whole world and were supremely unafraid.

'Come, child,' she said, and there was a thrill and a lilt in her voice. "We must return to our guests.'

Serena could only stare at her, and then half impatiently, half good-humouredly, the Marchioness stretched out her hand, took Serena by the forearm and turned her away from the cavern where the torches still spluttered their fierce revealing light, into the comparative darkness of the passage. Her fingers were like steel in their strength and resolution. They were warm, too, and Serena could almost feel energy and excitement pulsating through them.

It was as though that swift action, murderous in itself, intent on its achievement, had revived within the Marchioness her reckless, impulsive youth. She was vividly alive, tingling with a magnetism which made her look for the moment ecstatic as with requited passion. She must have looked the same when in the heyday of her beauty

127

she had lain satisfied and enraptured in the arms of a much-desired lover.

Pulling, half dragging Serena by the arm, the Marchioness walked swiftly down the tunnelled passage. Serena's feet kept pace with her almost automatically. For the moment she had ceased to reason, ceased to think; she was only conscious of a horror beyond expression and a physical coldness which seemed to penetrate into her very bones.

As they went, the Marchioness paused at every flickering candle to snuff out its light. They climbed the steep stone steps side by side in silence. The Marchioness still held Serena's arm and continued to do so down the last part of the passage which led them to the sliding panel and back into the house.

They stepped into the warmth and light, the secret panel closed behind them and it seemed to Serena as if she awoke from the ugly terror of a nightmare. The soft golden glow of the candles, the carved polished banisters and panelled walls, the thick carpet of crimson and blue were all familiar landmarks after a hideous fantasy of fierce flame and purple shadow, of wet rock and rough-hewn stone. Here it was hard to believe in craft and evil, in violent passions and bloody murder.

Trembling, Serena raised a hand to her forehead. The Marchioness regarded her with hard eyes and lips which curved disdainfully at such weakness.

'Pull yourself together, girl,' she said sharply. 'It is of no moment. There is one less rogue in the world and he will not be missed.'

'But, Ma'am . . . Ma'am . . .' Serena stammered, and her voice was strange and broken even to her own ears.

The Marchioness threw back her head, the light of the candles glittering on the jewels around her neck and sparkling in her tiny ears.

'Faugh, you are chicken-hearted. I thought better blood coursed through your veins, but it appears I was mistaken.'

Instinctively Serena reacted to the lash in her words and in the tone of her voice. Without replying she straightened her shoulders and held her chin a little higher.

'Come, that is better,' the Marchioness admonished. 'Pinch your cheeks, child, so that there is some colour in them, or I declare people will think you have seen a ghost.'

She laughed at her own joke and Serena shivered at the

sound. She had heard much talk of ghosts since she had come to Mandrake, and now there would be another spirit to walk the dark passages seeking perhaps his lost and injured body.

Rogue and smuggler, he had yet been a man, a human being who had lived and breathed and had his being on this earth. Now his blood, warm only a few minutes since, seeped into the mud and damp and soon the sea would take his body to her cold bosom. Serena felt a sudden impulse to go back, to stand again at the dying man's side. If there was nothing else she could do, she could at least pray for him.

But it was too late, for already the Marchioness had started up the stairs and Serena knew that she must follow her. For a few seconds there was only the rustle of their dresses and the soft sound of their feet on the stairs. Then as they reached the landing of the first floor Serena put out her hand pleadingly.

'Please, Ma'am,' she said, 'may I retire?'

The Marchioness looked at her with scorn.

'Of course not, you silly child; are you so bird-witted that you cannot see we must return to the drawing-room together? Our absence may have been noticed, but we have been in my bed-chamber titivating our faces. Come, and cease being in such a fidget. The loss of a rascally smuggler is of no importance, I assure you.'

As she spoke, the Marchioness linked her arm through Serena's and Serena knew that it imprisoned her as firmly as bars or chains might have done. They traversed the first floor and came to the landing above the Grand Staircase. As they began to descend it, the Marchioness said in a voice loud and high-pitched:

'I vow that my luck has changed. I shall win. I can feel good fortune at the tips of my fingers.'

She was speaking for effect, Serena was instantly aware of that, and then she saw that below them, coming from the direction of the banqueting-hall, was a little group of men—the Coastguards, the Dragoons, and with them Lord Vulcan. The Marchioness made as if she had seen nothing, but Serena knew by the sudden pressure of her fingers and by the tense alertness of her whole body that this was but a pretence. The Marchioness's voice was light as she continued:

'Lud, but gaming is a chancy business. You are indeed

fortunate that it does not yet concern you, my dear Serena. But I have heard people swear that marriage is also hazardous.'

They reached the bottom steps of the Grand Staircase, and with a little cry of astonishment the Marchioness glanced towards the group of men advancing into the hall.

' 'Pon my soul, more visitors!' she cried. Then, looking at her son, she added, 'Your friends, Justin?'

'Yes, friends, Mother,' the Marquis answered gravely; 'but unfortunately their call on us concerns business and not pleasure. May I present the officer-in-charge, Lieutenant Delham?'

A red-faced young man in the uniform of the Dragoon Guards bowed a little sheepishly.

'I am enchanted to make your acquaintance, Lieutenant,' the Marchioness said. 'Will you join us at a game of chance?'

'Unfortunately, Ma'am, I am here on duty,' the Lieutenant replied. 'The Coastguards have reported that they have viewed a boat at the very foot of your cliffs. I came to ask leave to search your garden and also to enquire if you had any knowledge of a landing-place where a boat might anchor or unload a cargo.'

The Marchioness's eyes were round with astonishment.

'A boat! Here!' she exclaimed, looking from one man to another. 'But what do you suspect?'

'Smugglers, Ma'am.'

The Marchioness gave a scream.

'Smugglers! La, but I declare that it is a thrilling notion. Smugglers at Mandrake! What do you think of that, Justin?'

'I suspect it is only a bubble,' he said quietly; 'as Lieutenant Delham was just saying, the cliffs are very dangerous at this point and it is unlikely that a boat would be able to land.'

'Oh, but let us pray that they can do so!' the Marchioness cried, clapping her hands. 'For I promise you, Lieutenant, that I shall never be satisfied until I have had a peep at their cargo. What would it contain, think you? Lace? Ribbons? Velvets for a new gown? And maybe a bottle or two of French brandy? Fie on you, Lieutenant, and the gentlemen with you, for seeking to spoil a game which is so beneficial to the community!'

There was a guffaw of laughter at this; but the Marchioness, dazzling those who listened with her brilliant smile, continued: 'You may laugh, but do none of you severe, Puritan-minded men, intent only on enforcing the law, remember the needs of us poor weak women? Everything we require has become much more expensive since the war, besides being often unobtainable. Think of us trying to remain your fair charmers without any of those aids to nature which only the Frenchmen can provide, and be a little sorry for us.'

'If we catch the smugglers, Ma'am, I will let you know what their boat contains,' Lieutenant Delham replied.

'That is a promise!' the Marchioness cried. 'Thank you, Lieutenant. You are indeed gallant, and you too, gentlemen.' Her gesture embraced the grinning Dragoons and Coastguards. 'But I must not keep you from your duty. Justin, have these gentlemen availed themselves of our hospitality?'

'Indeed we have, Ma'am,' the Lieutenant answered for him. 'His lordship has been most kind, but we must not linger any longer. May we have your permission to proceed?'

'But of course! You are certain it is the gardens which interest you? You would not rather search the house? For all I know, one of my guests may be in league with the smugglers. They may even be exchanging signals from a bedroom window.'

'I think it is unlikely, Ma'am,' the Lieutenant said.

The Marchioness sighed.

'Perhaps you are right. Most of them, I regret to say, are too cork-brained to have intelligence enough to plan let alone carry out such a scheme. One day when I have time I must turn smuggler myself and then, Lieutenant, I will give you a chase worthy of your wits.'

'Let us hope that day is not too far distant, Ma'am,' the Lieutenant said gallantly; 'to capture a smuggler like yourself would be a crowning achievement in a somewhat humdrum career.'

'Well spoken,' the Marchioness approved; and then, stretching out her hand to Serena, who had stood quietly and unobtrusively on one side while this conversation was taking place, she said. 'Come, child, we must to the *salon*. Faugh, but gaming will seem dull after our talk with the Lieutenant. There is real excitement and adventure for you.'

'Your servant, Ma'am.'

The Lieutenant made his bow and marched away with his little band of men.

Serena, at the Marchioness's side, heard Lord Vulcan instruct a footman to show the Lieutenant to the east door which led into the garden. It was a door which she well knew was the farthest away from the cliffs. It led directly into a walled-in herb-garden and from there into the intricacies of an ancient maze, and beyond that into the Rose Walk. It would take some minutes at least before the Lieutenant and his men found themselves finally on the lawns which bordered the cliffs, and even then there was no direct access on to the cliffs themselves save by the little door which she herself used, but which would be hard to find at night and without a guide.

Now she and the Marchioness were surrounded by friends who were listening, spellbound, to the Marchioness's gaily told story of what had just occurred.

'Pray heaven they do not search the house,' she was saying, 'for I swear that the barrels of brandy which were delivered from London three days ago look as if they have been smuggled. If they are found, the excisemen are certain to accuse us of having brought them over ourselves, and maybe even Justin will be accused of handling an oar in a guinea-boat.'

There was a roar of laughter at this, and the Marchioness continued:

'La, but I am sorry for the smugglers, whoever they may be. You never saw such determined, stalwart young men as those soldiers; and the Coastguards looked like bruisers. If it came to a fight, I would be sorry for the smugglers, 'pon my soul I would.'

'I'll take any odds that the smugglers can look after themselves,' a young fop drawled.

'I only wish I could encounter such game-cocks,' the Marchioness retorted. 'Now Isabel Calver and her brother can tell us all about them, for it was only yesterday that they went to Dover and conversed with one.'

There were exclamations of surprise at this, and several of the company went in search of Isabel and Gilly to question them as to what they had seen.

'And what does our sweet Serena think of all this?' a hateful voice said close to Serena's ear, and she looked up to see Lord Wrotham gazing at her intently.

While she hesitated for an answer, the Marchioness supplied one.

'She is afraid, poor child,' she said, but there was no sympathy only a sneer in her tone.

'And who shall blame her,' Lord Wrotham replied, 'when it is obvious to the most inexperienced eye that only Paris could have produced such exquisite material for her gown?'

The Marchioness raised her eyebrows for a moment, then she laughed.

'Harry, you are cursed sharp; does nothing escape your eagle eye?'

'Not much,' he said, 'and nothing where such beauty is concerned.' He leered at Serena, who turned her face sharply away from him. 'Harriet, I need your help,' he continued. 'Our sweet Serena, whom I have known since a child, is angered with me. I have proffered her my apologies, my most abject apologies, but she will not listen. Use your influence, Harriet, that I may at least have a fair hearing.'

He spoke lightly enough, but there was a deep undercurrent in his voice; an under-current so dark and treacherous that Serena could only turn to the Marchioness and say hastily:

'I beg you will hold me excused, Ma'am. My head aches and I would, with your permission, retire for the night.'

The Marchioness glanced at her. She was wise enough to realise that the girl had reached breaking-point. There was nothing further to be gained by keeping her.

'Go to your bed if it pleases you,' she said, 'for sure these rooms are hot enough to give the strongest of us a headache.'

'I am obliged to you, Ma'am. Good night.'

Serena dropped a curtsy. She did not even glance in the direction of Lord Wrotham. But as she moved away she heard him say quite clearly and distinctly:

'Harriet, I have a proposition to make to you, and one which I think you will find distinctly interesting.'

His voice was sinister, but that, Serena told herself, was nothing new where Lord Wrotham was concerned; at the same time she wondered. Could that proposition concern herself? Such an idea was absurd! and she assured herself that she was being stupidly imaginative. The events of this evening had frightened her so that she saw danger on every side.

She reached the Great Hall. It was empty save for two footmen waiting by the outer door. Then as she put her hand on the carved banister and her foot on the first step, a question arrested her:

'You are retiring, Serena?'

The Marquis had come out of the ante-room and was approaching her.

'Yes, my lord, I am . . . going to . . . bed.'

Her voice trembled a little despite her resolution to be quite calm.

'Something has upset you,' he said. 'I saw it in your face when you came downstairs with my mother.'

She looked up at him. For the first time there seemed something kindly and almost compassionate in his voice. He was at least human amongst what seemed to her overwrought imagination at this moment a crowd of inhuman monsters.

For the moment she was a little uncertain of what had happened only a short time ago. It was all so fantastic, so twisted in her mind which was full of tangled and distorted emotions and imaginings. She only knew that out of a nightmare of horror from which every nerve of her body shrank, Lord Vulcan seemed to her at that moment a man whom one could trust.

His eyes were looking down into hers. She had not answered his question, she had only stood there, very small and vulnerable, her face drained of all colour, her eyes dark with suffering. The Marquis put out his hand and took hers from the balustrade where it rested. It was very cold, and he held it for a moment in both of his as if he would warm it.

'What has occurred?' he asked gently.

In answer her fingers fluttered in his like a captured bird, and then for an instant they clung to him, clung with a pathetic effort at reliance, yet with the desperate clasp of someone who is drowning.

'I . . . I cannot . . . tell you, my lord.'

The words were hardly above a whisper, and he must bend his head to hear them.

'Do not try, then. In the morning things will seem better.'

'Better!' she echoed, as though such a word were an astonishment to her. 'I shall never . . . never forget—never.'

She was not far from tears now. The shock which had

held her numb was breaking. For one moment her fingers clung to his again, for one moment her other hand, quite unconsciously, sought the warmth of his clasp, and then like a frightened fawn she was free of him.

'I must . . . away.'

She knew only that she longed for the shelter of her own room. She wanted to be alone, wanted to forget. Her flying feet carried her up the staircase and along the passages; then in the seclusion of her own bedchamber she lay prostrate, face downwards on her pillows in an agony of mind which was beyond the relief of tears.

Next morning found Serena with a heavy head and eyes dark-ringed from sleeplessness. It was late afternoon before Eudora would let her rise, and then she made no effort to leave her own chamber, but sat on the window-seat staring out to sea. Eudora brought her food and milk. Serena drank the milk but refused the food, saying she did not feel like eating.

She had not told Eudora what had happened. Somehow she could not bear to put into words what she had seen; but the picture of it was there before her eyes—the flaming torches lighting the rough-hewn stone roof, the great sprawled figure on the dark floor, the dark red stream of blood. Would she ever forget it?

It was afternoon when Torqo, whining a little and thrusting his nose into the limpness of her hand, made her remember that he was missing his accustomed walk.

'I will go out, Eudora,' Serena said, rousing herself from her reverie with a vast effort.

' 'Twill do you good,' Eudora said, 'for you look as pale as a corpse. If you were a child again, I would be certain that you were sickening for an indisposition.'

Serena sighed.

'I am not a child, unfortunately, and what ails me is not what is about to happen but what has already occurred.'

Eudora waited for her confidence, but when it did not come, she said nothing. She knew well those moments of reserve which had been Serena's ever since she was tiny and how, when something perturbed or hurt her overmuch, she could not speak but could only suffer. Serena was suffering now; and while Eudora's heart bled for her, there was nothing she could do but tend her as best she could, and hope that sooner or later she would gain her confidence.

Moving to the cupboard, she fetched a bonnet of chip

135

straw, but when she brought it Serena shook her head.

'Give me my hood,' she said, 'I would rather wear that, for it hides my face.'

'You look fatigued, 'tis true, but even so immeasurably fairer than anyone else in this place.'

Serena smiled at Eudora's partisanship.

'I was not thinking of my looks in vanity, but it's that I have no heart to be seen. In my hood people are less likely to recognise me, and they will not think me impolite if I hurry away at the sight of them.'

She felt it would be impossible for her at this moment to talk lightly even with Isabel or Nicholas.

'If I see anyone,' she thought, 'I will run in the opposite direction.'

Isabel had already sent up a message earlier in the day to ask if Serena would ride with them, but she had sent back word to say that she was feeling extremely fatigued and hoped to sleep until dinner-time. It was unlikely that either Isabel or Nicholas would be in the gardens, but Isabel was as unaccountable and as changeable in her plans as a weather-cock, so that one could never be certain of her movements from one hour to another.

Serena's hood of pale-blue wool, trimmed with ribbons, was her own. Yvette was already engaged upon making one of velvet trimmed with sable, but it was not yet ready, and to-day she was thankful to be able to wear something which had been bought and paid for with her own money and was not a gift from the Marchioness.

It was silly to mind little things, Serena chid herself, when there were greater and far more important issues to be faced; nevertheless she felt a tiny pinpoint of satisfaction in the fact that the hood was hers and the Marchioness was not in any way connected with it.

When she was ready and Torqo, knowing that his walk was imminent, was bounding noisily about the room, Serena went to the window. She looked at the garden below and saw that it was empty. Then she opened the door into the little turret-room. The windows here looked both south and east and gave her a good view of the gardens. Here again there was no one in sight save a gardener tending the flower beds.

'Would you wish me to precede you,' Eudora asked, 'and see that there is no one on the stairs?'

She did not understand Serena's sudden desire for solitude, but she was prepared to respect it and to help her all she could. Something had happened, something which had brought her mistress to bed white and trembling like a frightened child. But what had been the cause of it she had not been able to ascertain, even from discreet enquiries amongst the servants.

Eudora was not friendly with Martha, whom she suspected because she was in attendance on the Marchioness, and his lordship's valet had nothing to report save that a party of Coastguards and Dragoons had arrived during the evening to search for a smugglers' boat and found nothing. Perhaps Lord Wrotham was responsible, Eudora thought, and she muttered darkly to herself, for she, too, hated the man who had seduced the pretty Charmaine. Serena turned to leave the turret-room.

'I will slip down the small staircase,' she said, and then she gave a little exclamation. 'I wonder where this door leads to,' she questioned.

She pointed to a door in the turret itself. It was low and narrow, with ancient wrought handles and a heavy latch.

'I have never tried it,' Eudora answered.

'I expect it is locked,' Serena said, but at the same time she put out her hand and lifted the latch. The door opened. 'Why, Eudora,' she cried, 'there are steps here; steps going down. Do you think this leads to the garden?'

Eudora came from the bedchamber to look. The steps were small and followed the curved proportions of the turret, twisting their way out of sight.

'I would not be astonished if the people who built this place used such stairs as a bolt-hole,' Eudora suggested.

'But of course,' Serena agreed, 'and it is obvious that the stairway leads direct to the garden. This solves my problem, Eudora. No one will see me and I can go in and out as I desire.'

She was smiling now, and Eudora felt relieved that something had roused her from her lethargy.

' 'Tis reasonable enough,' Eudora said. 'Torqo will protect you, and the staircase must have been intended for use or the door would have been locked.'

'Come on, Torqo,' Serena said, and set off down the steps.

She had to go slowly, for the way was narrow and twisted; but there was just enough light to see from the arrow-slits placed at intervals in the walls. Down, down they went until finally the stairs stopped and she came to another door. It was rather dark, and she felt with her hand until she found another latch similar to the one on the door above her. It was a little stiff, and she gave it a push so that the door was flung open suddenly.

She found herself, not as she had expected in the garden or in a passage-way, but standing at the top of a short flight of polished steps which led directly into a room. The room was lined with books and in the centre of it, sitting at a big desk which was also piled high with books, was an old man. For a moment it was difficult to know who was the more astonished—Serena or the occupant of the room.

Then, Torqo, impatient of being confined to the narrow stairway, pushed his way past Serena and bounded into the room. Without waiting for an invitation, he ran up to the man at the desk, sniffed at him and wagged his tail. The man put out his hand and stroked Torqo's head, then rose to his feet.

'Will you not be pleased to enter, Ma'am?' he asked Serena.

Serena came down the polished steps and walked across the room.

'I must offer you my apologies, sir,' she said, dropping a curtsy. 'I believed that these stairs, which lead directly out of my bedchamber, would bring me to the garden. I was about to take my dog for a walk.'

'This was originally the Guard Room,' was the answer, 'and those stairs led to one of the watch-out turrets. They have not been used for many years and I believed that the door at the top was locked.'

'I must indeed apologise, sir,' Serena said again.

'But please! I assure you, Ma'am, that you are very welcome.' He put his hand up absentmindedly to his bald head. 'Oh, dear me, where is my wig? We are so unused to visitors that I am afraid we are looking very untidy.'

He looked round the room and espied his wig hanging on a chair. He picked it up and clapped it on his head, slightly crookedly so that it gave him a rakish air. Then he went across to the fireplace and emptied a big arm-chair of the books which covered the seat.

'Will you be seated, Ma'am?' he asked, with a courtly grace which told Serena all too clearly that he was no ordinary librarian, as she had at first suspected. His shoulders were now bent, but it was obvious that in his youth he had been a tall man.

When he first looked up from the desk it had seemed to Serena that his face was familiar; but it had only been a fleeting impression, and now she saw that his face was lined with age and pallid as if with ill-health.

'What a number of books you have here!' she remarked, looking at the volumes which overflowed from the shelves on to the floor, to the chairs, the tables, and in fact everywhere in the room.

'My library,' the old gentleman said proudly. 'I am engaged in writing a history and I require a great many books for reference.' He glanced towards a parcel which stood unwrapped in the centre of the room. 'Those arrived yester eve by post-chaise from London. I have not yet found time to unpack them, but I fancy they will prove of great interest. Have you a partiality for books, Ma'am?'

'Indeed I have, sir, for we had a big library at my home. My father had no love of reading, but my grandfather was a scholar. You may perhaps have heard of him—Sir-Hubert Staverley?'

'Hubert Staverley! Why, God bless my soul, he was at school with me. A fair-haired fellow, I recollect, who put us out of all patience as he always gained all the prizes.'

Serena felt curiously pleased that here was someone who had an acquaintance with her own family.

'You were at Eton, sir?'

'I was indeed. All my family have been schooled at Eton.'

'And your name? Will you tell me your name . . .' Serena began, but at that moment the door opened. A little old man wearing the Vulcan livery came into the room.

'I heard voices, m'lord . . .' he began. Then he saw Serena and stopped with a start of astonishment.

'I have a visitor, Newman; and, dear me, I am forgetting my manners. Bring the lady a dish of tea, Newman.'

'Very good, m'lord.'

The valet's surprise at seeing Serena was almost ludicrous, and when he had left the room the old gentleman chuckled.

'Newman believed that you must have dropped down the chimney. There is only one entry into this part of the house and the door is bolted and barred.'

'You enjoy such solitude, sir?'

'Yes . . . Yes, I like solitude, and I have few enough visitors. My son, of course, visits me frequently, and very occasionally, my wife. But Harriet is always engaged. She has always been enamoured with entertaining.'

Serena stared at him. Then her mouth opened and she

gave a little exclamation. The old gentleman looked at her.

'Dear me, dear me, I ought not to have said that. Could you forget it?' There was a sudden twinkle in his eye. 'No, I suppose not. That is why I have no visitors. You see, m'dear, I cannot keep a secret, never could.'

He pushed his wig a little farther back on his head and it gave him almost a comical expression; then he pulled it forward again and now it was easy for Serena to see why her first impression of his face had been one of familiarity. Justin was like his father. They had the same clear-cut features, the same steel-grey eyes set beneath strongly marked eyebrows, the same jaw, the same thin aristocratic nose. But if this was Justin's father . . .

Serena suddenly clasped her hands together. If this was Justin's father, then Justin was not Lord Vulcan, not entitled to be styled 'the Marquis'.

The old gentleman was chuckling a little.

'I shall be in disgrace again. I nearly always am, one way or another; but I think I can trust Hubert Staverley's granddaughter! Will you give me your word that you will not reveal what I am about to tell you?'

'My hand on it, sir,' Serena exclaimed; 'and I think I have guessed your secret. You are the Marquis of Vulcan—Justin's father.'

'That is right, m'dear. That is right. But I ought never to have let the cat out of the bag. It is a long story, and in my humble opinion not an engaging one. But you shall judge for yourself. Ah, here comes our tea.'

The valet entered with a big silver tray. He set it down on a small table by the fireside which his lordship hastily cleared of books.

'I have made the tea, m'lord,' he said in a low voice.

'Quite right! Quite right!'

The old gentleman turned to Serena.

'You will excuse me, Ma'am, if I do not make your tea myself, but I am so absentminded. Sometimes I put in a great number of teaspoonfuls—far too many and very extravagant—at other time I forget to put in the tea altogether. Newman does it for me. He is very careful. We have to be with such a heavy duty to pay on tea.'

He poured Serena out a cup, and suddenly Serena felt a pang of pity. Had he any idea of the lavish expenditure that was accepted without comment in the other part of the house? Or had he ever guessed that the tea he drank might have entered the country without yielding its lawful tax?

The valet withdrew; and sipping his tea, the Marquis said:

'As you have discovered me, it is only fair that you should know the reason why I am here, otherwise you might be imagining all sorts of things, might you not?'

'I should be glad if you would trust me with your story, my lord; but if you would prefer not to inform me of anything so intimate . . . I shall understand.'

'And be curious for the rest of your life?' the old gentleman queried, then he laughed. 'No, no, m'dear, I was young myself once; fact is, I have never ceased to be curious when there are things to be learned and things to discover about other people. Nowadays I have a preference for discoveries in books, but at your age I preferred them to be walking about on two legs. Well, to begin. You have met my wife?'

'Yes, my lord.'

'And my son?'

'. . . Yes.'

It was difficult not to hesitate before she answered, but the old man seemed quite pleased with the monosyllable.

'He is a splendid fellow and I am proud of him. He never forgets me, never. Sometimes we read together, but usually we just talk. He tells me about the world outside. I have never regretted leaving it, but Justin makes certain that I shall have no regrets. A fine boy, a very fine boy.'

For a moment the old man seemed to have forgotten that he was about to tell Serena his story; then at last he continued:

'But you desired to learn of me why I am here. Well, the truth is it all began because I was a gamester.'

'A gamester!' Serena exclaimed.

'Yes, yes, I know what you are thinking. That I am like my wife. But that is not quite correct. My heart's not in it. I played a mildish hand when I was in London, but not overmuch, if you understand me. Now and then at Cocoa Tree or Waiter's I would while away the time before taking Harriet to Almack's. A game in some friend's rooms would pass the hour while she was being attired for a ball, but that was all gaming meant to me. I had no *penchant* for those rubbishing hells; it was books I loved, and I had already begun the history of Mandrake.'

141

'Is that what you are writing now?' Serena interposed.

'And have been for the last twenty years. It will be a fine tale when it is finished . . . if I ever finish it.'

He looked around the room with a little sigh, and then continued:

'To be frank with you, I have always cared for books beyond everything else in my life. That is what Harriet says; and she vows I ought to have married one! A jest, of course, but there's a grain of truth in it. I seem a dull dog to her. I suppose really I was too old to marry the lovely child she was when first I saw her, but she was like all the fairy-tales I had read when I was a boy rolled into one. There are no words really to describe her . . . that incomparable face . . . and I thought . . . I believed I could make her happy!'

The old man sighed and stared into the fire.

'But I was old, too old, I suppose. Soon I got tired of the social round, the gay life. It left me no time for reading, and undoubtedly no time for writing. I came back to Mandrake and left Harriet to herself. Then unexpectedly she returned. We disagreed for the first time in our lives, for she wanted to make changes in the house, she wanted to fill it with people. I suppose I had got used to being alone, for I did not like people in my house. Besides, I wanted to get on with my book.'

There was another gentle sigh, and Serena knew that the old gentleman was recalling disagreements and arguments. Then he went on:

'When things were at their most difficult, a friend of mine fell ill. He was a very distinguished émigre from France, Prince Charles de Fauberg St. Vincent. He was in the prime of life, but he suffered greatly with his heart— just as I have suffered with mine all through my life; in fact ever since I was at Eton with your grandfather! Being a foreigner and because he was in pain, the Prince thought he was about to die. No stamina, those foreign fellows, even the best of them. He was a friend of Harriet's and my wife begged me to talk with him, to rouse him. Having no pluck, he just lay there waiting for death to overtake him. I went to his bedside.

' "Charles, dear fellow," I said, "there is nothing wrong with you. Rouse yourself, come back to the world. There are a great many years of enjoyment left for you yet." "It is too late," the Prince answered, "too late, my old friend,

142

for I am dying." "Dying!" I cried. "You must be foxed, for you are no more dying than I am. Both our hearts play us false at times, but that is not to say that we are either of us for the grave for another quarter of a century."

'He did not answer me; so, being determined to rouse him, I said: "I will wager you, Charles, that I will die before you. How is that for a sporting offer?" He smiled at me weakly. "You will lose your money, Vulcan." I shook my head. "I shall gain yours," I said. "What will you bet?" "Anything you like," he replied, "because I am bound to win." "I will lay you ten thousand guineas," I retorted. "No, twenty thousand; twenty thousand that I am a dead man before you, Charles." For the first time in weeks he laughed. "I will live just to spite you," he cried.'

The old gentleman took a deep breath.

'Can you guess the end of the story?'

'I think so,' Serena answered.

'My wife wanted money. She needed it for Mandrake; I wanted solitude. I suppose now it was a wrong thing to do, but the Prince was a very rich man. Twenty thousand guineas would mean very little to him, and it meant a great deal to Mandrake. So I died; I died of the smallpox! Only my wife and my most devoted valet nursed me during the last days of my illness. The coffin was screwed down before anyone would see me and catch the infection. I was laid to rest with great pomp in the family vault. But·here I am—a living corpse!'

The old gentleman chuckled, and Serena had to laugh too.

'It is an amazing tale,' she exclaimed, 'exciting enough for a book.'

'I have often thought of that myself,' the old Marquis said; 'maybe one day I will write the story, but it could never be published.'

'And your son? Does he mind?' Serena could not forbear the question.

'Ah, Justin! He did not know for over a year. At first he was very angry; in fact I have never known him so angered. He swore he would reveal all. He made things very uncomfortable for us all, but we persuaded him—at least Harriet did. For one thing, the money was spent and nobody wanted to return it, and for another I was content. I prefer this life. I have everything I need—my comforts, my own servant, a view from my windows and the knowledge that I am here at Mandrake.'

The old Marquis made a gesture with his arms and added:

'What is more, I have the time to write. If you only knew how much I disliked the mutton-headed people I had to meet night after night! If they could read, they never did so except to make sure that they were invited to every fashionable rout. Oh, and those interminable dinner-parties! Thank God I am now spared the boredom of the *beau monde*.'

He spoke rather like a naughty little boy playing truant, and Serena had to laugh.

'I am vastly obliged to you, my lord,' she said, 'for entrusting me with your secret. It is, I assure you, safe in my keeping. And now I must leave you or I shall be encroaching on your solitude.'

'Ah, but I like visitors occasionally,' the old Marquis said, 'especially when they are young and beautiful like yourself.'

Serena smiled at him.

'Thank you, my lord, for the compliment. May I come again?'

'I shall be very grieved if you do not. But your visit must be a secret, remember, and you must never reveal to anyone that we have met.'

'I give you my word of honour, my lord, that no one shall know that I have found my way here. And if you wish to stop my coming again, it is very simple—you have but to lock the door.'

'I never thought of that,' the old Marquis said; 'but the door shall remain open, permanently open; and you promise me that you will return?'

'I promise you that.'

'And now you want to reach the garden. I have my own way, of course, and I go out at night to take the air. Newman and I walk together. There is something very wonderful about Mandrake in the moonlight. One night you must come with me and let me show you how beautiful it is.'

'I would like that,' Serena said simply.

The old man touched the bell, and almost instantly the door opened.

'Show this lady to the garden, Newman,'

Serena dropped a curtsy.

144

'Good-bye, my lord, and thank you once again.'

'Your servant, my dear.'

He raised her hand to his lips. For a moment, as he bent his head, his broad shoulders were silhouetted against the light from the window, and she thought it might have been Justin who kissed her hand.

Ten

'I AM exceeding envious of your riding-habit,' Isabel said, reining in her horse and drawing up alongside Serena where, mounted on a magnificent chestnut, she waited at the end of a long grass mile.

Serena smiled.

'I am so afeared of spoiling it,' she said, 'that I hardly dare to move. It was only finished for me yesterday.'

'I have never seen such velvet,' Isabel declared, pulling off her riding-glove and stretching out her hand to stroke Serena's skirt. 'I swear it is not obtainable in England.'

Serena blushed, and looking round, tried hastily to change the conversation.

'Surely that is Lord Vulcan coming towards us?' she asked.

'Yes, it is Vulcan right enough,' a voice said from behind, making both Serena and Isabel jump.

Lord Gillingham on horseback had approached them unseen, and behind him, also mounted, was Nicholas.

'Oh, there you are!' Isabel exclaimed. 'Serena and I are as mad as fire with both of you. We thought that you would have the courtesy to wait on us, even though we were a trifle delayed. Instead of which we were informed by the stable-boy that "his lordship and Mr. Staverley, becoming vastly impatient, had taken themselves off".'

Gilly laughed.

'What a fibber you are, Isabel! All the same, Nicholas and I were in revolt. We had waited long enough for wenches, however attractive they might be.'

'Hark at them, Serena,' Isabel said with mock severity. 'Did you ever listen to such abominable impertinence?'

'Well, do not get in a pet, Isabel,' Gilly begged; 'and you need not blame Nicholas. The poor fellow would have waited until to-morrow morning if I had let him.'

Nicholas looked embarrassed, but he said nothing, and

Serena wished she could chide him for his humility and patient acquiescence where Isabel was concerned. But now was not the moment, and at any rate the opportunity was lost for her even to defend him, for at that moment the Marquis galloped up on a great black horse which he had some difficulty in reining in.

'Gad, sir, but that is a fine animal,' Gilly exclaimed.

'Good morning, ladies,' the Marquis said, raising his hat, and then replied to Lord Gillingham: 'You are right! Thunderbolt is a splendid creature, but he is not easy to ride; there is too much Arab in him.'

As if Thunderbolt knew that he was being admired he pawed the air and pranced around. It was impossible not to admire the capable way the Marquis handled him.

'Be careful, Justin,' Isabel admonished. 'I declare I am frightened to death of such a monster. He looks to me as though he would be devilishly bad-tempered and might throw you at any moment.'

The Marquis smiled.

'I will be careful, Isabel, and Thunderbolt already knows who is his master. And now, if you will excuse me, I will gallop some of the devil out of him.'

The Marquis swept off his hat and went off at a fine speed, leaving the others staring after him.

'The cursed fellow can ride, I will grant him that,' Nicholas said sourly, and Isabel turned round in the saddle to laugh at him.

'Poor Nicholas,' she said, 'has that cast you into yet another despondency? But I vow that you yourself sit a horse as to the manner born.'

'Nicholas has always been very good with horses,' Serena said; but it was obvious that Nicholas was not to be consoled.

He rode well, but the quiet grey mare that he was astride gave him no chance to show off. It was difficult to emulate the picture which Lord Vulcan's elegant figure made astride a pure-bred horse.

The little party now set off to ride towards the end of the park, and Serena drew a little apart from the others, not wishing to join in their chatter. She did not seek solitude to think, for she was afraid of her own thoughts. So much had happened, so overwhelming had been the experiences that she had encountered within the last two days, that she wanted above all things to have a moment's respite, to cast away the clouds that overcast her and the

147

problems that beset her from every side; to remember only the sunshine, the freshness of the air and the movement of the horse beneath her.

She loved riding and had learnt to handle what horses there were at Staverley ever since she was a small child. But it was a very different thing to be riding at Mandrake. The horse she rode now was a fine, sensitive animal and, as its groom put it, was 'a niceish piece of blood for a lady'. Serena would not have been feminine if she had not known how vastly becoming was her new riding-habit. It was cut from that wonderful velvet, the texture of which had excited Isabel, and there was real lace at her neck and in her hat a curling plume which touched her shoulder.

Serena knew that she appeared the very figure of fashionable elegance, and as she rode she wondered whether the Marquis had noticed her, and if so what he had thought. 'The Marquis!' Even as her thoughts named him, she recalled that the title was incorrect. Vividly, before her eyes, there appeared the kindly aged face of his father. She had not been able to sleep last night, but had lain awake seeing picture after picture forming itself in the darkness.

There was one of the aged Marquis surrounded by his books, others of the long dark tunnel through which she had passed in search of the Marchioness, of the cavern with its flaming torches lighting the rough-hewn ceiling, of the faces of the smugglers, the Marchioness standing amongst them, beautiful, glittering, fantastic . . . and then . . . that dark stream of blood pouring from the dying man's open mouth.

She dared not dwell on that thought, which horrified and haunted her, and it required her utmost resolution to force it from the surface of her mind even while it remained underneath, recurring again and again like an uneasy ghost.

Serena, after her walk in the gardens, which she had reached through the old Marquis's private entrance, had returned by her usual route to her own apartments. She had hurried along the panelled passage feeling an uncontrollable shudder of horror and disgust shake her as she reached the foot of the staircase and knew that, if she sought in the panelling, she would find the spring which opened the secret door. For one wild moment she had been half inclined to press the spring and pass through, to go down the long, steep steps and find out if the cave was empty, and if, as the Marchioness had commanded, the man she had murdered had been taken away.

What had they done with him? Serena questioned, and she knew the answer even while her nerves shivered at the thought.

The impulse to such madness was little more than a passing thought, and Serena had hurried up the stairs to the safety of her own chamber. She had sent Eudora with a message to the Marchioness to say that she was indisposed and to beg that she might be excused from appearing at dinner.

It was indeed the truth. She was in fact suffering from shock; and when Eudora had undressed her, she slipped between the cool linen sheets, to lie shivering and trembling until Eudora brought hot bricks for her feet and warm milk for her to drink. But youth is elastic, and despite a second night when she had lain in sleeplessness, Serena found that the morning brought her renewed health and a desire to escape from the company of her own sombre thoughts.

She had been glad enough when Isabel had sent word to say they were going riding and hoped that she would accompany them. The dark fears and the horrors of the night seemed to pass away, or at least they appeared less formidable in the summer sunshine. Last night Serena had believed that the only course open for her was to flee from Mandrake, to run away and find somewhere else to dwell, however humble, however unattractive.

This morning her better judgment made her realise that running away would solve nothing. She was still under an obligation to pay her debt to Justin if he required it of her. She was still as completely in his debt as she had been when she left Staverley. His mother's behaviour, however horrible, however lawless, was not her concern. She was Justin's prisoner, imprisoned by a debt of honour which could only be cancelled by him; and until he gave the word, to leave Mandrake would be merely the action of a coward and one who desired to evade a just claim.

She would not allow the Marchioness to bleed her of her courage. That at least was her one armour against the future and against anything which might befall her now. Serena threw up her head, forgetting for the moment that she was not alone, until Isabel's voice, amused and teasing, asked:

'Who has vexed you, Serena? I declare you look quite fierce.'

Serena laughed a little shamefacedly.

'I am not really vexed,' she answered. 'I was but thinking.'

'Thinking!' Isabel exclaimed. 'Then it is of someone who has made you sore. But, of course, it is that odious creature, Harry Wrotham.'

'I am not surprised Serena dislikes the fellow,' Nicholas said. 'He is an outsider if ever there was one.'

'He is repulsive enough, I will grant you that,' Isabel said, 'but it is no use Serena making such a dust about him. It is obvious that he will stay here a long time, for the Marchioness makes much of him.'

'I cannot think why, for he wins vast sums from her,' Lord Gillingham remarked.

'That is so,' Nicholas agreed. 'He took several hundred guineas from her last night, for I saw him making a note of them.'

'Maybe, but she is going to get some of it back,' Isabel answered.

'What do you mean?' her brother asked.

'I do not know exactly what it is about,' Isabel replied, 'but last night . . . no, the night before . . . I saw that Serena was retiring and I hurried across the room to bid her good night. But she was too quick for me, and as I reached the Marchioness's table where she had been standing, she disappeared through the door and I realised it was no use trying to follow her.

'I hesitated, intending to return to my own game, when I heard the Marchioness say: "Fifteen thousand, Harry. It is worth it to you, you know it is," and he answered in that horrid, oily voice of his, "Ten thousand guineas is all I am prepared to give you, Harriet, and that, of course, when the goods are delivered, not before." He said "the goods" with a strange accent on the words, and with that I realised I was eavesdropping on a private conversation. I turned away, but not before I had heard the Marchioness say, "You are cursed mean, Harry, you want this . . ." '

Isabel stopped speaking, and after a moment her brother prompted.

'This what?'

'That is all I heard,' she replied.

'Demme, Isabel, having listened to so much and whetted our curiosity, you might have paused a second longer.'

'Just what I thought myself later,' Isabel said; 'but what do you make of it? What do you think, Serena?'

Serena turned her face away.

'I do not know . . . I have no idea,' she said quickly, stammering a little. 'Oh, it is too lovely a day to talk of such creatures as Harry Wrotham. Let us race. Look, there is a small temple over there. Are you game?'

They all accepted her challenge and she was thankful for the moment that she had diverted their attention to another subject. It was only too obvious to her what the Marchioness's conversation had meant. How foolish she was, Serena thought, to speak openly of things which involved danger not only for herself, but for so many others! Were it to be discovered that there were smugglers at Mandrake, Serena knew that not only would the Marchioness suffer the utmost penalty, but her son and everyone else were likely to be involved. It would mean a huge and ghastly scandal, and who knew what other secrets would be brought to light or what other revelations would follow?

Even the existence of the old Marquis might be discovered. Serena shuddered when she thought what the world would say of a son who took his father's name before he was dead, and how Justin's pride would be humbled to the very dust. He knew now, his father had made that quite clear, but who would believe that he had not known of the arrangement until it was too late for him to protest?

He had been loyal to his mother even while Serena guessed that it must have been terrible for him to be part of such a deception. However much she disliked Justin, she was fair enough to admit that it would be against the whole basis of his character to lie and dissemble or to practise daily and hourly a deception such as this. No, it must have hurt him bitterly, and perhaps, Serena thought, that accounted for his air of cynicism, for his detachment and his indifference to everything which in the ordinary way would gladden the heart of a young man. She could almost find it possible to pity him—and yet, was it possible to believe that he played no part in the lawlessness which took place beneath the pomp and ceremony of Mandrake?

What about the smugglers? He had known where his mother was when the excisemen called. Was he, too, benefiting from the illicit cargoes brought from France? Somehow Serena could not believe it. Perhaps like his father's pretended death the smugglers had been something else he had learnt about when it was too late to do anything about them.

'Oh, I wish I knew. I wish I understood,' Serena thought, as she rode swiftly towards the little temple and reached it a length in front of Nicholas.

'I have won!' she cried excitedly, triumphant that she had beaten the other three.

'Well done, Serena!' Lord Gillingham cried, as he came in third, and then another voice also congratulated her.

'You rode well.'

Flushed and excited, she looked round to see that the Marquis was sitting his horse in the shadow of the trees. He rode forward to be beside her. She looked up at him, smiling and a little breathless.

' 'Tis your horse that should be congratulated, my lord.'

She bent forward as she spoke to pat the neck of her mare. Lord Vulcan watched her, as Isabel came trotting up. She had been left a long way behind and had made no effort to hurry.

'La, you are too fast for me,' she said as soon as she was within earshot. 'I tried to keep up with you, but I began to lose my hat, and as it is not even paid for I decided to follow you in a more leisurely and certainly a more genteel manner.'

Her brother and Nicholas both burst out laughing at such a demure statement from the reckless Isabel; but ignoring them, she rode across to Justin and putting out her hand laid it on his arm.

'Stop admiring that haughty creature Serena,' she said, 'and tell me if I am not in looks this morning.'

Justin's eyes twinkled. The command in her voice was not without a note of jealousy. It would have been difficult not to admire Isabel in her scarlet habit with green facings. She was very lovely and very alluring. He answered her promptly.

'You need no words of mine to tell you, Isabel, that you will always be the toast of . . . the town.'

For a moment she looked pleased, then she made a little grimace.

'But not of Mandrake! Thank you, Justin, for a very one-sided compliment. I appreciate your subtlety.'

For a moment there was a cloud over the youthful lightheartedness of the party. It was difficult to define what had happened, but somehow the morning seemed darker, and sunshine less brilliant, and Serena felt suddenly weary.

'Let us go back,' she said, and without waiting for a reply she started to canter towards the house. She reached it ahead of the others and, giving her horse to a groom, went indoors and up the stairs to her own bedchamber.

'Have you enjoyed yourself?' Eudora asked. 'It has certainly brought the colour to your cheeks.'

'Yes, I have enjoyed myself,' Serena said, and knew that it would be both ungracious and untrue to say different. She had enjoyed herself.

'Will you be dining downstairs to-night?' Eudora asked.

Serena nodded.

'I cannot keep indefinitely to my room,' she said, 'and I have no excuse as I have been out riding this morning.'

'What will you wear?' Eudora asked.

'I care not,' Serena replied; 'choose for me.'

She suddenly stretched her arms above her head. 'I am sleepy. It must be the fresh air.'

'Lie down a little while,' Eudora suggested. 'If you sleep past the luncheon-hour, I will bring you something to eat when you wake.'

'I shall not sleep for long,' Serena said, but as soon as her head touched the pillow she fell into a dreamless slumber.

She slept on and on, and Eudora, creeping into the room at intervals to see that she had not tossed the bedclothes aside, did not waken her. It was evening when she finally opened her eyes, and even then she lay in drowsy contentment for some time, wondering why she felt both well and at peace within herself. Then at last she realised that the curtains were drawn.

'Eudora,' she called, and instantly Eudora was at her side. 'What hour is it?'

'After six o'clock.'

Serena sat up in bed.

'You are funning, Eudora.'

'By no means! See the clock on the mantelshelf.'

'Have I slept for so long?'

'It has done you good.'

'That is true enough,' Serena answered. 'I feel a different person, ready to face anything and everybody.'

She slipped out of bed, and was pulling a shawl round her, went to the window. The sun was sinking in a blaze

153

of crimson and gold, the moon was rising up the sable sky. The sea was very calm, and there were no waves to break the deep sapphire blue of the water. 'How lovely it is!' Serena said, more to herself than to Eudora, and turning her head with a little smile, she added, 'I am ashamed to admit it, but I am hungry.'

'I will get you something tasty to eat,' Eudora said. 'But not too much. I do not want to spoil your dinner.'

Serena laughed. It was a remark such as Eudora had often made to her when she was a child.

'I could eat an ox,' she said, 'so do not worry about my dinner. I shall doubtless be able to eat a second one then.'

'In which case you will not be able to get into the dress I have chosen for you,' Eudora said tartly.

Serena laughed again because Eudora always had the last word. She sat at the window-seat clad only in her nightgown and shawl while she waited for Eudora to return. She was not cold, and she thought what a wonderful night it would be to go to sea. Even as the thought came to her, she remembered the smugglers. Would they be crossing to-night? She knew little of their business, and did not know how long they rested in between trips, or whether everything depended on the smoothness of the sea or the firmness of the weather.

She looked at the moon doubtfully. It was not yet full, but it would give enough light to constitute danger to those who wished their presence on the water to be a secret. She imagined a sea mist or a fog would be best to escape the observation of the excisemen. 'I will not think about them,' she told herself fiercely. 'I have got to forget them. If I go on remembering, it will drive me mad.'

Eudora came back with a tray containing cold chicken and slices of ham, a cake made of layers of pastry and cream, and a small basket filled with crimson strawberries.

'They are the first of the season,' Eudora said. 'His Lordship's valet was good-natured enough to obtain them for me from one of the gardeners. Even her ladyship has not tasted them yet.'

'How exceeding clever of you, Eudora,' Serena exclaimed. 'You know how fond I am of strawberries, and as they are the first of this year I must wish.'

As she said the words she thought of Madame Roxana's words. 'One day you will know your heart's desire, and you will gain it.' In the meantime, what should she wish for? She picked up a strawberry.

'This reminds me of Staverley,' she said. 'Do you remember, Eudora, how I used to steal into the strawberry beds and how angry old Meakam used to be? Nothing will ever taste as good as those strawberries tasted—warm in the sunshine and sweet because I had picked them for myself.'

Memories of her childhood came flooding back to Serena and she sat for a moment without moving.

'Take a little something to eat,' Eudora said. 'It does no good to repine continually for the past.'

'That is true enough,' Serena said, with a sigh.

She looked at the strawberry.

'What shall I wish for?' she asked.

Unbidden a wish formulated itself in her mind—'to love and to be loved'. For a moment it repeated itself over and over again; and almost as if she defied the Fates, Serena ate the strawberry she held in her fingers.

The plate of chicken and ham was soon finished, and Eudora took it away well satisfied. Serena ate the cake and turned again to the strawberries. Then she had an idea. She took the little basket off the tray and placed it on the window-seat.

'I have finished with the tray, Eudora.'

'What about the strawberries?' Eudora enquired.

'I have set them on one side,' Serena replied. 'I desire to carry them to a friend.'

'A friend?' Eudora enquired.

'A rather special friend,' Serena said in a mysterious voice, 'and I wish to begin to dress now so that I shall be ready early.'

Eudora sniffed slightly suspiciously, but she asked no more questions, busying herself with bringing hot water for Serena to wash in and putting out the diaphanous garments she would wear beneath her ball gown.

Eudora's choice for the evening was a robe of white satin trimmed at the low-cut neck with frills of lace which also formed the tiny transparent puff sleeves. It was worn with a scarf of diaphanous blue gauze. The colour brought out the golden lights in her hair and the soft pink of her cheeks. Her shoes were blue and there were tiny bows of gauzy ribbon to hold her curls in place. When she was ready, she stared at her reflection in the mirror, while Eudora gave a little cry of pleasure.

'You look beautiful, my little love,' she said; 'I only wish

155

that those who knew you when you were a child could see you now.'

Serena smiled tenderly, but she asked:

'Do you think my gown would impress them? Most of them loved me for myself not for how I was dressed. As for my father . . .' She paused for a moment. 'Let us be honest between ourselves, Eudora. He was never particularly interested in me.'

'He cared for no one after her ladyship died,' Eudora said slowly.

'Not even for his only child,' Serena said. 'I tried to love him, Eudora, and sometimes I feel ashamed that I do not mourn him more, but I meant so little in his life and he in mine. If we had cared for each other, he would never have made that last cruel wager.'

Her voice broke for a moment, then resolutely she smiled.

'But why are we being so morbid? Do not let us dwell on such things. We were saying, were we not? that this dress was vastly becoming.' On an impulse she bent down and kissed Eudora on the cheek. 'You are the one person I have always loved, Eudora,' she said; and then before she received a reply she moved across the room and picked up the basket of strawberries. 'Now,' she said gaily, 'I am ready to visit my friend.'

Her hand was on the door of the room which led into the turret before Eudora exclaimed.

'Are you going down that way again?'

Serena nodded.

'Do not admit anyone into my bedchamber while I am gone. This stairway is a secret, Eudora, between you and me.'

Eudora's reply was to bolt the outer door of the bedchamber, and Serena, entering the turret room, lifted the latch of the door which led down to the old Marquis's library.

Lifting her gown with one hand to prevent the hem touching the dusty steps, and with the basket of strawberries in the other, Serena went slowly and carefully down the winding stairway. It was difficult to see, for already it was nearly dark outside. But she knew her way and when she reached the door which led into the library, she listened for a moment, knowing it would be imprudent of her to make herself known should anyone else be with the Marquis.

There was silence, and after listening for a second or

two, she opened the door very, very gently. The curtains were drawn over the library windows and the tapers in the big silver candelabra on the writing-desk were lit. As Serena expected, the Marquis was sitting at the table writing. Very softly, so as to surprise him, she pushed open the door and entered the library. Then she came on tiptoe down the three steps which led into the room, and as she reached the floor she said:

'Good evening, my lord.'

She thought for a moment that in her white dress and the deep shadows around her she must look almost like a ghost, and she was not unprepared to hear the exclamation which came from the Marquis's lips as he raised his head. But as she looked at his face full in the candlelight, it was for her to exclaim. Sitting at the desk was not the old Marquis, but Justin!

For a moment they stared at each other, and then Justin got to his feet and in a voice startled out of its usual complacency he asked:

'What are you doing here?'

Serena was so surprised at the sight of him that she could not answer him, and when at length she did reply, her tone sounded faint and frightened even to her own ears.

'I . . . I came . . . to visit . . . your father.'

'My father?' Justin gasped, and coming from behind the desk he walked towards her. 'Is there no secret in this house which can be kept from you?' he enquired.

There was so much irritation in his tone that despite her fear and the fact that her heart was beating quickly, Serena could not help but see the humour of the situation.

'I . . . I am exceeding sorry,' she replied, and her voice was so apologetic that Justin, standing looking at her, felt his anger recede.

'How did you find your way here?' he asked.

'Down the stairway, my lord, which leads from my bed-chamber.'

There was now a definite twinkle in his eye, and as if he had suddenly remembered his manners he made a gesture with his hand indicating a high-backed chair beside the fireplace.

'Since you have come, Serena, will you not be seated?'

She moved towards it, and then looked down at the little basket of strawberries she carried in her hand.

'I was bringing your father a present.'

Justin glanced in the basket.

157

'Strawberries!' he exclaimed.

'The first of the season,' Serena replied.

'Have they come from London?'

'No . . . my lord, from . . . the gardens of Mandrake.'

Now he threw back his head and laughed—a hearty, boyish laugh that seemed unmuffled by the dusty shadows of the room.

'I declare you are incorrigible.'

Serena felt the tension lessen within her. Her heart was still beating hard and she could feel her pulse throbbing, but she was no longer afraid. The slight stammer left her lips.

'It was by mistake that I found my way here yesterday,' she said, 'but your father invited me to visit him again.

'And how did you know he was my father?'

Serena looked at him from under her dark eyelashes, and then she said demurely:

'I might well have recognised him, my lord, but . . . the truth . . . slipped out.'

'The devil it did!' Justin exclaimed.

'I have sworn to reveal it to no one,' Serena said. 'Can you trust me?'

'Can I?' Justin asked the question, and in answer Serena's chin went up and she widened her eyes at him.

'Do you doubt me, my lord?'

'You are a stranger, and yet within such a short while of your coming here the most guarded secrets of Mandrake are in your keeping. I think I am a little afraid of you, Serena.'

'Afraid? You are pleased to tease me, my lord.'

'No, I speak truthfully.'

'I promise you that the secrets of Mandrake, strange though they be, are safe with me.'

In answer he put out his hand.

'Do you swear that?'

She laid her hand in his and was surprised at the sudden strength of his fingers.

'I give you my hand on it,' Serena said. 'What I have learned here shall never pass my lips.'

'Thank you, Serena.'

Lord Vulcan spoke gravely, then to her embarrassment, instead of relinquishing her hand, he held it in both his. She was conscious of the warmth of his fingers, of some strange feeling his touch aroused within her. She could not explain it, she only knew it was there. She felt herself tremble, and was suddenly afraid of him again.

'Such a little hand,' Lord Vulcan said softly, 'and yet it holds the honour of Mandrake in its palm.'

Suddenly and unexpectedly he bent his head and pressed his lips on her open palm. For a moment she was too astonished to speak, but even while she drew in her breath quickly and quivered with a sudden inexplicable pain, her hand was released and Lord Vulcan rose to his feet. For a moment he stood with his back to her, his hand on the mantelshelf, then he spoke in a normal, unhurried manner.

'I regret that for the moment you cannot see my father. He was slightly indisposed this afternoon. He suffers, as perhaps you know, from his heart. He had an attack this afternoon and his valet has put him to bed. At the moment he is asleep.'

'I am sorry . . . he is not well.'

Serena's voice was low. Somehow she found it impossible to speak steadily or to quell the fluttering in her breast which made her voice shake.

'When he wakes, will you give him these strawberries, with . . . with my love?'

She rose to her feet as she spoke, and putting the strawberries down on the desk was turning away towards the door through which she had come, when Lord Vulcan stopped her.

'I am glad, Serena,' he said gravely, 'that you have found something, or rather somebody, to love at Mandrake. For you have also found much to hate.'

Almost against her will she looked up at him. The candlelight was full on their faces and there was something in his eyes which seemed to hold her spellbound. She had no idea there could be so much expression in Justin's eyes. No longer cold, no longer cynical, they seemed to be lit by some inner fire which held her and drew her . . . towards what she had no idea. She only knew in that moment that it seemed as if Justin had a message for her, that there was something he was striving to say, something which could not be put into words.

They stood there as if they were both made of stone, and then Serena was conscious that her breath was coming quickly, that her lips were parted. She was afraid, yet strangely excited. She felt that she must go, yet something within her longed to stay.

159

A log falling in the fire broke the spell which bound them. The sound, slight though it was, drew Justin's attention, his eyelashes flickered and Serena was free. With an incoherent murmur of farewell she moved across the room, climbed the polished steps and slipped through the door in the wall. It closed behind her and the latch fell. Then there was silence.

Eleven

THE Marchioness was dressing for dinner. Martha was arranging a spray of jewelled flowers in the curls of her hair. Yvette was putting a few finishing touches to a gown of silver gauze which had been completed only that afternoon, and the black boy stood beside the dressing-table holding in his hands a salver on which reposed a crystal decanter filled with wine and a glass engraved with a monogram.

'A trifle more to the right, woman,' the Marchioness said to Martha, and then with an exclamation of annoyance: 'Pish, how clumsy your fingers are! You pulled my hair; I felt the pain of it shoot right through my head.'

'I am exceeding sorry, m'lady, but if you will move about it is difficult to avoid hurting you.'

'Do not argue with me,' the Marchioness snapped. 'Arguments are the weapons of fools. What are you fidgeting at, Yvette?'

She moved her feet restlessly.

'Ze hem is ze right length in ze front, m'lady,' Yvette said, 'but ze back is still *trop* long. Your ladyship must have ze patience.'

'Pah! That is one thing I have not got,' the Marchioness said. 'So hurry, for heaven's sake, hurry.'

'Your ladyship will be dressed in plenty of time,' Martha said soothingly.

'I am well aware of that,' the Marchioness snapped, 'but I would speak with Madame Roxana.'

Martha sniffed. She disliked the gipsy, and the mere mention of her name was enough to make her scowl and draw from her one of these disapproving sounds of which the Marchioness had been unable to cure her even after thirty years' service.

'I cannot but 'collect,' the Marchioness said in a quieter tone, as though she were speaking to herself rather than to her maid, 'that Roxana has been right over many things that she has predicted for me.'

161

'Only those which were of no matter to your ladyship,'
Martha said. 'If she could give you some reliable information at cards, 'twould be more useful.'

' 'Tis true that the stars are vague,' the Marchioness said.

'Purposely so, if you ask me,' Martha retorted.

'But she assures me that the planets will soon be in my
favour,' the Marchioness said, her eyes glowing. 'Soon,
soon, Martha, and then all your croakings will be con-
founded.'

'I only hope your ladyship will not be disappointed,'
Martha said primly, in a tone which conveyed only too
surely her conviction that she would be.

The Marchioness laughed and suddenly her mood of irritability vanished.

'La, Martha, but you are always the same. On the sun-
niest day you would swear it was about to rain. I believe in
Madame Roxana. She has promised me gold to-night. Yes,
to-night . . . we shall see.'

'Your ladyship is confident that you will win to-night?'

'No, Martha, I did not say that. I said I was expecting
gold.'

Martha looked at her anxiously.

'Your ladyship is not planning anything new?' she enquired.

She would have said more, but as if she realised that
Yvette and the black boy were listening, she tightened her
lips while her eyes searched the Marchioness's face as if for
information.

'Now, do not get into a fidget, Martha,' the Marchioness
said. 'I have a new plan, and it is a mighty good one.'

She got up from the dressing-table and stared at her
reflection in the glass.

'I am not so old and decrepit but that my wits can still
intrigue, and to-night we shall see just how fortunate those
wits can be.'

Martha looked worried. The Marchioness, reaching out
her hand, pushed her sharply on the arm.

'Go along, you old crow, and fetch Madame Roxana to
me. Yvette, not one moment longer will I stand for you.'

'It is finished, your ladyship.'

Yvette rose from her knees and stood back. She was a
middle-aged Frenchwoman, but there was an expression of
ardent admiration in her face as she looked at her mistress.
She threw out her arms.

162

'Mais, madame, vous êtes ravissante, vous êtes exquise!'

The Marchioness preened herself a little.

'It is a charming gown, Yvette.'

'Your ladyship will be ze most beautiful person in ze room to-night.'

The Marchioness smiled at her own reflection complacently. It was true there were few women with her beauty, her looks, or with her brains. Beauty, power and money! She had them all, and although money had proved elusive lately, to-night her luck would change. She turned to the black boy and poured some wine from the decanter into the glass. She sipped it for a moment reflectively, then drained the glass to the bottom.

She felt excited and elated. But at the same time there was a fear, a tiny, insistent fear, clutching at her heart. She turned the great diamond ring round her finger until it glittered and shone in the light of the candles. Why should she be afraid? Her plan was perfect. It was well conceived, well thought out, and its reward—well, ten thousand guineas was a prize worth winning. And yet, persistently, that tiny chord of discontent nagged at her. What would Justin say? He should not mind, but Justin was often incalculable in his reactions.

How angry he had been with her yesterday! Despite an effort at defiance the Marchioness felt again that sense of dismay which had been hers when he had raged at her. She had not known until then that he knew of her smuggling activities. It had indeed been a shock to her when Serena came to her, stepping from the shadows into the lighted cavern, saying that she had a message of warning from Justin.

There had been so much to think of at the time and immediately afterwards that it was not until she had retired to bed that night, secure in the knowledge that the soldiers and the excisemen had discovered nothing, that the Marchioness remembered that she must face her son on the morrow.

Justin knew! How hard she had tried to keep such knowledge from him! How cleverly she had succeeded until now! And yet had she really been so clever? Had he not known for some time, suspected and yet shut his eyes to the knowledge because there was nothing he could do to stop her?

She had teased him, pretending that the materials for her

new dresses, bottles of brandy and other objects which were bound to attract his attention because he saw them at Mandrake had been smuggled to her by friends or by devoted fisherfolk who plied their trade along the coast.

She had thought it amusing to divert his attention so that never for one moment would he guess the real explanation of their appearance of the vast skilful organisation which enabled her to send thousands of pounds of gold across the Channel and to receive in return double its value in easily disposable goods. Even now she told herself that it might be possible to keep Justin from knowing the whole truth. But morning had brought disillusionment.

He was angry when he came to her with an anger such as she had never known before. It made his eyes like steel, his mouth hard and bitter, and his tongue a lash which hurt her even in the very sparseness of the words he used. She knew then for the first time that she was afraid of her son; that he was no longer a boy whom she could keep in adoring subservience, as she had kept her lovers, but a man who sat in judgment on her; a man who saw her piteously and without any illusions, but who would protect her not because he cared for her personally, but because he would save the honour of the name she bore.

She had even shed a few tears, hoping to soften him, hoping to drive that cold expression of dislike from his face, but he had been unrelenting. She could only pray that he would never learn more of what had happened than he knew already. She had been half afraid that Serena would have spoken to him of the murdered man, but the shock had evidently kept the girl silent, and while she found that Justin had learnt much, including the fact that the cargo was carried to London and sold there, he was not aware that one of the smugglers had died at his mother's hand. What he did know was, however, enough to make him angry with a cold fury which was worse than if he had shouted and stormed at her.

'It has got to stop,' he said, and his voice rang out authoritatively.

'And if I refuse?' the Marchioness asked, watching him through veiled eyes.

'Then I shall have the passages beneath the house blocked up.'

The Marchioness gasped.

'You would not dare! It is a secret that has been handed down through the ages. It is part of Mandrake itself.'

164

'So is our good name; so is the fact that we have ruled this land generation after generation; that we at Mandrake have stood both for dignity and for order. My father should never have told you of the secret passages. That knowledge should have been passed on to me alone. But you learnt of it and you have used it for your own ends. I have been weak enough not to interfere until now; weak as I have been all my life where you are concerned. I have allowed you to use me, I have gambled for you, gained for myself a reputation of being cruel and calculating because I have been prepared to take money from any man who was fool enough to wager his good fortune against mine. I have always loathed games of hazard, and yet I have played them because I believed that the money was for Mandrake. Even as time passed and I was suspicious, I was fool enough to continue to credit what you told me, even while my instinct warned me that you were false. Now it is finished. I shall give you no more money, and your smuggling activities will cease forthwith.'

'You dare to speak to me in such a tone!' the Marchioness cried.

'Yes, I dare,' her son replied, 'and this time, Mother, you will listen to me and obey me.'

He left her then, and for a long time she had lain against her pillows, her fingers plucking feverishly at the lace-edged sheets. What could she do? What could she say? She knew that it was impossible for her to draw back now, to give up her wild pursuit of gold. It was part of her, as much a part of her body as any of her limbs, and to live without gambling would be to crucify herself afresh day after day. She was getting old. There were few other passions open for her and besides, the thrill of gambling consumed her. She needed it as a drunkard craves drink.

She had lain for a long time tossing in her bed, then she had remembered that for the moment she had another plan to distract her, another plan which, if successful, would at least assuage her more immediate needs. That plan would be successful. She was as sure of it to-night as she was sure of her revived and restored beauty in the silver gown.

Once her beauty had been enough. To know that men's hearts would beat quicker at the sight of her had been all that she asked of life. There had been excitement for her in beholding the burning desire within their eyes, in the knowledge that their lips were hungry for hers and that she had but to smile or frown to give or withhold happiness.

She had been thrilled then by the power of her beauty, but she had soon found that to tantalise and tempt a man was not enough in itself. She wanted more, her passions were easily aroused. She, too, desired love.

But she was easily satiated, quickly bored, not with love and passion itself, but with the man who shared it with her. Lover succeeded lover. She dazzled them, gave them a glimpse of Paradise, then discarded them coldly and without even a passing interest in their misery or their broken hearts.

Yet insidiously, so subtly that she was hardly aware of its happening, time caught up on her. Her lovers grew fewer and not so ardent. Passion entirely replaced love so that those she dismissed no longer pleaded for her favours but shrugged their shoulders and sought other and younger charmers.

It was bitter to know that her power was waning, to learn that she must strive to hold those who attracted her where before she had but to command. Where she had reigned supreme she would not supplicate; she wished for something to take the place of men in her life . . . and found it.

Yet even so, besotted and immersed in gaming, she could never lose entirely that joy and pride which came from an awareness of her beauty. Sometimes she even cried that crows-feet must encroach on the smooth magnolia surface of her skin, and that the firm ivory contour of her neck must sag and wrinkle. At other times the kindly glow of candlelight and a sudden spring within her blood would create for her the illusion that she was incomparably glorious again as she had been in her youth.

To-night she felt that lilt and gladness within her which was an echo of the swift receding past. Her mirror told her she was young and beautiful and she could pretend for the moment that she was also desired and adored.

There came a knock at the door and the Marchioness called out:

'Come in.'

Madame Roxana came creeping from the shadows. To-night she seemed darker and more sinister than ever. Her hooked nose cast a strange shadow over her mouth and her eyes glittered in the candle-light. As soon as she came into the room the black boy trembled so violently that the glass on the tray tinkled against the decanter. Hearing it, the Marchioness made an impatient gesture and thankfully he

166

put down the tray and crept to his familiar corner of the room, his eyes rolling wildly in their sockets.

'I had to see you, Roxana,' the Marchioness said in a low voice. 'So much is at stake to-night. Put out your cards and tell me what you see.'

'I already asked the cards this morning, my Queen,' the gipsy answered, 'but they were silent. It is not wise to force an answer.'

'But why should they be silent?' the Marchioness asked. 'Nothing can go wrong. How can it? You told me that this man would bring me gold—the man with the left hand. You remember, you saw his coming two days before he arrived, and now . . .'

The gipsy went across to the fire and held out her hands to the blaze.

'It is a warm night,' she said, 'but my bones are cold.'

'You mean that my plan will not be successful?' the Marchioness asked.

'I did not say so,' Madame Roxana answered. 'Come, hold the cards in your hand, and if it pleases you, my Queen, we will ask them once again.'

The Marchioness took the pack and shuffled the cards to and fro. It was very hot in the room, and yet it was true that Madame Roxana's hands held out to the leaping flames in the fireplace looked blue and cold. Despite a conviction within her that she would triumph, the Marchioness felt herself shiver. Ten thousand guineas meant so much to her at the moment.

'Put out the cards, Roxana! Put them out,' she cried imperiously, holding out the pack to her.

Serena, coming downstairs five minutes before the appointed hour for dinner, saw the dark figure of Madame Roxana slipping along the landing from the Marchioness's room. Her head was bent forward, her shoulders pinched, and it seemed to Serena that in some extraordinary way she gave the impression of being afraid. There was something sly and crafty in the way she moved, but even so there was something more than that. It was almost as if she were scuttling along, hurrying, flying, going somewhere.

'How imaginative I am to-night!' Serena told herself; and yet, as she watched the gipsy, who had not seen her, out of sight, the impression remained. Roxana was afraid. She was flying from something.

Serena went slowly down the Grand Staircase. The usual

167

chatter came to her from the Silver Drawing-room where the guests were assembling for dinner and where the footmen were passing round glasses of sherry. Instinctively as she reached the foot of the staircase Serena held her head a little higher and straightened her shoulders. It was always an effort to enter the room alone. Sometimes there would come a little hush at her appearance, as though people had been talking of her; at others a woman would laugh a little spitefully following a whispered word which, judging by the spiteful glances which followed, had been none too complimentary.

It was always a relief to see Isabel smiling at her across the room and to know that Nicholas' good-humoured face would light up at her appearance. To-night Nicholas was standing alone, for Isabel had not yet made her appearance. Serena hurried to his side.

'That is a very becoming gown, Serena,' Nicholas said approvingly.

'Thank you, dear cousin,' Serena answered, dropping him a curtsy. 'I am honoured that you should notice what I wear.'

'Between ourselves I am getting well trained,' Nicholas replied. 'All women's frippery used to look much the same to me, but Isabel likes a man to discriminate. I am getting nearly as knowledgeable about ball gowns as I am on the cut of cravats.'

Serena laughed.

'Dear Nicholas! Do you not often long for the comfortable lazy days at Staverley when we used to lie in the hay and talk about ourselves, or ride our ponies in the park and never give a fig for how we appeared to each other?'

' 'Twas fun, was it not?' Nicholas said. 'But when I 'collect what happy days those were, I wish Isabel had been there.'

'Oh, Nicholas, must she share your past as well as your future?'

Nicholas smiled for a moment and then he scowled.

'So long as she does share my future, and sometimes I think that she cares a trifle more for me than she used to; at other times I am cast into such a despondency that I wish I had never been born.'

There was nothing Serena could say except to press his arm, for at that moment she noticed the Marchioness had come into the room. There were exclamations from all around at the beauty of her new gown, but Serena thought that the Marchioness looked a little pale as if something had perturbed her. Strangely enough as she looked across the room their eyes met and it seemed to Serena as if on the Marchioness's face there was an appeal for her personally.

'How ridiculously I am mistaken!' she laughed at herself, and a moment later had forgotten her impression as her partner for dinner proffered his arm.

There was dancing again this evening, and Isabel upset Nicholas by refusing to dance with him until she had been partnered by the Marquis.

'If you refuse me, Justin,' Serena heard her say, 'I shall sit alone and forlorn the whole evening, and everyone will know that I am wearing the willow on your account.'

'That regrettable state of affairs must be avoided at all costs,' Justin said; 'I will dance with you, Isabel, but these gentlemen are witnesses that I do it because a pistol is held at my head.'

There was laughter from the group of young men who always clustered round Isabel, and Nicholas stalked angrily away.

'Now Nicholas is in a miff,' Serena said in a low voice to Lord Gillingham.

'There never was such a fellow for being hipped,' he replied, 'but Isabel is certain to dance with him later. Come to the drawing-room and let me get you something to drink.'

'Thank you, I am thirsty,' Serena replied.

She glanced over her shoulder and saw Isabel smiling up at Justin as they took the floor together. The Marquis had never asked her to dance, and now she wondered at the omission. It was true that he seldom graced the floor, but there was no doubt that when he did he was an elegant dancer.

Lord Gillingham went in search of a glass of iced punch, and for the moment Serena stood alone. A footman came hurrying up to her.

'Pardon me, Ma'am, but her ladyship instructed me to inform you that there has been an accident to your dog and to ask you to come at once.'

'To Torqo?' Serena gave a little cry. 'Oh where? What has happened?'

'If you will come this way, Ma'am.'

He led her through an adjacent door into a passage which ran parallel with the drawing-room and ended in the

169

Great Hall. Serena ran along it hastily. Waiting in the hall was the Marchioness's black boy, and the moment he saw her he led the way through the main door and out into the night.

Serena wanted to ask questions. What had happened? Why was Torqo not in his kennel? But she had never spoken with the black boy and had the idea that he could not speak English. Also he was moving so swiftly and she had breath for little more than to keep up with him. She pulled her gauzy scarf round her shoulders so as to leave her hands free to lift up her satin skirt.

They went through the inner courtyard and now through the high iron gates on to the drive outside. Here the way was no longer lit by the light from the windows of the house, but it was not dark. The moon had risen and its silver light flooded the park and turned the sea to molten magic.

Serena hurried along, the sharp stones of the drive hurting her feet through the thin soles of her shoes, but she was oblivious to everything save the thought of Torqo. Had he been run over? Had he been snared by a trap? What had happened to him?

Suddenly ahead of her she saw a coach and horses. Now she understood. One of the horses must have kicked Torqo or he had run under the wheels of the coach. Outstripping the black boy, she ran forward.

'Torqo!' she cried. 'Torqo!'

Seeing a footman holding open the door of the coach she called out to him.

'My dog! Where is he?'

He made a gesture as if inviting her to look into the coach. She hurried to the door and stared in. It was dark, and for a moment she could see nothing. Then she felt herself lifted bodily in somebody's arms; she was thrown forward on to the seat; the coach door slammed quickly behind her; and with a jerk the horses started.

For a moment Serena was too astonished, too bewildered to do anything; then with a cry she bent forward and wrenched at the door. Even as she did so a voice from the shadows said:

'I am afraid you will find it impossible to open, my sweet Serena.'

She gave an exclamation of sheer terror. Then a hand went out and pulled the shade from a silver lamp. Slowly, very slowly, because her breath was coming with difficulty, she turned her eyes from the lamp to the thin white fingers of the hand which held the shade, and finally to the face watching her from the corner. There was silence for a minute, a silence in which the horses' hoofs flying over the gravel sounded unnaturally loud, and then Serena whispered:

'What do you want with me?'

Lord Wrotham leant back in his corner and regarded her with an expression in his eyes that matched the hateful smile on his full lips.

'Surely you are woman enough, my sweet Serena, to know the answer to that?'

'But Torqo? I was told that he had had an accident.'

'A slight inexactitude, my dear. It was easier to ensure your presence here that way than to invite you to accompany me.'

'You know I would have refused,' Serena said hotly and added: 'Enough of this farce. I have no desire to go riding alone with you at this time of night.'

'That is a pity,' Lord Wrotham said suavely, 'for I have every desire to drive with you, Serena, and as it happens, there is quite a journey ahead of us. Shall we not make the best of each other's company?'

He bent a little towards her and instinctively Serena backed away, moving until the width of the seat was between them and her shoulders were tense against the padded green satin which lined the coach. Serena was frightened, but she was determined not to show her fear if she could help it. Her voice betrayed little of her agitation as she said:

'A journey, Lord Wrotham? Perhaps you will explain yourself, for at any moment my presence will be missed at Mandrake.'

'I think not! Your hostess will assure those who are anxious on your behalf that you have withdrawn to your bedchamber with a slight headache. Your absence, my sweet Serena, will not be discovered until to-morrow morning and by then we shall be far away.'

'Where are you taking me?'

'To a very charming place,' Lord Wrotham answered. 'It is a trifle lonely, perhaps, but you shall not lack for company while I am with you. And when we have sojourned together long enough to know each other well, we will return to the fashionable world together . . . as man and wife.'

171

'As man and wife!'

Serena repeated the words and her voice rose a little.

'You must be indeed deranged, Lord Wrotham, if you think I would wed with you.'

'I think you will have little choice in the matter, my dear,' he said drily; and though he said no more, she understood with a sudden horror what he meant. He was taking her away, taking her somewhere where she would be utterly at his mercy, and after that . . .

If she did not marry him, what sort of life or what position would she have as Harry Wrotham's discarded mistress? She looked wildly out of the window. Already they had passed through the park gates and were in the open country. In the moonlight it was easy to see the open fields and hedges high with dog roses. There were few houses, there were even fewer passers-by at this late hour of night. If she screamed and shouted, what chance had she of being heard? Besides, who would interfere with a nobleman's coach complete with grooms and footmen?

As if Lord Wrotham had read her thought, he smiled again.

'It is no use, Serena, I have caught you, my pretty bird. It is better for you to accept the inevitable and to love me as I wish to be loved by you.'

'Love you, my lord?' Serena asked. 'I shall die before such a word shall ever pass my lips where you are concerned. I hate you, do you understand? I hate you, and you had best let me go before I strive with all the strength that is in me to do you an injury.'

Lord Wrotham laughed, and it was not a pleasant sound.

'Egad, but I like your spirit,' he said. 'It will be amusing to watch your ineffective efforts to prevent me claiming you as my own. One grows tired of easy conquests, my sweet Serena, and a trifle of hatred will give our life together a spice and a piquancy which will make a new appeal to my somewhat jaded palate.'

He came nearer to her as he spoke, and though Serena moved away until she was close in the corner of the seat, there was no escape.

'If you touch me, my lord,' she said between her teeth, 'I will . . .'

'Well, and what will you do?' he enquired.

Before she could move, he had slipped his arm around

172

her and drawn her close. His action pinioned both her arms to her sides, and with a strength of which she had not thought him capable he held her as though she were in a vice. Then, slipping his hand beneath her chin he forced her head back until it lay against his shoulder. He looked down into her face.

'So lovely,' he smiled, 'and so untouched. It is surprising that Justin was not more interested in his winnings.'

His mouth pressed down on hers. She felt his lips, greedy, brutal and possessive, before she forced her head to one side, sick and disgusted and at the same time terribly afraid.

'Let me go!'

She made a frantic effort to free herself, and then, as she realised the impossibility, was conscious with a sudden sense of despair that her efforts not only amused but excited him. He was strong, and her ineffective struggles to escape did not perturb him in the slightest. He held her firmly, and now his hand moved from beneath her chin down the white column of her throat and over her bare shoulders. It was more than she could bear, and now for the first time there were tears in her eyes and a sudden pleading in her voice as she said:

'Let me go, my lord, for God's sake!'

His thick lips were still very near to hers.

'Ah, that is better,' he said softly. 'So now your anger is going. You are no longer so fierce with me. You are a trifle frightened, I think, for I can feel your heart beating beneath my hand.'

'Be merciful, my lord.'

'Merciful!' Lord Wrotham laughed. 'Would you have been merciful to me had I asked it of you? No, my sweet Serena, you were very bitter and very cruel to me; but it is that which made me desire you all the more. It will amuse me to teach you to obey me and I promise you that in time you will come to love me—even as Charmaine loved me.'

He said the words deliberately to rouse her to a frenzy. Now the tears were gone.

'You beast!' she stormed. 'How dare you remind me of the girl who loved you and whom you abandoned so heartlessly! You seduced her . . . you . . .'

'There was no difficulty about it, I assure you,' Lord Wrotham interposed. 'She came willingly enough. It is that very willingness which becomes after a little while so in-

173

finitely boring. Now you, my sweet Serena, will never bore me. Besides, you are lovely; lovelier by far than any woman I have ever beheld.'

Again his hand, soft, caressing, touched her throat, and then slipped lower to the delicate laces at her shoulders. Serena twisted and writhed to be free, but she heard the lace tear; and now as the lantern light revealed the full beauty of her white skin, Lord Wrotham's voice took on a thicker note.

'You are lovely, Serena,' he said hoarsely, 'Lud, but you are lovely.'

It was then that Serena screamed, screamed despairingly, and even as she did so there was a sudden jerk. The coach pulled up and there was a sound of voices raised in altercation.

'Demme, what has happened?' Lord Wrotham exclaimed, but even as he asked the question the door was flung open. A masked face came into view and a voice, strong and resonant, called out:

'Get out of there, and be swift about it!'

Quickly Lord Wrotham bent forward towards the place under the seat where his pistols were concealed, but the highwayman anticipated him.

'Do as ye are bid,' he said gruffly, 'or I will blow a hole through you.'

There was nothing for it but for Lord Wrotham to alight, cursing beneath his breath. He stepped from the coach to see that his coachman on the box had his hands above his head and his two footmen behind were in a like position.

'I have little money on me, fellow,' he said furiously, 'but take my purse and begone.'

'So the gentleman is in a hurry,' the highwayman said mockingly. 'Well, I am often pressed for time myself. Hand over your purse, your ring, your watch, and that gaudy pin in your cravat. Now for the lady.'

He shot a sharp glance towards Serena who had just descended.

'She has no jewellery,' Lord Wrotham said abruptly.

'Odd's truth, but my luck is out tonight. A fancy mort like that ought to be stiff with gems. Are you too mean-pocketed to buy her a trinket or have you concealed the ware under the seat?'

'I have told you, thief, that the lady has no jewellery.'

'Is the old gudgeon telling me a cock and bull?'

174

The highwayman spoke to Serena. She was standing in the moonlight concerned only with the arrangement of her torn gown. Her arms were marked from Lord Wrotham's fingers and there was a long red scratch low on her chest where in her struggles she had caught against one of the diamond buttons on his cuff.

'It is the truth,' she answered quietly, 'I have no jewels.'

The highwayman stowed Lord Wrotham's purse and his personal jewellery away in the deep pocket of his black coat.

'No peck or blooze,' he jested. 'I'll hope for better luck next time.'

'I hope I see you hanged by the neck for this, fellow,' Lord Wrotham said savagely. 'And have we now your permission to proceed?'

'At your convenience, m'fine gentleman,' the highwayman said with mocking politeness.

He stepped back a pace or two, still pointing his pistol.

'Keep your arms raised,' he said to the coachman, ' 'til I am out of sight.'

He swung himself on to his horse which stood patiently waiting for him beneath a tree; and then, just as he was about to move off, Serena spoke.

'Oh wait,' she cried, 'please wait.'

He looked down at her in surprise.

'Well, lady, what is it?' he asked.

'Would you help me?' Serena asked. 'This . . . man . . . is abducting me. If you could only give me the chance, I can escape him now.'

Lord Wrotham moved forward and put a hand on Serena's arm.

'Good lord, Serena, are you mad? You cannot ask favours from a fellow like that.'

'Better a thief,' Serena replied, 'than a beast such as you, my lord.'

The highwayman looked from one to the other of them, and then he laughed.

'Here's a queer rig!' he said. 'Now what is it all about? Is it a fact, lady, that this swell mort is carrying you off against your will?'

'Quite true,' Serena answered. 'This gentleman,' and there was scorn in her voice, 'has brought me away from Mandrake. You know the house, it cannot be far from here.'

175

'Aye, I know Mandrake,' the highwayman answered. 'Do I take it you wish to return there?'

'Yes, if you please,' Serena said. 'I will walk there if you would be so obliging as to point me the direction and give me the chance to get away without the coach following me and this gentleman capturing me again.'

'It will take you some time on your trotters,' the highwayman said.

'Enough of this nonsense,' Lord Wrotham interrupted angrily. 'Serena, I command you to get back into the coach and not to bandy words with this common fellow. You will land yourself into far worse trouble if you throw yourself on the mercy of a road thief—a highwayman.'

'Nothing could be worse than to be in your power, my lord,' Serena retorted, and going up to the highwayman, she put her hand on his horse's neck. 'Please help me, sir,' she said.

The moonlight was full on her face and she looked very young and childlike with her fair hair disarranged, one hand holding her torn white gown over her breasts. The highwayman stared and then threw back his head and laughed.

' 'Tis the strangest request I've ever had from a lady, strike me if it isn't. But who'll dare say in future that a gentleman of the road can't help a damsel in distress. I believe your story, lady, or at any rate I'll take a chance on it. Can you ride pillion?'

'Of course I can,' Serena answered.

'Serena, you foolish chit,' Lord Wrotham cried. 'Are you bereft of all your wits? This cursed fellow will never take you to Mandrake.'

He stepped forward, but the highwayman's pistol was pointing straight at his stomach and he stopped uncertainly.

'The Devil take you, then,' he swore.

'You keep your break-teeth words to yourself,' the highwayman remarked, 'or I'll make you bleed freely of them. Stand back, gabster.'

He dismounted, and still holding his pistol in his hand, lifted Serena and set her on his horse's back. Then he sprang into the saddle again and Serena, reaching out her arms, placed them round his waist. The highwayman gathered up the reins, slipped his pistol into his holster and took off his hat with a courtly bow.

'A very good night to you, my lord,' he said to the figure standing glowering beside the coach.

'You will be deuced sorry for this madness, Serena,' Lord Wrotham said furiously.

Serena did not deign to make reply. The highwayman spurred his horse and in a moment or two they were out of sight.

Twelve

IT WAS extremely uncomfortable balancing herself somewhat precariously on the horse's back, but Serena thought of nothing save escaping from Lord Wrotham; and when finally they were out of sight of the coach and the highwayman turned his horse away from the road to a grass path leading across some fields, she gave a deep sigh of relief.

As if he heard her, the highwayman pulled at the reins and his horse dropped from a trot into a steady walk.

'Has that knocked you, lady?' he asked over his shoulder.

'No, I am all right,' Serena replied, 'and I am vastly obliged to you, sir, for coming to my rescue.'

' 'Tis a bully jest,' he said, 'for I had no thought till now of being of service to a lady such as yourself.'

'Of great service, sir,' Serena answered.

Even as she said the words she shuddered to think of what had befallen her when the highwayman stopped the coach. Her arms were badly bruised from the fierceness of Lord Wrotham's hold, but worse than any pain she had been forced to endure had been the feeling of his fingers caressingly sensuous against her bare skin. Involuntarily at the memory she glanced over her shoulder.

'They cannot catch us?' she questioned.

'Nay, you are safe,' the highwayman answered, 'at least from that particular devil. But tell me, lady, are you not afeared of being with me? Those who pursue my trade have, I am told, none too savoury a reputation.'

'I have nothing that you can steal,' Serena answered innocently.

The highwayman laughed.

'Methinks the gentleman in the coach was not after money, fair lady.'

Serena felt her muscles grow tense.

'I am prepared to trust you, sir,' she said in a low voice.

The highwayman was silent for a moment before he put up his hand and pulled the black handkerchief from the lower part of his face. 'If you can trust me, lady,' he said, 'I can trust you, and this kerchief is making haste to stifle me.'

He turned his head as he spoke, and Serena had a glimpse of coarse but not unkindly features. She saw, too, that he was a man nearing middle age, that there were streaks of grey in his hair, and deep lines running from nose to mouth. His voice was rough and uncultured, but it had a humorous, rather pleasant note in it. He was well shaved and his coat, against which she was forced to lean when the horse trotted, smelt of tobacco and the fresh fragrance of the countryside. His linen was clean, too, and there was nothing repulsive in being in such close proximity to him.

Yes, she trusted him! Why, she could not be sure, but it was as instinctive as had been her loathing and distaste of Lord Wrotham, which had now been amply justified.

They moved steadily forward, the bridle path ascending a sharp incline so that to Serena's satisfaction the highwayman made his horse take its time and move slowly. It was not a cold night, but Serena with nothing over her bare shoulders save her gauzy scarf and with her torn dress slipping a little with every movement, felt the light wind chilly. She shivered.

' 'Tis not over more than another two miles to Mandrake this way,' the highwayman said, as if he guessed her thoughts. 'You will soon be home, lady.'

Home! The word seemed to echo itself in her heart. Never had she believed that she would look on Mandrake as home, or crave for the sight of the building because it stood for safety and security. Yet now she longed for it, but even as she thought of its massive solidity as a refuge, she remembered with an almost startling sense of dismay the circumstances in which Lord Wrotham had been able to abduct her.

It was of the Marchioness's contriving. That was clear enough; but bemused by the horror of Lord Wrotham's advances and the disgust she had experienced at the feel of his hands, it was only now that she remembered she had been enticed from the drawing-room by a false message given her by the footman on the Marchioness's instructions. She had been guided to the coach by the Marchioness's own personal servant.

Clearly, as though someone had rung a bell in her ears, the pattern of the intrigue fell into place and Serena beheld the whole plot. Lord Wrotham, desiring her, had promised the Marchioness in payment for her—10,000 guineas! Yes, that was the sum, and she had been 'the goods' which Isabel had overheard spoken of in such a strange accent that the intonation had made her remember she was eavesdropping. Ten thousand guineas, payable of course when she was in Lord Wrotham's power and when, having forced her by such circumstances into marriage with him, he became possessed of her fortune as well as herself.

It was a clever plan, clever indeed if it had succeeded; and there was no reason to think that it would not have been successful had not the unexpected intervention of the highwayman set all Lord Wrotham's scheming awry. The Marchioness wanted the money. She had also wanted to be rid of a girl who threatened her son's independence. It had indeed been an admirable scheme, killing two birds with one stone. Unfortunately, as far as the Marchioness was concerned, it had been unsuccessful. What would she say? What would she do when confronted by . . . failure?

Serena gave a little gasp at the thought. Here was a situation in which she could not expect the merciful intervention of a stranger.

'Are you cold, lady?' the highwayman's voice broke in on her thoughts.

'A trifle,' Serena admitted, 'but methinks it is likely to be caused more by fright than by the temperature of the air.'

'Strap me not to have thought of it afore!' he exclaimed. 'I have a medicine with me which will cure that ill. Steady, for I am going to dismount.'

He drew up his horse and then, as Serena transferred her hands from his waist to the saddle, he swung himself to the ground. They had reached the summit of the small hill they had been climbing and now to the south of them Serena could see the silver line of the sea.

'Mandrake is over there,' the highwayman said, pointing to the left where a thick wood of trees sheltered the house from view.

'It is not far,' Serena said eagerly.

'Not across the fields,' the highwayman answered. 'Rufus and I usually know the shortest cuts.' He put out his hand and patted his horse; then he drew a flask from its place in the saddle. 'Step down, lady,' he said. 'I am going

180

to proffer you something to warm the cockles of your heart.'

'I assure you that there is no need, sir, for such drastic measures,' Serena answered, but as she shivered again she changed her mind and let him assist her to the ground.

The flask was a long one of thick glass. The highwayman drew the cork and passed the bottle to Serena.

'Take a sip of this,' he said, ' 'twill not harm you.'

She took a sip. The flask was filled with a fiery spirit which seemed to scorch her throat, but instantly she felt the warmth within her body reviving her, driving away both her coldness and the sense of shock.

'Again,' he commanded.

She obeyed him, and now she felt a sudden flush of colour in both her cheeks. She handed the flask back to him.

'My most grateful thanks, kind sir.'

'You are better?'

'Much better. It is indeed a warming mixture.'

He raised the flask to his own lips, throwing back his head and taking a deep draught.

'A ball of fire,' he said, smacking his lips, 'distilled in the vineyards of France, and never a penny o' duty paid on it.'

He peered at her in the moonlight as if to see the effect of his words; then laughed.

'What rogues we be!'

His laugh was infectious and Serena felt herself smiling in response.

'Roguery is a dangerous trade, sir,' she said. 'Are you never afeared that you will be captured?'

'Afeared?' he questioned. 'There are moments, no doubt, when I am hard pressed, when I wish I had chosen a less hazardous profession, but usually I am in luck's way.' He crossed his fingers superstitiously and spat upon the ground. ' 'Tis never safe to boast,' he muttered; 'and now, lady, in case yon amorous cheat has thoughts of revenge—we are wise to be on our way.'

He set his hand on each side of her waist and swung her up on to the horse's back.

'Gawd's truth, but you're no weight,' he said; then he stood looking up at her. The moon was full on her face, and he glazed at her for some moments. ' 'Tis no surprise that swell-bleater was over eager to be off with you,' he said. 'You're a pretty wench and a game pullet too.'

'You are pleased to be complimentary, sir.'

Serena smiled down at him. As if he were suddenly aware of her regard, he put his hand up to his face.

'Taking a hard look at me?' he asked. 'Well, forget what you have seen. 'Tis dangerous for me to show my phys to anyone, let alone to one of the gentry who have no reason to care for such activities as Rufus and I pursue.'

'Do you think I would ever betray you after your kindness to me?' Serena asked. 'I trusted you, sir, and you have paid me the compliment of trusting me. I shall ever be in your debt for your kindness to me to-night.'

The highwayman looked at her for a long moment. It seemed to Serena as if he were not only staring at her but looking back into his own past. Perhaps he was linking the two together, for there was an expression on his face such as made her think that he was recalling thoughts of something or someone which made his eyes grow tender and his mouth soft.

Instinctively, because anyone in trouble drew her heart, Serena said softly:

'You are lonely!'

The highwayman sighed.

'You remind me of someone, lady. She had hair the colour of yourn! Gold like the wheat when it first ripens.'

He sighed again and there was a deep hurt in his eyes.

'Your wife, sir?' Serena asked.

'My wife!' he answered. 'Aye, Nellie was my wife for nigh on ten years.'

'Did she . . . die?'

'Nay! At times I think I could bear it better had she gone from me by death, but I lost her to another. To a gabster whom I would not soil my hands by throttling; a bagman, the type of cove who is only at his ease in a boozing-den.'

'Oh, but I am sorry for you!' Serena cried.

'Maybe I was in part to blame,' the highwayman answered gruffly. 'Maybe I was over content with my pretty Nellie, with my inn—yes, I was an innkeeper and a good 'un too—and with the bag of gold under my mattress which grew fatter month by month. Respected I was and no man found me short or mean-pocketed. Then this mealy-mouthed fellow came snooping around. He had no oof. Why, the very bread he put into his mummer I paid for! And before I guesses what is up, off he lopes with my Nellie. Takes me gold with him too. That was cruel, to think she'd shown him where I hid it.'

'It was cruel indeed,' Serena said.

'I tried to cotch 'em, lady, but the world is a big place. I was blue-devilled fierce, and I'd have plugged him cold as a nail had I caught up on him. Then as the months dragged on I knew Nellie was gone from me for ever. I took to boozing, for what else is there ever for a lonely man to do with himself? Fierce I was often when the spirit was in me, and one eve a squint-eyed cove got me pucker up. I let fly my fist at him and down he went for the count. Dead as a herring he was when they picked him up, and it was out of the back door for me with only Rufus for company.'

'So that is why you became a highwayman?' Serena said.

'Aye, there's the reason sure enough. But if Nellie hadn't left me, that squint-eyed 'cull would still be walking this earth and Rufus and I wouldn't have a price on our heads. Fifty guineas they offer for me, lady! What say you?'

The highwayman suddenly laughed as if it were a good joke.

'Methinks you are exceeding brave to laugh,' Serena told him, 'for I swear your tale makes me want to cry.'

'Nay, 'tis not bravery, lady, but the fact that I was born with a jest on m' lips. Do you know what they calls me on the road?'

'No. Tell me!'

'The Joker! That's my name and that's my nature. If I forks your pockets, 'tis with a laugh.'

'I shall always remember you, sir, as a man who could laugh at himself,' Serena said softly. 'It takes a brave man and great courage to be able to do that.'

'Pray Heaven then, when you do pray,' the highwayman replied, 'that when the time comes for them tó put a rope round my neck, I may die with a laugh in my throat. I'm told 'tis bone-eating cold on a gibbet.'

Serena gave a little cry.

'Oh, give it up, sir! Give up this life! There are places here you could settle and no one would know who you are or from where you have come. The risk is too great— the penalty of failure too horrible to contemplate.'

The Joker laughed again.

'Lady, I've made your flesh creep. Do not trouble your pretty head about the Joker. They've got to cotch me first and Rufus and I have a cunning beyond belief. Nay, I shall live many a year as yet and I've grown to like the game I play. There's a spice to be found in bleeding the swells of their gold and plucking the fancy morts of their gems.

Waste no sympathy on the Joker, lady, but wish him luck.'

'Indeed I do that.'

'And now we must lope off post haste,' the highwayman said.

Without another word he pulled his hat a little further over his eyes and sprang into the saddle in front of Serena.

'Gee-up, Rufus boy,' he commanded, and they set off at quite a sharp pace in the direction of Mandrake.

Now they were over the brow of the hill there was no protection from the sea wind. It was not strong, but it blew in their faces, lifting the curls around Serena's forehead and blowing the ends of her gauzy scarf behind her so that she thought whimsically that their silhouette against the sky must look as if Rufus sprouted wings.

The swift movement caught her breath and she felt the chill of it strike her. She knew that if it had not been for the spirit she had drunk her teeth would have been chattering. Even so, the tip of her nose and her fingers were numb with cold; but at length they came into the shadow of the trees around Mandrake itself. They crossed the road and before them Serena saw the park gates and the lights of the lodgekeeper's house.

'Would you leave me here?' she asked.

'Nay, I can take you nearer,' the highwayman replied. ' 'Tis safe enough in the park of Mandrake. Rufus and I have lain there before now.'

'Oh, be careful,' Serena said. 'I would not have you run any risks for my sake.'

' 'Tis a better reason than I usually have for trespassing,' the highwayman answered.

They passed by the gates and finding a gap in the hedge he guided Rufus in through the trees. The branches were low and Serena was forced to keep her head down to avoid being entangled. When she raised it again they were through the wood, and Mandrake itself lay before them in the moonlight. She caught her breath at the sight of the house. It was lovely at any time, but now, bathed in silver and silhouetted against the sky and the gleaming horizon, it looked like some fairy palace. Its windows were bright with golden light, but there was mystery as well as beauty in the darkened turrets, in the great sweep of the roofs and chimneys and in the stone terraces encircling it like a necklace.

The highwayman drew in his horse in the shade of one

184

of the great oak trees about two hundred yards from the house.

'Can you find your way from here?' he asked.

In answer Serena slipped down from the back of the horse to the ground. There she straightened her gown, wrapped her scarf more closely around her and held out her hand.

'Thank you with all my heart,' she said. 'I wish there was something I could offer you with which to show my gratitude, but alas, I have nothing with me.'

'The service I have been able to give you, such as it is, was yours very willingly,' the highwayman replied.

'Then thank you, sir, for being a true gentleman of the road.'

He chuckled at her jest and bending, raised her hand to his lips.

'Take care of yourself, lady. Another time such a journey may not end so pleasantly.'

'I will indeed be careful,' Serena said, 'and if it is not presumptuous, may I say the same to you—take care of yourself, Mr. Joker, and God speed you.'

She turned as she spoke and started to hurry towards the house. She was well aware that the highwayman ran a risk in coming so near to Mandrake and she had no desire to endanger him by keeping him longer in conversation than was necessary. She had gone a little way when she turned round. He was still watching her go, almost indistinguishable in the shadows of the trees, but she could just see him there, his face white against the darkness. She waved to him and hurried on.

As she reached the gravel of the drive, she went more slowly. Now she was suddenly conscious of a deep fatigue. She was cold too. The highwayman's spirit had revived her momentarily, but now its effects had gone and she felt not only cold, but stiff and bruised. Her arms hurt her, and glancing down she could see dark marks where Lord Wrotham's fingers had pressed, and on her chest there were dried drops of red blood from the scratch his button had made.

She came into the courtyard of Mandrake and made straight for the main door. Vaguely she thought it would be wiser to go round the house and find some less important entrance, but she was so tired that she felt it was impossible for her to drag herself any further. Besides, there

185

was every possibility that the doors into the garden would be locked at this time of night.

As she approached the main door, she saw there was a carriage waiting outside and guests were descending the steps. Two people stepped into the carriage, a footman hurried forward with fur rugs and then as the carriage door was slammed and the horses started forward, Serena stepped into the house. If the lackeys stared at her, she took no notice.

The Great Hall was mercifully at the moment empty. She hurried to the staircase, holding on to the balustrade and ascending it as swiftly as her fatigue would let her. In the light of the chandeliers she was well aware how strange she must look. Now she could see that her new white gown was crumpled and dirty, and that the lace at the neck of her dress was in tangled tatters. But for the moment she did not care.

She had one idea and one idea only and that was to reach her own room, to find sanctuary and rest and the soothing consolation of Eudora's presence. Later, she thought wearily, she would have to face the Marchioness. Later, there must be scenes and recriminations, but for the moment all that could wait, could stay in abeyance until her body was rested and she could find some warmth to dispel the coldness which seemed almost to paralyse her.

The door of the drawing-room opened. There was a sudden burst of laughter and voices and the sound of music coming from the long gallery. Serena moved a little faster, but it seemed to her that the stairs were endless. It was an effort to climb each one of them. Only the fear that she might encounter someone kept her going. She had no wish to meet Isabel, who would undoubtedly ask embarrassing questions, or Nicholas, who might feel that as a relative he could demand an explanation.

Lord Wrotham had failed in his nefarious plan to abduct her. That was all that mattered and even the thought of facing the Marchioness paled into significance beside the utter relief of knowing that she was back here at Mandrake.

She reached the top landing and turned along it towards the smaller staircase which would lead her to the second floor. Then as she moved, dragging her feet in her utter weariness, she was aware that someone was coming in the opposite direction. She drooped her head, turning it aside in an instinctive action which hoped to escape recognition.

But a few steps further on something compelled her to see who approached. She was aware who it was almost before her eyes moved, for something within her had already told her the truth.

The light from the candles set in the gilt wall brackets revealed the expression on the Marquis's face. Serena thought she had never seen him look so severe, so stern, and somehow it seemed to her too, that he had grown immeasurably bigger.

He towered above her and she felt very small and utterly helpless. She had thought of the other people as she ascended the stairs, but she knew now with a sudden innermost conviction that it was Justin she wished to avoid more than anyone else. Deep down within her a question had been asking itself insistently during the ride home, a question she could not permit herself to formulate even in her own mind. Now she could not deny it had been there. It leapt out of her, written as clearly as if it were inscribed on the very walls. Had the Marquis contrived at her abduction by Lord Wrotham? Had he wished to be rid of her? Had he been glad that the problem of her future should be solved without discomfort to himself?

Even as the questions asked themselves, even as they rose tumultuously within Serena's breast, she knew that they were utterly false and without foundation. In reality they did not even exist because, whatever else she felt about him, she knew that Lord Vulcan was honourable and that he would not lower his pride or his self-respect to pursue such methods, however much they might benefit him personally.

And now they were face to face. He was staring down at her, taking in, Serena felt, every detail of her windswept hair, of her torn gown. Instinctively her hands flew to her breast, raising the satin a little higher, pulling her scarf with trembling fingers around her naked shoulder.

'Where have you been?'

The Marquis's voice was harsh, so harsh that she started, for she had never heard him speak like that before. She looked at him dumbly. She wished to speak, but somehow the words would not come to her lips.

'I looked for you,' he said when she did not answer. 'My mother told me you had retired for the night. Why are you here? Why are you so dishevelled?'

Still she could not answer him. She could not imagine what had come over her; she only knew that the harshness in his tone seemed to take all initiative from her, to leave her weak and suddenly near to tears.

'So you will not answer me.'

His voice vibrated with anger, and suddenly he stepped forward and gripped her shoulders with both hands.

'Who have you been with?' he asked. 'Who has had the privilege of disarranging your hair? It is the lure of the moonlight, I suppose, and you could not keep within doors. You are like all the others, lustful for excitement, and yet I would have staked my life that you were different. But you are silent; let us learn what gallant has had the honour of escourting you.'

The grip of his hands was hard, and Serena, looking up at his face, was afraid of his fury. There was a light behind his eyes and his mouth curled contemptuously.

'Well, answer me,' Lord Vulcan continued. 'Or are you so ashamed that you cannot speak? Is it your cousin Nicholas that you crept out to meet secretly in some hidden arbour? Or was it my Lord Gillingham? Faugh, so you will not tell me. Perhaps such affairs are best kept locked in a maiden's heart.'

He spoke furiously and then as suddenly as he had taken hold of her, he released her shoulders.

'I bid you good night, Miss Staverley,' he said, and there was so much scorn in his voice that Serena felt as if a whip had been lain across her body.

As he left hold of her, she staggered. For a moment she almost lost her balance and then she fell against the wall, putting out her hands to save herself from stumbling. As she did so the scarf slipped from her shoulders, the torn laces of her dress dropped lower over her white breasts, revealing the great red scratch which Lord Wrotham's button had made. Even as he turned on his heel the Marquis saw it and stood transfixed.

'You are hurt? Who has dared to do that?'

His voice was different now. The bitter cynicism had given way to a note half of alarm, half of concern. For a moment Serena stood there, her arms against the wall, her shoulders drooping, careless for the moment of how she appeared or what she looked like. She was fighting a sudden faintness which threatened to overpower her, and then valiantly, with a courage which seemed to come to her from nowhere, she forced herself to raise her head again.

'I would . . . retire, my lord,' she said, her voice very low.

But he barred her way.

'Not until you have told me what has occurred?' he said. 'I have no wish to plague you, but I must know, Serena.'

He spoke urgently and now that his anger had gone there was a sudden gentleness in the way he spoke her name.

'It is of . . . no significance,' she answered.

'It is to me,' he said. 'You are hurt, and . . .'

He gave an exclamation, for he had seen the bruises on her arms.

'Serena, tell me the truth,' he cried. 'Someone has dared to harm you. You cannot hide it from me.'

'I have nothing to say, my lord . . . Not at the moment. . . . Perhaps to-morrow, perhaps never. . . . I do not wish to speak of what has taken place. . . . I only want . . . to go to bed.'

Justin's mouth tightened ominously.

'You prefer that I believe that you have enjoyed your struggle, for struggle it has been if one can judge by the mark on your breast and the condition of your gown.'

'Enjoy it?'

Serena was stung at last. If Justin could be angry, she could be angry too.

'As I have said before, the moonlight was obviously a sufficient inducement to entice you into the garden.'

'Entice me! These are indeed the right words,' Serena cried. 'And how was I enticed, my lord? By a trick! A trick played on me in your mother's name and by your mother's servants. I was told my dog had had an accident; and when I rushed from the house, I found . . .'

Her voice faltered and suddenly her anger was all gone and was supplanted by a tempest of tears which swept over her.

'Oh, but why should I speak of it?' she said, her voice breaking. 'Is it not enough that I have had to suffer the indignity of being abducted? Of being touched and kissed by a man I loathe more utterly than anyone else in the world? Is it not enough that I reach home bruised and exhausted only to be bullied by you and insulted by infamous suggestions that I have been enjoying myself? I hate you! Go away and leave me alone! Leave me, I tell you!'

She stamped her foot and then inexplicably in that second lost all control. She covered her face with her hands, her shoulders shaking with her sobs. Then suddenly she felt herself caught up in Justin's arms. He lifted her as if

189

she had been a child, and she was too bemused to do anything but submit. She laid her face against his shoulder and continued to cry.

He carried her along the passage, up the staircase, and towards her own room. Miserable and broken though she was, Serena was well aware of his great strength, of a soothing sense of security that came from feeling herself held so closely. But she could no more have stopped her tears than she could have prevented the tide from encroaching upon the shore. For too long had her feelings been subdued and repressed. All the misery and loneliness and apprehension she had felt ever since she had come to Mandrake was released now in a storm of unhappiness.

The terror and horror which had beset her when she had seen the smuggler die, the horror of Lord Wrotham's advances, were all mingled and mixed into an agony which could find its relief only in the collapse of self-control. In some curious way she was almost thankful to be able to cry, to hide her face against Justin's shoulder, and to know no dismay in feeling the rich cloth of his coat grow wet with her tears.

The door of her bedchamber stood open. He carried her in and laid her down very gently on the bed. As she felt him relinquish her, she gave a little cry as if in regret. Then as he stood looking down at her, she turned her head away from him, her eyes hidden by her fingers.

'It was Wrotham, wasn't it?' he said.

His voice was quiet and very grim.

She made no reply and after a moment he said:

'You must answer me, Serena.'

'Yes, it was,' she said, as obedient as a child, 'but I escaped from him with a highwayman who brought me back here . . . on his horse. It is a huge jest . . . only I . . . I cannot laugh.'

Her tears flowed again, but she was conscious that Justin stood looking down at her. Then abruptly he turned his head. Eudora was standing in the doorway.

'Take care of your mistress,' he said authoritatively, and was gone.

Serena heard his footsteps going swiftly down the passage and she listened until she heard them no more.

Thirteen

THE Marchioness opened her eyes, groaned and shut them again. She felt exceedingly ill, so ill that for the moment she craved oblivion more than anything else in the world. But sleep had deserted her and instead consciousness swept over her insistently so that she was unpleasantly aware of her throbbing head and dry mouth.

She had taken laudanum last night when she went to bed, for she knew that otherwise she would lie awake the whole night, tense and sleepless, haunted by her own thoughts.

Now, though she regretted the impetuosity which had made her double her usual dose of the drug, she still felt it had been worth any after-effects to obtain forgetfulness. But with wakefulness she could no longer forget, and she reached out her hand to pull the silken bell-rope which hung beside her bed, groaning again as the movement jarred her head into a fresh agony of pain.

The door opened a few seconds later and Martha came in. She began to pull back the curtains, but a hoarse voice from the bed commanded her:

'Let not the light shine on my face, fool. I could not endure it this morning.'

Martha looked towards the Marchioness and snorted. She knew that tone only too well and there was no need for her actually to see the laudanum bottle standing on the dressing-table, she was so certain it would be there. She drew the curtains of the windows furthest away from the bed, but left the others closed; then she picked up the silver dress which lay in tipsy untidiness half on a chair, half on the floor, and collected the scattered under-garments which were like little islands of frippery on the wide expanse of the blue carpet. The Marchioness's jewels were thrown in a tangle on the dressing-table as though she had taken them off in great haste. There was a stocking on the hearthrug, one shoe under a stool and the other at the foot of the bed. Martha sniffed again. Furiously a voice from the bed said:

'How much longer am I to wait for brandy, you fool? You know 'tis that I need.'

Martha's thin lips tightened, but she said nothing and went to the door. A moment later, as if he had been just outside and waiting the summons, the black boy entered with his silver salver bearing a decanter of wine. The Marchioness, lifting herself on her pillows, groaned audibly, and raised her hand to her forehead as if to support her head. Martha hurried to her side with a bed-jacket of velvet and swansdown, and set lace pillows behind her.

'I feel cursed ill this morning,' the Marchioness muttered.

'Is your ladyship wise to take more brandy?' Martha asked.

'More?' the Marchioness snapped. 'You think I was foxed last night, woman, but you are mistaken. 'Twas not strong wine which made me turn to the laudanum bottle, I assure you.'

Martha said nothing but looked unconvinced. It was usual, when the Marchioness had taken too much to drink, for her to swallow a sleeping draught when she retired. The Marchioness reached out her hand for the glass of brandy and sipped it. Then she set it down again.

'Faugh, but it makes me feel sick,' she said. 'Fetch me a small enamel box which stands in the top drawer of my dressing-table; the one I have always forbidden you to touch.'

Martha moved across the room to find it. She pulled open the drawer, and carrying the snuff-box gingerly in her fingers as if it were something with which she was not anxious to come in contact, she brought it to her mistress. The Marchioness opened the box with hands that trembled. Inside was a smooth white powder. She looked at it for a moment and then, taking a pinch in her finger and thumb as if she were taking snuff, she applied it to her left nostril. She sniffed once, then twice, and repeated the action. Breathing shallowly, she lay back against her pillows with her eyes closed.

A moment or two later she took a deep breath and looked around her. Already she seemed better, her eyes were no longer partially closed, heavy and lustreless, but brighter, the pupils beginning to dilate. A faint colour seemed to be creeping into her white cheeks and into her pale lips. Martha held out her hand.

'Shall I put the box back, m'lady?'

'No, let it be,' the Marchioness snapped. 'I may need it again.'

'No, m'lady! No!'

The Marchioness stared at her.

'You heard what I said, woman; leave it where it is.'

Martha went away and there was a look of consternation in her face. The Marchioness smiled to herself. A delicious feeling of well-being was creeping over her, dispelling the heaviness and depression of the sleeping draught. She could feel life seeping through to her brain, she could feel energy and a sense of power coursing through her blood, reviving and revifying her. She was better! Nay, more than that, she was well.

She put out her hand again, took the glass of brandy and drank it off. Then she gave a little laugh. Now she was herself again. Thank God that the powder was hers to use when she wished. She thought of the man who had given it to her.

He was a Russian, a Prince of the Royal blood, and he had made love to her for one esctatic and entrancing summer when he was on a visit to England. They had loved each other madly and with a recklessness which even at times threatened to sap their strength. It was then that he told her of a magical powder which could be used when the body failed to keep pace with the desires of the brain.

'Give me some, give me some,' Harriet had said greedily, and amused at her insistence he had initiated her into the art of sniffing a very little of what he called jokingly 'the snuff of passion'. It took her a long time to persuade him to give her some into her own keeping.

' 'Tis dangerous for those who like you, my beloved, are reckless and impetuous,' he said, 'and it should be used with the greatest care and only very occasionally.'

'I understand,' Harriet whispered. 'It should be kept for moments such as this.'

She had flung back her head and her flaming red hair, unbound, had fallen over her neck and shoulders. He bent forward to press a kiss at the base of her white throat.

'For moments such as this, my beautiful love,' he echoed softly.

Later they had spoken of it again and he repeated his warning.

'The powder is mixed by a very learned apothecary in the Court of the Czar. There are very few people to whom he will entrust even a tenth of an ounce because it is so potent, and an overdose, a misjudgement in sniffing the powder, will result not in renewed strength but in madness. Yes, madness, Harriet. I cannot warn you too strongly. If you take it, you must be exceeding careful. It intensifies everything you feel. If you love and you sniff the powder, then you will love with an ardency that surpasses the highest flights of imagination. If you hate and you take the powder, then you will hate equally fiercely.'

'I shall take it for love,' Harriet said softly.

He had looked down at her as she lay there, the diaphanous material that she wore barely covering her perfect figure. He had looked at her eyes half closed with the languor of love, her crimson lips parted as if in invitation, and then with a smile on his lips he held out the box in which reposed the powder of which he had spoken.

For years Harriet had kept her promise. She had used the powder sparingly and only when the occasion was romantic enough to justify her need of it. There was so much superstition within her that it was in things like this that she could be utterly punctilious while she was careless over other promises far more solemn.

But this morning, she told herself, there was every justification for her using the powder. Never in her memory had she felt so ill and never had she needed her wits more about her. She had got to think, it was imperative she should do so. This was not a moment to be squeamish about anything which would clear her mind. She needed the full use of all her senses.

'Will your ladyship take a little something to eat?'

Harriet looked from the shadows of the bed at Martha and considered the question.

'Maybe it would be wise,' she said. 'What is the hour?'

' 'Tis near noon, m'lady.'

'Then order me something tasty, not too much. Tell the chef he must tempt my appetite.'

'Very good, m'lady. And to drink?'

'A bottle of champagne, and bring that here to me swiftly.'

Martha made one of her sounds denoting disapproval, but the Marchioness took no notice of her. She slumped back against the pillows, not even bothering to pick up the hand mirror which Martha had put beside her and in which she usually regarded her face first thing in the morning. There was no time to waste in titivating. She had got to think, and to think quickly.

It wss fortunate that at this moment her brain had never been clearer, and what was better still, the powder had dispersed that sickening sense of fear, a fear which had driven her last night when she had come to her room to seek consolation from the bottle of laudanum. And yet who should blame her? For Justin would have inspired fear in anyone, however courageous, however stalwart.

The Marchioness reconstructed the events of the night before. Slowly what had occurred passed before her mind in procession and she examined every detail and every aspect, seeking arduously and with a sharper precision that she had ever employed before for some loophole, some escape, or if not that, for some flaw in the indictment against her.

She had been so certain that her plan would succeed. In fact as she had watched Serena hurry from the drawing-room after the lackey had spoken to her, she had felt a sudden elation and excitement as though the ten thousand guineas which Harry Wrotham had promised her were already within her grasp.

She had been playing *ecarté* with a rich and rather stupid young man, who had been brought to Mandrake by the Courtess of Forthampton. It was the first time for weeks that the Marchioness found herself winning, not small sums, but large ones. Two hundred guineas, four hundred and then a thousand. She had been so excited that it was impossible for her to conceal her satisfaction.

'The stars have changed in their course,' she said to herself. 'I knew that I must be successful to-night, and now everything will go right.'

Ten minutes later she saw the black boy come back to his position in the corner of the room where he habitually waited her bidding. She looked across at him and he nodded his head.

Triumphantly she staked again and hardly noticed that she lost.

'You are in amazing good looks to-night, dear Harriet,' a beau at her elbow remarked. She laughed up at him, raising her glass to toast him with sparkling eyes.

It was not difficult in such a mood to gather admirers around her. The Marchioness found herself being scintillatingly witty and knowing once again that admiration which was even more heady than an excess of wine. She lost another five hundred guineas and rose from the table with an exclamation.

'Faugh, but my heart is not in the game to-night.'

'Come and talk to me instead,' an old admirer suggested, and laughingly acquiescent she linked her arm in his and allowed him to draw her aside into a secluded alcove where he made somewhat ponderous love to her.

But she was too restless to remain with any one person for long, and soon she was amongst the gay crowd again, darting from table to table and from game to game, making a bid here, laying a stake there, swift, excited and like something mercurial in her silver dress and glittering gems.

The hours passed, but the Marchioness was untiring. She drank a great deal but the wine itself had no effect on her. Her inner excitement was far more potent and intoxicating; and then, while she was surrounded by a group of men amused by her jokes and vying with each other in paying her extravagant compliments, Justin crossed the room and stood at her side.

Before he spoke, the Marchioness was aware that something was wrong. Even before he opened his lips she felt as though a heavy hand, cold and commanding, was laid upon her. She looked up in her son's face and what she saw there made her heart throb with a frightened, apprehensive violence.

'I wish to speak with you, Mother,' Justin said quietly. 'Would you oblige me by coming with me to the library?'

The Marchioness was sophisticated enough not to reveal her feelings.

'La, Justin,'she said, 'what a time of night to choose to approach me! Is the house on fire? Are there thieves about? 'Tis obvious that you are a bearer of ill tidings.'

'Fie on you, Vulcan,' someone said, 'for taking your mother from us at this moment. I declare she has never been in better spirits. She has set us all laughing.'

'I regret my inopportuneness, gentlemen,' Lord Vulcan said; but there was a note of cold determination in his voice which Harriet knew only too well meant that he would have his way and that she must accompany him whether she willed it or not.

'I will go quietly to the guillotine,' she said jestingly; and taking Justin's arm she allowed him to lead her from the drawing-room, across the hall and down the passage which led to the big library.

The moment they were out of earshot of her guests, the Marchioness looked up into his face anxiously.

'What is it, Justin?' she asked, and now there was a note

of irritability in her voice. 'Could not that which you have to impart to me have waited until the morning?'

He did not answer her, neither did he quicken his pace. They moved slowly across the marble hall, and then, as he opened the library door so that she might precede him into the room, the Marchioness felt a sudden spasm of fear. What could this be about? Had Padlett brought the guinea-boat through the secret channel without her instructions? Had Justin discovered the murder of the drunken smuggler? Or worse still, had . . . no, she hardly dared to suggest even to herself that her plan with Harry Wrotham had gone astray.

The library was a vast, gloomy room which the Marchioness had never liked. She hated books. They had in her married life stood for something infinitely boring. The library walls lined with them from floor to ceiling gave her, as she phrased it to herself, 'a sense of the creeps'. It had been her husband's favourite room and now Justin had taken it for his own. All his work for the estate was trans-acted there, and she seldom if ever crossed the threshold, preferring when she desired her son's presence to send for him to come to her own newly decorated and colourful

The fire was not lit in the grate and the Marchioness shivered.

' 'Tis odiously cold in here,' she said. 'Hurry, Justin, with what you wish to impart, for I desire to return to my guests.'

Lord Vulcan closed the heavy door behind him, and it seemed to the Marchioness that there was something ominous in the very deliberation with which he saw it was secure before he walked across the room to the hearth. There he faced her. Despite her apprehension she could not help but admire him for his looks and his handsome presence. He was so big, so strong, and the Marchioness had always admired strength in a man.

She was well aware that Jstin's great strength could be put to good use. She had seen him tame and train a wild horse when no one else would go near it and the grooms had shrunk away in terror. She had seen him, too, knock out two foot-pads who had held up her sedan chair one night in the darkness of Berkeley Square, and on another occasion she had seen him rescue three women from drowning when their pleasure boat overturned in the sea. He had brought them safely to the shore while a company of men had stood by helplessly shouting instructions and making no effort to effect a rescue. Yes, Justin was strong, and he was outstandingly handsome too, for all his face now was set sternly and there was a steely quality about his eyes, which made her afraid.

Even as she was conscious of her fear she chided herself for it. After all, he was her son—the little boy who had once adored her, who had followed her about because, as he had said: 'You are so beautiful, Mother. The angels must be all like you.' She had laughed at the remark and had made much of it, repeating it at dinner parties and re-counting it even to the Queen herself. But she had little use for a child around her in those days. Justin had been assigned to the care of nurses and tutors. She believed that he spent long hours with his father, but she never made it her business to enquire closely into how he passed the time.

Then as he grew older, a slim attractive boy, it had been amusing to know that he adored her, still thought she was the most beautiful person he had ever seen. She would call him to her and pat his cheek, delighting in the admiration they aroused as mother and son.

But it was very different if Justin wanted to see her when she was engaged with a lover. Then she would send him a curt message telling him that he must amuse himself as she was otherwise engaged. It was unfortunate that he discovered the truth about those times when she was not available. She would never forget how angry he was, that young idealistic Justin who had set her on a pedestal of his own making. He had been both angry and hurt, but it had not worried her unduly. Children, she had thought, were part of oneself. They must accept their parents as they were and not wish them to live up to some story-book standard which was obviously incompatible with real life. A smile and a few kind words, an occasional moment of ten-derness—why should a son ask more of his mother?

Harriet truly believed that she had treated Justin well She was also equally sure that could hold him and do what she wished with him. He adored her. She was as certain of that as she was of the admiration she could command from any man who looked long and deeply into her eyes. Justin was hers, a possession as personal and as intrinsically a part of herself as were her jewels, her diamonds, or the many other attributes which fêted her vanity.

Dear Justin! She was fond of him so long as he did not interfere with her wishes, so long as he was co-operative and not obstructive in her little world in which she reigned supreme. As he crossed the room towards her now, she smiled. She was thinking how much she had done for Mandrake and how proud Justin should be of his mother.

'Well?' she questioned. 'Say what you have to say to me, and be swift about it. I have no desire to catch my death of cold in this gloomy mausoleum when there is light and laughter elsewhere.'

'I wish you to tell me the truth,' Justin said, 'the exact truth—for I will be content with none other—about your arrangements with Lord Wrotham to abduct Serena.'

The Marchioness gave a little cry of astonishment. It was admirably acted and would have deceived nine people out of ten.

'Heavens above, Justin, but of what are you speaking? That Harry Wrotham should abduct Serena? I declare 'tis an amusing hum, but 'tis the first I have heard of it.'

'It is no use pretending, Mother,' Justin said quietly. 'I am not deceived for one moment. You connived at this nefarious plot which would have succeeded had not Serena with extreme cleverness managed to escape from my lord.'

'She has escaped?' she asked quickly. 'How do you know?'

'Because she has returned here.'

The Marchioness sat down suddenly in one of the big armchairs beside the fireplace.

'She has returned,' she said, and there was a metallic note in her voice. 'Harry must be deranged.'

She had forgotten for the moment all that she wished to disguise from Justin and was concerned only with the news that her plan had failed and that with it, as she well knew, had gone her chance of gaining ten thousand guineas. She had counted on the gold, she had been so certain that it was hers that the loss struck her with an unsuspected severity.

'Yes, she has returned,' Lord Vulcan repeated; 'and now, Mother, you will oblige me with the truth.'

The Marchioness looked up at him. Her eyes were flashing.

'What a cursed fool Harry is,' she said, 'to carry off the wench and then let her run away from him! Can one imagine such foolishness?'

She spoke impetuously and then suddenly the words died on her lips as she saw the look on her son's face.

'What did he offer you for your part in this scheme?' he demanded.

His words were spoken slowly and each one was like a

199

hammer, weighted and dangerous. Too late the Marchioness realised the trap into which she had fallen. Her original attitude had been the right one, she should have denied all knowledge of what had occurred.

'I know not what you mean, Justin,' she said, but her words lacked conviction.

'Answer me,' her son thundered, and now she was afraid of him as he towered above her.

But she had never lacked courage. With an effort she rose to her feet.

'La, Justin, what a fuss you are making about this silly chit. You do not want her for yourself and Harry Wrotham was prepared to marry her. 'Twas a good marriage, a splendid one. Any mother would have welcomed it for her daughter. But Serena was stupid enough to show Harry a cold shoulder because she believed he had seduced one of the servants at her father's house. If 'twas true, 'twas of no significance; but Harry assured me that the stupid wench would not listen to reason, so we concocted a little plan together, Harry and I. 'Twas for Serena's own good, and one day she would have thanked me for it when she was Lady Wrotham and châtelaine in that charming house of his in Dorset.'

The Marchioness spoke quickly, but Justin's voice was slow as he said:

'That is not what I asked you, Mother. I asked you how much gold Lord Wrotham had promised you in payment.'

'Dear Justin. Have you no decency of mind? As though I could be paid by any gentleman. I am certain that Harry intended to give me a little present, just as I should have given him and Serena a wedding present once the ceremony had taken place. He was grateful to me and I was sure Serena also would have been grateful later. But you tell me the silly chit has returned. I will go see her and find out what occurred.'

The Marchioness turned away. Then she gave a little cry as Justin's hand came out and took her by the wrist.

'Listen, Mother. I want the truth.'

'Insolent boy,' she flamed at him. 'How dare you touch me! You are hurting me. Take your great hand away.'

'The truth,' Lord Vulcan repeated.

The Marchioness faced him for a moment defiantly. Their eyes met and after a second she capitulated.

'Very well then,' she said furiously. 'Know the truth if you will and the devil take you for your insistence. Harry promised me ten thousand guineas. 'Twas little enough by all accounts when you 'collect that he would get eighty thousand when he married the girl—if he did so after he had taken all that he wanted of her. Yes, ten thousand guineas, and I needed it badly enough. Now are you satisfied?'

She pulled her wrist from her son's grasp, then took a step backwards as she saw the blazing white anger in his face.

'How dare you!' he said. 'How dare you sell a guest! It was bad enough that you should contrive at the seduction of an innocent girl, a child whom I entrusted to your care because I believed that with all your faults you were at least a gentlewoman. But that you should plot against someone who has accepted the hospitality of our house and our home, that you should sell her and betray her for filthy money is a disgrace which will for ever stain with utter shame our pride and our honour.'

'Gammon,' the Marchioness snapped at him. ' "Our pride and our honour"—You mean Mandrake. You and your father are the same. You think not of me, nor of human beings, you think only of this house. The Vulcans of Mandrake—that is all that life means to you. The history of the family, the history of the house.

'Lud, I am sick of it! I have listened to it all my life. Have I no existence of my own? Am I not a woman with feelings? Have I no interests, have I not a life to live which is apart from the everlasting tentacles of family and place? Your father married me and that, I truly believe, because he thought I was beautiful enough to grace a house which he loved to the exclusion of all else. There was no room for a woman in his life. He wanted not living flesh and blood, he wanted a mistress for Mandrake and because the place was sacred to him, that mistress must have beauty and breeding. That was why he married me and you are behaving even as he behaved. It is Mandrake. . . . Mandarake all day, every day. Nothing else matters. People can die or sob out their hearts in misery, they can want and go hungry so long as Mandrake is safe—nothing else matters. I am a woman and I want more. I am not content with bricks and mortar, with history and tradition, with heraldic signs handed down the centuries. I want gold, I want excitement. I want the thrill of gaining what I need for myself. I am not afraid of Mandrake. Mandrake may be your mistress, but it is not my master.'

201

The Marchioness's breath was coming very quickly. She almost spat the words between her red lips, but her son was unmoved.

When she had finished speaking, there was a sudden silence, a silence which was even more frightening than the passionate words which had preceded it. The Marchioness waited a moment; then it seemed as if her hot blood, ebbed away and almost apprehensively she looked up at Justin.

'Well,' she said. 'Have you nothing to say? Have I silenced you at last?'

'I have a great deal to say,' Justin said, 'and a great many things to do. I shall speak with my father and then I shall tell you what decisions I have come to about this, and about many other things. 'Tis likely that the house will be closed and you must go elsewhere. The passage beneath the cliff will be blocked up. These are but a few of the things that must be done and done quickly. After that we will see. But there is something else that must be done first now that you have told me what I wish to know.'

He spoke so quietly that for a moment the Marchioness did not grasp his meaning. Then when she did she drew in her breath and her face paled.

'Justin,' she said, 'you cannot mean it. To close the house, to send me abroad?'

Her hands went out to him, but he turned aside. For a moment she felt as though he had taken every support away from her and she must fall to the floor. Her world, the world she had built so laboriously about her, was crashing in ruins. She had a sudden vision of the rooms empty, of the Silver Drawing-room shrouded in dustsheets, of the curtains drawn against the sunshine. She saw only the night watchmen with their swinging lanterns traversing the long halls and passages, the servants' wing vacant save for a few caretakers, the bedrooms closed and curtained, the stables empty of horses.

She gave a sudden cry. It was the cry of a frightened child.

'No, Justin not that. You cannot close the house, that would be cruel and unjust. Besides, I would not let you.'

Even as she spoke the words she knew how ineffective they were. She had no power, no strength to match against his. In the eyes of the world he was the Marquis of Vulcan. He owned the house and the estate, he was master of everything and she was dependent on him even for the allowance

202

with which she might pay her gown-makers and her jewellers.

Too late she saw that she had fallen into a pit of her own digging. The husband might have been coerced, pleaded with and even seduced into a fairer frame of mind. But the son was ruthless. She had driven him too far and too hard, and now she was up against an obstacle which she could not circumvent, for she had not the means within her power.

'Justin,' she cried again. 'Please, please listen to me.'

But already he was moving towards the door.

'We will speak of it, Mother, to-morrow, or maybe the day after,' he replied. 'Now I will beg you to excuse me, for there is something I have to do.'

'But what?' the Marchioness asked bewilderingly. 'What . . what are you going to do.'

He smiled a smile to which she could find no explanation and less consolation, and then with a little bow he left the room. She stood alone, bewildered, astonished and afraid; and for the first time since she had opened the great *salons* of Mandrake to her friends she did not wait to say good night to them but went upstairs alone to her own bed-chamber. She felt tired with a tiredness which weakened her whole body and made her mind feel clogged and thick so that, however hard she tried, she could not think coherently.

She walked about her room until weakness caused her to sit down in a chair and stare at the dying fire. Martha would be waiting up for her as usual, but she did not ring for her. She wanted only to be alone, to sort out this tangle. In some strange manner her life had suddenly become coiled and distorted into something horrible and meancing. She could not believe it was possible, having been so happy earlier in the evening, to know such sheer despair at this moment. She tried to tell herself that she need not be afraid, that Justin did not mean what he had said; but all the time the cold logic within her brain told her that he had spoken with a deep conviction and that there would be no gainsaying him.

A lighted coal fell from the grate. The Marchioness shivered. She pulled off her clothes, flung them down in haste, and taking the bottle of laudanum from the cupbaord at the end of the room, put it on the dressing-table. For one moment she thought wildly that she would drink the whole bottle; then her courage, still raising its head from what seemed a shambles around her, told her that there must be a way out, a loophole of escape.

For the moment she would seek only oblivion, and it was with a steady hand she poured a double dose, drank it off and got into bed.

A loophole! That was what she wanted now. That was what she had got to find this morning before Justin came to see her again, before the final judgment fell from his lips. She was thinking, thinking hard, thinking against time. Fretfully she stretched out her hand again and rang the bell. Martha came into the room.

'Where is his lordship?' the Marchioness asked. 'Do not send for him, I do not wish to see him, but I wish to know where he is.'

'I will find out, your ladyship,' Martha answered.

She went from the room and the Marchioness lay back against her pillows again, thinking, thinking. Would pleading help? no, she knew that was hopeless, for she had tried it in the past and it had proved useless. Justin held the reins in his hand. What then could she do? With a miserable sense of impotence she flung wide her hands against the sheets. To be old, to be growing old, to lose one's power was bitter—bitter indeed. Once she had been beautiful, far more beautiful than this silly chit who had caused all this trouble.

At the thought of Serena the Marchioness suddenly sat bolt-upright in bed. The powder was working. She felt that her brain was rising quickly, that her heartbeats were accelerated, that the blood was coursing quickly through her veins. She was not finished yet. Serena! Yes, that was the name of the one who was at the bottom of all this trouble. It was that girl, that pale-faced country miss who, coming into the house, had upset everything. She had brought bad luck, the Marchioness was certain of that now. Things had not been easy before she came, but never had they been as desperate as they were now. It was she who should be blamed, it was she who should pay, and pay dearly for what had occurred.

The Marchioness's fingers tightened until her nails were cutting deeply into her palms. The door opened and Martha returned.

'I have ascertained, your ladyship, that his lordship left the house last night on horseback and has not returned.'

'Left last night?'

The Marchioness's voice was shrill with astonishment.

'Yes, m'lady. The grooms report that he asked for a horse about three o'clock in the morning. He left no message for your ladyship, nor did he tell anyone where he was going.'

The Marchioness stared at her.

'My God,' she said, 'he has gone to fight Harry Wrotham!'

She fell back against her pillows. Her face was so white that Martha bent over her solicitously, fearing that she was about to faint. The Marchioness closed her eyes, then opened them again.

'Martha,' she said in a deep voice. 'They will kill each other! Justin was in a blue-devilled rage, and I know, fool that I was not to have thought of it before, that he went to call Lord Wrotham out.'

'Perhaps it is not as bad as that, m'lady.' Martha said. 'Your ladyship may be mistaken. And his lordship left no message.'

'No message,' the Marchioness repeated. 'Why should he? I should have known at the time. I should have stopped him. Martha, Martha, what can we do?'

'Nothing, m'lady,' Martha said practically. 'If his lordship is fighting a duel, it will have taken place by now.'

'At dawn,' the Marchioness cried. 'The Lord save us, Martha! How are we to know what has occurred?'

For a moment she covered her face with her hands. She had forgotten her anger and her fear of Justin. It was her son who was in danger, someone who was part of her blood, one who was part of her life.

'Now, now, m'lady, do not upset yourself,' Martha said. 'You will get yourself all worked up over these things and that's a fact. There is something coming up for you to eat in a moment and you will feel better then.'

'Fool, you fool! I don't want food,' the Marchioness snapped. She sat up suddenly, pushing aside Martha's ministering hands. 'I am all right, leave me alone, I tell you. And fetch Miss Staverley to me at once . . . do you hear?'

Fourteen

WHEN Serena awoke the summer sun was high in the sky, its golden rays shining brilliantly through the partially curtained windows of her casement. The whole room seemed golden, and she lay with her eyes half closed, letting the loveliness of it seep into her consciousness so that it was some seconds before the events of the night came crowding back on her.

Then she stretched her arms high above her head and sat up. She felt exceedingly well and refreshed. The hot posset which Eudora had brought her and which had sent her speedily to sleep had taken the chill from her limbs and brought her a dreamless slumber in which she had had no nightmares.

Now in perspective with the sunshine warm on her face it was easy to forget her misery and tears and to remember only that she had outwitted Lord Wrotham. There was satisfaction in recalling that. How angry he must have been! Serena gave a little chuckle to herself before she called out for Eudora.

'Eudora!'

'So you are awake at last, Miss Serena.'

Eudora stood in the doorway, twisted and deformed, but so dearly familiar that impulsively Serena held out her arms to her.

'Yes, awake, and oh, Eudora, I am so glad to see you. I might not have been here this morning.'

'So I understand from your bletherings last night,' Eudora whispered; 'but before you tell me what occurred I will fetch you a dish of hot chocolate.'

'I would like that,' Serena said, 'and maybe a little fruit Eudora. I have no fancy to eat.'

'We will see about that,' Eudora said severely. 'You will need to keep your strength up if there are many more such goings-on.'

She spoke with ominous bitterness, and Serena laughed at her.

'I feel strong enough to face the most formidable occurrence,' she said. 'Hurry up, Eudora, there is much I want to tell you.'

When Eudora had gone and she was alone, Serena slipped from the bed. She crossed the room to the window-seat, and pulling the curtains back so that no sunshine should be excluded from the room, she sat there bathed in glory, the waves below shining iridescently before her eyes. How lovely it was! Serena gave a little sigh, and then looked down on the gardens beneath as if searching for someone.

Her eyes had wandered across the well-kept lawns before she shook herself and a faint flush stole into her cheeks. She knew for whom she was looking, yet why she should imagine he should be there it was not easy to explain, even to herself. She only knew that she could still remember the strength of his arms, the gentleness with which he had laid her down on her own bed.

'Surely I am being exceeding absurd,' Serena told herself.

But she was answered by the soft throbbing of her heart, by the blood flooding into her cheeks.

When she came back with the tray, Eudora exclaimed at the sight of Serena.

'You will catch your death of cold without even a shawl on your shoulders,' she scolded. 'Besides, 'tis not decent.'

'There are only the seagulls to see me,' Serena teased.

'That's as maybe,' Eudora retorted. 'There are enough loose ways in this house without your adopting them.'

Smiling, Serena allowed Eudora to drape her pelisse over her shoulders.

'By rights you should be in bed,' Eudora went on in her complaining voice.

'Stop finding fault with me,' Serena commanded, 'and I will tell you what occurred yester eve.'

She sipped her chocolate as she spoke and discovered that she was hungry. She was glad to sample the dish of eggs, the pat of guinea-yellow home-made butter and a pot of freshly gathered honey. As she ate she talked, and when she had finished her tale Eudora's eyes were round with astonishment and anger.

'The rascal! Was there ever a more black-hearted knave,' she exclaimed, 'to lure you away, and to believe that by such methods he would force you into accepting him in wedlock!'

'Methinks I should have had little choice when the moment came,' Serena said drily, 'but luckily no harm is done.'

'No harm indeed!' Eudora retorted, 'when his lordship brought you up here blue with cold, bruised and bleeding, and crying your heart out! Where did he find you?'

'Who?' Serena asked, knowing full well to whom Eudora referred.

'His lordship, of course.'

'Oh, I . . . I encountered him on the stairs.'

Serena's tone was purposefully light, but she knew that Eudora was not deceived. Her tale had ended with the highwayman bringing her within a few hundred yards of Mandrake. She felt curiously loath to speak to anyone of her meeting with Justin. Not for worlds would she have recounted his accusations or later her own anger in response to his taunts. It was he who had caused her to lose her self-control and to break down, but Eudora attributed her tears as being the result of Lord Wrotham's attentions. And who should say it was not the truth?

'I have finished now,' Serena said, pushing the tray from her and anxious to change the subject.

Eudora sensed that this was her desire and her brows knit together. It was with worried eyes that she watched Serena move about the room.

' 'Tis a lovely day,' Serena said. 'I will get dressed and take Torqo for a walk.'

'And her ladyship?' Eudora asked.

'Oh, the Marchioness!'

Serena's heart suddenly stood still. She had forgotten the ordeal that lay ahead of her. What should she say? What should she do? Then suddenly as quickly as her fears had arisen they subsided again. But, of course, how stupid of her to be worried! Justin would have told his mother that she had returned and doubtless appearances would be kept up in one way or another.

Perhaps the Marchioness would not speak of the episode at all, perhaps a tactful silence would cover such recriminations as might have been on either side. It was sufficient in itself that Lord Wrotham had left the house and was not likely to return.

'I wish to go for a walk,' Serena repeated out loud, and Eudora brought her clothes and assisted her into them. She was dressed and a footman had been despatched for Torqo when there came a knock at the door. Eudora opened it, Martha stood outside.

'Her ladyship would be obliged by Miss Staverley's presence in her bedchamber.'

'I will see if Madam feels disposed to accept her ladyship's invitation,' Eudora said, her voice hostile, her whole body bristling with enmity. 'Be kind enough to wait a minute,' she added, and shut the door sharply in Martha's face.

Turning round, she looked across the room to Serena.

'Will you go to her ladyship?'

Serena hesitated; then she made a little gesture of compliance with both her hands.

'I have got to face her sooner or later, Eudora. I somehow expected that . . . well, never mind! Tell the maid I will give myself the pleasure of waiting upon her ladyship within a few minutes.'

Eudora opened the door, repeated Serena's words in a voice which suggested that there would be no pleasure in the meeting, and closed the door abruptly as she finished speaking. Serena put her bonnet back on the chair.

'Keep Torqo here,' she said. 'I will be as swift as I can and then return for him.'

'You are not afraid?' Eudora asked.

Serena was, but she would not admit it.

'Methinks her ladyship will be genteel enough to hide her anger,' she said. 'She may even be preparing to offer me an apology, Eudora. 'Tis unlikely, but let us give her the benefit of the doubt.'

Serena smiled, then walked slowly down the passages which led to the Marchioness's bedchamber. As she went, it was impossible not to remember that the night before she had come this way held high in Lord Vulcan's arms. Had he despised her weakness? For a weakness it had been to betray her feelings in so uncontrollable a fashion. What should she say to him when she saw him? Should she thank him? How difficult it was to know what to do!

Serena reached the Marchioness's bedchamber. A footman who was on duty outside the door opened it for her. She entered. The room was dim, for some of the windows were still curtained. For a moment she wondered if the Marchioness was indisposed, and then as she drew near the great curtained four-poster she saw that there was no need for anxiety on that score.

The Marchioness was sitting up in bed and her eyes, bright and shining, were more intensely alive than Serena had ever seen them before; her mouth, to which she had just applied a crimson salve, was vivid and startling against the whiteness of her skin.

'Ah, there you are, girl!'

The Marchioness's voice was strong and resonant and seemed to echo loudly in the great room.

Serena curtsied.

'You sent for me, Ma'am.'

'Indeed I did! I wish to hear what you have to say for yourself.'

'Say for myself?' Serena repeated.

'Do not pretend to be stupid, child,' the Marchioness snapped. 'You know full well to what I refer.'

'To last night, Ma'am?'

'Of course!'

There was a moment's silence, then Serena said:

'Do you wish me to recount to you what occurred or have you already heard it from your son?'

'My son!' The Marchioness gave a little scream. 'Yes, that is what I wish you to tell me. What you said to my son, what wicked lies you concocted to incite him, to drive him—yes, drive him—to take this crazy action. For it is your fault and your fault alone.'

Serena looked bewildered.

'What action, Ma'am? I am afraid I do not understand.'

'You understand well enough,' the Marchioness retorted angrily. 'You drove him to it. 'Twas you with your exaggerated and doubtless false witness against an old friend who sent Justin off on this wild chase.'

'I have sent . . . Lord Vulcan?' Serena asked. 'But where has he gone?'

'Where do you expect he has gone? What alternative was there for him after listening to you?'

"You mean that he has gone to find Lord Wrotham?"

'Find!' the Marchioness cried. 'Find is indeed a good word. He has gone to call him out, girl.'

'A duel!'

Serena whispered the words. Her face had suddenly gone ashen, her hands clasped together.

'A duel! Yes, indeed, a duel!' the Marchioness repeated grimly, 'and all on account of an insignificant country chit who . . .'

She broke off suddenly, for the door was opened hastily and Martha, looking pale and agitated, came swiftly into the room.

'M'lady,' she cried, 'a groom from Grosvenor Square has arrived. He has news, m'lady.'

'News? News of his lordship?' the Marchioness cried. 'Bring him in here, bring him swiftly, woman, do you hear?'

'Yes, yes, m'lady, he is outside.'

Martha bustled from the room. Serena stood waiting. It seemed to her at that moment as if a great hand squeezed her breath from her body; she felt as if she could not breathe and could do nothing but stand at the end of the Marchioness's bed feeling as if she were turned to stone. It seemed to her almost an eternity, though it was in reality only a few seconds before Martha returned, followed by a groom in the claret and silver Vulcan livery.

He was twisting his cap awkwardly in his fingers, and his boots were splashed and stained with mud; and though he was a red-cheeked country lad of a robust constitution, he looked tired, and his face was streaked with dust and sweat as if he had travelled hard and fast to reach Mandrake. He was obviously tongue-tied at the sight of the Marchioness. Impatiently she said to him:

'What news, lad? Speak.'

The groom moistened his dry lips, then stammered:

'Your ladyship, I . . . I came to . . . to tell you that . . . this morn . . . morning . . . at dawn . . . his lordship fought . . . a du . . . duel.'

'Yes, yes, I guessed that,' the Marchioness said. 'Tell me the result, boy—the result?'

'His lordship fell, m'lady.'

'Fell!'

The Marchioness shrieked the word.

'Yes, m'lady.'

'You mean . . . Lord Wrotham . . . ?'

'Fired before . . . the ready, m'lady. 'Twas a trick! 'Twas wicked! I seen it all.'

'And . . . Justin fell?' the Marchioness repeated.

Her voice was dull as though she could not comprehend what had happened.

'Aye, m'lady. His lordship had said to 'um, he said, "If anything happens to me, Jansen, post at once to Mandrake an' inform her ladyship." I thought he was but jesting, for I'd no idea that anything could rattle his lordship. Strong as a lion he seemed. Then t' gentlemen met. They chose their pistols an' started to pace it out. Ten yards 'twas to have been, m'lady.'

'Ten yards! It was murder.'

'Aye, m'lady. But his lordship's opponent turns at three an' fires.'

'The devil he did!' the Marchioness exclaimed.

'His lordship fell. I didn't wait to see more, m'lady. I came aloping off here as his lordship has instructed me.'

'Then he may not be dead, for you did not wait to see what had happened. He may not be dead. Who was with him?'

'Sir Peter Burley, m'lady, another gentleman, an' his lordship's own groom with t' horses.'

'Where did this take place?' the Marchioness asked.

'About five miles outside London, m'lady. A place called Cross Trees.'

'I know it well,' the Marchioness said. ' 'Tis a quiet and lonely spot.'

She put her hand to her head.

' 'Tis queer to think that Harry Wrotham should do such a dastardly deed as to fire before Justin was ready.'

She put her hands over her eyes, and Martha, who had been hovering solicitously in the background, said:

'Now, now, don't you distress yourself, m'lady. His lordship may only have been wounded. 'Twould have been better if the lad had waited to see what happened than to come chasing here upsetting you with his wild tales.'

'I only does what his lordship told 'un to do,' Jasen said sullenly.

'That's enough,' Martha said. 'You get downstairs and ask for something to eat. We have heard enough of your ill tidings for the present.'

The boy shuffled awkwardly from the room, and then, as the door closed behind him, the Marchioness uttered a cry.

'Don't let him go! Don't let him go! There may be more he can tell us.'

'He has told us all there is to know. Now don't you take on, m'lady. Ten to one the silly fellow has got the wrong end of the stick from beginning to end. Why, his lordship is the equal of any man in a duel.'

'But not if there were treachery, not if he were struck down in such a dastardly manner. Besides . . .' The Marchioness raised her voice suddenly. '. . . Roxana warned me. She warned me that there was death coming to the house. She saw it, she saw it in the cards. "There is death,"

212

she said, ". . . death and blood." She meant Justin. Oh, God, she meant Justin—my son.'

The Marchioness's voice was vibrant with misery.

'If anyone ought to be shot it ought to be that old witch for frightening your ladyship like this,' Martha said sharply. 'I don't believe a word of her gruesome tales, and never have.'

'Death and blood!' the Marchioness repeated. 'Send her here. Let us learn from her own lips whether Justin is dead. Fetch her, woman, fetch her.'

The Marchioness made an imperious gesture with her arms. Martha looked at Serena.

'Will you stay with her ladyship while I go and find the gipsy?' she asked.

Serena nodded. For the moment she found it impossible to speak. She still felt numb. The shock of what she had heard seemed to have petrified her to the very spot on which she stood. She could not move, could not even feel the pain of her own fingers knit together until the knuckles showed white.

Martha went from the room and with an effort Serena moved a little nearer to the Marchioness, who had fallen back against her pillows, her face crumpled and wrinkled, her shoulders hunched and her fingers spread across her eyes. Her whole attitude was exaggerated, and her voice was distorted out of its usual tones into a note of shrill suffering. There was something strange and unpleasant in the abandon of her grief, for the Marchioness had always had dignity. Now with her mouth twisted in a grimace and her knees drawn up under the bedclothes, she looked like a sick monkey and there was something utterly distasteful about her. Yet, because she felt she must say something Serena forced the words of consolation to her lips.

'It may not be as bad as you fear, Ma'am,' she said softly.

'As I fear?' the Marchioness repeated. ' 'Tis not what I fear but what the fates have told me. Death and blood! Roxana saw it! Last night she warned me.'

Serena remembered then how pale the Marchioness had seemed when she came down to the *salon*. She remembered, too, how she had seen the gipsy move along the corridor stealthily and yet quickly as if she fled from something. She felt her heart beating in a frightened way. Had there really been a warning? Had Roxana seen clair-

213

voyantly and predicted truly what had now occurred?

Even as she wondered Serena felt again that suffocation, that difficulty in drawing her breath that she had experienced a few minutes earlier. She felt the room swim around her, she felt dazed and utterly bewildered.

The door opened and Martha came in. At the sound of her footsteps the Marchioness took her fingers from her eyes.

'Where is Roxana?'

'M'lady . . .' Martha said, then paused.

'Well, speak, woman. Where is she?'

'She has gone, m'lady. She left early this morning.'

'Left?'

The Marchioness's question was a shriek.

'Yes, left, m'lady. She called for a conveyance to take her to Dover. It is understood that she took the stage coach from there to London.'

'Left!'

The Marchioness threw herself back against her pillows.

'She saw it coming! Death and blood! Death and blood!' Her voice rose higher and still higher. 'Death and blood!' She shuddered, gave a shrill, horrible, ghastly shriek, then flung herself frantically from one side of the bed to the other. 'Death and blood!' Again she shrieked and yet again; her hands clawed at the neck of her bed-jacket as if she could not breathe.

'Pull yourself together, m'lady.'

Martha bent over her, taking her hands and holding them; then over her shoulder she whispered to Serena.

'Leave us, miss. 'Tis better when there is no one to hear her.'

Quickly, only too glad to go, Serena reached the door and let herself out. The Marchioness was still shrieking. Serena heard her cries as she ran from the room down the corridor, and even when she was out of earshot she could still hear those ghastly sounds echoing in her ears. It was horrible, beastly; but more important than that, far more urgent in Serena's mind, was the thought of Justin. He had fallen. If he was not dead, he was wounded, and how long must they wait to know the truth?

She stood suddenly very still on the landing and realised that it was the very spot where the night before she had met him. It was here he had spoken to her with such sharpness. It was here he had reached out his hands and gripped her by the shoulders. It was here that she had collapsed, here he had released her to fall against the wall, when her very weakness revealed to him the scratch on her white skin, the bruises on her arms.

She could see now the expression on his face as it had changed from contempt and anger to consideration and concern. She could recapture for a moment the feeling that had been hers when he had taken her up in his arms. She could feel again his arms around her and know the comfort of finding her head against his shoulder. And now Justin—Justin so strong, so invulnerable and authoritative, had fallen!

For a moment Serena felt an overwhelming sense of dismay envelop her. Almost blindly she stretched out her hands and felt the cool solidity of the wall against which she had fallen the night before. Death and Blood! Again she could hear the Marchioness's voice, her shrieks, her cries.

Suddenly Serena knew what she must do. She could not wait, could not let the day pass slowly until a second messenger brought the dread tidings. She would find out for herself, she would wait for no one. There was only one thing she could not face and that was to be alone with her fears, alone with the horror of that voice repeating over and over again 'death and blood'.

She started to run down the corridor and sped along the staircase which led to her room. She burst into her bedchamber where Eudora was tidying her things.

'Quick, Eudora, quick,' she said, 'my riding habit.'

Eudora stared.

'What has happened?' she asked.

'I have no time to answer questions,' Serena replied. 'Give me my habit, Eudora; I am for London.'

'London,' Eudora exclaimed, but even as she stood still in astonishment, Serena was pulling the habit from the wardrobe where it hung.

'His lordship has fought a duel on my behalf,' Serena said. 'He is wounded, perhaps . . . perhaps worse.'

She could not bring herself to say the word.

'But you cannot go alone,' Eudora cried.

'I will take a groom with me,' Serena said.

'Have you ordered a horse?' Eudora asked.

'No, I shall go myself to the stables. I do not desire to see anyone and I wish no one to prevent me from going.'

Swiftly, so swiftly that she had no time for further speech, Serena attired herself. Eudora fetched her hat from the cupboard and she put it on her head, hardly giving herself a glance in the mirror. She picked up her riding whip and gloves, and then just for a moment she paused.

'I shall be all right, Eudora; do not worry about me.'

'You must do as you think fit, Miss Serena,' Eudora answered, and there were tears in her eyes. 'God guard you.'

'Pray not for me, but for his lordship,' Serena said, and bending down she kissed Eudora's cheek and hurried from the room.

She reached the stables without encountering any of the guests staying in the house. The head groom came hurrying towards her as soon as she appeared.

'Ye desire to go a-riding, Ma'am? I was not informed that a horse was required.'

'I sent no orders,' Serena answered, 'for I am pressed for time.' And seeing the surprise in the man's face, she added: 'I have to proceed to London on business which closely concerns his lordship.'

'To London?' he repeated. 'Now I wonder which horse would be best for you, Ma'am. "Starlight" is a sweet goer.'

Serena took a deep breath.

'Saddle Thunderbolt,' she said.

'Thunderbolt!' The groom stared at her as if she had taken leave of her senses. 'But, Ma'am, only his lordship rides Thunderbolt.'

'His lordship informed me that I could ride the horse when I wished,' Serena said authoritatively. ' 'Tis the fastest horse in the stables and there is no time to be lost.'

The groom scratched his head.

'Blow me, but I dunno, to be sure. Ma'am.'

'Those are my orders,' Serena said sharply; 'carry them out quickly, please.'

The man went away to do her bidding, but he was muttering to himself as he went. Serena waited tapping her whip impatiently against her boot. After a moment or two he came back to her.

'If ye are set on a-riding Thunderbolt, Ma'am, 'tis certain sure that the groom'll never be keeping up with ye. He'll strive a push, Ma'am, and I'll fit young Joe with the swiftest piece of blood in t' stables, but Thunderbolt'll lope off without him. Strike me if he won't.'

'I will not blame the groom,' Serena said. 'He must follow as close as he can and if Thunderbolt throws me, he can doubtless pick up the pieces.'

She meant it as a jest, but it was obvious enough that the groom took her seriously.

'Pieces is about all that'll remain o' ye, Ma'am,' he said grimly.

Determined though she was, Serena felt apprehensive as Thunderbolt was brought to the yard. Two grooms held him, and a third was trying to tighten the girths. He was plunging and rearing, his ears back, his eyes rolling wickedly, and it was with some difficulty that the grooms could bring him alongside the mounting block.

Joe was already mounted on a young chestnut mare, but no sooner was Serena in Thunderbolt's saddle than he shot out of the yard like an arrow from a bow. Even as she guided him into the driveway she knew that all her strength would be ineffective to hold him, and without worrying about the groom behind she let Thunderbolt have his head.

His first pace, which seemed almost winged in its swiftness, gave place after a mile or two to a steady gallop. He was fresh, so fresh, and so full of fire and spirit that Serena knew it was useless making any attempt to pull him in until some of his exuberance had subsided. She had ridden many horses in her life, but never one which approached in any way the magnificence or the breeding of Thunderbolt, and when her first nervousness had passed she began to enjoy the movement of the great horse and the ease with which he could carry her.

On they galloped. Serena knew that by heading north they should meet some five miles from Mandrake the main Dover road. Sure enough she perceived it in the distance but kept to the fields and the bridle paths knowing they would move more swiftly off the highway where there was the constant interruption of traffic. They had been going for nearly an hour before Thunderbolt responded to the curb and dropped from a gallop into a trot, then at last Serena could turn her head and look behind her. As she had expected, there was no sign of the groom.

'He will catch up with us,' Serena said aloud, and Thunderbolt cocked up his ears as if in surprise at the voice.

She bent forward and patted his head.

'Take a breather, old boy,' she said. 'You will tire yourself out and we have a long way to go as yet.'

They were passing through some wooded country and she was thankful that Thunderbolt was content to go a little more quietly or she might easily have been swept off his back by the low-hanging branches. He was still inclined to be playful. A pile of potatoes in the corner of the field would cause him to shy, the sudden cry of the pheasant rising in the undergrowth would start him galloping again.

But it was as if Thunderbolt was showing off a little to the strange rider he found on his back and was not being intentionally malicious. Serena talked to him. She had learned many years ago that animals are soothed by the sound of the human voice, and grow speedily accustomed to taking orders from someone they can hear.

She had gone another five or six miles when an open desolate piece of country brought a frown between her eyes. Look as she would she could not see any sign of the Dover road.

'We must not lose our way, Thunderbolt,' she said.

Coming in from the fields she found a lane winding its way between high hedges bright with dog roses and convolvulus. Serena looked eagerly for a milestone, but she saw none. Then suddenly Thunderbolt began to move in a curious manner.

'What has happened to you?' she asked, and knew the answer.

Once before it had happened to her. She knew the gait of a horse which had cast a shoe.

She drew Thunderbolt up to a walk.

'This lane must lead to somewhere,' she said anxiously.

They went on some way. There were no cottages, no houses, only the lane and occasional clumps of trees. The sun was hot and Serena felt thirsty.

'If we come to a village,' she told Thunderbolt, 'you shall have a new shoe and I will have a drink of water.'

She guessed by the position of the sun that it must be after three o'clock. She wished now that she had been sensible enough earlier on to wait for her groom. She could have taken his horse and left him with Thunderbolt. But now he must be miles behind.

'I wonder where we are,' she sighed, and then suddenly a rough voice behind her remarked:

'Stand and deliver!'

She gave an exclamation and turned her head to see under the shadows of some trees another horse and a man astride it; but even as she turned the voice said:

'Strap me if it isn't the little lady from Mandrake.'

With a cry of gladness Serena turned Thunderbolt around to face the Joker.

'How exceeding glad I am to see you!' she cried. 'My horse has cast a shoe and I am for London post-haste.'

'Odd's truth, but you are escaping from yet another well-breeched swell?' the highwayman laughed.

'Nay, going in search of one,' Serena answered. 'Help me, Joker, for 'tis mighty urgent.'

'Help you I will,' he replied. 'But are you alone?'

Serena nodded.

'I lost my groom from the moment we left the stables at Mandrake.'

'That provokes no astonishment,' the highwayman exclaimed, 'for you're riding the finest piece of blood I have seen for many a long day.'

'It is the Arab in him,' Serena exclaimed, 'but even an Arab needs four shoes.'

'Which he shall have,' the Joker replied. 'Follow me through these trees and I will take you to a smithy not a mile away.'

He led the way, bending his head beneath the branches. Soon they were out in the open again with Thunderbolt prancing and preening himself a little beside Rufus.

'You've a longish ride ahead of you,' the highwayman said; 'not that it should be of any great moment with a horse such as yourn.'

'I fancy that I am more likely to be tired than Thunderbolt,' Serena replied.

'You're a game pullet,' the highwayman said, 'as I have told you before.'

'Thank you, sir.'

'I thought you'd be tired enough last night to sleep the clock round.'

'I awoke to hear serious news of . . . of a friend.'

'A friend?' the highwayman questioned with a smile. 'Be honest, lady, 'tis your heart's desire this time.'

Serena looked at him, and then quite suddenly, before she could answer him, she knew the truth within herself. Yes, her heart's desire—was Justin. How absurd she had been not to realise it before! How blind, or if not blind, hypocritical even to herself! She loved him! Why pretend? Had loved him, it seemed to her now, for a long time.

'He's a lucky cove whoever he may be,' the Joker said with a chuckle. 'When you marries him, give him m'kind regards and tell him how I rescued you from a scoundrel.'

'He knows that already,' Serena answered.

219

'He does?' the highway asked in surprise. 'I dunno how he can do that seeing he's in London.'

'He went there this morning, or rather last night, to fight a duel,' Serena said, and even as she said the words they sounded ominous even to her own ears.

'A duel!' the Joker exclaimed. 'Then he's a game 'un too, and who shall blame him? If ever a cove wanted a hole blown through him, 'twas that tallow-faced cull you had with you last night.'

Serena gave a sigh which seemed to come from the very bottom of her heart. If only it had been Harry Wrotham who had fallen, she would have been glad. Yes, glad, for he would have got his deserts.

There was no time to say more before they came to a tiny village. A few thatched cottages nestled round a grey church and on the village green there was a smithy's forge. The highwayman led the way to it and dismounting, shouted:

'Hey, Ted.'

A huge man, naked to the waist, his skin almost as brown as the leather apron he wore, came out into the sunlight.

' 'Lo, Joker. Are ye in trouble?' he asked, and then seeing Serena gave a low whistle. 'Ah, 'tis queer to see ye with such a fancy piece,' he added jovially.

The highwayman looked almost embarrassed.

'Keep your mummer shut, Ted,' he said, 'don't you know a lady when you sees one?'

'Oi beg your pardon, m'lady,' the smithy said to Serena. 'T' Joker is an old friend o' mine.'

'And of mine,' Serena said softly. 'Will you shoe this horse for me?'

The blacksmith walked towards Thunderbolt, who instantly reared in the air as if in fright; then surprisingly as he put a hand on his bridle, the horse became as quiet as a lamb. The smith spoke to him in a quiet voice, and as Serena slipped from his back the great animal allowed himself to be led obediently to the anvil.

Serena looked at the highwayman in surprise.

'Ted's grandmother was a gipsy,' he exclaimed, 'and he has learned much of their gabble. He's a rare 'un with a horse is Ted.'

Serena remembered her dry lips and parched throat.

'Do you think I could have a glass of water?' she asked.

'I'll get you one,' the Joker said. He left his horse loose

and went to a near-by cottage bright with flowers outside. He came back not with water but with a glass of milk.

'Fresh from the cow,' he said; ' 'twill do you good.'

Serena thanked him and sipped it slowly. Thunderbolt was behaving in an exemplary manner. It was pleasant to rest, but she was consumed by an anxiety to be on her way.

She looked round the quiet village. Children were playing at the far end of the green and several of the cottagers were tending their gardens. She glanced up at the highwayman.

'You are safe here?'

He nodded.

'I have friends I can trust.'

Serena sat down on a log of wood just inside the forge. Rufus cropped the grass outside and the highwayman leant against the door watching Ted as his hammer rang out metallically, the gleaming sparks shooting upwards.

Suddenly at the end of the village where the road wound from the open green into a narrow lane there appeared two horses and a flash of scarlet. They were followed by more scarlet—soldiers on foot marching behind their officers. Serena gave a little gasp.

'Joker!' she said warningly.

He turned round and saw the men approaching. For a moment he hesitated and Serena knew he was contemplating instant flight; but as the little band approached, she saw that the horses of the officers were fresh and might easily prove speedier than Rufus'. Instinctively she knew what it was best to do.

'Go into the forge,' she said. 'Take Thunderbolt by the bridle.'

The Joker glanced at her and as swiftly as she had thought it he understood her plan. Thunderbolt had been tied by his bridle to the wall. He loosed the rein and stood at the horse's head speaking to him in soothing tones.

The band of soldiers came nearer. They drew up with a sharp word of command outside the forge. One of the officers, a dark man with bold eyes, stared at Serena and then, dismounting, walked up the pathway, swaggering a little arrogantly in his self-importance.

'Ho-there, smithy,' he called.

Ted gave four noisy blows with his hammer before he answered, then he raised his great head. There was insolence in his bearing even though his words were civil.

221

'Ye called me, sir?'

'I called you, fellow. Have you seen ought of a high-wayman? A gallows-dodger that goes by the name of the Joker?'

'How should Oi know him if Oi did see him?' Ted asked. 'No doubt he wears a mask o'er his phys?'

'Maybe, and maybe not,' the officer replied. ' 'Tis said he has accomplices in this neighbourhood. A middle-aged man I understand him to be, brutal looking and pock-marked, but with a ready jest for those from whom he thieves. Do you know of him?'

The blacksmith turned again to the horseshoe he was shaping.

'Nay,' he said. 'Oi've heard no talk of 'un in these parts.'

The officer peered into the shadows.

'Who is that with the horse?' he asked suspiciously.

Serena rose from the log.

'Sir,' she said imperiously. 'If you wish to question my groom, it would be more polite to beg my permission. I have urgent business in London and wish not to be delayed in pursuing my journey.'

The officer turned to look at her. Slowly, and almost reluctantly, he swept off his hat from his head.

'Your pardon, Ma'am. I did not know that 'twas your groom of whom I spoke.'

Serena inclined her head.

'I accept your apology, sir,' she said; 'but I would be vastly obliged if you would postpone your enquiries until the blacksmith has finished shoeing my horse. I am on business of the utmost importance.'

The officer scrutinised her. He missed nothing of the rich velvet habit, of her air of breeding and authority, and he noted too that Thunderbolt was no ordinary horse. He bowed.

'I will command my men to withdraw, Ma'am, until you have been served.'

'My thanks, sir,' Serena said, then turned from him as if in dismissal as coolly and as disdainfully as any great lady of fashion would have behaved in like circumstances.

Slightly put out, but unsuspicious, the officer went back to his troop. He gave the word for them to fall out and they withdrew to the shadow of a great oak tree on the green, propping their muskets against its trunk and throw-ing themselves down in the shade of its branches. As soon as they were out of earshot, Serena spoke to the blacksmith.

'How long will you be?'

'But a couple o' minutes,' he answered; 't' shoe is ready.'

He was as true as his word and in a few minutes Thunderbolt had been shod and the Joker led him out of the smithy, himself keeping on the side of the horse out of sight of the officers who had dismounted and were talking together but a few yards away. He offered Serena his knee and she mounted; then deliberately she wheeled Thunderbolt about so that he was between the highwayman's horse and the two officers. The Joker sprang into the saddle; Serena felt in her pocket and threw a guinea to the blacksmith who had come from the forge and was blinking in the sunlight. He caught it deftly, and then with their spurs on their horses' sides Serena and the Joker clattered away down the road. They did not dare look back and Serena held her breath, fearing at any moment that she would hear the hoofs of horses pursuing them or the sound of a musket shot.

They were half a mile away before she turned her head and smiled at the Joker. It was then she saw the beads of sweat upon his brow.

' 'Twas a near thing, lady,' he said, 'but you piked them on the beam.'

'They would have recognised you?' she asked.

'Nay,' he replied, 'but if you had not out-jockeyed them, they would have taken me for questioning. 'Tis not amusing to be questioned these days by the military.'

'Oh, sir, how can you bear such a life?' Serena asked.

' 'Tis better than dying of boredom' he replied. 'Weep not for me, lady, if you hear I am a-dangling at the rope's end.'

Serena shuddered.

'Do not speak of it.'

The Joker laughed.

'You are too squeamish, lady. It is a hard life, but me-thinks you also choose the hard way. You have a lonely journey in front of you.'

'Will you put me on the right road?' Serena asked.

'That I will,' he replied. 'But a quarter of a mile from here we strike the Dover road. Do not leave it again. 'Tis easy to lose your way and there are often unpleasant people about—highwaymen and the like.'

223

He laughed at his own joke. They hurried on, drawing rein only when the winding country lane opened on to a crossroad and a milestone told the distance both to London and to Dover. Serena reined in Thunderbolt and held out her hand.

'Methinks I am once again most deeply in your debt, Sir Joker.'

'Nay, this time 'tis for me to thank you,' he replied.

Their hands touched, but when he would have kissed her fingers Thunderbolt plunged around, startled by a few leaves blowing aimlessly across the road.

'God speed,' the highwayman cried, and Serena waved her whip in response as she cantered up the road.

She kept Thunderbolt on the grass beside the highway. He soon settled down into a long comfortable stride, seeming to enjoy the unexpected demands upon him and giving little trouble to Serena save when a stage-coach thundered by or a swift curricle made him plunge furiously as if he wished to turn and race the horse traveling in the opposite direction. Nothing passed them going northwards for they were travelling too fast to be overtaken.

After an hour or so Serena reined in the great horse and made him walk, proffering him water at a near-by stream on one occasion and at a village pond on another. But as if he sensed her own eagerness to arrive at her destination, he was interested in nothing but continuing their journey, seemingly fresh and untired, although Serena herself was beginning to feel stiff and her arms were aching. Thunderbolt had been by no means as difficult to ride as she had feared after his first headward rush when he had dragged her arms nearly out of their sockets, but he still taxed her strength by shying or prancing around at the least provocation.

She was beginning to feel almost overwhelmingly weary as the daylight faded and the sky became overcast. The warmth of the day had given way to a chill wind blowing from the east and presently Serena felt a spot of rain against her cheek. It was followed by another and yet another and soon they were battling their way against a storm.

There was no question of finding shelter nor did Serena wish to waste the time. There was only one thing to do and that was to plod on. Thunderbolt did not care for the rain and slowed his pace. They kept on the road now, the miles passing slowly as the rain drenched down, until Serena could feel it soaking through her velvet coat and trickling in small rivulets down her back.

And yet her physical discomfort did not equal the despondency of her mind. All day she had striven to keep her mind on the importance of her journey and had not let her anxiety over Justin take possession of her. Now in the rain and the gathering darkness and with Thunderbolt easier to manage, a spectre of what might have occurred loomed up to frighten her. Now she knew in all truth what she had admitted to herself earlier on, that she loved Justin.

It had taken the Joker's light words to dispel the pretence with which she had blinded herself. Now she admitted fully and unreservedly that she loved Justin with all the fibre of her being. She had known it, she thought, that day when he showed her the models and had asked, 'Shall I make you love me, Serena?'

She had fled from him then. Now she wished above all things that she had stayed. Had he been mocking her? Had he been merely jesting or had there been a deeper and more tender reason for his question? How she wished she knew the answer! How she longed to know if she mattered to him in any degree, even the smallest! She had shrunk from his anger last night and then he had carried her to her bed. What had he thought as she lay sobbing in his arms? She wished now that she had glanced upwards at his face, that she had read the expression in his eyes. If she had looked at him then, would she have known? Would something have told her the truth?

Humbly she told herself that it was too much to expect that he should love her; it was enough that she should interest him, that he should find her attractive. She thought of Isabel, vivacious and inviting, her crimson lips held up to Justin. If he were able to resist Isabel's blandishments, was it likely that he would care for her? What had she to offer? Little save an untouched heart and a love which seemed to her greater and more consuming than any love there had been since the beginning of time. She loved him, she loved his face, the handsome clear-cut features, the eyes steely as the sea must be in winter, the mouth firm and usually curved downwards cynically as if at some inner disappointment, yet sometimes wide with laughter—boyish and spontaneous.

She loved his shoulders, the great strength of his arms, his long thin aristocratic fingers. Yes, she loved him. How foolish she had been not to know it before, how crazy to have avoided him during those days and weeks at Mandrake rather than to have sought him out! Fool that she was! Was anything so bitter as a vision of what might have been?

It was dark now. Still Thunderbolt plodded onwards. Now the countryside seemed more populated. There was a house here and there, an uncurtained window warm with orange light, the sound of laughter and of joyful voices inside an inn. Still they went on. She felt that even Thunderbolt was tiring, annoyed with the beating rain and hoping perhaps that soon he would find the warmth and comfort of a stable and the consolation of a good meal.

Serena shivered. She was soaked to the skin and her fingers had become numb with cold. Had Thunderbolt set off now in the opposite direction, she would have been unable to prevent him.

London at last! The first streets, the first sound of a night watchman wandering over the cobbles with his lantern. 'Eight o'clock, gentlemen, and all's well.' So late! Serena had hoped that she would have been at Grosvenor Square before now. She stopped to ask her way of a watchman. He directed her and on they went again.

There were houses now on either side of the street, gutters running fast with the recent rainfall. They were coming into the more fashionable London. A coach rumbled by, a postillion in crimson astride one of a team of perfectly matched jet-black horses. A sedan chair with the crest as large as a saucer was preceded by a linkman in a livery of peacock green embroidered in silver.

Wearily Serena turned Thunderbolt into Park Lane. It was not much further now. There were lights and the sound of music coming from one of the great houses overlooking the park, powdered footmen were assisting the guests to alight on to a red carpet, and there was a row of carriages one behind the other.

On Serena went, thinking only of what she would find. Justin had fallen! The words repeated themselves over and over again in her mind and linked with them were the cries of the Marchioness, her screams echoing and re-echoing from the vastness of her curtained bed.

Grosvenor Square at last! And Vulcan House with its white pillars and high railings. She pulled Thunderbolt up outside the door. A linkman ran forward. Slowly, and half afraid that she would be unable to stand when she reached the ground, Serena dismounted.

'Take the horse round to the stables,' she said, and her voice was hoarse. ' 'Tis the property of his lordship, the Marquis, and must be attended to instantly.'

The linkman stared at her; and Serena knew he was wondering who she was, surprised at her appearance, damp and bedraggled, at this time of night.

She walked swiftly up the wide marble steps. The door was flung open, and light streamed out enveloping her. For a moment she was too dazzled to distinguish anything; then she saw that a butler was standing looking at her. With a tremendous effort she spoke to him.

'I have come from Mandrake. His lordship? Is he here?'

She could hardly bear to say more, could not put into words the question which mattered to her more than all else.

'Your name, Madam?'

'Miss Staverley.'

'Will you come this way?'

The butler preceded her. She followed him because it seemed to her that for the moment she had neither the will to question him nor to do anything but what was expected of her. She crossed the hall with its black and white marble squares like a giant chessboard. The butler flung open a huge mahogany door. Serena entered the room. It was a big room, brilliant with light, colourful, with embroidered curtains and furniture. She had an impression of gaiety, she heard voices and laughter which suddenly ceased as she entered. For a moment it was difficult to focus her eyes, then she heard the butler's voice boom:

'Miss Staverley, m'lord, from Mandrake.'

And then she saw him, saw Justin whom she had come so far to seek, saw the man whom she thought was dead or at least mortally wounded. He was sitting in a chair by the fireplace and his arm was in a sling, but he was laughing, and in his other hand he held a glass of wine.

There were several other men in the room. One was standing with his back to the fire and another was opposite Justin, his legs outstretched and an arm flung over the back of the chair nonchalantly. But next to Justin, sitting on a low stool beside him, one white hand resting on his knee, was a woman—a woman such as Serena had never seen before in the whole of her life.

227

Instinctively and insistently she took in every detail. She saw a lovely face, unusual in its beauty and unusual in its construction. She saw dark eyes under narrow winged eyebrows, dark hair powdered with specks of real gold, a gown also of gold cut so daringly low as to give the impression that the wearer was partially naked. She saw, too, a mouth curved in laughter; and she guessed without being told that it was some sally from these crimson lips which had caused Justin such merriment.

She took it all in. And she knew in that moment it was a picture that she would never forget. Then even as she saw Justin start to his feet, even as she heard his voice enunciate her name in astonishment and surprise, she felt the floor come up to meet her and a sudden darkness descend on her. As she fell, she knew with an agonising sense of despair that her ride—like her love for him—had been in vain.

Fifteen

SERENA awoke to find herself in a big green and gold bedroom which she had never seen before. For a moment she wondered wildly where she was, and then the door opened and Eudora came in.

'Eudora! Oh, Eudora!' Serena said, sitting up in bed and holding out her arms, and a moment later she felt the familiar roughness of Eudora's weathered cheek against her own. 'Where am I? What has happened? How did you get here?' The questions tumbled out of Serena's mouth one after another.

'It is all right, m'dearie,' Eudora answered, and Serena saw that there was a suspicion of tears in her eyes. 'I arrived late last night, passing late it was, and you were asleep.'

'Asleep?' Serena exclaimed. 'But . . . ? Oh, I remember now. I remember seeing . . .' She broke off suddenly. 'Everything went dark . . . I can remember nothing after that.'

'You fainted from exhaustion,' Eudora said. 'The housekeeper told me all about it. They carried you up to bed, and the doctor who was called in by his lordship prescribed a soothing draught for you. You drank it and you have not moved until this very moment.'

'Yes, I remember now. I remember drinking something. It was still dark and there were voices.'

'You were dead tired,' Eudora said. 'Oh, my little love, why did you do such a foolish thing, for foolish it was.'

'Foolish indeed,' Serena said slowly, and her voice was suddenly bitter. Then quickly, as if she would escape from her own thoughts, she added: 'But you have not told me how you came here. Oh, Eudora, I have never been so glad to see anyone.'

'I must fetch you your chocolate,' Eudora said, as if she suddenly remembered her duties, but Serena caught at her hand.

'Not until you have told me—all.'

Eudora smiled.

'After you had gone from Mandrake I started thinking and I 'collected, poor cork-brain that I am, that I should never have allowed you to go chasing off on such a wild scheme, but 'twas too late. I ran down to the stableyard and was told by the head groom that you had been gone nearly a quarter of an hour. Gloomy as a gravestone he was, too, swearing that monstrous horse of his lordship's would be the death of you. The things he said made my very heart come up into my mouth, and I hurried back to the house in search of his lordship's own man. I was not a minute too soon, either, for there he was with his lordship's valise packed and leaving on the instant in a phaeton for London.

' "His lordship will be needing me," he says, and I replies to him, "And what about my lady? She will be needing me too. Take me with you if there is a drop of God's mercy in your veins." Well, Miss Serena, he gave me five minutes, five minutes by his timepiece to get ready. I throws your gowns just as they were into a small trunk and I was there on the doorstep beside him when the phaeton comes round.

'We should have been in London sooner, but we were delayed at one of the posting houses. Slow as snails they were and all that we could say and not even the gold his lordship's man offered them would make them hurry with the changing of the horses. I was nearly crying with impatience when we got here, and thankful I was to find that nothing worse had happened than that you were safe in bed.'

'Yes, I was safe in bed,' Serena repeated.

Then she lay back against her pillows.

'Now let me cease my plattering and attend to you,' Eudora said. ' 'Tis something to eat and drink that you are needing. I will not be a moment longer than I can help and the housekeeper is a vastly obliging woman, I will say that for her.'

Eudora hurried from the room. Serena lay still, looking around her, but with listless eyes. Now the whole events of the evening returned to her, the fatigue, the misery of the last part of her journey, the feeling of cold, being soaked to the skin and dishevelled as she dismounted at Grosvenor Square, and then . . . yes, then she saw again, clearly as if it were painted on the wall, the picture that had met her eyes as she was announced to Justin and his friends.

Never, she felt, would she be able to forget the exotic beauty of the woman sitting beside him. She could still see those wide-set eyes, the enticing curve of that laughing mouth. Serena drew a deep breath. She knew now who the woman was. She had heard Nicholas speak of her two weeks ago at Staverley; she had listened to Isabel deride her bitterly and with spiteful jealousy. *La Flamme!* It was she, of course, and it was understandable how her beauty had made her the toast of St. James's. The bucks had flocked to Vauxall Gardens to see her dance, and Justin had taken her under his protection.

Serena shivered and felt suddenly cold; then turning over with a little convulsive movement she hid her face in the pillow. Why not be honest with herself, why not admit that she, too, was jealous, madly, crazily jealous? She loved Justin, and he . . . well, he had *La Flamme*.

In a few moments Eudora came back with a dainty tray set with silver dishes. To please her Serena made a show of eating, but she felt that every mouthful must choke her. Then, while she was still making a pretence under Eudora's watchful eye, there came a knock at the door. Eudora went to open it. Serena, listening, heard a voice say:

'His lordship's compliments, and he would be greatly obliged if Miss Staverley would hold converse with him as soon as it is convenient in the morning-room.'

Eudora came to the bedside and repeated the message. Serena's eyes were suddenly bright.

'Tell his lordship I will be with him as soon as I am attired,' she replied, and as Eudora went to give the message, she sprang from the bed.

Serena had never taken long to dress herself, and this morning she was unusually swift. How thankful she was that Eudora had had the sense to bring some gowns with her! There was a new white dimity with an entrancingly demure fichu at the neck, and with it went a blue sash and blue slippers. The clock in the hall was only striking the eleventh hour as Serena came from her room and walked down the wide staircase.

A footman flung open the door of the morning-room. Justin rose as she entered. His arm was in a sling, but he contrived to be amazingly immaculate. He raised her fingers to his lips.

'Your servant, Serena.'

Somehow it was impossible for her to say anything, try as she would, and after a moment he added:

'You are rested? I was vastly troubled over your health last night.'

'I can only apologise for my most unseemly weakness,' Serena answered.

She tried so hard to keep her voice steady, but it sounded tremulous, a little faint.

'You should certainly not apologise for what was an amazing feat,' Justin replied. 'To have ridden here all the way from Mandrake was in itself no mean achievement, but to have ridden Thunderbolt was a miracle.'

'He carried me well,' Serena said quietly. 'He is none the worse?'

Justin shook his head.

'I have just been out to see him in the stables. He is in fine fettle. A little extra exercise has been no hardship to him. But you? You are certain that you are not indisposed?'

'Quite certain,' Serena answered.

She found it hard to look at him as she spoke. Her heart was beating almost suffocatingly, and she was afraid, desperately afraid, that he would read her secret in her eyes. She steeled herself to speak slowly and with a distinct coldness. Not for a moment must she forget that it was *La Flamme* who interested Justin, and that she must never, never humiliate herself by letting him know how much he mattered to her.

'Won't you sit down, Serena?' Justin asked. He hesitated for a moment and then he added, 'I wish to speak with you.'

She obeyed him, choosing a rather stiff, upright chair, and sitting with her back straight, her hands clasped together in her lap as if she were a child attending to a lesson. She fancied there was a faint smile at the corner of Justin's lips as he looked at her; but when he spoke, his voice was grave.

'Serena . . .' he began, 'I deeply appreciate your action in coming here last night. I have learned from my valet that one of my grooms, a silly, excitable fellow, rushed to Mandrake after he had seen me bowled over by the shot fired from Lord Wrotham's pistol. It was the blast that caught me, the bullet itself has made but a faint flesh wound in my arm. I turned, hearing the referee shout, and as I did

232

so, a flash from the pistol caught me off my balance. Perhaps it was as well that it did or I might have been more seriously injured.'

'It was a monstrous action,' Serena said, 'and . . . what happened to . . . his lordship?'

'Lord Wrotham has, I understand, left for Holland,' Justin replied. 'If he returns, he will doubtless retire to his country seat. St. James's will know him no longer.'

'Oh, I am glad.'

Serena's voice was a little breathless.

He will not trouble you again,' Justin said; 'but unfortunately the consequences of his crime are far-reaching.'

'What do you mean?' Serena enquired.

'I mean,' Justin continued, 'that his lordship's ill-considered treachery and Jansen's impulsiveness were responsible for bringing you to London. A brave action, Serena, and one which I commend in all humbleness. At the same time you forgot that I am living here as a bachelor.'

He paused ror a moment as if to let his meaning sink in, and now Serena raised her eyes.

'I . . . do not understand,' she said.

'You stayed here last night,' Justin said very gently, as if explaining something to a small child. 'It was impossible to make any other arrangements at so late an hour. Besides, when you arrived I was entertaining some friends —gentlemen friends of my acquaintance. The story of your arrival, of your resolution in coming unattended from Mandrake, will by now be the talk of the Clubs. It is impossible, as you well know, to prevent people talking.'

'You mean,' Serena said, 'that I should not have come?'

'I mean nothing of the sort,' Justin said firmly. 'What I am trying to tell you is that your arrival, courageous, if a little unexpected, merely necessitates us moving a trifle more swiftly than we have been inclined to do these past weeks. In short, Serena, it is time that we made haste to settle our lives, yours and mine.'

Serena's hands moved convulsively from her lap to her breast.

'You mean . . . ?' she faltered.

'That I have made arrangements for our marriage to take place immediately,' Justin said. 'I have procured a special license and the Vicar of St. George's Church in Hanover Square is waiting for us.'

Serena sprang to her feet. Her face was suddenly drained

of all colour; then as she stared at Justin he reached out his hand and took her fingers gently in his.

'I have the very great honour, Serena,' he said quietly, 'to ask you to become my wife.'

For a moment her fingers quivered in his as if she would snatch them from him, and then she was very still. It seemed to her as if her heart was beating so hard that it must burst through the confines of her body. At the same time she felt dazed, too dazed to reply, too bewildered to do anything but stand there with her hand in his, her face turned aside so that he should not see her eyes.

'Well, Serena?'

His voice was low, and yet she somehow sensed that he was impatient.

'It . . . it shall be . . . as you desire, m'lord,' she answered.

She felt his fingers suddenly tighten on hers, was conscious of the strength of him and of that strange magnetism which she had known before, compelling her against her will to raise her eyes to his, but even as she resisted him, even as she fought against something invisible and unspoken, the door of the room opened.

Instantly Justin's hand released hers, and she was free.

'Sir Peter Burley, m'lord,' the butler announced.

Sir Peter, dressed exquisitely in a coat of bottle green, came into the room.

'Justin, dear fellow, I hope I am not late,' he said; 'that clumsy manservant of mine was as fat-fingered as hell with my neck-cloth this morning.'

He crossed the room to Serena's side, lifting her fingers to his lips.

'Your servant, Miss Staverley.'

'I am glad to see you, Peter,' Justin said, and turning to Serena, he added, 'Sir Peter has promised to act in the capacity of best man at our marriage.'

It was with difficulty that Serena prevented herself from giving a cry. It was too much for Justin to speak openly of their marriage as if it were something which had been arranged for some time. As if he sensed her discomfiture, Justin said quietly:

'We shall be leaving in a few minutes for the church.'

Serena murmured something incoherent and sped from the room. She ran up the flight of stairs and burst into her own bedroom. Eudora was tidying away her clothes.

Serena flung her arms round her and half laughing, half sobbing, said:

'Oh, Eudora, I am to be married. I am leaving now, this minute, for the church. What shall I do? How can I bear it?'

'I know, dearie,' Eudora said. 'His lordship's valet told me that his lordship had gone off early this morning to obtain a licence.'

'You knew?' Serena gasped, 'and you did not tell me?'

'No, dearie, it was for his lordship to do that. But oh, Miss Serena, I am glad for you. His lordship is a fine man and a decent one, for all that there are those who say the contrary. You will be happy with him, I am sure of that. I was blind with hate when we went to Mandrake, but since we have been there I have learned many things. Her ladyship is as bad as can be, but his lordship is a different story. He will look after you, my little dear, and you need not be afraid of him.'

'Afraid of him!'

Serena whispered the words and turned away towards the dressing-table. How could she explain to anyone, even Eudora, that she loved Justin, loved him so desperately that it was agony to be beside him, agony to know that he did not love her? She could but remember that woman's hand on his knee, see the rounded loveliness of her throat as she flung back her head to look up into his eyes.

Serena drew a deep breath. The only thing left for her was pride, she still had that. Whatever happened, she would never let him know, never reveal what lay within her heart until the day came—if come it ever did—when he loved her too. One thing she would never ask of him was pity. That would be too much to bear. If they were married, maybe he would learn to care for her, maybe as time went by she would become necessary to him.

She remembered how Lord Wrotham had said that he was bored with love; she vowed that she would never risk boring Justin with her love. If he wanted it, he must seek it.

As she looked at herself in the mirror, Serena instinctively straightened her shoulders and raised her chin a little. The strenuous events of yesterday had left no mark upon her beauty. Her eyes were a little tired, perhaps, and she was paler than usual, but the pallor was peculiarly becoming, especially in a bride. Eudora re-arranged her

235

fair curls and fetched from the cupboard a bonnet of chip straw, trimmed with blue ribbons and three azure blue feathers. Serena tied the ribbons under her chin, and taking her handkerchief, stood up for Eudora's inspection.

'You're lovely,' Eudora exclaimed. 'Lovely, my sweet dear . . . my child whom I have loved since you were but a tiny babe.'

'Oh, Eudora!'

Serena put her arms round the little woman, felt tears shake her body and turned away to hide her own. There was no time to say more, there was no time to cry. As she reached the door, she heard Eudora call.

'Good luck! . . . God bless you now and always.'

Eudora's lips were smiling, although her eyes were blinded with tears.

Serena came down the stairs. Justin and Sir Peter were waiting for her in the hall. Outside in the square she could see the big claret and silver coach drawn by a pair of perfectly matched white horses. Justin offered Serena his arm; she placed the tips of her fingers on it and he led her from the house. They sat side by side on the claret satin seat of the coach, and Sir Peter sat opposite them.

' 'Tis only a short distance,' Sir Peter remarked.

The footman closed the door and sprang up behind.

'Will you carry these?' Justin said quietly to Serena, taking from the seat beside Sir Peter a bouquet of white flowers.

There were roses, orchids, and lilies-of-the-valley. Serena raised them to her face.

'How beautiful!' she exclaimed. 'Thank you.'

'And they are as fresh and fragrant as the bride herself,' Sir Peter said gallantly.

Serena smiled at him.

'I have no words to answer such flattery, Sir Peter.'

'There's not flattery but truth in what I say,' Sir Peter protested. 'It would be impossible to draw too long a bow, eh, Justin?'

But Justin did not answer. Yet Serena knew that he was watching her and she felt her cheeks flush, so that to hide her confusion she bent her head low over the flowers. He said nothing until they arrived at St. George's Church. The coach drew up and the footman opened the door. Sir Peter alighted first. Serena would have followed him, but as she moved, her eyes looked into Justin's and were held. They both were very still for a long second, and then he said:

'It is not too late if you would rather draw back.'

She felt her pulses throb suddenly. At this eleventh hour was it his desire to be rid of her? Then she saw that there was consideration in the expression on his face and an unexpected gentleness in his eyes. There was something else too, but of that she did not dare to think.

'Draw back?' she repeated, realising that he was waiting for her answer.

He made a sudden movement.

'No, no,' he said, almost as if he spoke to himself rather than to her. 'It was but a passing thought.'

They alighted from the coach. At the door of the church the priest was waiting for them. It seemed to Serena from that moment as if she were made of ice, incapable of all feeling. Someone else, someone who wore her body yet was not herself made the responses, held out her hand to Justin, felt him place the ring on her finger. Someone else, cool, detached and utterly composed, went from the grey sanctity of the church to the vestry and signed the register; someone equally at ease placed her hand on Justin's arm and was led from the church and back to the waiting coach.

It was only when once more the three of them were travelling back to Grosvenor Square that she became alive again. The numb feeling passed, the composure which had carried her through serenely and without any inner disturbance began to evaporate. Now she was conscious once again of the thumping of her heart, of something quivering and sensitive within herself. She was afraid and yet enchanted.

She did not speak to Justin on the homeward journey. Sir Peter chattered gaily. Serena made no attempt to listen to what he said, and was well aware that he thought her silence was due to a becoming shyness.

In Vulcan House the servants were lined up in the hall to greet them. The butler, slow, pompous, and unassailably dignified, was the spokesman.

'On behalf of the staff, my lord, may I offer your lordship our most hearty congratulations and add our heartfelt good wishes for her ladyship's and your own long and continued happiness.'

Justin thanked them in a few appropriate words; then he and Serena shook hands with all the servants from the housekeeper, in her stiff black silk dress, down to the goggle-eyed pantry boys and the scullery maids who giggled a little from sheer nerves.

Wine and sweet cakes were waiting for them in the library. Sir Peter toasted them both, and again Justin replied; then luncheon was served and they all three lunched together. Surprisingly Serena found herself laughing and unexpectedly at ease.

'If only Gilly were here,' Sir Peter said. 'He will be as mad as fire at missing your wedding, Justin.'

Serena gave a little start. There was someone else, too, who would be angry. Isabel! What would she say when she heard the news? She glanced apprehensively at Justin, but he was smiling at Sir Peter and apparently he, too, had forgotten Isabel.

When luncheon was over, Sir Peter made his farewells. Then at last they were alone. Serena was acutely conscious of how alone they were as the morning-room door closed and Justin rose from the chair on which he had been sitting and stood in front of the fireplace.

There was a moment's silence, a long moment it seemed to Serena, and then he spoke:

'I am expecting the doctor in a few minutes. After he has gone, we can discuss our plans for the future. As a bride you are entitled to a honeymoon, you know.'

There was something in the way he said the words that brought the blood to Serena's cheeks, and then, even as she would have spoken, the butler opened the door and announced that the doctor had arrived.

'You will excuse me,' Justin said with a little bow.

He was gone and she was alone. Yes, alone, as she had never been before. She knew that now, knew, as she sat with her hands to her eyes, that this was a loneliness such as she had never known before. Far worse than the loneliness she had experienced when she had left Staverley, worse than anything for which her life to date had prepared her. To love and to be alone in one's loving was indeed to know a solitude and a desolation beyond words.

She walked to the window. A beggar outside had a tiny monkey attached to him by a chain. The monkey jumped on to the pavement and held out its small brown wizened hand to passers-by. Two men passed without even glancing at it and the beggar jerked the chain impatiently. The monkey, chattering, sprang back on to his shoulder.

Serena watched; but though her eyes saw what was

going on, her mind was otherwise preoccupied. It was a warm and sultry day, yet dull, but now a shaft of sunshine came through the low clouds and shone on the garden in the square, on the shivering under-fed monkey and his ragged master, and in at the windows of Vulcan House. It touched Serena's fair hair, transforming it for a moment into living gold, then glinted on a ring which encircled the third finger of her left hand.

She caught the gleam of it and as it attracted her attention she took her hand from the curtain and turned back into the room. Her eyes were drawn almost as if it were against her will to the narrow band of gold. She stared at it for a long moment before she made a strangled sound which was almost a sob in her throat.

Uneasily she glanced towards the end of the room where there were big double mahogany doors. They were closed, but through them she could hear the murmur of voices. She stood for a moment listening, then she sat down in a chair. She tried to force herself to be calm, to steel the restlessness of her fast-beating heart, which made her afraid to think, afraid even to contemplate all that the ring—plain and ungarish as it was—meant.

Instinctively she put both her hands up to her face; then feeling the coolness of the precious metal against her cheek she started away from it as if it were something dangerous. She stared at her hand again. She half contemplated pulling the ring from her finger, but as her right hand went out to touch it she knew such an action was merely childish. Jumping to her feet, she walked across the room and back again, then she went to the window.

The beggar with his monkey was still there. He had been joined by another man now—an ex-soldier, in a tattered, dirty uniform, a black patch over his left eye and a stump of wood where his right leg should have been. The men were arguing, and it seemed likely that at any moment a quarrel would break out between them. Indifferently Serena turned from the window.

How long the doctor was! She wanted him to be finished so that she could speak with Justin, and yet . . . yet she shrank from the very idea. Justin—who was now her husband! The thought was impossible, and yet it had happened. How little she had imagined yesterday that to-day she would be wearing his ring, would be entitled to bear his name.

Once again Serena's hands crept up to her face and now

they stayed there, her fingers over her closed eyes. Yes, she was entitled to bear Justin's name, but how little it altered the great gulf yawning between them.

Hearing the deep tones of Justin's voice in the next room even though she could not distinguish what he said, she felt a sudden wild desire to rush to him, to fling herself on her knees before him and to tell him all that was in her heart. She almost heard her own words tumbling over themselves, felt them warm and pulsating with the yearning that was within her. Probably he would put his arm round her and lift her a little so that her head would rest on his shoulder as it had done once before. She felt her whole body quiver at the thought of his hands, of the strength of his arms, of his lips. . . .

Suddenly Serena sprang to her feet. She must not think like this, she must control her body, control the aching desire in every limb which cried aloud for Justin. . . .

She walked about the room again, and yet nothing could still the fever within her. She knew then in that moment that something must be done, something desperate, something which would prevent her doing in reality what she had imagined so wildly. She knew now that her love was beyond her control! If he touched her, if . . .

Her white teeth bit into her lip. It would be impossible then not to cry out, not to reveal how much she adored him. Oh God, fool that she was, to imagine for one moment that she could keep such a secret hidden. She tried to lash herself with the thought of *La Flamme*, to recall all too vividly the beauty of the woman whom Justin had chosen; but even while such thoughts hurt her, she knew that when the moment came she would be capable of remembering nothing but the weakness of her own flesh, the overwhelming strength of her own desire.

'I must escape,' she thought wildly. 'I must leave him! I cannot stay here!'

But even as she thought such things, the door opened and Justin came in.

' 'Tis good news,' he said smiling, 'the doctor is pleased with me. The flesh has knit and I need only keep a bandage on it. The sling is dispensed with.'

'I am glad,' Serena said, 'very glad.'

Her voice was small and breathless, but Justin seemed not to notice. He walked across the room to stand beside her.

'So now,' he said quietly, 'we can make our plans—you and I.'

Serena quivered and then was very still.

'Shall we stay here?' Justin asked. 'Shall we go to Bath? Or is there any other place that you would prefer?' Still she did not answer and after a moment he said very gently, 'I thought maybe you would like to visit Staverley.'

It was then she gave a cry, a cry that to her own ears was not far from tears.

'No, no, not . . . not Staverley.'

'Then not Staverley,' Justin said gravely.

'I . . . I think I . . . would . . . return to Mandrake,' Serena said wildly, feeling that she must say something and conscious of being caught in some trap from which there seemed no way out.

'To Mandrake?' Justin said in surprise, and then added: 'But of course—if you wish it. We go together, you know—together.'

It was then that Serena moved away from him, moved to the window, conscious of some relief in being away from his compelling nearness even though it were but half the length of the room.

'There is no need for us to go together,' she said in a muffled voice. 'I perfectly understand the situation . . . and your chivalry; but there is no need to keep up the pretence when we are alone.'

A silence followed her words, a silence so pregnant that it was with the utmost difficulty that she prevented herself from turning round. And when at length he spoke there was a hint of amusement in his voice.

'Who is talking of pretence, Serena?'

'I am,' Serena said quickly. 'Can we not be frank with each other?' she asked, and now she turned again to face him. 'My lord,' she said, 'you have married me and I am, in the eyes of the world, your wife; but let us not forget the conditions under which we came to know each other. You won me at a game of cards, and I have paid my father's debt. Furthermore, last night I foolishly dug a pit for my own destruction. I came here unchaperoned, unattended, and you have been good enough to save my reputation. Duty is satisfied on both sides, my lord—no more is required of us.'

As she finished speaking Serena saw that Justin was smiling, and now without moving from his position in front of the mantelpiece, he said:

'Come here, Serena.'

His voice was low and deep, and somehow in spite of its command, caressing. For a moment she almost obeyed him instinctively, and then quickly, because she was so afraid of her own desire to go to him, she answered:

'No!'

'No?' he questioned, raising his eyebrows, 'and you have but a few minutes ago promised to obey me.'

'What do you want of me?' Serena asked.

'Come here and I will show you,' he answered.

But she dare not, and her hands hanging loose at her sides clenched together suddenly in the folds of her white dress so that the nails bit deep into the palms.

'Serena,' Justin said, 'I told you to come here. I want you.'

Very, very slowly she moved towards him, knowing that with every step she was walking towards her own betrayal, knowing that her heart was beating suffocatingly, that her lips were dry. He was waiting for her. There was a light in his eyes that she had seen once before. His mouth was no longer cynical and downturned, it was curved in a secret smile, and then suddenly as she came within but a few feet of him and it seemed to her as if in very weakness she would run the last few steps and throw herself into his arms, pride came to her rescue. Wildly her brain seeking for an avenue of escape found one and clung to it.

She stopped a few feet away from him behind a chair, holding on to it for support.

'I have something to tell you, my lord,' she said in a low voice.

'Yes?'

His voice was suddenly sharp as if he sensed her change of mood.

'You asked me once,' Serena said, her words tumbling over each other, 'you asked me if I was . . . in love. I told you that I was not. It was the truth at the time, but now . . . things have changed. I . . .'

Her voice died away.

'You are trying to tell me that you . . . you love someone,' Justin said, and there was a question in his voice as if he hardly believed such a thing were possible.

'Yes,' Serena answered, 'I love someone.'

'Who is it?' Justin snapped, and then quickly covered the words. 'Your pardon, I should not presume such a question. You tell me that you are in love. This is a new state of affairs, surely?'

'Yes, my lord, quite new.'

'It has but recently happened?'

'Yes, recently.'

Justin suddenly strode across the room to the window. Serena raised her eyes and watched him go, then she turned her head because she dare not look at him again.

Justin stood looking out of the window. Outside the beggars were still arguing, but he did not appear to notice them. After a moment he said:

'I had no idea. It is Gilly, I suppose, but I will not question you. I understand now your reluctance to visit Staverley.'

Serena swallowed a sob in her throat. Could anything be more near to heaven than to be at Staverley with Justin if he did not care for her? To show him the places where she had played as a child, the trees and bushes she had made especially her own, the rooms where she had dreamt happy dreams, to wander down to the lakeside, to stroll through the woods and hear the pigeons cooing . . . Oh, to be at Staverley with Justin—a Justin who loved her!

'What then would you wish to do?' came the voice from the window, and this time the voice had no caressing note in it, but one of harshness.

'I would like . . . to return to Mandrake,' Serena repeated.

It was somehow the only place she could think of where she would not be alone. It was the only place which seemed at the moment a kind of refuge because of the many people who were there, because of the chances it afforded of escaping further intimacy with . . . the man she loved.

'It shall be as you wish,' Justin said abruptly. 'I will order the coach. Your maid can travel with you, and I will come down a trifle later this evening in my curricle. Is that as you desire it?'

'Yes . . . and thank you.'

Serena's voice was faint. This ordeal had taxed her more than she would have believed possible.

Justin turned from the window. He walked across the room to face Serena where she stood still holding on to the chair. As he faced her, she looked up, and he thought for the moment of some wild creature who had been trapped and who had prayed for death as much as for freedom. He looked down into her face and his eyes were cold and grey.

'You little fool,' he said slowly, 'why didn't you tell me this before?'

It was as if his bitterness and his anger were too much for Serena. She had suffered so much that this was the last straw. She gave a little convulsive cry and turning, ran from the room. As she fled across the hall and up the stairs, she thought she heard Justin's voice call her name; but she was not sure, and anyway, she was consumed only by a desire to get away from him.

She reached her own room and slamming the door behind her, flung herself face downwards, on the bed and lay there trembling.

Sixteen

'I'LL BET a monkey we have to endure a thunder-storm before nightfall,' Lord Gillingham said, staring out over the sea from the windows of the Orangery.

' 'Tis too hot to bet, too hot to be anything but odiously unpleasant,' Isabel replied.

She was seated in a low, cushioned chair in front of an open french window which led down on to the green lawns. The Orangery was one of the most beautiful pieces of architecture in Mandrake. It had been built in the reign of Queen Anne and its designer had arranged that the windows, opening on one side to the sea and on the other to the lawns, should give one the illusion of being afloat in a boat filled with fresh greenery and golden fruit.

In the centre of the Orangery there was a tiny fountain, and the water made a rhythmic tinkle as it played into a shallow pool where fish swam amongst the waxen petals of the water lilies.

'The ground is badly in need of rain,' Lord Gillingham remarked.

Isabel picked up a painted fan and used it languidly.

'Can you talk of naught but the weather, Gilly?' she asked crossly.

The Marchioness, who had been sitting in another chair with her eyes closed, got to her feet.

'I was fool enough to say I would not be "at home" to-night,' she remarked, addressing herself neither to Isabel nor to Gilly, nor yet to Nicholas who, leaning against the wall, was watching Isabel with brooding eyes.

There was a moment's pause and then quickly, as if she feared their silence was impolite, Isabel said:

'Now that you have learnt that Justin is not seriously wounded, Ma'am, it would be easy to send your friends word that you will be pleased to entertain them.'

The Marchioness moved towards the window. She stood still for a moment looking out. A light wind from the sea blew her dress of finely embroidered muslin tight against her figure.

'But am I pleased?' she asked. 'Do I really wish to see them? Those chattering, bird-witted persons whom I am mistaken enough to speak of as friends?'

There was raw misery in the Marchioness's voice, and Isabel rose from her chair.

'You are depressed, Ma'am,' she said softly; 'would you not be wise to rest a little? The events of yesterday have upset you and in very truth it is not surprising.'

The Marchioness put her hand to her forehead.

'Yes, yes, I am upset,' she said. 'I will go to my room. And yet there . . . yes, there . . . I shall be alone . . . alone with my thoughts.'

She spoke wildly, her voice so desperate that both Nicholas and Gilly looked startled and then embarrassed.

'Oh, but, Ma'am . . .' Isabel began, but before she could complete her sentence the Marchioness had turned abruptly away and passing swiftly down the length of the Orangery, she went into the house.

All three of her guests watched her until she was out of sight; then Isabel gave an exclamation of astonishment.

'What ails her?'

'I fear she is indisposed,' Gilly answered. 'She was remarkably strange last night. I thought just now as she walked away that she was like some wild animal in captivity—in fact she reminded me of a caged tiger.'

Isabel laughed.

'Oh, lud, Gilly, you are growing imaginative! But 'tis true, the Marchioness has not been herself of late. What think you, Nicholas?'

'It is Lord Vulcan's fault,' Nicholas answered sullenly. 'That stupid stable-boy bringing the news that he was dead or mortally wounded would have distressed any mother.'

'I was deeply grieved for the Marchioness,' Isabel agreed. 'And I should have been vastly disturbed myself had I not awoken only after the crisis was passed and good news had been received.'

'That is so like you, Isabel,' Gilly said. 'You save yourself from every possible fidget. And that reminds me, has anything been heard of Serena?'

'No,' Isabel replied. 'And I am mad as fire with myself for not having accompanied her when she set out for London. Had she but informed me of her intention, I would, of course, have gone with her.'

'But not on a horse,' Gilly said with brotherly sarcasm. 'Your ladyship would undoubtedly have travelled in comfort!'

'Had I thought like Serena that Justin was in danger,' Isabel retorted, 'I would have gone to him by the swiftest way available, whatever the discomfort to my person.'

Nicholas moved suddenly and walking to the window stared out. It was obvious that he was in a sullen mood and that Isabel's talk of Justin did not improve his temper. Isabel looked at him and her eyes twinkled mischievously.

'If I had been awake when the news came, I would have sped to Justin in a fast curricle. You would have driven me, wouldn't you, Nicholas?'

There was a moment's pause before he answered, and as he turned round his eyes were dark.

'No, I would not,' he replied in a voice so deep with anger that Isabel's eyebrows rose a little in astonishment.

'La, how ungallant of you, Nicholas,' she exclaimed. 'Perhaps Serena was wise in that she went off on her chase unchaperoned save by a groom.'

Nicholas looked even angrier.

'It was a most regrettable action on the part of my cousin,' he said stiffly. 'I would never have expected her to do such a wild and thoughtless thing. I can only hope that you, Isabel and Gilly, will not allow the story of her indiscretion to spread further.'

Nicholas spoke with so much dignity that even Isabel was impressed.

'Good heavens, Nicholas,' she said, 'is it likely that Gilly or I would chatter maliciously of Serena? I love the girl, I swear it, though I vow it was a most unfriendly action on her part not to have taken me into her confidence. I . . .'

She was about to say more when she saw that the Marchioness was approaching them. She came back down the Orangery, still with a wild, haunted look upon her face, and flung herself down in the chair she had but recently vacated.

' 'Tis oven-hot in the house,' she said after a moment, as if she suddenly realised that some explanation of her return might be expected of her. 'I declare that even the Great Hall is like unto purgatory. There is more air here than elsewhere.'

'Could not the footmen bring you a couch, Ma'am?' Isabel suggested. 'If they put it in the open window and we withdrew you might sleep and wake refreshed.'

'Sleep!' the Marchioness exclaimed. 'No, Isabel, I could not sleep . . . my brain feels as if it is on fire . . . there is something strange within my head. . . a monstrous queer feeling and one . . . one which I cannot explain.'

Isabel glanced at Nicholas as if for help, but he was silent and after a moment she said timidly:

'Won't you let me escort you to your bedchamber, Ma'am? I know it is wise that you should take some rest.'

'No, no,' the Marchioness exclaimed almost frantically, 'I cannot, I tell you, I cannot!'

There was the sound of footsteps and all four people turned their heads in the direction of the sound. It was only a lackey bearing a silver salver, but they were silent as he approached the Marchioness and, bowing low, proffered the salver on which lay a note.

The Marchioness sat up suddenly in her chair.

' 'Tis from Justin himself!' she cried. 'When did this arrive?'

'A groom brought it from Grosvenor Square, m'lady. He arrived but a few minutes past.'

The Marchioness took the note, staring for a moment at the writing as if she had never seen it before.

'Oh, do open it, Ma'am,' Isabel said impatiently. 'I long to hear how Justin is, and he may tell us if Serena has reached London in safety.'

'Serena!' the Marchioness repeated the name and her voice held a snarling note. Then very slowly as if it were difficult for her to control her long white fingers, she opened the letter.

Isabel bent forward in her chair, her eyes bright with eagerness and curiosity. Even Nicholas' sullenness lifted for a moment and he drew a little nearer as if he were afraid he might miss what was being said.

The Marchioness read the note slowly. After a second or so she blinked as if it were hard to focus her eyes on the words. Her three guests watched her face. They saw her eyes widen, they perceived that she took a deep breath and then suddenly she sprang to her feet, crumpling the note in her hand and holding it away from her as if it were something vile.

'No,' she cried. 'It cannot be true, it cannot.'

'What, Ma'am? What is it?'

' 'Tis untrue! A monstrous untruth!' the Marchioness cried, trembling all over.

'What has happened, Ma'am? Please tell us,' Isabel said

agitatedly. 'I pray you not to keep us in suspense. Is it Justin?'

The Marchioness, still with her hand held straight in front of her, replied, 'Yes, it is Justin.'

The words seemed to come with difficulty from between her lips, and then suddenly spitting out her words so that both Isabel and Nicholas moved back a pace in alarm, she said: 'He is wed! Justin is wed!'

'Wed?'

Isabel echoed the word hardly above a whisper.

'But to whom?' Gilly enquired.

It was the first time he had spoken and now the Marchioness turned to face him. He thought in that moment that he had never seen a face more contorted.

'To whom but that scheming, sly-faced chit whom he brought here but a few weeks past.'

'To Serena? My cousin?'

It was Nicholas who spoke now.

'Yes, to Serena,' the Marchioness hissed, and then sharply. 'Out of my way! I wish to retire!'

She pushed past Nicholas and went hurrying down the Orangery, swaying as she walked a little unsteadily so that Lord Gillingham cried:

'She is about to have the vapours, I swear it. I will go with her and put her in charge of her maid.'

He sped after the Marchioness, leaving Isabel and Nicholas standing as if petrified to the very floor on which they stood. It was Nicholas who spoke first.

'Isabel!'

She rounded on him immediately, her eyes sparkling with anger, a patch of colour coming into both her cheeks.

'Don't Isabel me! This is pleasant news indeed, very pleasant! So Justin is married—and to your cousin. Doubtless you are relieved and delighted, no doubt you even contrived it, pretending to us that you had no knowledge of her movements, but all the time assisting her in her wild flight to be at his side. A pretty story, a very pretty one, and one which speaks unpleasantly of intrigue.'

Isabel suddenly threw the fan that she held in her hand to the floor. Its ivory sticks smashed against the marble, but she did not even glance at the damage she had done. Instead she walked to the window facing the sea and stood looking down on the sharp rocks far below them.

'Isabel, I beg of you,' Nicholas said quietly. His face had grown very pale while she attacked him.

'Beg what of me?' Isabel asked. 'Faugh! I am sick and tired of your begging, that I promise you. I at least thought you were honourable—you and Serena—and what do I get in return for my trust? The bite of a serpent! Serena pretended to be my friend. She knew I loved Justin, I told her so often enough, and she vowed—yes vowed to me that she had no personal interest in him and was but bound to him by a debt of honour incurred by her father. So much for Serena! And you . . . you have—' Isabel obviously sought for words—'You have bored me with your pleadings and your beggings, with your continual whining of unrequited love while contriving with Serena to wed her to Justin. How foolish you have made me appear! Justin is married and there is naught that any of us can do about it save . . .'

Isabel paused and leant a little further out of the window.

'I have a mind,' she said wildly, 'to throw myself from the window on to the rocks below. 'Twould be a fitting wedding present for the returning bride and groom—the broken body of a woman who had presumed to love him too much.'

'Isabel, I beg of you,' Nicholas said, moving forward apprehensively.

'Beg of me! There you go again,' Isabel said, and throwing back her head she laughed a little hysterically. 'It is funny, you beg of me and I beg of Justin, but in vain. 'Tis better that I should die than live without him, for there are not two men like him in all the world.'

Again she leant dangerously out of the window and this time Nicholas moved forward and took her by the shoulders. He pulled her back into the Orangery, his face white, for he had been seriously frightened by her action.

'Will you have a care for yourself?'

Isabel struggled against his restraining hands.

'Let me go,' she said furiously, 'how dare you touch me!' To her surprise Nicholas did not relinquish his hold.

'I dare to save you from yourself,' he answered, and his voice was unsteady.

'Let me go,' she repeated. 'I shall do what I desire to do.'

'You will do nothing of the sort,' he replied, and then suddenly the strength of his fingers increased. 'Damn it, Isabel,' he exclaimed, 'but you would try the patience of a saint.'

She laughed then, laughing a high hysterical laugh, and fought him once again.

'Stop it!' Nicholas said. 'Do you hear? Immediately!'

He shook her, shook her as she were a child, shook her so hard and so violently that Isabel's breath was shaken from her, and in her astonishment her mouth remained open a little stupidly.

'Stop it!' Nicholas repeated, still shaking her, and then he lost complete control of his temper. 'You, idiotic, stupid girl,' he stormed. 'How dare you behave like this, frightening and disturbing people! Besides, your love for Justin was nothing but a hum. It was never real, never anything but a wild desire to get your own way. He did not love you, so you wanted him. You have no use for people who really care for you because they treat you with decency. Well, it is the outside of enough! I have finished with waiting on you. You have cast me into despondency for the last time, do you understand? But before I leave I will give you what you deserve, what you have deserved over-long.'

He shook her once again, then suddenly taking one of his hands from her shoulder, he slapped her hard across the face. Isabel gave a cry—a cry of shrill surprise. Her curls had become loosened and disarranged from the shaking Nicholas had given her, and now from the sheer pain of his blow the tears started into her eyes. The marks of his fingers were crimson against her cheek. Nicolas still gripped her with his other hand.

'That will teach you,' he said roughly, 'to play with men as you have played with me. You have made a cursed fool of me one way and another, and now I am free of you. I am leaving and you will never see me again!'

He stared down at her, his eyes still dark with rage; and then as he noticed for the first time her confusion and dishevelment, he became aware of the loveliness of her eyes filled with tears, of the enticement of her red lips which were trembling. Without a word, in one swift movement he swept her into his arms. He held her so tightly that she was breathless, and he kissed her—kissed her hard and brutally, his mouth pressed on hers until her lips were bruised. As unexpectedly as he had taken her he let her go.

'Good-bye!'

His voice was hoarse now, but not only with anger. He strode away down the Orangery, while Isabel breathing quickly steadied herself for a moment against a chair. Then even as Nicholas reached the door, as his hand was on the latch, he heard feet flying after him.

'Nicholas! Oh, Nicholas!'

Isabel's voice seemed caught in her throat, but he heard her. He hesitated and half against his will turned and saw her coming towards him—her ribbons flying, her curls tumbling against her scarlet cheek. He waited grimly, his mouth set in a hard line. Isabel reached him.

'Oh, Nicholas,' she panted, 'You cannot leave me like this. Oh, Nicholas, I did not understand. I . . . I did not know 'til now.'

She looked up at him, her eyes swimming with tears. Suddenly and unexpectedly her arms were around his neck, she was pulling his head down to hers, and her lips, parted and eager, were very near his.

'Oh, Nicholas!' she whispered, and had no chance to say more.

Serena, travelling towards Mandrake in the coach, with Eudora beside her, was planning what she could say to Isabel of her hasty marriage. She felt that she owed her some explanation, but at the same time it was difficult to know how she would put it into words. She felt that Isabel would think she had behaved if not treacherously at least with a complete lack of consideration, and it hurt to think that she must offend someone of whom she had grown so fond. She sighed, and instantly Eudora asked:

'You are fatigued, dearie?'

Serena shook her head.

'No, Eudora, only worried.'

'But you should not be worried on your wedding day.'

'No?' Serena asked listlessly, thinking of what a strange wedding day it was and how little she felt like a bride.

As Justin had wished her a formal good-bye in the hall of Vulcan House, the thought had come to her that she would never see him again. She did not know why such an idea should enter her head and yet it had been there. She had felt an almost sudden overwhelming desire to tell him that she had changed her mind and had no wish to return to Mandrake but would go with him anywhere he suggested. Even the thought of being alone with him brought her such a strange, sweet pain within her breast that it was with difficulty that she kept her fingers from holding tightly to his as he kissed her hand formally in farewell.

'There are a few matters which require my attention,' he said in his usual voice of cynical indifference, 'and then I shall have the pleasure of waiting upon your ladyship at Mandrake.'

'That will be delightful, my lord,' Serena replied, knowing that the servants were listening.

She dropped him a curtsy and stepped out towards the coach. As the footman shut the door, she bent forward. She half hoped that Justin would be waiting to see her go, but there was only the butler and the attending lackeys in sight.

'He is doubtless planning to visit *La Flamme*,' she told herself jealously, and the mere thought of that woman had the power to bring the colour to her cheeks and make her breath come quickly. Would *La Flamme* be perturbed by the news of Justin's marriage? But why should she worry? Serena thought bitterly. It would make little difference to such a person whether her protector was married or not. Besides, in the fashionable world most married men had 'a ballet dancer' or 'a bit of muslin' under their protection.

She sighed again, and Eudora put out her hand and touched hers.

'You are going to be happy, Miss Serena,' she said softly. 'I feel it in my bones, and though I am no gipsy like that trashy Madame Roxana, I know what I know and 'tis the truth.'

'You are wrong this time.'

Eudora looked bewildered.

'Why, dearie, what has occurred between you and his lordship? I was so sincerely glad this morning when you went off to be wed, and his lordship's valet told me in strictest confidence that his lordship planned that you would spend the honeymoon at Staverley. My heart leapt at the news! I imagined you there—as handsome a pair as ever graced the place. And I thought as how we would make up the bed in the Rose bedchamber. 'Twas always your mother's favourite room and . . .'

'Please, Eudora, do not torture me,' Serena cried, turning her head away.

'But I fail in understanding,' Eudora complained. 'You marry a fine young blood like his lordship and here you are travelling back to Mandrake with only silly old Eudora beside you.'

Serena's fingers tightened on Eudora's hand; then in a voice shaken with tears, she said:

'You are not . . . silly or old . . . and I am glad to be with you. I would rather be with you than with anyone else in the world, except . . .'

'. . . Except his lordship,' Eudora said. 'There, there, my

pretty dear. But how has this come about? What has happened?'

Serena could contain herself no longer.

'Nothing . . . nothing has happened! Oh, I love him so! But . . . but, Eudora, he does not care for me! You think I do not wish to be with him at Staverley. . . . I would like it above all things. . . . Yet . . . how could I endure it when . . . only yester eve . . . that . . . that woman was with him?'

Eudora stiffened.

'What woman?' she enquired.

'*La Flamme,*' Serena sobbed. 'She is lovely, Eudora, far lovelier than I could ever hope to be. No wonder she holds his heart.'

'Fiddlesticks!' Eudora said sharply. 'Never have I heard such a pack of nonsense in the whole of my life. 'Tis indeed a pity that you did not relate all this rubbish an hour or so ago. If it were not for the thought that maybe his lordship would have left and we would miss him, I would have the coach turned back this instant and return with you to Grosvenor Square.'

'What do you mean?' Serena asked.

Eudora was speaking to her in exactly the same voice that she had used when as a child Serena had done something particularly naughty and Eudora had taken her to task.

'All this talk of *La Flamme!*' Eudora snorted. 'As though the like of her would count with his lordship one way or another.'

'But she did . . . and she does,' Serena said. 'You do not understand! Nicholas told me, and Isabel. It is true, Eudora!'

'Mr. Nicholas and her ladyship ought to be ashamed of themselves,' Eudora said severely, 'especially her ladyship, who shouldn't be speaking of such things. I am not saying, mark you, that his lordship did not take a passing interest in the woman, but what does it signify when it was but a passing interest and before he had met you?'

Serena sighed.

'Poor Eudora, you are trying to console me, but I myself saw her at Grosvenor Square last night.'

'Alone?' Eudora asked.

'No, not alone,' Serena admitted. 'There were other gentlemen there, several of them, to be truthful, but . . .'

'And Sir Peter Burley amongst them, I'll be bound,' Eudora said.

Serena nodded.

'Why, yes, I believe he was among the gentlemen. I could not be sure of them all . . . for I fainted . . .'

'And no wonder after such a ride,' Eudora interrupted; 'but if that saucy piece was there in the place, it was Sir Peter who had brought her and you can be as sure of that as you can be sure that you are living and breathing at this very moment.'

'But what has Sir Peter got to do with . . . with *La Flamme*?' Serena asked in bewilderment.

'Everything for that matter,' Eudora said in a voice of triumph. 'It was Sir Peter who took her off his lordship's hands, to put with vulgar bluntness. I heard the whole story from his lordship's own man over two weeks ago when we happened to be speaking of such things. In fact, his lordship's valet was remarking how extremely fortunate it was for the woman—I would not soil my lips by calling her a lady—that such an arrangement had been made, for Sir Peter is exceeding wealthy and has provided her with a truly elegant house in the village of Chelsea and a carriage with two horses. Two, mark you, though 'tis seldom such a one as that gets more than one.'

Serena drew in a very deep breath.

'Sir Peter! Oh, Eudora, is that really true? Really?'

'May I fall dead this minute at your feet if I am telling you a falsehood,' Eudora said. 'Oh, child, child, how can you have been so stupid as to believe the . . .'

'The evidence of my own eyes,' Serena said miserably. 'She was sitting familiarly by his lordship . . . her hand on his knee.'

'What does it matter what she was doing?' Eudora said crossly. 'For the likes of those there is no true elegance of behaviour. How should there be, poor creatures, when they know no better?'

'But she is beautiful,' Serena said, still only half convinced that Eudora was speaking the truth.

'So are you—you stupid child,' Eudora said. 'Have you not looked at yourself in the mirror? Did you not see the expression in his lordship's eyes when you came back from your wedding to-day?'

'I did not look at him.'

'More's the pity, for if ever I saw love in a man's face it was there in his lordship's.'

'Love!' Serena repeated the word in a whisper. 'Do you really think . . . ?'

255

'I do not only think, I know.' Eudora snapped; 'and here we are going back to Mandrake when we might have been heading for Staverley.'

'Oh, if only I could be sure,' Serena said; 'and now he thinks . . .'

'What does he think?' Eudora enquired curiously.

'That I am in love with somebody else.'

There were tears in Serena's eyes.

'Was there ever such a coil!' Eudora exclaimed. 'Lawks a' mercy, but you would twist a straight road into a tangle!'

'If I could believe you . . .' Serena began; 'but I was not certain, I . . .'

'Well, his lordship won't be far behind,' Eudora said. 'You can speak with him to-night; you can ask him if I have not told you the truth.'

'Oh, I could not,' Serena said, her cheeks burning suddenly at the thought.

'Why not?' Eudora asked. 'It is not difficult to speak of anything to a man with whom you are wed.'

'I wonder. I think it would be very difficult to speak of some things,' Serena answered more to herself than to Eudora.

And then suddenly she was conscious of the singing within her heart, a feeling as if a dark shadow, which had pressed down upon her, were lifted and had gone. How silly she had been not to make sure! And yet, how could she have known? Seeing *La Falmme* there at Vulcan House, seeing her beside Justin and so obviously at her ease with him had seemed indisputable evidence, and yet . . . if Eudora was to be believed . . .

Suddenly, clearly and unmistakably, Serena knew she was to be believed, knew that she had been crazy even for a moment to think that Justin would have taken her to the altar unless his reason for their marriage had been more than the wish to save her reputation. How blind she had been! How stupid! But now the journey was no longer tedious, no longer arduous. She was warm and radiant with her own thoughts, for soon she would be at Mandrake, and soon, perhaps in an hour or so, Justin would be with her again. She prayed that he would not be long delayed. His curricle would carry him more swiftly than they could travel even in this coach built for speed.

The miles and hours went by as if they were on winged feet and Serena was surprised when Eudora broke into her reverie with the words:

'We are approaching the park gates. Will you tidy your bonnet, for all eyes will be on you when you arrive?'

'All eyes?' Serena asked, startled. 'Why?'

'Did you know that his lordship has sent word to his mother that you are wed?' Eudora asked.

'No,' Serena replied. 'He did not speak of it to me.'

'A groom was despatched some time before we left,' Eudora explained. 'He will have arrived before us.'

'Oh!'

This was news to Serena and she digested it soberly. She had somehow forgotten, when there had been so much else to think of, that the news of Justin's marriage would cause a commotion at Mandrake. What would the Marchioness say?

She had little time for reflection before the coach turned into the courtyard and drew up with a jerk. Serena alighted slowly. She knew by the very smile on the old butler's face that the news had reached Mandrake; but when he made her welcome and wished her every happiness, she could only smile shyly and hold out her hand.

'I will find out which room has been prepared for you,' Eudora whispered. 'You had best find her ladyship and pay her your respects.'

Serena asked for the Marchioness, but she was told that her ladyship was resting.

'In that case I will not disturb her,' Serena said hastily, glad of the respite.

She walked up the staircase. It seemed to her that the house was very quiet. Although it was already twilight, the candles did not appear to have been lit in the great drawing-rooms. At the top of the stairs Mrs. Matthews, the housekeeper, was waiting. She curtsied deeply.

'Good evening, your ladyship. May I offer your ladyship my most humble good wishes for your ladyship's happiness.'

'Thank you, Mrs. Matthews,' Serena said.

She paused for a moment expecting the housekeeper to lead her to another room, and then, as nothing was said, proceeded on her way towards her old bedchamber.

She reached it to find Eudora was there already, having come up the back stairs. Torqo was lying by the fire. He bounded at her, almost crazy with joy at seeing her again. She put her arms round the dog and hid her face against his neck.

Eudora shut the bedroom door and said:

'I asked which room you were in and was informed that by her ladyship's orders you would remain here. We will see what his lordship has to say to this when he returns.'

'No, no, Eudora,' Serena cried, 'do not make a disturbance. There is plenty of time for me to move when things are more settled. It must have been a shock to all of them and I am afraid that her ladyship must be exceeding annoyed.'

'What does it signify if she is?' Eudora asked truculently. 'Don't forget that you are the Marchioness now!'

Serena said nothing, but her thoughts ran instantly to the old Marquis in his library away down below her. Later, she thought, she would go and see him, but it would be best to allow Justin to break the news to his father. Perhaps they might even go together. She smiled shyly at the thought. How magical that word could be—together!

There came a sharp knock at the door. Eudora opened it and Martha stood outside.

'Her ladyship's compliments to Miss Staverley—' she began.

'The Marchioness of Vulcan,' Eudora corrected.

'Her ladyship sent a message to Miss Staverley,' Martha repeated. 'She will see her at dinner which will be in an hour's time. She wishes to have no private conversation with her before his lordship arrives.'

Eudora stood almost quivering with rage at what she considered was an insult.

'The Marchioness of Vulcan thanks the Dowager Marchioness for her message,' she said at length and slammed the door triumphantly in Martha's face.

Serena could not help laughing.

'Oh, Eudora, you are like a bulldog at bay. What does it matter what they say?'

'It matters a lot,' Eudora said grimly. 'You will take your rightful place in this house and the sooner the better.'

She went downstairs to get Serena a warm drink and came back with the news that there was to be no party tonight.

'The guests were turned away last night too,' she said. 'It seems strange, but they tell me the Marchioness has been indisposed ever since the news of his lordship's duel.'

Serena shivered a little as she remembered that voice shrieking from the bedroom.

'Where is Lady Isabel?' she asked.

'I know not,' Eudora answered, 'but you must be about attiring yourself, for you have not long before it will be the dinner hour.'

Obediently Serena started to change her clothes. She had washed and was robed in her evening gown when her bedroom door, burst open and Isabel came in. Never, Serena thought, had she seen her look more radiant. She had expected her to be very different—reproachful, even melancholy—and she could only stand gasping as Isabel flung her arms around her with cries of delight.

'I had no idea you were back, dear sweet Serena. No one told me and I have been waiting all of a twitter the whole evening for you. Are you happy? Where is Justin? What time is he arriving?'

Serena gasped.

'Isabel . . .' she said.

'La, but here I am, plaguing you with questions and not giving you the chance to answer any of them. But tell me first, are you happy?'

'Oh, Isabel,' Serena said, 'are you angry with me?'

'Angry?' Isabel said. 'No, of course not! Oh, Serena, I cannot wait to tell you. I am madly, crazily in love, for the first time in my life. I had no idea it could be such . . . such enchantment. This is different—wonderfully, divinely different from anything I have ever known before.'

'But . . . I thought . . .' Serena began.

'Oh, Serena, he is so splendid, so strong, and so brutal. I declare I am terrified of him every minute. Look!' She turned her cheek to Serena and pointing to a very faint bruise against the whiteness of her cheek, said: 'Do you see it there? 'Tis the imprint of his fingers.'

'But, Isabel,' Serena cried, 'who has done this? Who has dared?'

Isabel looked at her and laughed.

'You would never guess, not if I gave you a thousand guesses. 'Tis Nicholas!'

'Nicholas!' Serena thought that her hearing must be at fault. 'Nicholas dared to strike you?'

'Only because he loves me, because we are going to wed. Oh, Serena, I am so happy.'

Serena sat down on the bed in sheer astonishment.

'I declare it is all beyond me. Start at the very beginning, Isabel.'

259

They were both late for dinner, and only as they reached the hall after the footman had been sent to tell them that her ladyship was waiting did Isabel say.

'Why, I declare I have forgotten to ask you where Justin is.'

'He should be here at any moment,' Serena answered, 'if he has not already arrived. He has to travel by curricle while I came in the coach.'

'How ungallant of him!' Isabel pouted. 'Nicholas says he will never leave me for one moment. He is so jealous that he vows that if I so much as smile at a lackey he will break his head open. Did you ever hear such a brute? And how . . . I adore him!'

Serena was laughing as she entered the small drawing-room where the Marchioness was waiting for them, but as she saw the Marchioness's face, the smile died on her lips. Never had she seen anyone look more severe, never had she been more frightened of the almost ominous quietness of the Marchioness's greeting.

'So you have returned!'

Serena dropped a curtsy.

'Yes, Ma'am.'

'And my son, I understand, is following later on?'

'That is correct, Ma'am.'

'Then we will await his arrival and his instructions before we speak of things which concern you both.'

'Very good, Ma'am.'

Serena curtsied again, and the Marchioness led the way in to dinner. It was an uncomfortable meal. The guests who had been in the house the day before had left that morning, but whether of their own free will or at the request of the Marchioness Serena did not discover. There only remained the three people whom Justin had invited—Isabel, Gilly and Nicholas.

Isabel, it was true, was quite unperturbed by the unpleasant atmosphere during dinner. She was so entranced by Nicholas that she had eyes only for him, and regardless of good manners they spoke together in low voices or exchanged glances which excluded everyone else from a world in which they were completely happy by themselves.

Lord Gillingham tried to hold a conversation with the Marchioness, but she sat staring ahead of her and saying nothing. There was a wild, haunted look in her dark eyes, Serena thought, which seemed to have become very deep-set and ringed around with shadows. There were more lines about her mouth and there was something unwholesome in her extreme pallor. She ate nothing, but drank brandy, and immediately after dinner she announced that she would retire.

'I also wish to retire,' Serena said when she had gone. 'It has been a long day and I am fatigued.'

'You will not wait up for Justin?' Isabel asked curiously.

Serena shook her head, but when she reached her own room she took up the big white quill pen and wrote a few lines on a piece of paper. When she had finished, she sanded it and read it over again and yet again.

There is something I would fain impart to your lordship [she wrote]. *It is of the utmost urgency and if you agree we could speak on your arrival. I await your lordship in my bedchamber, but have not retired for the night.*

Serena.

She gave the note to Eudora.

'Can you arrange it that his lordship receives this the moment he arrives?'

Eudora smiled at her.

'I give you my word it will be done,' she said and added: 'A few words, Miss Serena, will explain everything. Do not be shy; there is happiness waiting for you and you need not be afraid to grasp it.'

Eudora went down with the note and Serena settled herself beside the fire. Torqo was still there. He had not yet been taken back to the stables. The logs were burning brightly and there were only a few candles burning in the room. It was very quiet and yet somehow pleasant. Serena wondered how long she would have to wait. She was not sleepy. She felt as if every faculty within her body were wide awake, waiting, waiting for this moment.

She was glad that her gown was becoming. It was one that Yvette had only recently finished and was trimmed with frills of ruched net and sprigged with tiny pearls—like teardrops. She thought of Isabel's shining happiness with Nicholas and was both glad and envious.

'One day,' she thought, 'when I know Justin well, I will ask him to give them Staverley . . . but not before we have been there ourselves . . . Justin and I.'

261

Her cheeks burned at the thought.

'Oh, Justin,' she whispered in the silence of her room, 'how greatly I need you . . . come quickly . . . quickly!'

Eudora came back with something in her hand.

'I met her ladyship's maid in the passage,' she said. 'She said that her ladyship had been perturbed to see how tired you looked at dinner. She had noted, too, that you drank nothing, and she thought maybe that you had contracted a chill on the journey. She sent this glass of mulled wine—with her compliments.'

Serena looked surprised.

'It is unexpected considerate of her ladyship.'

Eudora snorted.

'Not before 'tis time. If you ask me, she has thought things over and realised that her day is ended. 'Tis always better not to quarrel with the new mistress of the house.'

'Actually I do not feel at all tired,' Serena said; 'but I thought the Marchioness looked sadly indisposed.'

'Well, a glass of wine won't do you any harm,' Eudora said.

There came a knock at the door. Eudora, the goblet still in her hand, opened it. The Marchioness's black boy stood outside. He handed Eudora a note on a silver salver. She took it to Serena, who opened it.

' 'Tis from the Marchioness,' Serena exclaimed. 'It says:

"Sleep well, my dear Serena. Be pleased to give the boy the goblet when you have drunk the wine".'

Serena looked at Eudora.

'You are right, Eudora,' she said. 'Her ladyship wishes to be pleasant. But why does she want the goblet back so urgently?'

Eudora held it up. The goblet was of gold and had, set in its base, semi-precious stones which sparkled in the firelight.

' 'Tis a special one,' she said. 'Look at the gems on it. It is doubtless very valuable.'

'How pretty!' Serena exclaimed.

'You had better drink the wine,' Eudora said; 'the boy is waiting.'

She held out the goblet to Serena who took it, raised it to her lips, and then exclaimed:

'Indeed I cannot! The truth is I am too excited either to eat or drink.'

262

Eudora smiled.

'I understand, my dearie.'

'Throw the wine away,' Serena said. 'I would not offend her ladyship by refusing her kind offer.'

'Nay, why be wasteful? I will drink it myself.'

Eudora drank the wine quickly and going to the door, handed the empty goblet to the boy outside.

'With her ladyship's grateful thanks,' she said and shut the door again.

Serena bent down and fondled Torqo's ears.

'I wonder how long we shall have to wait, Eudora,' she said. 'You made sure that my note would reach his lordship as soon as he arrived.'

'I gave it into the keeping of his lordship's own man,' Eudora said, 'with . . . my . . . own . . .'

She stopped suddenly and put her hand to her head.

'I . . . feel . . . queerly . . . dizzy . . . Miss Serena . . . it .. must . . . be . . . the . . . heat . . . it's . . .'

She put out her hand blindly as if she would grope for support.

'Eudora, what has happened? What is the matter?'

Serena rushed to her side and helped her to a chair.

'I . . . think . . . I . . . have . . .' Eudora murmured, then suddenly slid from the chair to the floor in a crumpled heap.

Serena raised her head. At first she thought she had fainted and fetched some water from the wash-stand. She tried to force it between Eudora's lips, but it trickled back, and then she went to the dressing-table for a vinaigrette. She brought it back and held it under Eudora's nose.

'Eudora,' she cried. 'Oh, Eudora!'

There was no response and Serena thought wildly that she had been poisoned.

'Oh, Eudora,' she gasped; 'do not die . . . Eudora. I cannot endure this . . .'

Eudora's lined face seemed to bear the pallor of death. Serena felt a sob of fear and of unutterable misery rise in her throat. She thought of crying out frantically for help or of running to fetch someone. Then pulling herself together and controlling her panic, she felt first for Eudora's heart; it was beating faintly but regularly.

Serena stood irresolute. What should she do? If only Justin were here! Suddenly Eudora gave a tremendous snore. Serena stared at her and then bent down, felt again for her heart and then her pulse. She was alive, there was no doubt about that. A sudden suspicion made Serena very gently and with fingers that trembled, ease back one of Eudora's closed eyelids. Eudora's eye stared sightlessly at her. The pupil had contracted to the tiniest possible pinpoint!

Serena knew then the truth, for in her mother's last illness the doctors, to deaden the pain, had dosed her repeatedly with laudanum.

Eudora had not fainted! She was drugged—drugged because she had drunk the wine which the Marchioness had sent to her new daughter-in-law. Serena opened the door and half cried, half dragged Eudora into her own room. With some difficulty she lifted her on to the bed and covered her with warm blankets. Eudora's snores repeated themselves rhythmically. Serena knew that she would sleep now for a long time. She had no idea how much laudanum there had been in the wine, but it must have contained a very strong dose.

Serena shut the bedroom door and went back to her own chamber. She stood for some time deep in thought. What did this mean? What did this portend? Why had the Marchioness wanted her to be unconscious? Was it to prevent her speaking with Justin when he arrived? Or was there some other and more sinister reason?

She was suddenly aware that she had left the door ajar. She did not know why, but the dark opening frightened her. She moved across the room swiftly, closed the door, then bolted it. For the first time since she had come to Mandrake she examined the bolt. It was a light thing, made merely of a thin piece of wood, and it seemed to Serena that it was loosely fitted so that it would not stand much strain. She did not ask herself why she was noticing these things so minutely. She only knew that her attention was drawn to them insistently and she must obey her own instinct which warned her of approaching danger. Through the wall she could hear Eudora snoring deeply. Why had the Marchioness sent that goblet of wine drugged with laudanum?

Serena put her hand on the door latch. Should she go downstairs and enquire? Then suddenly, even as she would have gone, she was afraid—afraid of the dark passages, afraid of the long lonely way down the narrow staircase which led to the first floor. She went back to her seat by the fire. Now she no longer sat thinking of Justin. She waited for him, her muscles tense, her longing for his presence physical in its intensity.

Suddenly Torqo lifted his head and growled slightly in his throat.

'What is it, Torqo?' Serena asked.

He growled again and now she could hear someone coming softly along the passage.

Serena jumped to her feet, her heart beating wildly. There came a knock on her door.

'Who is it?' she asked, and tried to keep her voice steady.

In answer the latch was lifted and someone pushed against the door.

'Who is it?' Serena repeated, and her voice was sharper this time.

The latch was lifted again. Now suddenly Serena was desperately afraid. Who was seeking an entrance without betraying his or her identity?

'Open the door, Serena, I wish to speak with you.'

It was the Marchioness who spoke, in a voice so contorted by emotion as to be almost unrecognisable. There was something ugly in the sound of it, something uncanny and terribly frightening.

'What is it you want, Ma'am?' Serena asked, trembling.

'I desire to come in. Open the door.'

Torqo growled deeply in his throat.

'It . . . it is very late, Ma'am,' Serena stammered. 'I have . . . re . . . retired. Can we not speak on the morrow?'

'Open the door,' the Marchioness repeated, and now there was something so menacing, so horrible in her voice that Serena knew beyond any shadow of doubt that danger and hatred were lurking there in the passage, a hatred that was menacingly vibrant even though its author remained invisible. She could feel evil reaching out to envelop her. She saw, too, that Torqo sensed it, for his hackles were rising.

'I have retired, Ma'am,' Serena repeated, but her voice was weak.

In answer the latch clicked up and down again. There were several thumps against the door as if the Marchioness had put her shoulder against it, and then, through the gap between the lintel and the door itself there appeared a long thin shining blade of steel. It was like the long poisonous tongue of a reptile.

Serena saw it, gasped and felt in a moment a terror which made her so weak and faint that she could hardly stand. That sword, stained as she well knew with the blood of a murdered man, was no figment of her imagination, it was real, it was there. Soon it would be within the room at her throat, piercing its way through her warm flesh. There was only a bolt, fragile and insecure, between herself and a maniac obsessed by a hatred and a bestiality beyond all reason and all sanity.

Trembling, Serena looked wildly around her. She glanced at the window and knew there was no escape that way. Then she remembered. The door in the turret! She sped towards it and wrenched it open. Swiftly, with fingers that shook so violently that she could hardly control them, she lifted the latch of the smaller door which led on to the staircase. Even as she did so, she heard the sound of splintering wood and knew that the bolt on the door of the bedroom was giving way. But already she was on the stone steps and was running down them, feeling her way in the pitch of darkness. Behind her came Torqo.

As she flung open the door into the library she heard a crash and knew that the Marchioness had found her way into her bedroom. But she was in the library. The lights were on, and she saw that the old Marquis was sitting at his desk. She ran across the room to him.

'Oh, my lord,' she panted. 'Help me! I. . .'

She stopped suddenly. He was leaning forward and she thought at first that he was writing, but now she saw that, while the quill was still in his hand, his head was on his arm, his face hidden. She stood very still. There was no need to speak again, no need to touch him. She knew, without the need of words, that the Marquis was dead. He had died at the writing of his history, the way, Serena thought, that he would have wished to go.

For a moment she forgot everything, her own fear, her own danger, in a sudden overwhelming sense of compassion. In the death of the old Marquis she had lost a friend. And then a sound startled her, a sound which recalled everything, for it was the footsteps of someone coming slowly down the stone stairway.

It was at that moment that a panic beyond anything ahat she had ever known in the whole of her life swept over Serena. It was almost beyond comprehension to be alone with a dead man and know that she was being pursued by a woman who was determined that she, too, should die.

Seeking escape frantically like a cornered animal, Serena ran through the library door. Fortunately she knew the way down the main stairway which led into the garden. She reached the door and pulled back the bolts. Then the fresh air was on her face and she was free.

With Torqo bounding beside her she rushed wildly across the lawn, down the rose-walk, across another part of the garden and on and on until she reached the gate on to the cliffs. She was guided in her flight entirely by instinct, neither thinking nor reasoning, driven by a terror which bereft her of everything save the thought of evading the Marchioness.

Just as she reached the cliffs, a storm broke. There was a sudden clap of thunder, a streak of lightning, and the rain came pouring down as though the skies had opened; but she ran on. The thunder was in her ears, and lightning in her eyes, the rain beating against her and soaking her to the skin, seeming in its force almost to tear her clothes from her.

She ran on, the thunder roared again, and it seemed to her in that moment that the Marchioness was just behind her. The lightning seemed linked with that streak of cruel steel—the steel that she had seen buried in the smuggler's throat. The rain lashed her face. Blinded she could see nothing; she was alone in the darkness with her own fear.

Still she ran.

She gave a sudden cry of terror. She had stepped forward into nothingness. She felt herself fall and strove against her falling, but it was useless. The thunder drowned the sound of her voice—and then there was only Torqo's deep baying and below the splash of the waves against the cliffs.

Seventeen

THE Marchioness stopped and stared down at her dead husband. Her mind was so inflamed with the desire for revenge, so bemused by a fire which seemed to consume all thought save that of a hunger for blood, that she did not for the moment recognise him or remember who he was.

Then through a red mist reason returned to her for a split second and she called him by name. He did not reply and she made a movement as if she would have touched him, but the hand that she outstretched held the naked rapier-like sword and the glint of the steel reminded her whom she sought and what was her avowed purpose.

Serena! That girl, that minx, who had defrauded her of so much and who should be made to pay not only for the bad luck and ill-fortune she had brought to Mandrake, but also for presuming to marry Justin. Craftily the Marchioness remembered that with Serena's death her fortune of eighty thousand pounds would become theirs. Yes, theirs, because in this moment she was linked with her son, linked against all who threatened to disrupt the personal kingdom which was Mandrake—a fortress, as it had always been, against all who were alien.

Yet her mind, chaotic and entangled, could not for long sustain the thought of sharing that fortress or that kingdom with anyone, even her own son. What ever the title deeds might say, she believed that the real Mandrake was the one which she created, and that was hers and hers alone. Yes, hers, for whatever her husband and Justin might say to the contrary, this great home existed to-day merely because the fashionable world found it a tolerable gambling place.

She had made it a rendezvous for the people who mattered, and she would defy anyone, whoever it might be, who challenged her supremacy here. The Marchioness threw back her red head as if she faced a hostile mob and once again the mercury-like glint of steel recalled her resolution.

She would kill Serena! That was what she intended to do, to rid Mandrake of her once and for all, to rid Justin of her, too. The white powder she had sniffed so freely but a short time ago had created a wildness that was an intoxication within her veins. She knew that her strength was equal to any task, however formidable. She knew she was unconquerable, nothing and no one could stop her.

She turned away from the old man lying silent and still. She saw beyond him the open door which told her all too clearly the way Serena had taken. She went through it and then hesitated, for there were steps leading downwards into the garden and a passage in front of her which led back to the house. Which way had Serena taken?

'I will find you, wench! I will find you!' the Marchioness cried out. 'Do not think you can escape me.'

Her voice brought the old valet from his room at the far end of the passage. He opened the door, the light shining behind his grey hair. He saw who it was and came forward.

'Did you call, m'lady?'

'Where is she?' the Marchioness asked in a deep resonant voice which seemed to echo down the passage.

'Where is who, m'lady?'

'That girl. She came this way.'

'I know not of whom you speak, m'lady. I was waiting for his lordship to ring. 'Tis time he retired to bed.'

'I seek—a girl,' the Marchioness said menacingly, and then the old valet saw what she carried in her hand.

'M'lady . . . oh, m'lady,' he exclaimed.

'Out of my way, fool,' the Marchioness cried. 'I will find her. You can be sure of that. I will find her.'

The man fell back against the wall. He saw the madness in the Marchioness's eyes, heard it in her voice, and he was afraid.

She swept past him. The old valet stood trembling when she was gone, then hurried towards the library.

The Marchioness swept on. For the moment she had lost her sense of direction and was not certain where she was going or why. Suddenly she found herself on the first floor of the landing, and running towards her with agitation written all over her features was Martha.

'Oh, m'lady,' she cried. 'I have been searching for your ladyship everywhere.'

'Where has she gone?' the Marchioness asked in a savage, frustrated tone.

'Where has who gone?' Martha enquired.

'That crafty chit, Serena . . . Staverley,' the Marchioness snapped.

'Why, she is in her room, m'lady.'

The Marchioness turned as if she would retrace her steps to the second floor, but Martha clutched her arm.

'Wait, m'lady,' she said, 'I have something of grave import to tell you.'

'What is it?' the Marchioness enquired. 'I have no time to linger.'

Martha looked over her shoulder and spoke in a whisper.

'The smugglers, m'lady, they are here.'

The Marchioness looked at Martha for a moment as if she did not quiet understand what she said, then she repeated slowly.

'The smugglers! Here? To-night?'

'Yes, m'lady. Have you forgotten that your ladyship sent for them? You said you had urgent work for them. Don't you recollect, m'lady? I took the message for you myself this very forenoon.'

'Yes, yes, of course,' the Marchioness said.

'Quickly, m'lady. They are waiting for you. You have gold for them? Can I find it for you?'

The Marchioness turned, as if reluctantly, towards her own bedroom.

'Now think, m'lady,' Martha entreated. 'Oh, God in heaven,' she said suddenly, 'it is that devil-mix powder you have been taking.'

'Silence, fool,' the Marchioness said. 'What I take is my own business. Maybe that is what I want this moment, more of it, more to make my brain clear.'

' 'Tis clear enough,' Martha said soothingly. 'But look, m'lady, you have dropped the sheath from your sword-stick.'

The Marchioness stared at the sword in her hand.

'I have got to find her,' she muttered. 'I have got to find her.'

'Yes, yes, m'lady,' Martha said. 'But hurry now, the men are waiting.'

They reached the Marchioness's bedroom. The Marchioness stood in the centre of the room while Martha went to the dressing-table.

'The gold? Where has your ladyship hidden it?' Martha asked.

'I have none!'

'No gold?'

Martha was horrified. Her mouth dropped open and she stared stupidly at the Marchioness. 'Then why, why did your ladyship send for the men?'

'Because I need money, fool. Because they will obtain it for me. Bring me my jewel-case.'

'Your jewel-case, m'lady?'

'Yes, and swiftly too,' the Marchioness said impatiently.

Staring at her as if she had taken leave of her senses, Martha fetched the big leather-covered jewel-case from the locked drawer in the wardrobe. When her back was turned, the Marchioness went to the dressing-table and pulled open the drawer which contained the snuff-box. She sniffed once and yet again, and then she drew a deep breath. She glanced at herself in the mirror. She saw that the pupils of her eyes, enormously dilated, were dark and menacing. She saw that her skin was very white, her lips quivering. Then she gave a laugh of triumph.

'Egad, but I am in looks to-night! More beautiful than I have been for many a long day.'

'Yes, yes, your ladyship, but do not linger. The men are waiting.'

'Let them wait,' the Marchioness replied. 'Open the box, woman, and let us see what we have within.'

Martha turned the key and swung back the heavy lid. Inside, each one in a velvet-lined compartment, lay the Vulcan jewels. The Marchioness put out her hand and picked out two great necklaces, one set with rubies the size of pigeons' eggs, the other with diamonds which seemed to glitter with a strange fire as the light of the candles was reflected in them.

'The next tray,' she commanded sharply.

Martha obeyed her, lifting the tray to reveal bracelets and tiaras to match the necklaces. The Marchioness gathered two or three of them into her hands and turned towards the door.

'M'lady, where are you going?' Marsha asked. 'You cannot dispose of the jewels. They are his lordship's, m'lady.'

'And what would my son need them for?' the Marchioness asked lightly.

'They are his, m'lady—his to give to his wife.'

'His wife!'

The Marchioness turned round swiftly on her, her face contorted almost beyond recognition.

'That is whom I seek—Justin's wife. Where have you hidden her?'

Martha gave a cry.

'I have hidden her nowhere, m'lady. Oh, go now, go. The men will be getting impatient. Speak to them, send them away and ask them to come another day, for there is danger for your ladyship and for us all while they linger here.'

'I am not afraid.'

The Marchioness laughed again, then she turned with a swagger, the light gleaming on the great tangle of jewels she held in the one hand and on the sword she carried in the other.

'Shall I come with you, m'lady?' Martha asked in a low voice.

The Marchioness looked down at her scornfully.

'And what help would you be? No, wait for me here. I will be back in a few minutes and then together we will seek for that baggage.'

She went forward as if she were walking on air. Indeed she felt at that moment as if she had wings and they bore her down the narrow staircase to the hidden door in the panelling. She made no effort to light the candles in the tunnel. She knew her way by instinct and as she moved forward in the dark she did not falter, not even when she came to the top of the stone steps.

Down, down she went, the damp, cool air coming to meet her as she descended. Every now and then there was a distant crash of thunder which seemed to reverberate, echo and re-echo ominously, but the Marchioness paid no heed. Soon she saw the lighted cave ahead of her, and when she entered, it was to find the torches flaring and the men standing round waiting for her arrival.

She swept in suddenly amongst them, a creature from another world with her bare shoulders glittering with jewels, her red head held high, her eyes compellingly dark and strange. Padlett came forward.

'Good evening, your ladyship.'

'So you are here,' the Marchioness said.

'Yes, your ladyship. You sent for us—we are ready.'

The Marchioness looked at him, and for a moment she did not speak, then as if to hurry her he said quietly:

'Your ladyship has the gold for us?'

'Gold! No, I have no gold,' the Marchioness said. 'I have

272

these. Take them! They are exceeding rare and should purchase all you can carry and more.'

She threw out her left hand with a flamboyant gesture. As she did so one of the bracelets fell from her hold and lay glittering on the damp floor. No one moved to pick it up. The men stared at her and there was a murmur between two or three of them in the background.

'Jewels, m'lady,' Padlett exclaimed. ' 'Tis not easy to sell such ware across the Channel. 'Tis better that we have gold to take with us.'

'But I tell you,' the Marchioness said impatiently, 'that I have no gold for you. Take the jewels! They will sell for thousands of guineas. They are valuable, I tell you, exceeding valuable.'

Padlett glanced towards the men for whom he was spokesman. What he saw in their faces strengthened his own reluctance.

'I'm sorry to disoblige, your ladyship,' he said, 'but 'tis not easy in France to dispose of such things. There are spies everywhere. And they will as like as not think such rare pieces are stolen. 'Tis yellow gold those Frenchies want.'

'You will do as I command you,' the Marchioness said, and for a second her eyes narrowed and there was an ominous note in her voice.

Padlett turned to the other men as if to seek their advice. One of them, a big hulking fellow with a beard and a broken nose, said:

' 'Em be dangerous ware; 'tain't reason to take ought but gold, an' us be a-wanting more for t' journey too. Five guineas, 'tain't enough. There's other nobs that'll pay seven jacks an' more. Also us be a-wanting our pickings. A bottle o' blood-an-thunder per man, an' summat for each o' us t' take home an' all.'

'You will have neither brandy nor anything else from the cargo,' the Marchioness said furiously. 'You know my rules. You have been told them often enough.'

'Aye, but us be a-going t' make our rules anow,' someone shouted.

'Dogs, curs, do you defy me?' the Marchioness screamed.

She faced them angrily, the sword in her right hand glittering a little as her fingers tightened on the handle.

'An' what'll ye do t' us if us do?' someone asked in a low undertone. 'Spike us as ye spiked young Adam?'

The Marchioness stood there, her breath coming quickly, the nostrils of her thin nose quivering a little with sheer rage.

'Thieving scoundrels,' she said, 'scum of the earth, miserable sapskulls, do my bidding this instant or 'twill be the worse for you.'

'She's crazed,' one man whispered to another; but the word, soft-whispered though it was, swept round the cavern so that the Marchioness heard it.

'Crazed, am I?' she cried. 'Yes, crazed to have ever trusted such riff-raff as you. Do as I command you, or, by heaven, you shall feel the bite of this.'

She made a sudden lunge with her sword. The man nearest to her fell back a pace or two.

'*Touché*' she laughed; 'shrink back, you cowards; I will teach you who is master here. Obey me or I will call in the Dragoons and hand you over. I am not afraid of you, but you shall be afeared of me. You shall learn of my power and my strength and you shall do my bidding or pay for your disobedience . . . pay for it with your lives.'

There was a sudden startled silence and then Padlett said hastily:

'In God's name, your ladyship . . .'

But he said no more, for a stone flew from the back of the cave. It hit the Marchioness on the shoulder. For a second she staggered and then she screamed:

'Stone me, would you, thieves? For that you shall cry on your knees for mercy.'

She made a swift movement forward; her sword caught a man unawares on his bare arm and ripped his flesh open. But she got no further. Another stone, a big one, caught her between the eyes, and as she staggered with the impact of the blow, there came another and yet another. There was a sudden cry of voices, harsh and inhuman, and for one moment Padlett's voice was high above the rest.

'Stop it . . . do you hear? Stop it. . . .'

Then he was heard no more. Stones were flying through the air, one after another they crashed against her, beating the Marchioness to her knees and then to the ground.

She gave one cry, but it was lost in the general *mêleé* of sound. There was a noise, guttural and thick, such as an animal makes when it pulls down its prey, and then suddenly there was only the sound of footsteps running down the tunnel towards the open sea. There was a shout, an incoherent noise, a splashing of oars as if they hastily and without caution struck the water. Then there was silence.

The torches lit the great cavern. At the far end a pile of stones partially covered the body of a woman. Her hand out-thrown on the damp earth was still clutching the great necklaces of rubies and diamonds which glittered and sparkled in the leaping light. There was the lap of the waves and an occasional rumble of distant thunder. It was damp and cold and very quiet.

Justin, driving in at the gates of Mandrake, heard the thunder receding into the distance. He had still been some miles from Mandrake when the rain started, but catching only the edge of the storm he had been amply protected by his thick, many-caped driving coat. As he drew nearer to the house, however, he could see great puddles of water and realised that the storm must have been particularly sharp over the house itself. He drew up in the courtyard, flung the reins to the groom, and strode towards the house.

The door was opened before he reached it and he saw the old butler standing there with a row of attendant footmen. He walked in and as the butler began the speech he had been rehearsing the whole evening after the news had come of his lordship's marriage, he gave him such a look that the words died on the man's lips. He could only stand staring after his lordship, who passed from the outer lobby into the Great Hall. Here Justin dragged off his coat and gloves, still with that frowning darkness in his expression which seemed to freeze the very lips of those who would speak to him. His valet, however, who had been waiting in the far corner of the hall, came forward with a note on a silver salver.

'What is it, Wilkins?' his lordship enquired, and his voice was harsh.

' 'Tis urgent, m'lord,' his valet replied.

'Urgent?' Justin questioned, in a tone of voice of one who finds such a suggestion intolerable.

'From her ladyship,' Wilkins said quietly. 'She asked that it should be handed to your lordship the very instant of your arrival.'

'Her ladyship?' Justin said, and it was a question.

'Yes, m'lord. Her ladyship made a good journey and was not over-tired on arrival.'

Justin put out his hand for the note and opened it swiftly. Then it seemed to those who watched as if the darkness disappeared from his face and he was suddenly measurably younger. Without a word he turned and went up the wide staircase two steps at a time. It was only as he reached the landing that he hesitated for a moment, giving Mrs. Matthews, the housekeeper, the opportunity to advance towards him, a speech of welcome hovering on her lips. She dropped a deep curtsy.

'Good evening, your lordship. I have the honour to wish you . . .'

'In which room is her ladyship?' Justin interrupted.

The housekeeper drew a deep breath.

'In the room where she has always been, m'lord. Your lady mother gave instructions that no changes were to be made. . . .'

'So this is the way you treat my wife, is it?' Justin said sharply. 'How dare you not receive her correctly? Prepare the Queen's bedroom immediately. You know as well as I do. Mrs. Matthews, that it is a tradition that the bride of every heir to Mandrake sleeps in the Queen's bedroom.'

Mrs. Matthews looked flustered.

'Yes, m'lord. Of course, m'lord. I beg your pardon, m'lord, but your lady mother said . . .'

'Do as I command you,' Justin said, and then he was gone, leaving the housekeeper still murmuring her apologies and dropping one agitated curtsy after another.

He hurried along the landing and went up the narrow staircase to the second floor. Only as he reached the passage which led to Serena's bedroom did he pause for a moment and glance down at the note in his hand as if for reassurance. Then he went on again. He saw that her door was wide open and he slowed his pace a little as he drew nearer to it.

He reached the bedroom and knocked at the door. There was no reply and after a moment he spoke.

'Serena!'

But there was no answer. He entered the room. It was empty. The fire was burning brightly in the grate, the canles were lit, and then he saw, to his surprise, an over--turned table which in falling had split a work-box so that the contents were scattered over the carpet. For a moment he stared around him, then looked down at the bolt of the door lying broken on the ground. He gave a gasp, and as he did so was conscious of sounds from the room next door. He knocked impatiently but without waiting for a reply lifted the latch and entered.

The candles were lit and he saw Eudora lying on the

bed, deep snores coming stentoriously from her open mouth. He moved across to her.

'Wake up,' Justin said angrily. 'Where is your mistress?'

He bent down and shook her by the shoulder. It made not the slightest impression, and then, even as Serena had known, he realised that such sleep was unnatural. He turned and went from the room and back into Serena's bedchamber. He stood looking about him and saw the door into the turret. An expression of relief came to his face. He hurried across to it, entered the turret room and saw that the smaller door was open too, revealing the twisting staircase. He hurried down, his feet clanking noisily on the stone steps. The door into the library was also open and he hurried in.

When he reached the room, it was to see his father's old valet whom he had known ever since he was a child, kneeling at his father's side.

'Newman,' he exclaimed. 'What is the matter?'

The old man got to his feet. Tears were streaming down his cheeks, the slow, difficult tears of old age.

'His lordship's dead, Master Justin,' he said. 'He died at his work. It was as he would have wished to go . . . but . . . he has gone.'

Justin crossed slowly to his father's side. He put out his hand and gently touched his father's cheek. It was already cold, and then, as he felt the hand still holding the pen stretched over the white paper, he gave a sudden exclamation, for he saw that the last word his father had written was 'finis'.

'He finished his history,' he said quietly. 'That was why he died, Newman, his work was completed.'

'Oh, Master Justin. . . . God rest his soul!' the old man sobbed.

'Has anyone been here, Newman?' Justin asked quickly. 'The young lady who came the other day? She must have passed through here.'

'I did not see her,' Newman answered, 'but I saw her ladyship, and oh, Master Justin, it was in a terrible way she was, with a naked sword in her hand.'

'A naked sword? Are you sure?'

'As sure as I am standing here, Master Justin, and she was seeking someone. She too asked me if I had seen a girl.'

'Oh, my God!'

Justin said the words beneath his breath as he pulled

277

open the library door. He glanced down the passage and then he started. The door into the garden was open. He could feel the cool air and smell the damp fragrance of the earth which had been recently wet by the rain. He ran down the flight of steps. Yes, the door was open and now he went out into the gardens, standing there listening, his head turned first this way and then that. For a moment there was only the sound of the thunder away over the sea, and then he heard something else, a dog barking, the deep baying note of a mastiff.

He began to run towards the sound, running more swiftly than he had run since he left school. It was Torqo who led him to the very spot where Serena had fallen over the cliff. Torqo, rushing to the cliff's edge and then back again, barking distractedly and trying his intelligent best to attract attention to his mistress's plight.

Justin leaned over to see where Serena had fallen. The ledge was very narrow and it was a miracle that she had not fallen directly down on to the pointed, treacherous rocks hundreds of feet below. Her dress had saved her, for it had caught on the roots of an old tree. It was obvious that she must be moved with the greatest care for there was only a breath between her and utter destruction.

It took Justin but a few minutes to run back to the house, rouse the staff and return with several stalwart young footmen and a strong rope. Carefully they lowered him over the cliff. He would let no one but himself attempt it. It was dangerous both for him and for Serena, for the slightest miscalculation might send them both hurtling down on the rocks below. Very cautiously they lowered him and when at last he held Serena in his arms and cried to them to pull him up, the men dragged them both to safety.

They reached the top of the cliff where hands were outstretched ready to take the precious burden from Justin's arms; but curtly he refused them. Shaking himself free of the rope, he carried Serena across the garden into the house and up the stairs to the Queen's bedroom.

In the light of the candles in the Great Hall he thought for one frantic moment that she might be dead. She was so pale and her fair hair, soaked by the thunderstorm, streamed on to her shoulders, giving her an almost frightening appearance of frailty.

'Serena!' he whispered urgently. 'Serena!'

But she could not hear him. Only as he reached the

bedroom and was lowering her on to the bed did her
eyelids flutter and one of her hands, blue with cold, made
a feeble movement.

Very gently Justin laid her down and took his arms from
beneath her.

'Gracious, but her ladyship is soaked to the skin,' the
housekeeper exclaimed, peering anxiously from the opposite side of the bed.

'Get blankets, hot bricks, brandy,' Justin said sharply.

'They are coming, m'lord. Pray heaven they will not be
too late.'

'Serena!'

There was an agony of fear in his voice now.

'Serena!'

Serena gave a convulsive movement and her lips moved.

'Justin,' she cried. 'Justin, oh, save me, save me!'

Her voice was very low and hardly audible, but even so
there was such sheer terror in the cry that those around the
bed felt the tears start to their eyes.

'You are safe—quite safe,' Justin answered. 'I have
saved you, do you hear me?'

He took one of her hands in his and started to rub it
gently. With a sudden surprising strength she wrenched it
from him.

'Justin,' she called. 'Justin, save me!' Then in a voice of
almost pathetic pleading, she added: 'Oh, Sir Joker, show
me the way. I must get to him. 'Tis urgent; he has fallen!
. . . Justin! Justin! . . . Yes . . . yes . . . he is my . . . my
heart's desire.'

'Poor lady, she is delirious,' Mrs. Matthews exclaimed;
and then, as she said afterwards, her breath was taken
from her by the expression on his lordship's face.

Eighteen

SERENA pushed open the casement window and stood looking out at the garden. The sunshine was warm and golden and the sea reflected the deep blue of the sky. A flight of white pigeons passed over the green lawn.

Serena turned her head as Eudora entered the room carrying a bouquet of flowers. She brought them to Serena and placed them in her hands.

'From his lordship,' she said.

Serena took them eagerly.

'They are even lovilier than usual.'

Eudora nodded.

' 'Tis true,' she said. 'Never have I beheld such exquisite bouquets as his lordship has sent you day after day.'

Serena thought of the deep red roses which Eudora had brought her yesterday, of the purple orchids the day before and the coral pink carnations the day before that. Then she saw that to-day's flowers were white roses, white orchids and lilies-of-the-valley. She looked at them and then down at her dress. She had not realised when she put it on that it was the one she had worn at her wedding. She glanced at Eudora and saw that she, too, had noticed the coincidence.

'I am dressed like a bride,' she said, her voice a little shy.

' 'Tis about time you began to behave like one,' Eudora retorted.

Serena felt the colour rising in her cheeks; but before she could speak, Eudora went on:

'His lordship sends his compliments and if you are in good enough health he would be mightily pleased to speak with you at your ladyship's convenience in the library.'

'Oh!'

Serena scarcely breathed the word; and then, as she did not reply, Eudora said:

'Methinks you are in good enough health.'

Serena laughed.

'But of course I am! I have been well enough these past two or three days, but you and the doctor have bullied me into staying in bed.'

'We wisely wanted you to recover,' Eudora said, 'and recover you have. Besides, 'twas better that you should stay in your room while there were funerals and such like taking place.'

Serena's eyes darkened for a moment. She looked out of the window.

'You went?' she asked.

Eudora nodded.

'We all went,' she said; 'his lordship's orders, but none were invited save the staff and tenants of the estate. I have not spoken of it afore, dearie, for fear it would distress you, but 'twas a simple quiet service and somehow I felt that the poor lady had found peace at last.'

'That is what I hope she has found,' Serena said—'peace!'

She was silent for a moment as deep in her heart she prayed that the Marchioness's restless, turbulent soul might indeed be at rest. Then a thought struck her.

'You spoke of funerals, Eudora?'

Eudora nodded.

'There was someone else buried at the same time. I know not who it was, but 'twas some relation who was entitled to a place in the family vault.'

'So they were buried together,' Serena said softly.

'Yes, together,' Eudora answered. 'But let us talk of something more cheerful. It is over and forgotten, dearie, all that you have suffered, all that you have been through. There is the future ahead of you.'

Serena put her hand up to her cheek.

'Yes, I know, but oh, Eudora, I am afraid.'

'Afraid of his lordship?' Eudora asked. 'Why should you be that now that you know there is no reason for you not to be kind to him.'

'. . . Kind to him!' Serena repeated the words with a little sob, and then quickly, as if she would hide her emotions even from Eudora, she asked, 'He has enquired for me since I have been . . . indisposed?'

'Every day,' Eudora answered. 'You know that.'

Serena looked round the room. How lovely it was! The Queen's room, the room where all the brides of the Vulcans slept when they first came to Mandrake. It was a room which seemed as if it were made for love; its white satin curtains were embroidered with cupids, posies of flowers and true lovers' knots of blue ribbon. The great four-poster bed, too, was hung with embroideries made by loving hands hundreds of years ago; and the brocaded walls were covered with silver-framed mirrors reflecting and re-reflecting the windows which opened on to the terrace. It was a room of sunshine, a room made for happiness; and Serena thought now, when she had lain in the secret vastness of the great bed, she had hidden her face in the pillow because of the thoughts that it had brought her—thoughts of Justin. And now the moment had come when she must go downstairs to meet him.

It was strange to think that she had not spoken to him since her wedding-day, since that moment when she had left Grosvenor Square because she thought that he loved *La Flamme.* How crazy it seemed to her now! How foolishly impetuous she had been not to have made certain before she turned away from her heart's desire and subjected herself to all the dangers that were waiting for her at Mandrake. Yes, she had been foolish; and now the moment of reparation was upon her and she was afraid. She glanced out of the window and then once again at Eudora. Eudora gave her a smile.

'Go down to his lordship,' she prompted. 'He has waited patiently enough this past week.'

Slowly Serena walked towards the door, holding her flowers in her hand as if they were some talisman which would give her courage for what she had to do. Slowly she descended the Grand Staircase. The house was very quiet and yet it seemed to her that the atmosphere was one of gaiety and happiness. The sunshine was coming in at every window. There was no chattering voices nor the throb of music from the great drawing-rooms, but through the open doors she could see that the rooms were filled with light and with flowers.

Never had Mandrake appeared more beautiful. There were no long lines of liveried lackeys waiting for guests, no footmen hurrying by with trays of crystal glasses, there was no sound of horses and coaches in the drive outside nor the clink of money on the gaming tables. It had all gone. There was just sunshine and flowers, and in the gardens the song of the birds.

Serena walked across the hall. At the library door she paused for a moment. A tremor of fear shot through her.

Only once before had she peeped into the library. It was a dark room, she had thought, sombre with its rows of books rising from the floor to the ceiling. It was as dark and sombre as Justin could look when he was annoyed, as impersonal, too, as he could appear in his indifference to what went on around him. But Justin had been so close to her in her thoughts these past days that now it was difficult for her to realise that he was a very different person in the flesh—one, mayhap, who was still angry with her, incensed by the confession she had made him the last time they had met.

She turned the handle of the door and for a moment thought she had come to the wrong room. There was sunshine here, too, sunshine golden as it poured scintillating in through the great bow-window which looked over the sea. Here, also, there were flowers, great bowls of them on every table.

She came into the room and Justin rose from the bureau set against the wall, where he had been writing. He moved across to her and she strove hard to read the expression on his face. They met in the centre of the room and stood for a second looking at each other. Was it really necessary to put anything into words? Serena wondered. She felt that he must hear the beating of her heart, must read in her eyes all that she had to say. Shyly she dropped him a curtsy.

'You are better?'

It seemed to her that his voice was unexpectedly low and deep.

'Yes, thank you,' Serena answered. 'I am recovered entirely.'

Instinctively, because she was trembling, she moved a little away from him. She went towards the window, her flowers in her hands, the sunshine behind her so that it haloed her fair head. Because she was so afraid that she would falter in what she had to say, she began quickly:

'I want to thank you, my lord, first for the flowers you have sent me every day, and then for saving me. I understand that . . . you put yourself in grave danger when you came down the cliffs to me.'

'It was not difficult to save you once you were found, and Torqo should be thanked for my finding you. If it had not been for him, things might have been very different.'

'I have told Torqo how grateful I am,' Serena replied, 'but I must thank you too.'

'And now you have thanked me, forget about it,' Justin said. 'It is past, a closed chapter. Let us never speak again of the events of that night.'

'No, let us not speak of them,' Serena agreed.

There was a moment's silence, a long moment, and then Justin said quietly:

'But there is one thing I wish to hear and one which I think I am entitled to be told.'

'What is that?' Serena asked.

'What you were going to impart to me when you wrote asking me to speak with you in your bedchamber,' Justin said. 'I came in response to your note, but I was . . . too late.'

Serena was very still. Then she took a deep breath and her lips moved, but the words would not come. She looked down at her flowers before she placed them on a little table beside her. Justin was watching her, and after a moment he said:

'Will you not tell me, Serena?'

Serena moistened her lips and linked her fingers together.

'Yes,' she said. 'Yes, I want to. It is just that it is very difficult to put it into words.'

'Very difficult?' Justin enquired.

'Very difficult,' Serena answered gravely.

Again there was a pause and then at last she began.

'My lord . . .'

'My name is Justin!'

Serena blushed. Somehow it was terribly difficult to say his name.

'Well . . . Justin . . .' she stammered at length. 'When we were at Vulcan House after we . . . we were . . . married, I . . . I told you something.'

Justin frowned a little as if he were trying to recollect the conversation.

'You told me something?'

'Yes, my lor . . . I mean, Justin,' Serena went on. 'I told you that . . . that I was . . . in love with . . . with someone.'

'Oh, yes, I 'collect now.'

'I promised you once,' Serena said in a very low voice, 'that I would always tell you the truth. Well, what I told you then . . . was the truth but . . . not the truth . . . as you . . . as you believed it.'

Justin looked puzzled.

'I regret I do not exactly take your meaning.'

284

'It is so terribly difficult . . . to explain,' Serena said desperately, 'but . . . when I said I was in love . . . with someone . . . I was in love . . . with someone.'

'That makes it much plainer!' Justin said with an amused smile.

'Oh dear,' Serena sighed. 'You see . . . I was in love . . . I mean . . . I am in love . . . with somebody . . . but . . . but it is not who you think it is.'

'Ah, now I am beginning to see daylight,' Justin said. 'You mean I am suspecting the wrong person.'

Serena nodded.

'Yes.'

'But if my recollection is not at fault, you did not reveal this most fortunate person's name.'

'Oh, no!'

There was a pause.

'Yet now I think of it,' Justin said, knitting his brows, 'I believe I ventured to mention someone whom I suspected of receiving your favour.'

'Yes . . . yes, you did.'

'But my supposition was incorrect?'

'Entirely.'

'Then I must apologise in all sincerity.'

'Thank you.'

'And now you will tell me who the right and most enviable person may be?'

'Yes,' Serena murmured.

'That is excellent,' Justin said. 'Such frankness will clear away all misunderstanding.'

'It is . . .'

Serena paused. First she was pale, then her cheeks were crimson, now she was pale again. Her fingers, linked together, were twisted in each other a little desperately.

'Won't you trust me?' Justin asked softly.

She was looking down at her hands, but suddenly she raised her eyes to his, and he saw that they were full of tears.

'I . . . cannot,' she whispered. 'I cannot . . . say it.'

In two strides he was across the space between them and was beside her.

'Oh, my darling,' he said, 'what a brute I am to tease you! It is only for the exquisite joy of watching your face, of wanting to hear your lips speak the words I so greatly desire to hear—more than I have ever wanted anything in the whole of my life.'

For a moment the world stood still and then, with an effort, Justin went on speaking.

'I dare not touch you yet,' he said, and his voice was hoarse. 'There are things that I must say to you or else they will never be said. I wish you to know, my beloved, that I have loved you from the very first moment I saw you when you stood at the top of the staircase at Staverley Court. I loved you because you were so utterly different from anyone I had ever known or seen in my life before; and yet, because I was cynical, because I had been disillusioned so often and so completely by other women, I doubted what I saw with my own eyes. Always I was afraid to obey the instincts of my own heart, always I was trying to catch you out, to find you less pure, less fine, than you appeared. I could not believe, you see, that anyone could be so beautiful, so perfect as you—and come to me unsullied, unspoilt.

'Though I have loved you, I have crucified myself with my own doubts. There are many things you will have to teach me, Serena, one of them being to have faith. I lost my faith many years ago because all the ideals I cherished fell in fragments about me. But in you everything in which I once believed and everything which I know is good and perfect has been recreated. Together, darling, we can live for those things—the real things in life—because you have always known them and you can show me what is worth having.'

His voice ceased and he stood looking down at her. Then at last he held out his arms with a gesture of utter simplicity and yet utterly commanding.

'I want you, Serena,' he said softly, 'but first of all I want to hear you say whom it is you love.'

Now, at last she could resist him no longer. Her eyes were held by his for one moment, her lips trembled and as the colour rushed headlong into her cheeks she whispered:

'I love . . . you, Justin.'

Then her face was against his shoulder, hidden there, and his arms were round her. He held her closely for a second before he placed his hand under her chin and turned her face up to his. She was trembling, but in utter happiness. There was so much ecstasy in that moment that it seemed as if something divine enveloped them both. Then his mouth was on hers. She quivered for one second before she surrendered herself, utterly and completely. She knew then his strength, she knew then how strong and masterful he would always be, and she gloried in it.

His kiss, demanding, possessive, passionate, seemed to draw her very soul between her lips, and then she felt herself lifted high against his heart and heard him say in a tone of supreme triumph:

'Mine—my darling, my wife—my perfect love.'